W9-BFH-166

© Urszula Soltys

Joseph O'Connor's *Shadowplay* was named Novel of the Year at the 2019 Irish Book Awards and was a finalist for the prestigious Costa Book Award. His novel *Star of the Sea* was published in thirty-eight languages and won France's Prix Millepages, Italy's Premio Acerbi, the Irish Post Award for Fiction, the Nielsen Bookscan Golden Book Award, an American Library Association Award, the Hennessy/Sunday Tribune Hall of Fame Award, and the Prix Litteraire Zepter for European Novel of the Year. He is the author of nine novels and is the Inaugural Frank McCourt Professor of Creative Writing at the University of Limerick.

ALSO BY
JOSEPH O' CONNOR

NOVELS
Cowboys and Indians
Desperadoes
The Salesman
Inishowen
Star of the Sea
Redemption Falls
Ghost Light
The Thrill of it All

SHORT STORIES
True Believers
Where Have You Been?

THEATRE/SPOKEN WORD
Red Roses and Petrol
True Believers
The Weeping of Angels
Handel's Crossing
My Cousin Rachel
Whole World Round (with Philip King)
Heartbeat of Home (concept development and lyrics)
The Drivetime Diaries (CD)

SHADOWPLAY

Joseph O'Connor

SHADOWPLAY

Europa
editions

Europa Editions
1 Penn Plaza, Suite 6282
New York, N.Y. 10019
www.europaeditions.com
info@europaeditions.com

Library of Congress Cataloging in Publication Data is available
ISBN 978-1-60945-698-6

O'Connor, Joseph
Shadowplay

Book design by Emanuele Ragnisco
www.mekkanografici.com

Cover image: Sir Johnston Forbes-Robertson, *Dame (Alice) Ellen Terry*
© Alamy Stock Photo

Prepress by Grafica Punto Print – Rome

Printed in Italy, at Puntoweb

CONTENTS

ACT I
ETERNAL LOVE - 17

ACT II
DO WE NOT BLEED? - 157

ACT III
ARRIVING AT BRADFORD - 303

CODA
FRIDAY 12TH APRIL, 1912 - 321

CAVEAT, BIBLIOGRAPHY, ACKNOWLEDGEMENTS - 385

For Carole Blake

SHADOWPLAY

Abraham "Bram" Stoker, clerk, later a theatre manager, part-time writer, born Dublin, 1847, died London, 1912, having never known literary success.

Henry Irving, born John Brodribb, 1838, died 1905, the greatest Shakespearian actor of his era.

Alice "Ellen" Terry, born 1847, died 1928, the highest paid actress in England, much beloved by the public. Her ghost is said to haunt the Lyceum Theatre.

In every being who lives, there is a second self very little known to anyone. You who read this have a real person hidden under your better-known personality, and hardly anyone knows it—it's the best part of you, the most interesting, the most curious, the most heroic, and it explains that part of you that puzzles us. It is your secret self.

—EDWARD GORDON CRAIG (Ellen Terry's son)
from *Ellen Terry and Her Secret Self*

ACT I
ETERNAL LOVE

Victoria Cottage Hospital, Near Deal,
Kent.
20th February, 1908

My dearest Ellen,
Please excuse this too-long-delayed response. As you'll
gather from the above, I'm afraid I've not been too well.
Money worries & the strain of overwork weakened me over
this wretched winter until I broke down like an old cab-
horse on the side of the road. What's good is that they say
little permanent damage is done. My poor espoused saint
has moved down here from London, too, to a little boarding house on the sea front & comes in on the 'bus to read
to me daily so we can continue irritating one another contentedly as only married people can. We enjoy quarrelling
about little things like sandwiches and democracy. I am still
able to type write as you see.

Last night, I had a dream of You-Know-Who—he was in
Act Three of *Hamlet* — & somehow you came to me, too,
like a rumour of trees to a tired bird, & so here I am, late
but in earnest.

How wonderful to know you are putting together your
Memoir & how frightening that prospect will be for
untold husbands. You ask if I have anything left in the
way of Lyceum programmes, costume sketches, drawings
or a Kodak of Henry, lists of First Night invitees, menus,

so on. I'm afraid I haven't anything at all in that line of country. (Are you still in touch with Jen?) Almost everything I had I stuffed into my *Reminiscences* & then turfed the lot (five suitcases-full) into the British Library once the book was published, apart from a couple of little personal things of no interest or use to anyone. You're correct to recall that at one time I had a file of letters from poor Wilde but I thought it wise to burn them when his troubles came.

What I do have is the enclosed, a clutch of diary pages & private notes I kept on and off down the years & had begun working up into a novel somewhat out of my usual style, or perhaps a play, I don't know. The hope was to finish the deuced thing at some point before my dotage. But I can't see that happening now that I seem to have lost the old vigour. In any case, since I have no savings & the London house is heavily mortgaged, I must marshal what forces I possess & find employment that will pay, which my scribblings have never done. The plan is to ship ourselves to Germany, perhaps Hamburg or Lübeck, the cost of living is lower there & Florence speaks the language. God knows, we are a little old to emigrate at our time of life, but there it is.

As to the scribbles: some parts are finished out, others still in journal form. I had intended changing the names but hadn't got around to it—your own name, being part of you, seemed too beautiful to change—& then, some months ago, I happened across a curious tome by an American, one Adams, in which he writes about himself in Third Person, as a character in a fiction, an approach that rather tickled me, & so I thought let the names be the names.

Since you appear in the proceedings yourself, you'll find, looking through the ruins, a curiosity at any rate & it might raise a smile or two at the old days of fire & glory, the madness of that time. Among the pages you will encounter a couple of smidgeons from an interview given by a certain peerless actress some time ago to *The Spectator*: the transcription of her answers is there but not the questions, don't know why. If any plank of the shipwreck is of use (which I doubt) for your Memoir, salvage rights are yours. Well, perhaps check with me first.

Much of it is in Pitman shorthand, which I think you know. If you don't, a local girl in the village will, or there is Miss Miniter's secretarial service near Covent Garden—I can see the street clear as daylight but can't think of its name. You may remember her. She is in the Directory.

Some of it is in a code even its maker has forgotten. I wonder what I can have been trying to hide & from whom.

Well then, old thing—my treasured friend—it is a holy thought to imagine my words moving through your heart's heart because then something of me will be joined with something of you, and we will stand in the same rain for a time under the one umbrella.

All fond love to you and your family, my dearest golden star,

And Happy Birthday next week I think?

Ever Your Bram.

P.S.: Like a lot of thumping good stories, it starts on a train.

* * *

I

*In which two gentlemen of the theatre set out
from London for Bradford*

Just before dawn, October 12th, 1905

Out of the gathering swirls of mist roars the hot black monster, screeching and belching its acrid, bilious smoke, a fetor of cordite stench. Thunder and cinders, coalman and boilerman, black cast iron and white-hot friction, rattling on the roadway of steel and olden oak as dewdrops sizzle on the flanks. Foxes slink to lairs. Fawns flit and flee. Hawks in the yews turn and stare.

In a dimly lit First Class compartment of the dawn mail from King's Cross, two gentlemen of the theatre are seated across from one another, in blankets and shabby mufflers and miserably threadbare mittens and a miasma of early morning sulk. Their breath, although faint, forms globes of steam. Not yet seven o'clock. Night people, they're unaccustomed to being up so early unless wending home from a club.

Henry Irving has his boots up on the opposite seat and is blearily studying the script of a blood-curdling melodrama, *The Bells*, which he has played hundreds of times throughout his distinguished career, from London to San Francisco, from Copenhagen to Munich, so why does he need a script and why is he still annotating it after all these years and why is he muttering chunks of the dialogue, with half-closed eyes, at the fields passing by the window? His companion sits erect, as though performing a yogic exercise intended to straighten the spine. The book he is reading is held before him like a shield. The train creaks onward, towards the northern outskirts of London.

Several centuries have passed since they last exchanged a syllable or even one of those wincing, gurning, eyebrow-raised stares in which, like all theatre people, they are fluent. The sheep's trotters and pickled eels bought hurriedly at King's Cross remain uneaten—somehow sweating despite the cold—in grubby folds of old newspaper. A bottle of Madeira on the floor has suffered an assault. A few drops remain, perhaps to reassure the drinkers that they are not the sort of gentlemen who would start on a bottle of Madeira in the cab to the station not long before seven o'clock of a morning and finish it in the train before eight. There is between them that particular freemasonry of the elderly couple who have long sailed the strange latitudes and craggy archipelagos of monogamy, known much, seen much, forgiven almost everything, long ago said whatever needed to be said, which was never that much in the first place.

"What is that rubbish you are reading?" Irving asks, in the tones of a maestro demonstrating "sophisticated boredom" to a roomful of the easily amused.

"A history of Chislehurst," Stoker replies.

"Sweet Christ."

"Chislehurst is in several respects an interesting town. The exiled Napoleon III died there in terrible agony."

"And now a lot of people live there in terrible agony."

The day could be long and tense.

A bloodstained, scarlet sky, streaked with finger-smears of black and handfuls of hard-flung gold. Then a watery dawn rises out of the marshlands, pale blues and greys and muddied-down greens, like daybreak in a virgin's watercolour. Staggered beeches here and there, sycamores, rowans, then a stand of queenly, wind-blasted elms and the Vs of wild geese breasting across the huge sky like arrows pointing out some immensity.

Beyond the steamed, greasy window, the beginnings of the

midlands: the distant lights of towns, the smokestacks and steeples, the brickfields and quarries served by new metalled roads. Between the towns, the mellow, dreeping meadows with their byres and barns and crucified scarecrows, the towpaths by the green and calm canals, the manors and their orchards and red-bricked boundary walls, the mazes and lodges and rectories. It is so like the Irish countryside yet not like it at all. Something different, undefinable, a certain quality of light, a sadness, perhaps, an absence that is a presence. Welcome to an absence called England.

The chunter of the train as it strains up Stubblefield Hill, the leaden sway and spring as it descends and rolls on, its momentum disconcerting on the downhill curve, and from time to time a sudden heaviness, a sort of worrying drama, as the carriage gives a skreek or a shuddering lurch. The roped-up trunk shifts in the luggage rack above them—the porter wanted it in the cargo carriage but Irving refused—and now the edges of a town.

The backs of little houses inch by in the rain. Twines of washing slung from window ledges or strung across midden-heaps serenaded by furious dogs. A dirty-faced child waves from a glassless window. A chillingly scrawny greyhound pulls at its chain. The navy-black sky and a broken fingernail of moon and a downpour so sudden and violent it causes both men to stare out.

Portly, bearded, in the fourth decade of life, Stoker still looks like the athlete he once was. At Dublin University he boxed, rowed in the sculls, swam. He once saved a man from drowning. His suit is a three-piece Gieves & Hawkes of Savile Row, a subtle herringbone tweed, fashionable thirty years ago. The Huntsman greatcoat is of heavy frieze, like a general's. He has a talent for wearing his clothes, looks comfortable, always, though everything he has on this morning has been repaired more than once, re-seamed, let out, taken in, patched up, not unlike the friendship. The bespoke if re-soled brogues are newly blacked. His hands are veined and knotty, a bit obscene, like hands hewn from lumps of bog oak.

Irving is frailer, sunken-in since his illness, skeletal about the emaciated, equine face. He is ten years older than Stoker and looks more. But flamboyant, long-limbed, uneasy remaining still. Purple velvet fez, organdie and linen scarves, fur-collared cloak, mother-of-pearl pince-nez. Lines of kohl around the lakes of his dark, tired eyes, dyed-black hair dressed in curls by his valet every morning, even this one. Walking-cane with a miniature skull as knob ("the shrunken head of George Bernard Shaw"). Like any great actor, he is able to decide what age to look. He has played Romeo who is fourteen and Lear who is ancient, on the same tour, sometimes on the same night.

He lights a short, thick cigar, peers out at the rain. "*Die Todten reiten Schnell*," he says. The dead travel fast.

Stoker's response is a disapproving glower.

The train enters a tunnel. Flicker-lit faces.

"Put your eyes back in your head, you miserable nanny," Irving says. "I shall smoke as and when I please."

"The doctor's advice was to swear off. You know this very well. I may add that the advice was expensive."

"Bugger the doctor."

"If you could remain alive until tonight's performance, I'd be grateful."

"Why so?"

"It is rather late to cancel the hall and we'd forfeit the deposit."

"Rot me, how considerate you are."

"But if you wish to be a suicide, that is your affair. The sooner the better, if that is your intention. Don't say I didn't try to prevent you."

"Yes, Mumsy. What a caring old girl."

Stoker declines the bait. Irving pulls insipidly on the cigar, rheumy eyes watering as though leaking raw whiskey. He looks a thousand years old, a mocking impersonation of himself.

"I say, maybe I'll be lucky, Bramsie, old thing."

"In what respect?"

"Perhaps I'll turn out like the feller in your ruddy old pot-boiler. The un-dead, my dears. Old Drackers. Mince about Piccadilly sinking the tusks into desirable youths. Chap could meet a worse fate, eh?"

"I am attempting to read."

"Ah, Chislehurst, yes. The Byzantium of the suburbs."

"We are thinking of moving there, if you really must know."

"You mean Wifey is thinking of moving there and you're thinking of doing what you're told, as usual."

"That is not what I mean."

"The lady doth protest too much."

"Do shut up."

"She'd look jolly good wearing the trousers, I'll give her that. Tell me, how do you squeeze into her corset?"

"Your alleged witticisms are tiresome. I am now going to ignore you. Goodbye."

Irving chuckles painfully in the back of his throat, settling into a fug of smoke and sleepiness. Stoker reaches out and plucks the cigar from his fingers, extinguishing it in an empty lozenge-tin he always carries for the purpose. Thing like that could cause an accident.

He watches the wintry scenery, the swirl of snow among oaks, the long stone walls and hedgerows. All the endless reams of poetry this landscape has inspired. Burn an Irishman's abbey and he'll pick up a broadsword. Burn an Englishman's, he'll pick up a quill.

Ellen is with him now, her mild, kind laugh, one evening when they walked near the river at Chichester, one of those streams that is dry in summertime. What is the word for that?

He blinks her back into whatever golden meadowland she came from.

An old song he heard years ago in Galway has been with him all morning like a ghost.

> *The sharks of all the ocean dark*
> *Eat o'er my lover's breast.*
> *His body lies in motion yon*
> *His soul it ne'er may rest.*
> *"I'll walk the night till kingdom come*
> *My murder to atone.*
> *My name it was John Holmwood,*
> *My fate a cruel wrong."*

Who can explain how it happens, this capability of a song to become a travelling companion, a haunting? In the dark of early morning the strange ballad had swirled up at him out of his shaving bowl or somehow stared back at him from the land behind the mirror, for no reason he understands. And now, he knows, it will be with him all day. He is trying to recollect more about the first time he heard it.

All writers who have failed—and this one has failed more than most—develop a healing amnesia without which their lives would be unbearable. Today, it isn't working.

Carna. County Galway. His twentieth birthday. Near the townland of Ardnaghreeva. He'd been there for his work, attending the courthouse, taking notes, when an adjournment was announced in the trial for murder of Lord Westenra's land-agent, one Bannon. The planned twenty minutes became an hour, then two. He went out to find a drink.

The people were speaking Gaelic. He felt lost, uneasy, frightened of something he couldn't name. Many were barefoot. The children gaunt as old keys. He couldn't understand it. Twenty years had passed since their wretched famine; why were the people still cadaverous and in rags? Why were they here at all?

A balladeer so thin that you could see the bones of her arms was singing a song but the ballad was in English. "Little Holmwood," someone said it was called. And then came the dreadful news from inside the courthouse. The magistrate had died, alone in his chamber, sat down to sign the death warrant but at the instant when he'd donned the black wig his heart and eyes had burst. Blood had gushed from him in torrents, drenching the floor of his chamber, until only his flesh and bones were left, like an empty suit. The prisoner had escaped. "The devil's work" had been done. Some of the people nodded coolly while others crossed themselves or walked away. The ballad-maker never stopped singing.

Returned to Dublin, he'd been restless, shaken by what he'd witnessed. There was something terrifying about the singer's imperviousness, if that's what it was. Behind it, dark murmurings nagged at him, as though the song had caused the death.

Unable to sleep, he had resorted to laudanum but it hadn't worked, left him feeling worse, disconnected, prey to red visions. The following night he attended the theatre, arriving late from his work at Dublin Castle. A few months previously he had begun reviewing for the literary pages of a newspaper. There was no money but it afforded free passes."

The play was into its third act by the time he arrived. A rainstorm was roaring outside. Soaked, cold, in the darkness he couldn't find his seat so he stood in the aisle near the prompt chair. Lightning sparkled through the high windows of the theatre—like many old playhouses, it had once been a church. The gasps of the thunderstruck audience.

Henry Irving stopped in mid scene and stared down at them grimly, his eyes glowing red in the gaslight. Paint dribbling down the contours of his face, like dye splashed on a map, droplets falling on his boots, his doublet and long locks drenched in sweat, his silver-painted wooden sword glittering in the gaslight, shimmering with his chain-mail in the lightning. For what felt a long time he said nothing, just kept up the stare, slinking towards the lip of the stage, left hand on hip, wiping his wet mouth with the back of his sleeve. Sneering, he regarded them. Then he spat.

As the gasps arose again, he resumed speaking his lines, insisting he'd be heard, that their revulsion didn't matter, that in fact it was essential, a part of the show, a gift without which this play about evil couldn't happen.

"'Tis now the very witching time of night, when churchyards YAWN"—he opened his maw wide and let out a rattling groan—*"and HELL ITSELF breathes out contagion to this world!"* He shook, clutched at his throat, as though about to vomit. *"Now could I drink hot blood and do such bitter business"*—gurgling the terrible words—*"as THE DAY WOULD QUAAAAKE TO LOOK ON."*

By now the people were screaming. He began to scream back. Not a shout, not a bellow—a womanly scream. Plucking the sword from its scabbard, swirling at the air, screaming all the while like a banshee. It was frightening, too discomfiting. A man shouldn't scream. Some in the audience booed, tried to leave, others rose in stampedes of operatic cheers, from the gods came the thunder of boot-heels on the floorboards. Stoker, in the thronged aisle, felt thirsty, faint.

He turned and looked at the cheap seats, behind the cage.

Punks, drunkards, the disgorged and disgusting. Warted, thwarted vagabonds, rent-boys in drag. Madwomen, bad-women, gougers on the make. Fakers, forgers, mudlarks, midgets, Bridgets on the game and rickety Kitties. Oozers, boozers, beaters, cheats, picklocks, urchins, soldiers on leave, poleaxed goggle-eyed poppy-eating trash, refugees from the freakshows and backstreet burlesques. And the smell. O dear Jesus. It buffets you like a gust, layers of fetid fetor and eyeswater yellow like the smoke from a train to Purgatory.

Why do they come here? Stoker doesn't know. All he knows is that they do come, they always will. If they screamed at the pain of their irrelevance, no one would listen. They need someone to scream for them. Henry Irving.

On the train for Bradford, memory comes to Stoker in Present Tense, as though recollecting the other man that every man contains.

Weak, trembling, the young critic makes his way to the street and walks around the building to the stage door. Already the crowd has begun to assemble. The play is still *on*—you can hear the muffled shouts of the actors—but the people are here, in the rain. Dozens, scores, soon hundreds. A covered carriage clops up, the horses nervous, stamping, the driver shouting at the people to move away, there'll be an accident. Policemen arrive and try to hold them back, the crowd pushes towards the doorway, chanting his name.

Irv
Ing.
Irv
ing.

Suddenly, roughly, two ushers emerge, one carrying an umbrella, the other a truncheon, hurrying him out like a boxer from the ring, through the storm of little notebooks pleading for autographs, through the macabre forest of outstretched scissors pleading for locks of his hair, and up the folding steps to the carriage. He's still in his stage clothes but with a raincoat thrown over him and a bottle of champagne in his hand.

As the carriage pulls away down Sackville Place, the police manage to barricade off the rabble.

"Stay where you are if you'd be so good, sir, this street is closed."

"I work at Dublin Castle," Stoker says quietly, showing the credential badge in his wallet. "I am on government business. You'll want to let me through."

Why does he follow? What is he doing? The last tram for Clontarf is about to leave from the Pillar and he needs to be on it, but he's not. Ahead of him, the carriage is now approaching the bridge. He walks slowly at first, stumbling on the greasy pavement, straining to see, now hurrying.

On the southern side of the bridge, the carriage is stopped by a herd of cattle being driven to market and he catches up. When it jolts off again, through a minefield of cowpats, he continues. Round by Trinity College, where he took his mediocre degree, along Nassau Street, up Dawson Street, along by the Green, the shop windows shining with rain.

Under the arms of a dripping aspen on the edge of the park, he watches as the tall-hatted cabbie dismounts and opens the carriage door. The Shelbourne Hotel is shining like a palace in an illustration of Christmas, the crystal lamps on its pillars blaze.

For some reason there is a delay. He pictures the rooms, sees himself moving through them, the great splendour of the ballroom with its Italian marble and gilt, its orchestra playing Mouret's "Sinfonie de Fanfares," portraits of judges and aristocrats in the alcoves, ice-buckets, upended bottles, shucked oysters, innocent apples, maids tactfully dusting nude statuettes. In his mind's eye he sees Irving striding through the furnace-like opulence, waiters take his hat, his gloves, his cane, the maître d' beckons towards a discreet table behind the ferns.

Rain on the aspens. A concierge and a pageboy hurry out through the glass doors with umbrellas. From the carriage alights a gracious woman in a long fur cloak. She pauses a moment, looks up at the sky, enters the hotel. The carriage clops away.

Winterbourne: a river that is dry in summertime.

* * *

II

In the night-traders' hut off the back laneway near the Fruit Market, he summons up a mugful of what purports to be coffee and souses it with a measure of hard Jamaica rum, the cheapest, most intoxicant brand. To be here among the whores and drunken squaddies, the dregs of the late night city, the outcasts. He likes to listen to their prattle, the juice of it, the spite. They address him as "Your Honour," not entirely ironically. They regard him as an oddity, a kind of queer mage; it disconcerts them that he writes in shorthand.

Sometimes they ask him to explain the runes in his notebook, finding it hard to believe that a squiggled symbol could be a word. They're right. It *is* hard. He is careful to speak to everyone here with respect. Being among the night people, it settles something in him. At home in his room, he can't write. The words turn to ashes. Here they bubble and spew, in the wake of the rum. He likes to watch the weary farmers arriving, bog-eyed, from the country with their carts, the traders returning in wagons from the quays, hefting boxes of American apples, Dutch flowers, English cornmeal; the butchers in their bloodstained whites. To think of the city sleeping while so much life is thrumming on—it makes him feel a co-conspirator.

As he bends to the page and continues to jot, among the inconvenient, the filthy, the deliciously malicious, he realises the song is with him, circling like a phantom in Dickens, an imprecation of guilt, and he wonders if it will ever let him be.

O Mother, where's the bonny boy
Come here last night to stay?
"He's dead in Hell, no tales can tell,"
Her father he did say.
"Then Father, cruel Father, you shall die a public show
For the murder of John Holmwood,
Who ploughed the lowlands low."

Now he's walking the north quays of the Liffey, breasting into the slab of wind, through a swirl of dirty gulls and old newspapers. The strange forlornness of Dublin on a midweek night, empty, ghostly, murderous. At the weekend there might be the hope that Lady Wilde will be having one of her soirées, the cultured young men and women, the wit, the fine food, the flirtations on the elegant staircase where one might meet someone beautiful, even a better version of the self. But a Wednesday night in Dublin is the loneliest in the world, dark windows, shuttered doorways, locked shops, empty offices, night-thoughts monkeying at him if he tries to sleep. The only way he can endure it is to walk.

First light coming now. Smacks heading down the estuary, trailing petticoats of nets, out towards the expanse of the sea. The last bedraggled tarts streeling home to their rooms. He's afraid to glance at his fob watch, doesn't want to know the time.

The bay looms in his mind, the surge of the breakers, the lugubrious moan of the lighthouse foghorn. The ghost of a drowned sailor chained to the mast of an ice-caked ship with a sail stitched from hanged men's shrouds. An image from a play he's been trying to write. But he doesn't have a shape for it yet.

Other Irish writers he knows about are interested in Ireland. He has tried to read them, to feel at one with them, but he has failed. They have organised themselves into clubs, little academies of pipe-smoking and mysticism, which meet on a Monday evening to bathe in the Celtic twilight or translate epic poems nobody sane wants to read in any language, before everyone trams home to the suburbs. The folktales, the myths, the faeries, the banshee, the stuff his Sligo mother used to mumble about after a sherry or two. All that dusty old fustian Hibernian rubbish, only remembered by the expired and the mad. While he can see it contains momentum of a certain clunking sort, it leaves him unmoved, it's like looking at drizzle. The mannequins who ponce and howl across this island of sodden failure, shown but never said to be vainglorious thugs, said but never shown to be heroic or admirable, seem to him devoid of shadowplay, pallid imitations of something not quite named, children's drawings where a Caravaggio is needed. At least in the theatre, there must be an audience. If there isn't, the play will close early.

He passes the Customs House, enters a gloomy old office building that for a hundred years has despised its reflection in the Liffey, crosses the flagged floor, climbs the steep dark staircase, his strong body now creaking with tiredness. On the third landing, he comes to an office door on which a plaque announces NIGHT EDITOR. Before he can knock, it opens. Mr. Maunsell regards him.

"Bram, my dear gossoon. You're out early. Isn't it horrid cold?"

"Actually I am out late."

"Won't you step in for a moment, I was about to wet the tea? What's that you have there? I wasn't expecting anything from you this week."

"My review. Henry Irving. In *Hamlet* last night."

The night editor rubs his right eye and utters a yawn of withering bleakness as he starts looking over the pages. The clay pipe in his mouth is empty but he sucks on it nonetheless; the whistling slurp is one of those little unpleasantnesses that seem worse when we are tired. He is a small man who looks smaller, somehow, during the hours of semi-darkness, a minor dandy in emerald green eye-shade, shabby porcelain-buttoned waistcoat and scarlet braces. They say he has a fancy-woman in Kimmage.

"*Hamlet*, eh, Bram? Doubt thou the stars are fire."

"Indeed."

"I don't know, lad, I don't know. Bit rich for our blood? Heaven bless them, the readers of the *Dublin Mail* wouldn't be experts on the Bard."

"One needn't be an expert to appreciate a play. I am not an expert myself. Neither was Shakespeare."

"Shakespeare wasn't an expert on Shakespeare?"

"He saw himself as a craftsman. Like one of the carpenters in his theatre."

"I'd been meaning to have a word with you about the theatre, Bram. Not quite the thing? Bit lacking in properness, the ladies a tad loose, one or two of the chaps a bit—you know."

"A bit what?"

"A bit Haymarket Harvey? I'm a man of the world myself but I've advertisers to think about. Maybe you'd widen your purview?"

"How so?"

"You don't happen to have a cat?"

"No I haven't."

"The readers love a heart-warming little article about a cat. Especially if it's missing a leg."

"I shall bear that in mind."

"Or the poor auld faithful hound won't leave his master's grave? They lap that stuff up and come cantering back for more. Or some good respectable hard-working lad but he falls into bad company and takes to the gin until it drives him astray in the head and he strangles the fiancée, you know, a morality fable? Or he ruins her and she's left with no choice bar going on the game. Temperance sells a barrow-load of papers these days."

"Irving has stated in many interviews that he means to make theatre respectable."

"A rose by any other name, though. You don't mind me

speaking frankly? There's those who do be saying your beloved Irving is a bit off."

"Meaning?"

"A glorified panto showman, bit of a carnival barker."

"I consider him a great artist and a peerless genius."

"That's lovely. I consider him my bum."

"I can offer the review elsewhere. Since you're not paying me, there can be no hard feelings."

Mr. Maunsell chuckles. "Doesn't the queen pay you, mister honey? She's well able to, God knows."

"So you'll take it?"

"What's the hurry. Hold your hour and have tea."

"I need to know. Now."

"You're a strange piece of work, young Stoker."

* * *

The alarm clock rattles out its shattering-glass summons. He gropes from the bed and quiets it. For a moment, his dead father is in the wardrobe mirror's reflection, black birdcage in hand; after-image from an uneasy dream. The reek of the chamber-pot rising from the corner, sleet beating angrily on the window. Forty minutes of sleep are better than nothing. But only by forty minutes.

Quarter of an hour later, he's running on Clontarf Beach, barefoot, in jockey's jodhpurs and a boxer's singlet. He runs two miles every morning, no matter the weather, has been doing it daily for years, a part of his routine. As a child he was often ill, confined to bed for months, years. That won't be happening again.

He listens to the pounding of his feet on the sand, the slop of the wavelets as he slaps across the runnels, the buffeting wind, the hiss of the creaming foam, the interior metronome of his breath. He stops and shadow-boxes, then a hundred press-ups and a dip. The shocking cold of the water, the zest of the salt.

Above him, the vast bowl of the Irish sky, placid, glassy, hardly ever changing, a bell jar beneath which the specimens writhe as they await the latest experiment. Now he sees the Kingstown ferry, far out in the bay, bobbing towards the Muglins before it faces out for Holyhead.

The pull of London is so strong for him that he senses danger in the magnetism. His few visits to the capital for his work have left him wheezy, feverish, as though there is something in Piccadilly's dust designed to resurrect his ashen boyhood. The city has seen him too hot in the summertime, petrified in winter, thirsty in vast parks, hungry in galleries, awestruck in huge museums stashed with imperial lootings, afraid to open his mouth for fear the indigenes might form views about his accent. The beggars of Holborn seem so ardent, as though it is they who secretly rule, as though the gentry are unwitting extras in the show.

And London has too many hidden streets, too many alleys and back lanes where everything is available for a price. The hovels behind Paddington Station, the pleasure garden in Chelsea, the secret map of a city that roils with availability. A whisper in the club, a nudge, a nod, these are the signposts. He fears the destinations.

There are times when he has considered the United States, perhaps Chicago or Boston or New York. It's said that men and women may remake themselves there, start the journey afresh with new outlooks and policies, new ways of speaking, even a new name if required. No one cares where you came from. You write your own story. But he wonders if that can be true.

In his daydreams he sees the greatbuildings, the long canyons of the avenues, hears the iron-jawed clatter of factories, the blowsy, brash place-names: Cincinnati! The Bronx! Baton Rouge! But this pitch and bopping punchiness of a new republic doesn't appeal to him. He imagines he'd find it tiresome.

The consolation about Ireland is that nothing will ever

happen here now. The fighting days are done, the years of wars and revolutions. The gallows won out in Ireland, as in India, as everywhere. To assert that the pen is mightier than the sword is only to float a fiction, a means of encouraging the sort of rebelliousness that changes nothing.

He shadow-boxes on the beach as the ferry glides by and the jockey's boy goes walking the horses. Nobody minds what you'll be doing because you won't be doing anything. Not that it would matter if you did.

Returned to his little room in the boarding house on the seafront, he puts a kettle on the bachelor's stove in the inglenook and prepares to shave. His ninth home in sixteen months, always little flats and bedsitters around the northside coastal villages, rooms at the tops of staircases. Probably he'll move again soon.

The thought of the evening meal with his fellow boarders settles like dust. A quintet of perfect, mutually uncomprehending misery, failure, mummery, and halitosis. A *tableau vivant* (on a good day) of chances-all-gone, of peas-on-the-knife-eating hideousness. What dystopia of roaring shame has he wandered into that he must share a table with this confederacy of the damned? Mr. Miggs, Mr. Briggs, tall Mr. Lawlor, small Mr. Lawlor and Mr. Strange. Beige-eyed Mr. Miggs, a bean-counter in Guinness's, from some godforsaken wind-lashed crossroads in the midlands. Getting away from it had sapped every bubble of manhood he had. Scallops evinced more life. Mr. Briggs, so it was whispered, had been a girls' school teacher in Exeter but, following a series of apprehensions in that city's public parks, seemed unlikely to be allowed to be one again. Small Mr. Lawlor had flakily poor skin, his lank namesake a goitre and a habit of picking his ears. Dribbling Mr. Strange was painfully meek but was not going to inherit the earth. "Ah, Stoker," the ruined would ask as he sat to the cabbage soup. "How goes the gay life of the Castle?"

On the crooked windowsill, his old copies of Sheridan Le Fanu, Maturin, *Wuthering Heights*, *Frankenstein*, their pages loose and spilling, his often-pawned *Complete Shakespeare*. *The Black Prophet* by William Carleton, stolen from Marino Library. *A Guide to the Munich Dead-House*. On the corkboard above the monkish bed, souvenir postcards of actors he loves: William Terriss, Henry Irving, Ellen Terry.

Seven times he has seen Irving play, Ellen Terry thirteen. Her gift, her presence, enthrals him. Like the changelings he has read of in his mother's mouldering storybooks, she has a magic that seems otherworldly, dangerous.

In a pewter frame on the window ledge, a daguerreotype of two people on their wedding day: white-eyed, stiff, in funereal black. To imagine these waxworks participating in the act that made them his parents is beyond his wildest powers. They emigrated to Brussels some years ago, with his sisters, to save money. He decided to remain in Clontarf.

Shave completed, he prepares a pot of tea with the seaweed he has gathered and begins lifting his dumb-bells in sequence, huffing with the effort, wrists throbbing. Eight o'clock now. He needs to hurry on. The two-pounders, the sixers, the half-a-stone. He tries to keep his grunting to a minimum so as not to upset the landlady downstairs or her elderly mother, the latter having the hearing of a dog. ("Go up and tell that Stoker article this is *not* that sort of house." "Mr. Stoker is at his exercises, Mammy, for the love of God stop shouting." "I'll exercise him in a minute. With the tip of my boot. The queer-looking Protestant shitehawk.")

Pain rippling through the sinews of his forearms, tautening, straightening, and he finds himself wondering if Irving lifts weights; it would be wise for all actors to do so. Acting is about the body as much as the words, and the body gets lazy, resentful of being inhabited. The Roman Catholics believe in pain, think it's redemptive, bracing; like the buttress of an old cathedral, pain stops you collapsing. They punish their bodies for the mortgage of their souls. It's good that the punishment is for something.

The little kettle on the stove starts whistling meekly, as though intimidated by the display of underclad manliness it has been forced to watch. As he crosses to damp the flame, he sees, through the yellowing lace curtains, a familiar figure downstairs on the street.

It's the walk he recognises first, its show-offy sense of performance, the saunter of a libertine wearing the most expensive clothes in this protectorate of the Empire, a man for whom being watched has become an art form.

Stoker ducks behind the pelmet. Doesn't want to be seen. Especially not by him.

What can he be doing out here in Clontarf, and so early? Why has he wandered from the city? The bell trings downstairs, followed by three sharp raps on the knocker. He hears the landlady lilting "The Verdant Braes of Screen" to herself as she limps through the hall, the clatter as she opens the sticky door. Then her crutches on the creaking staircase, her breathlessness as she knocks.

"It's myself, Mr. Stoker, sir? You've a caller below? Are you after going out to your work?"

He doesn't move. Scarcely blinks. Points at the kettle. "Keep quiet, you bastard," he whispers.

Minutes later, hurrying from the house, he collects the calling card and scribbled note from the hall stand.

My dear Bram. Was taking the sea air this morning and popped by on the chance you might be tempted to a constitutional. Quel dommage to have missed you. A pleasure deferred. Ever yours, Oscar Wilde.

* * *

III

*In which a young man receives counsel
on the avoidance of sinful occasions*

T he village seems asleep, its little shops darkened, the
storm-blown frontage of the funeral parlour bedecked
in lengths of sodden black crêpe, garlands of grey
rosettes. By the drapery, a scummy lake-like puddle where the
landlady's mother's dogs are nuzzling. Loamy smells from the
haggards, from the unseen yards. Wind flaps the faded Union
Jack on the post office roof, a sound like the guttering of a
flame as it furls itself around its trembling pole.

A girl in radiant yellow emerges from the shadowed alley by
the dairy, a yoke of blackened milk-cans borne crossways on
her left shoulder, and regards him for a moment as she passes
on the footpath with an after-aroma of sweet warm soap. Her
bare feet are white, her brown hair loose, a crucifix in the
bosom of her chemise. He finds himself recollecting a morning
in Paris, when, stopping on his way to visit the crypt at Notre
Dame, he had been approached in the street by a dark-eyed
girl who had asked him for directions to the Mabillon. She was
Irish, a Dubliner, she thought him an Englishman, and for
some reason he didn't say he wasn't. He knew what was happening, had read in his *Gentlemen's Guide to Paris* that this
was how such girls approached one.

She had spoken of the weather, of the bookstalls by the
Seine, as the students hurried by to their lectures at the
University and then she had asked, in almost a whisper, if he
wished to accompany her to a room. It was nearby, she said, off
the rue des Canettes. She spoke quietly, without shame. He'd

been afraid to do so, had sent her away. He had not the twenty francs, he told her. *Ten, then, sir. There is no need to be shy.* He had given her what he could spare but not gone with her.

He thinks about her now, as he walks damp Clontarf, through the dung and the mud of the almost empty street and the zizzing of unseen flies. That evening in Paris, the thought of what he had declined had blazed in him so fiercely that he couldn't sleep. At midnight he dressed quickly and hurried back to the rue de l'Université, drunk with a smoulder he didn't want to call lust. The thought of warm hands, of low, Irish laughter. The thought of being alone with another in a room.

The lobby of Clontarf Police Barracks is small, dimly lit, papered with advertisements for dog licences, interdictions, ordinances, tattered old warnings about gorse fires. A placard forbidding public meetings is nailed to the wall by the hatch.

Everything is quiet. Still not too late to stop. What he is about to do is insane. A worm of steely pain uncoils itself in his gut. His temples are drumming. From behind the counter the old constable looks at him assessingly, drawing a ledger tied on a string from some recess and opening it.

"You wish to report an intruder, sir. Your address if you please?"

"Number 15, The Crescent, on the far side of the village. It is my landlady's house. I lodge there."

"Mr. Stoker isn't it, sir?"

"How do you know my name?"

"By dad I'm not rightly sure, sir. People talk, I suppose."

The constable sips gloomily from a chipped enamel mug and riffles through the stiff pages in a methodical way, removing a length of leather strap doing duty as bookmark. The fingers of his right hand are nicotine-umbered.

"When did this incident occur, sir?"

"Earlier this morning. Dark fellow, muscular, rather flamboyantly dressed for a man. A middleweight. Felt hat. I happened to look out of my window and saw him in the side garden sort of mooching about."

"And then?"

"Then I opened the window and let him have it."

"Verbally, sir?"

"Of course verbally."

The constable nods as he writes.

"Go on, sir. Anything more?"

"My landlady's gardener, old Hoggen, has a potting shed there. I saw this character trying the lock and challenged him immediately. He let loose with a few remarks of the sort you can imagine."

"Of what nature were the remarks?"

"Remarks of a filthy and scurrilous stamp. Regarding Protestants and so on. 'West-Britons.' He took off pretty sharpish in the direction of the Strand when I told him I had a shotgun in the house."

"Have you, sir?"

"Have I what?"

"A shotgun in the house."

"Had I a shotgun in the house, I would have used it."

"Is anything afterbeen took that you know of ?"

"I'm not certain. I don't believe so. But I was concerned for my landlady and her mother. Her mother is an invalid."

"What class of height was our nice friend?"

"About my own, I should say."

"Anything distinguishing about him?"

"As I mentioned, his clothing. He was rather effeminately dressed. A Latin Quarter hat and a cloak affair with a fur collar."

"In Clontarf?"

"But look here, what concerns me most is that I have seen him hanging about near the gate of the house previously."

The constable raises his old eyes gravely as though this impartation is important.

"Excuse me a tick, sir," he says, sloping away into the dimly lit office behind him where his fellows are talking and smoking, a cloud of purple dusty smoke. He exchanges mumbles with a colleague, a bullet-headed man who looks as though life has been hard on him. Comes back to the hatch pulling on a raincoat.

"I'll stroll up to the house with you and take a gander about, sir."

"I say, must you? I am late for my work."

"It won't take but a few minutes. I'll require you to accompany me if you'd be so good. You've made a serious enough charge, after all."

Now he is walking back up the avenue with the elderly constable at his side. They make small talk about the weather, the birds. The constable is a Galwayman, "a blow-in" as he puts it, and the phrase seems to bounce in the air between them. A limping boy on the way to school with a string of books under his arm glances over his shoulder at the curious duo.

"And you work inside in the Castle, sir, unless I'm greatly mistaken?"

"You seem to know a great deal about me."

"That's a place seen a share of suffering, sir, God knows, down the years. Prisoners went into that place and never seen daylight again. Bricked up in the walls. Buried alive. But forgive and forget, that's what I says myself. Still, there's a ghost or two walking them battlements, I'll go bail. Wouldn't you?"

"I have never seen one if so."

"'Tis more than we see does go on in the world. And what sort of duties would you be having at the Castle, sir, if I may ask?"

"I am a clerk in the Office of Petty Sessions."

"The courts and so on?"

"Partly."

"'Tis a man of the law you are, so, sir. Like myself."

The constable opens the whiny little gate and walks around the front garden, staring silently at the grave-like mounds of earth, before approaching the potting shed and examining its lock. He tries the bolt a couple of times, wrinkles his nose. Wind moves the branches. A filigree of sunlight surrounds him.

Snapdragons lick their lips. Nettles unfurl. A thicket of briars begins drooling.

"It was here you saw My Nabs, sir?" the constable asks. "Over here by the door?"

"Yes."

"Quare there's no boot prints. With the ground being damp." He toes at the clay as though the action might uncover something.

"I saw what I saw."

"Certain sure you did, sir. You seen what you seen."

The constable bends heavily and plucks an object from the flower bed, testing its point with his uncommonly plump fingertips.

Tomatoes in the glasshouse wither open their skins.

"You'd want to let your garden-man know not to be leaving a dangerous auld yoke like that lying about. That's a thing could do a body a damage, so it could."

"He has been putting up a fence," Stoker replies, accepting the leaf-draped twelve-inch wooden stake. The constable lunges towards him, baring *small white incisors* –

"MR. STOKER."

Dry-mouthed, hot, he shudders awake at his desk. His superior, Mr. Meates, is standing in the door frame like an undertaker come to collect on his bill. A profoundly biblical Ulsterman, he talks with clipped contempt for anything he suspects might be human nature.

"At what time did you delight us with your appearance this morning, Mr. Stoker?"

"Some time after half past nine, sir."

"I am well aware that it was some time after half past nine, Mr. Stoker. I have not lost the use of my senses. My question, if you'd be so good—if I do not interrupt your reveries—is how *much* time after half past nine."

"I should say ten or fifteen minutes afterwards, sir. I was detained coming in to the office."

Mr. Meates approaches the desk slowly like a battleship bearing down on a disobedient island. He regards the sheaf of parchments on the blotter, the porcupine of unsharpened quills, the tall stack of files, the overflowing in-drawer, as he purses and unpurses the part of his face where his lips should be.

"When's this do you think I was born, Mr. Stoker?"

"Forgive me, I don't take your meaning, sir."

"He doesn't take my meaning, sir. Isn't that wild unusual all the same. Wouldn't you wonder what they do be teaching them in Trinity College nowadays? Lost in the fine web of thought."

This is another of his superior's odd mannerisms, the addressing in paraphrase of some invisible third party, the summation of what you've just said. When you hear it, you know you are facing sticky going, that it will not be too much longer before he starts yattering on about having known your father.

"This, Mr. Stoker, is a place where governance is practised. Not a doss house or"—he waves vaguely—"an opium den."

"Yes, sir."

"The work we do has importance. That may not always be evident to you, or even to me. But ours is not to question the will of our superiors on the mainland and the sagacity they have displayed in the organisation of our labours."

Please don't start on about the bees, Stoker thinks.

"I wonder if you are at all familiar with apicology, Mr. Stoker. Because in a hive, Mr. Stoker, everyone plays his part. If he didn't, the queen would expire. And it falls to you, Mr. Stoker, to attend here with punctuality and to give an example to the younger men, of dependability and calm purpose. You will have noticed that there are also a number of women working here, in subservient roles, cleaning, so on. What do you think would happen were the women to be given a poor example?"

"Chaos, sir."

"Chaos, Mr. Stoker. They would go out of their minds. And they wouldn't have far to travel."

"Sir."

"Do you understand the idea of presence?"

"I think so, sir, yes."

"Not to be away with the faeries when you are paid to be here at your work. Not to be dreaming up nonsenses for your so-called writings in pagan socialistic rags."

"If I may say so, sir—"

"In publications that, so far as I can see, do not have the betterment of white Christian society as we know it as their aim but its overthrowal and replacement by a sort of Zululand-on-the-Liffey. Bananas and anarchy. Bananarchy."

"Sir, I—"

"Do *not* interrupt me, Mr. Stoker. I have seen your literary efforts. Witches and goblins and the dear knows what. You would want to catch a good grip on yourself so you would."

"I don't believe I have ever written a story about a goblin, sir."

Mr. Meates empurples. His eyes are damp.

"Oh, wild smart, Mr. Stoker. A scholar and a wit. What do you think would happen if all of us surrendered to unmanly slackness and acted the layabout whenever we felt like it? If *I*, for example, remained at home all day, gardening or playing the fiddle or frightening myself? What do you think would happen *if I didn't come in here at all*?"

By any standards, an unfair question.

Without waiting for an answer the Lord of the Mummies

continues. "I knew your father, Mr. Stoker. We served many years together here in this office. It is to his intercession, I may tell you plainly, that you owe your position here. I was loath to accept you, I didn't like the cut of you, but I overruled my better judgement out of loyalty to a man of responsibility and punctilio. A man who did not gamble away the time allotted him by the Almighty consorting with triflers, buffoons and sensualists."

"In what way do you feel—"

"I'd as lief you didn't grin at me in that supercilious manner, Mr. Stoker. Dublin is small. You are a frequenter of the theatre, I am told. Don't deny it."

"I attend the theatre sometimes."

"He attends the theatre sometimes. Lucifer's recruiting station."

"If I may say so, sir, I think you're perhaps taking the matter a little too seriously."

"Och and heaven forfend that any of us would do that. It is certainly not a failing that could be ascribed to yourself. Was there ever a woman of thon theatre who was more than two steps removed from harlotry? Think on your father, sir. Think on your end. The theatre is the liar's house, a seething pit of idolatry. The fifth chapter of Ephesians counsels us plainly: 'Have thee no fellowship with the unfruitful works of darkness but rather reprove them.' How would your father feel to see his son lost to lewd entertainments designed to thrill poor halfwits and the scum of the tenements?"

"The play I attended most recently was by Shakespeare, sir. Last evening."

"And that absolves you?"

"Shakespeare was a Christian, sir, to the best of my knowledge."

"And Satan was one of the angels."

Mr. Meates reverses from the room like Methuselah on a trolley, a vision of admonition in bicycle clips. The other clerks are staring. Glumly they return to their work. Stoker gathers a thick packet of legal files sent up from the provinces and resumes noting the verdicts and sentences. Every fine and imprisonment, each pitiable committal: all must be recorded and processed. Failures, thieveries, libels, late rents, person-ations, arsons, evictions. A hungry girl in Sligo smashed her hand through a window to steal a loaf of bread. The woman at the table reached for a hatchet and chopped off the girl's hand in one blow, thinking "she had cholera."

Sometimes he wonders why the flames of suffering and struggle contained in these documents don't fan themselves into his stories, but for some reason they never do. The demands of putting together the reference book he must write are immense, the promised deadline is coming, and then there is the work on the census. The secret of Empire is that every-thing is written down.

At lunchtime he goes to the riverbank and sits beneath the sycamores, watches the longboats, listens to the calls of the stevedores. The sour smell of hops arises from the brewery. Slum children gather to watch the barrels of Guinness being barged to the world they will never see. Scenes and pictures from last night's play continue to flicker at him like afterimages of something looked at in sunlight. He waits almost an hour but his Florence doesn't come. On his walk back to the Castle, he happens into her maid buying fish on Usher's Quay. "Miss is unwell today, sir. One of her headaches."

Returned to the office, he is himself assailed by a headache, but there's nothing to be done, he must get on. The post-boy brings a sack of the afternoon mail, hundreds of envelopes containing census returns. The casement clock in the corner placks its stolid beat. From the distance, the siren in the gas-works sounds its shrieking wail. As he begins sorting the returns, whole handfuls of documents, all requiring transcrip-tion, he notices something odd.

The envelope is different, smaller, expensive looking, like the hand-rolled mourning paper they sell in Paris. Grey with a black border, watermarked with an upside-down cross in a circle. The cursive is elegant copperplate, graceful as a line of swans.

Personal
Mr. Bram Stoker
Theatre critic

As he opens it and reads, beads of sweat form on his face.

His first thought is that the letter is a trick, a practical joke got up by a colleague, a typical bit of Dublin snide cruelty masquerading as good humour. But when he turns, nobody is watching him, gauging his reaction. Every head is bent towards its desk.

He will remember this moment for the rest of his life. Bent heads, the clock, a letter.

* * *

Seven o'clock that evening finds him in St. Stephen's Green, smoking, pacing by the lake. His second-hand suit feels tight and he could find no clean collar, and, since payday will not come for another ten days, he doesn't have the wherewithal to buy one. The shirt he is wearing is turned inside out, its cuffs a little yellowed and frayed. In his mind, he has rehearsed what he wants to say, like an actor awaiting the scene.

The time will be short. Important not to forget anything. Vital to swallow down this crippling nervousness. Perhaps a gin for Dutch courage? Wiser not to. How terrible it would be to slur. Glancing up, he sees that oddball Yeats strolling over the little arched bridge, a silverback gorilla in a monocle.

Don't come in, says the Shelbourne Hotel. *You do not belong here. You'll only embarrass yourself, Fool. Run along.*

As he moves through the revolving doors, across the hundred-mile-long lobby, past the porter's leathered alcove, up the vast marble staircases, women on their knees are brushing the purple carpets and white-gloved maids polish porcelain doorknobs and a waiter pushes a trolley of glinting silver salvers, chivvied by the portly maître d'. The rich like silence. Everyone is whispering. He can hear the thump of blood in his temples.

From somewhere arises the sound of a woman's quiet laughter as he enters the gloomy corridor. The gas lamps are hissing. He walks along the long passageway, counting down the rooms, odd numbers on the right, even numbers on the left, until he comes to the door of Room 13.

He knocks. No answer. Knocks again. Stillness. Now he notices that the door is ever so slightly ajar. He pushes and it creaks open.

Inside the large room, heavy brocade drapes are closed. A fire spits and gusts in the grate. Red and orange light plays on the gloss of the dark wallpaper, on the droplets of the chandeliers, the crystal goblets and decanter, on the silverware that has been set in two places on the small mahogany table. Heads of deer stare glassily from their mounted shields. A single black candle is weeping its wax down the pillar of its alabaster candlestick.

"Good evening?" he tries.

Shadows, the crackle of the fire.

Now he perceives that the room is part of a suite, that there is a heavy-looking door with an iron-hoop handle in the oak-panelled wall to the right of the fireplace.

What to do? Should he approach? Or leave and start again?

"Someone there?" calls the voice from behind him.

Startled, he turns.

The firelight shudders.

In a doorway he had not noticed near the entrance to the suite, pale yellow candlelight is cast from a narrow passageway, towards which he crosses quietly.

In the parlour at the end of the passageway, Irving is seated on a chaise longue in dark grey evening dress. Three black candles placed on copper saucers burn on a bookshelf, a Turkish cigarette in a black onyx ashtray. He doesn't raise his glance to the visitor but continues staring at a pack of playing cards fanned out on an ottoman before him.

"You are in shadow," he says quietly.

"Sir?"

"My eyesight is poor. Step back half a pace, will you."

Stoker does as commanded. Irving looks up, his irises shining like new-minted coins, his black hair sleek as sealskin.

"The wizard of kind words," he says.

"I—didn't know whether or not to accept your invitation. I didn't want to trouble you."

"Oh, I knew you would accept. I saw it in the tarot. You had no choice in the matter, it was all ordained. Look."

He twirls the fingers of his left hand and produces the Hanged Man card from the air. Snaps them and it disappears. His buttery smile. "Little conjuring trick, Stoker. It's a skill I admire. You shall find an autographed photograph of me on the table inside. My thanks for your sensitive notice of my Hamlet last evening. Your writing casts quite the spell. Good night."

"I have taken the liberty, if I may, of bringing you a file of some ghost stories I have written and published. I should value your estimation. Should you feel any of them have possibilities as a piece for theatre. They have been published in little magazines. Tales of the imagination. But my greatest heart's hope is to write a piece for the stage."

"A theatre critic with imagination. You don't find that gets in the way? Like a pianist having three hands but not knowing what to do with any of them."

"I feel that life without imagination would be an unending hell."

"Is it not that anyway?"

"I did not come to trade clevernesses."

The actor yawns and bends his head to the cards again. "I have seen nothing in your writing that led me to believe you are an artist, Stoker. If you have come to me for affirmation, you shall be disappointed. Your criticism has sensitivity but you are not a creator. For which you should be grateful. The road of the artist is arduous. Loneliness is his lantern through the world."

"Perhaps—if you looked over the stories?"

"You have audacity, I see."

"Might I leave them on the table in the other room as I go? Or perhaps I might read one of them to you?"

"There is another come with you, Stoker. He is standing between us. I have the gift of sensing spirits, he wishes you not to be here. He begs you, for the sake of his soul's rest, to depart this room."

"I—"

"You are wondering, I think, why I have not invited you to sit with me. I never invite anyone. An old shibboleth among those of my sect. You must choose to step into the scene or remain in the wings. We theatre people have a weakness for superstition."

"If you are certain that I wouldn't be interrupting, I should think it a tremendous honour to sit with you a brief while."

"Then, do," he says quietly. "I don't bite."

* * *

IV

*In which a couple, perhaps to avoid a quarrel, become engaged,
and the voice of an old lady is heard*

B orn in his cage, he has never once left it, so the great
orang-utan believes life in the cage is freedom, that it is
those unfortunates beyond the bars who are imprisoned. How gloomy they appear. They gaze in at him longingly,
find diversion in their offerings of thrown nuts and grapes. It
bores him to accept their tribute but slavery is what they're
for. I could kill them with one blow. Why bother? Their forlorn, glassy eyes. Those rags they must put on. To think they
are my cousins. They're almost apelike.

Not far from the Monkey House in the Royal Zoological
Society Gardens, pallid Stoker and a young woman who has been
described as the most radiant in Dublin have paused by the cast-
iron drinking fountain in the rose arbour. Florence Balcombe's
skin is pale as Carrara church-marble, her auburn eyes large,
when she speaks out of deep feeling she moves her hands, like
an Italian. She is moving her hands a lot at the moment.

The orang-utan sometimes thinks them an unlikely couple.
Indeed, they have sometimes thought this of themselves. It has
been one of those loves that does not announce itself with satin
valentines but happens in spite of expectations.

They resume their walk now, wending down the lane by the
flamingo lake, then the Lizard House and back around
Anteater Hill. Nothing is said for some time. Which is a way of
saying much. The little tacit entr'acte has its purpose. They
know enough about one another to be aware that a brief cool-
ing-off is required if the appointment is not to end in a quarrel.

Nannies push children and children push hoops. A fez-wearing elephant is swayingly led along the white sawdust road by a boy in a loincloth but proper Irish wellingtons. Great ecstasies of squawking parrots gabble at the lions.

"On a holiday, do you mean?" the young woman asks coolly.

"Not on a holiday."

"This character you have never met before, about whom you know almost nothing—nothing of the slightest true importance at any rate—invites you to drop your life like a hot fork and scuttle off to London?"

"As his secretary, Flo, at his new playhouse."

"As his part-time secretary. On a part-timer's salary."

"It would be a new start in literary life. Who knows where it could lead? Perhaps to my writing a decent play."

"You can't write a decent play in Dublin?"

"I don't know that I can't. I know that I haven't."

"Bram—"

"Neither has anyone else."

"He has investment capital for this theatre of his? An actor? Helming a business? Who ever heard of such a nonsense? Like one of these chimpanzees managing a kindergarten."

"Everything is in place, he has shown me the plans. It's the old Lyceum near the Strand, a wonderful location. He has investors, influential supporters—his bankers are Coutts—a first-rate programme already subscribing. Shakespeare, the Greeks, the classic tales of all Europe. His idea is to make theatre respectable."

"Ambitious indeed."

"But admirable."

"My difficulty, Bram, is that I don't understand. It seems so sudden, so unexpected. You hardly know the man."

"I feel I've known him all my life."

"When you come out with these absurdities, it mystifies me."

"I see him on the stage and I somehow feel I know him. Everyone does, that's his greatness."

"If that is greatness, which I doubt, it sounds a little widely spread to me, and a little counterfeit, too. Who can be truly great to more than a few people?"

"You know what I mean. It's no different from what an audience hears in a great symphony or sees in a great painting."

"You're not running off to London to be with a painting."

"I am not 'running off' anywhere, Flo, it would be a temporary move. I merely thought we might talk it over, you and I."

"You sound as though you're a little in love with him, this walking symphony of yours. My rival."

"You will never have a rival, Dull, don't be silly. It's hard to explain. I don't know what's wrong with me today, do you not find it hot here?"

He leads her towards the gloomy coldness of the Penguin and Puffin House but the weird echoes and the rank odour of dead fish settle in like a fog and the forlorn clumsiness of the creatures out of water seems a sort of reproof and a cruelty, and he finds himself longing for sunlight. Emerged from the municipal imagining of Antarctica, they find a bench beneath a weeping willow and watch the peacock for a while. But chilliness has followed them out.

"You have a life here in Dublin, Bram. A pensionable position. It doesn't pay much at the moment, I know, but it is permanent and will lead to better things. You have friends—"

"I haven't."

"You have some."

He says nothing.

"You could have more," she continues, "if only you tried. If only you weren't so serious and private. Everything is laid out before you like a suit on a bed. Why turn your back on it? You don't even *like* London."

"It isn't that I don't like it. I have never felt at home there, that's all. The sky seems so big and Londoners so knowing, as though one's in a pantomime one doesn't quite understand. But in another way, London is my dream. It must be, for any writer who wishes to be more than a footnote. I feel this chance won't come again, Flo."

"And you and I?"

"What about you and I?"

"Isn't our knocking about together also a chance?"

"Of course it is very much more than that."

"You don't sound overpoweringly certain."

"I am."

"So, let me be clear that I understand my own minor role in the deliciously heroic drama devised and proposed by yourself and the Grand Pooh-Bah Mr. Irving. I am to trot down to the pier at Kingstown and wave you adieu with my tiny lace handkerchief like an obedient little puppy of a nicely behaved girl, is that it? For you to commence your exciting London life. Before toddling home to my embroidery and bible study over cocoa."

"Flo, please—"

Her eyes fill. "Rot me, you seem remarkably certain of my patience, old thing."

He takes her hand. "London is not far, pet. I would visit every other weekend. And the longest I should want to stay there is six months."

"Be still, my beating heart."

"My thoughtlessness has upset you. I am sorry. Let us discuss the matter another time. Come, let's not spoil our day."

"No doubt the girl is not supposed to say a thing straightforwardly. Which is a matter of tremendous convenience to the man, of course, and the reason why the world is in the state it's in. You are my lover. I am yours. I had hoped that we might be married. I imagine you must have known that. Anyhow. There it is."

"But I have hoped for the same, Flo. We're at crossed pur-
poses, I assure you. I *long* to be at your side. I always have."

She looks sad as she touches his face. "If you could see my
dreams, Bram."

He leans in to embrace her. She kisses him fiercely.

"Bram?"

"Pet?"

"What's that mark on your neck?"

"Nothing, love. Cut myself shaving."

* * *

THE VOICE OF ELLEN TERRY

*Recorded in 1906 on phonographic cylinder by the cos-
tume designer and writer Alice Comyns Carr as preparatory
material for a series of articles in* The Spectator.

Why he did it? One doesn't know . . . You'd have to ask
him directly . . . To throw over one's life, go tearing off to
London on a sudden. We never spoke of it, he and I. Hard to
credit, I know. Don't you ever feel it's the most obvious questions that never get asked?

Perhaps you could ask his wife. No, I never knew her well.
Bright woman, a lot of book learning. She intimidated me a
little.

All I can tell you is that Harry—by which I mean the
Chief—had a sort of mesmeric effect on one. Speaking in no
sort of metaphorical way but almost the literal truth. Ask anyone, he'll tell you. He or she. The same.

You'd meet him having prepared a soliloquy about why you
wouldn't do something he wanted and you'd leave ten minutes
later agreeing to. That sort. Splendid way of making you think

what he wanted was your own idea. Like a male novelist's idea of a wife.

One of those chaps able to make you think the rustling leaves are causing the wind. One adored him, of course. Devious cur.

. . . And there's that early bit in Bram's book, you know. Where he's going on about London. One always sensed that was how he himself felt. Have you a copy there? I say, you're well prepared. It's this bit, at the start. The old bloodsucker is a tremendous fellow for English literature, hadn't you noticed? Oh yes. He's practically got a ticket for Boots Book-Lovers' Library. Anyhow. Let me see. Just my spectacles. Ah yes. Then, this is from *Dracula*, page 24.

> Whilst I was looking at the books, the door opened, and the Count entered. He saluted me in a hearty way, and hoped that I had had a good night's rest. Then he went on.
> 'I am glad you found your way in here, for I am sure there is much that will interest you. These companions,' and he laid his hand on some of the books, 'have been good friends to me, and for some years past, ever since I had the idea of going to London, have given me many, many hours of pleasure. Through them I have come to know your great England, and to know her is to love her. I long to go through the crowded streets of your mighty London, to be in the midst of the whirl and rush of humanity, to share its life, its change, its death, and all that makes it what it is. But alas! As yet I only know your tongue through books.'

One sort of felt he was picturing him*self*, in a way. Provincial lad sort of thing. "The whirl and rush." Rather good. But it's only surmising, dear, one could be entirely wrong. Rather. One usually is. But crumbs, Dublin doesn't sound a lot of larks, though, does it, at the time? One adores the Irish people, darling, their romanticism and so on, such a delicious sense of doom and whiskey-flavoured rain and all the rest, but one shouldn't have liked to live there. Rather grey. Still wouldn't. Like Hull with rosary beads, one imagines.

And they can bore one, the Irish, the way they go on, forever assuming one's interested when a lot of the time one's just being polite. Well, the darlings feel they're so frightfully different to everyone else. Like Americans in that respect. Must be tiring.

I'd have jolly well scuttled out of the place, starter's orders, I should think. That's why we have youth, is it not? Young Brambles and his wife, off they pootled to London. Jolly good luck say I.

* * *

As the black, heaving steampacket inches her way out of Kingstown harbour, a couple married this morning are seen together near the lifeboats on the upper foredeck, hiding their little intimacy behind a white silk parasol.

Now he sits on a bollard, she perches on his lap. Together they look out in the direction of moonlit Howth Head, his lips caressing the back of her neck until she blushingly laughs and raises the knuckles of his right hand to her mouth. The twin lighthouses wink as though knowing more than they do. Clusters of fat guillemots hover.

The moon is almost full. Brightness shimmers on the water. When snow starts to fall, the sudden beauty thrills the couple, who have never before witnessed a snowfall at sea, a sight said by mariners to be lucky.

Later, in a cabin small enough for all four of its walls to be touchable from the bunk, they lie in one another's arms. He would like there never to be secrets between them now, he whispers, she must feel she can tell him anything, he will be her greatest friend. A storm-lantern dangles from the oaken ceiling. The golden glow flickering and shadowing the corners.

The creaks and moans of the turbulent ship rise up as the night wears on. Close to dawn, they see the hulk of Snowdonia through the spray-lashed porthole. Dressing, they breakfast together on slices of leftover wedding cake with hot tea and a mouthful of champagne.

Holyhead, the ugliest town in Britain. Cindery smoke already rising from the locomotive in the station. As they hurry through the belched filth, steam moistens a strand of hair to her forehead and he caresses her face with such tenderness that the porter, a Methodist, looks away and thinks himself on at least two of the commandments as he trundles their trunk towards Third Class. Great clouds of yellow light just above the horizon. Through the gorges of Snowdonia, the tunnels and passes, over miraculous bridges the envy of the world and across the flat plains to the Empire's capital. They sleep through most of the journey, only awakened in the end by the long slow skreek into King's Cross.

They are hungry, tired, as he drags their luggage up the steps to the street where thousands are making for work. Clerks in black bowlers, costermongers, chandlers, bankers, tailors, shop-ladies, telegram boys, messengers, maids, carriage drivers, navvies shouldering hods of brick and buckets of hot plaster, gangers digging the road, chimney sweeps, policemen, girls from the paper flower factory, American sailors on shore leave, their slangs and patois arising like a hot sweet mist benedicting the Euston Road. A gang of workmen on their knees with buckets and brushes, trying to scrub away a slogan that has been daubed across a library wall. VOTES FOR WOMEN.

The boarding house on the back alley off a carriage-lane near the Strand is small and lacks the hoped-for view of the Thames, but the pair of attic rooms to which they are shown by the Italian landlady are cleanly swept and neat enough and the stove has been lit. The vista of rooftops and chimneypots is pleasing, like a French painting. Away in the distance, the mountainous dome of St. Paul's.

While he unpacks his papers and books, his new wife goes to the market, returns with an armful of flowers: tall lilies, for-get-me-nots, meadowsweet. He makes tea on the stove, care-fully unhooks the curtains, beats the dust out of them down-stairs in the yard, using his tennis racket. After a time he notices her peering down at him, begins to dance about while he thrashes, cursing and threatening and menacing the cur-tains, which makes her laugh. Such a large man, her husband, a curious bear of a fellow, fuller of uncomplicated kindness than anyone she has known. Everything in him longs for peacefulness. He never speaks to her of his childhood, she gathers it was unhappy. He transmits that he doesn't want to be asked.

From time to time as she puts away his clothes into the wormwood dresser and the ancient wardrobe—heavy boots, tweed britches, a deerstalker, a threadbare overcoat—his pres-ence arises from a garment, something faint and clean and inti-mate behind the smell of thyme soap and launderer's starch. She holds a hem to her face, feels him enter her body, the pulse of his essence through her bloodstream.

His cufflinks and tiepins, a watch chain, a clothes brush with velvet back, a worn leather pouch containing an ivory comb and his shaving things, a sable brush, clippers, a razor and strop. How strange, the world of men.

In a beautifully made little ebony box, the mother-of-pearl comb that is a memento of his father; in the trunk's side pocket a roll of unused postage stamps, a book called *Sex Knowledge for Husbands* and a French letter. She is wondering what to do, whether or not she should let on to have found these things, when she notices, behind a fold of old newspaper, a loose panel in the floor of the trunk. Raising it, she finds a notebook

with padlocked binding, and the words STRICTLY PRI-
VATE—NEVER OPEN hand-inked across the cover.

"Flo, my dearest heart? Whatever are you doing?"

He is breathless in the doorway, his beard and brows grey
with dust, a living statue, tennis racket in hand, curtains folded
over his arm like a toga.

A picture she will always have of him.

Early the following morning they are awakened by their
landlady's husband, a Genovese with incredibly mournful eyes,
bearing a basket of fruit, bread and potted meats with boxes of
fine teas and a half-bottle of Madeira. A boy from the theatre
brought the hamper around just after dawn, he explains, "is
welcome gift of Signor Irving." They breakfast in the little
courtyard, watching the saddlers prepare the horses. When the
landlady and her husband admire the scent of the Indian tea,
an expensive blend that is hard to come by in London, the
happy couple insist on sharing it.

The morning is cold and bright. They put on heavy coats
and stroll the shaded side of the Strand, marvelling at the jew-
ellers' windows, the dressmakers' displays, such profusions of
colour and daring new cuts. A year of his salary wouldn't pay
for a gown here. On towards Piccadilly Circus—he points out
Giuliano's—then they pause before the majestic displays of
Solomon's the fruiterer, nectarines, greengages, mangoes,
Smyrna figs, boxes of candied peel and Turkish delight,
pineapples, Spanish oranges, berries whose names they don't
know.

The sinister windows of a doll shop on the corner of Regent
Street. Porcelain faces, tiny rosebud mouths, eyes that click
when they blink, the hair actually human, sold by girls of the
slums for black pennies. Turn the doll tummy down, she'll say
"mamma." Sit her on the counterpane. Dress her. Brush her.
She'll watch while you sleep. Almost lifelike.

Doubled back towards Charing Cross, they enter sweet-aired Green Park, with its bandstands and follies and arbours and rose walks, neater and cleaner than any park back in Dublin.

"How did you sleep, my darling girl? You look a little tired."

She takes his hand. "Not too well, I'm afraid. There were noises from the street, rough fellows or drunkards or something, serenading their girls. Every time I was about to drop off it seemed to start up again like clockwork. Almost amusing in that way."

"I'm afraid that goes with cities. We shall get used to it in a while, I expect. We are rather spoiled in Ireland with the quietness."

"And you snore like a walrus." She smiles. "You never told me."

He feels himself blush to the meats of his teeth. "Didn't know, I'm afraid. Rum state of affairs. My poor little sparrow, I kept you awake."

"There was another way you kept me awake that was nicer."

"Was it—what you had hoped?"

"In every way." She kisses him. "There is no happier woman in all of England this morning."

"How shall you amuse yourself this afternoon when I have gone to the theatre for my appointment?"

"I thought I might come with you for a bit? I should like to meet my opponent."

He laughs. "You shall never have an opponent so long as I live."

"So every Casanova would swear, in order to win a country maiden's heart."

"Don't tease, you owl. I should love you to come if you don't feel you would be bored."

"I shall say hello and murder any pretty actresses that might be wafting about in their underthings, then leave you and your precious Lyceum alone, never fear."

"Once you've been a good Protestant wife and saved me from a seduction, how shall you spend the rest of the day?"

"I am going to the British Library for an appointment at two o'clock."

"With a friend?"

"No, I intend to polish my German. They have a set of wonderful old grammars there at the Reading Room. It shall be pleasantly dull to study in that beautiful place, especially if it's raining. I love the sound of rain on glass, it gives one a scholar's headache."

"You don't find the German literature a bit abstruse, Flo, rather short on light?"

She chuckles. "At school, it was the austerity of the language that rather attracted me. The other girls adored French and we all had crushes on Sister Marie-Thérèse, but I could never master that 'r' sound, you know, or the genders of the nouns. And speaking Italian is so *vowelly*, like eating a never-ending marshmallow, don't you find?"

"Wouldn't know, I'm afraid. You shall have to teach me a little."

She squeezes his arm. "And then I am going to study the law of copyright and patents."

"Why so?"

"So that I can help you in your work. When you write a huge success for us."

"Honour bright, you have a mightily full dance-card for one day."

"Then later this afternoon I have an appointment with the Assistant Director of the Mechanics' Institute in High Holborn."

"What is that?"

"An organisation of working men and their families. I mean to offer a series of night-lectures there shortly, essentials of reading, writing, and algebra. There is a very great need among the poor."

"You intend to give lessons, dear? To labouring men?"

"And their wives, yes."

"But my love, this is a surprise. I am rather taken aback."

"I thought you should be pleased?"

"Nothing you do or think could ever *displease* me, my darling, but after all you have no experience—"

"O experience, my sainted aunt, don't be such an old fusspot. Experience is easily gained, it is merely repetition. Don't scowl at me so, Bram. Heavens you look so cross and jealous."

He touches her face. "Forgive me."

"You surely didn't think I would cluck about the nest like Mother Bird all day, laundering your shirts while I wait for you to come home?"

"Did I not?"

She pucks him softly. "You shall be busy. So shall I be. I mean to bloom where I am planted. In that way, we shall both be happy. What on earth is going on over there, Bram. Look?"

He glances towards the copse of limes a hundred yards across the lawn. A squadron of Beefeaters in scarlet and black livery, bayonets drawn, forms a human square around a group of expensively dressed ladies as an immense red rug is unrolled by servants across the grass. Butlers unpack picnic baskets and ice buckets under a forest of silver parasols. Among them, a photographer is setting up his tripod and hood. A cheer goes up from the watching crowd. Someone produces a Union flag.

"She appears younger," Florence says. "Don't you think so, Bram?"

"Who does?"

"Look again, silly boy. In the centre. Wearing the pretty silk slippers. You have many gifts but you are not tremendously observant, my dear. Fancy, our first morning in London and we have already seen the queen. Must surely be a good omen, don't you think?"

* * *

V

G ulls over Waterloo Bridge as a tall ship glides past, dreamlike. London's church bells pealing ecstasies for noon.

The Lyceum is chained up, the glass in its noticeboards cracked, the entrance steps thick with withered leaves and broken bottles. The portico has been used by street people as a latrine; the padlocks on the main doors are black with old rust. Down the street, the marble splendour of the Royal Opera House gives a look of pitying condescension. *You poor abandoned hovel.*

They walk around the Lyceum, into narrow Exeter Street, which is cobbled and dark, the gloom thrown by the height of the warehouses on either side. There must be a Stage Door but there's no signpost or notice. Tramps dossing in the alcoves. A tart peers down from her tiny cruciform window. Stoker is thinking: what have I done?

A portly little man in Jewish prayer shawl and black hat appears from around the corner, leading a dray horse and heavy wagon.

"You are maybe lost, my friends? Where is it you seek?"

"We are trying to gain entry to the theatre," Florence replies.

"Come with me. I am Yankel the woodman. Come along. You will come."

They follow as the elderly mare clops around to Burleigh Street, her affable master explaining that he delivers the fuel to the Lyceum's furnaces, has been doing so for years, has seen "many amusing sings."

"In there," he says, indicating a metalled wooden door with a Judas hole. "Knock thrice. Walter will admit. Go, go."

Before they can do as advised, the hefty door is hauled open, not by Walter but by a whey-faced girl of about thirteen who, without a word of greeting, turns and skips away down the dark corridor. Entering, they close the door.

Everything so quiet. Only the distant drip of water and the muffled calls of a costermonger out on the pavement.

"Dogs' meat here. Nice dogs' meat."

At the end of the passage squats a lopsided desk. From the blotter, their approach is regarded by a black, one-eyed cat, now hackling with a guttural hiss.

"Don't be so unpleasant," Florence laughs.

Now they see its three companions, staring from the shadows: scrawny, yellow-eyed, queenly, resentful. Clowns grin from ancient posters, harlequins caper. The gone-off-fruit stench of long-unlaundered linen. Mushrooms sprouting on the walls.

Up a staircase. Along a corridor lined in red velvet plush. Every picture on every wall is crooked or broken. More cats. Cats in alcoves. Cats on ripped chairs. Scrobbing their claws on the walls of the crush bar. Slinking out from between the filthy curtains of the opera-boxes. Ahead now, a pair of folding doors. Beyond, a hubbub of noise.

The auditorium is a forest of poles, rigs and scaffolding, platforms slung from the ceiling, ladders, guy ropes, lamp chains. There must be a hundred men working. Carpenters, scene painters, upholsterers installing seats, musicians on the stage in the midst of the racket, somehow attempting to tune up while booms of stage thunder rumble. Squeaky clarinets. Shouts. The shriek of violins. Navvies tearing out seating-boxes with jemmies and crowbars, smashing down lath-and-plaster partitions with lump-hammers. Bits of scenery being shunted—here a clifftop, there a battlement. And the curious sensation that all of it is being put on for your benefit, that nothing was happening until a moment before you arrived.

"I say," Stoker stops a man who is hurrying past carrying a wild animal that turns out to be an armful of wigs.

"How do, squire?"

"I am here to report to Mr. Irving. This is my wife."

"Who?"

From the flies above the stage comes a call—"*Look out, below*"—as an immense painted backdrop of a sea-storm is unfurled, dark blues and silvered greens, a great ship thrashing through vast breakers, the sky riven by slashing zeds of lightning but the canvas ruined by mould stains and asterisk-shaped holes and heavy parallel creases from having been rolled too long. Looking up at the forlorn spectacle, the musicians cheer bleakly.

"You are here, then."

Stoker turns.

Irving, grinning. His long, slim face blacked, sensual lips heavily rouged. The robe he has on is scarlet and silver with a druidic collar so high it comes up to his ears.

"Welcome to our little island of beauty," he says. "I hope you shall find the happiness here that has long eluded you."

The handshake is limp and lingering. Something impressive and yet absurd about him, like the tallest girl in the class, but the taut mouth unsmiling now, the eyes dead as whelks.

"Forgive me if my dress startled you. I have been sitting for a portrait photograph this morning as Othello. Some wretch asked me to do it and in a weak moment I agreed. Why does one wish to obtain the fleeting gratitude of fools? But I do not like to be portrayed. I always look like someone else. Men should be what they seem. Have you ever sat for a portrait yourself ?"

"No I haven't."

"You should. You have good features. Manly. About the chin. In a certain light you might be mistaken for handsome."

He turns the low flame of his gaze on Florence.

"You are here to apply as a hat-girl, dear? See Mrs. Reilly with your references. You will find her in her lair backstage. Only don't trip over her broomstick, will you."

"Mr. Irving," Stoker says. "If I might—"

"First names among theatre folk. Surnames bring bad luck."

"Henry, then, if you insist. May I present to you my wife, Florence."

"Your wife, do you tell me? Well now, my old beardsplitter. Forgive me, Mrs. Stoker. I didn't know Bram was taken. And what a handsome couple you make to be sure, to be sure. Such big eyes you have, Mrs. Stoker. As a wolf once said."

[At this point in the manuscript a 97-word paragraph appears in a code that has proven impossible to decipher. The text resumes in Pitman shorthand "rough note" form as follows, predominantly in dialogue.]

Flo nonplussed. As who would not? He behaving oddly, refusing to look at us.

He: I should have wept at your wedding had I only been invited. (*Now taking F by the arm*). I feel we shall be great friends, you and I. I have an instinct for such connections. Do you care for the theatre?

F: I care for my husband and what gives him pleasure and happiness.

He: A saint, not a wife. And you are named for my favourite of the great *quattrocento* cities. The stars are in alignment.

He spoke briefly of the renovations, huge expense of same.

Foremen kept fetching him documents to sign which he did without looking. He called for towels and a bowl of water the better to wash the colour from his face, which was not "make up" as I had supposed but plain watercolour and sloe oil, a system of his own devising. (Memo: the name of his dresser is Walter Collinson.) Presently a large black bull mastiff appeared in the wings and he called out to it. "This is Fussy." Its maw full of drool. Clearly adores him.

Then I said:

I thought we might go over some of my duties this afternoon? If you had a little time. Or I can come back later if you are busy, as you seem to be.

He: Seeming to be is my stock-in-trade.

I: Just so.

He: But how do you mean, "your duties"?

I: I assume letter-writing and so on, answering your correspondence? Assisting with booking the actors. Is that what a personal secretary does?

He: One supposes so.

I: I thought I could have a word with my predecessor and compile a list of the tasks. Or perhaps such a list exists already?

He: You haven't a predecessor.

I: But then, who has been attending to your correspondence?

He: Not entirely certain. Might I show you and your husband around the old ruin, Mrs. Stoker? The building I mean. Not myself.

F: I am sure you must be terribly busy. I have seen the stage already.

He: Oh the stage is merely the face, dear, the eyes of the body. We need to familiarise with the innards. As it were. *Allons-y.*

Led us out through Stage Left and into the backstage dock, which is in need of a fleet of handymen and scrubwomen but is magnificent, the original early 18th Century dock, hundred-foot ceiling, many lanes, 400 ropes. Scenery of Mountainous Pass being delivered (for *King Lear*), also the musicians store their instruments here. But rats and mice everywhere, despite the profusion of cats in proximity. Many buckets here and about to catch leaks from rafters. Generally a sorry picture of decrepitude and filth.

From there we doubled back through a passageway so narrow that we could go only one at a time, into the backstage itself, remarkable assortment of flywheels, sliders, traps, cogs, winches, backdrops on spindles, weighted guys, leads, pulleys, levers, sloats, like the belly of a ship but all candlelit, dusklike, strange gloaming. Thought of the Gaelic word *amhdhorchacht*, the twilight, taught me many years ago by Bridget something or another, our Roscommon maid of all work when I was six. Means "the darkness before it is cooked."

He enjoyed showing us the Thunder Run, a long tubed wooden track along which cannonballs are rolled to produce the rumpus of storms. Building was in the 1700s a chapel, he told us, later a Quaker meeting hall, then a picture-gallery, turned into a theatre a century ago. He has played here many times, before taking over the lease three months ago, "a long story, tedious, lawyers, a bank, the uttering of disingenuous promises."

Took the opportunity to ask him where on the premises was located the famous "Lyceum Beef-steak Room" of legend, where the rakes of olden times were wont to carouse and gamble and summon up Lucifer. He laughed like a chimp. Had *very* much hoped to find it, had read of it in old books, but no room in the actual theatre corresponded to its description in the naughty old stories, some of which would not be proper to discuss in front of Flo, and he suspected it had never existed or was an amalgam of other such dens. So much of theatre life was mirrors and smoke, he added, leading us on through the gloom. "Actors like a dirty story. It relieves the monotony of the job. There is a lot of standing about in our work."

He (*walking us*): We are not at our best just yet, my dears, as you see. Thank the fates you've arrived to sort everything out. But one rather likes the corruption in its way, don't you feel? Purity is so dull.

Up a winding staircase, very steep, past the Band Room and Green Room—"mind how you go"—through a long sort of annex, then down steps (stone) and into what must be an old Costume Store. Tabards, doublets, hosiery, gowns, Arthurian robes, all ruined by moths. No glass in barred windows.

He: A young dog like you won't know Wills' play *Vanderdecken*?

I: I twice saw you play it in Dublin.

He: Bloody Nora, you didn't? That was a thousand years ago. The moment in Act Four when the ghost answers Thekla's question?

I (*quoting*): "Where are we?"

He: "Between the living and the dead."

Then, to Florence:

He: You see, the hero is dead, dear. Terrifying thing. One thinks of it always, backstage in a theatre. For we, too, are neither living nor dead. A thought one finds strangely consoling. Don't you think?

F: These abstractions of the artist hold little interest for me, I'm afraid. I choose to live in the real world.

He: Ah, the real world, that vile dungeon of cruelty and hunger. You are welcome to it.

F: It must be a very heavy burden to think that of the world.

He: I never trust a thinker—to feel is the only calling. But without what we do as artists your real world would be less bearable, no?

F: I distrust those who say life would not be possible without art. For millions of the poor it must be. They have no choice in the matter. Life would not be possible without little fripperies like food. Or shelter. The contention of anything else is a pose.

He: You have spirit, Mrs. Stoker.

F: I have a good deal more than that.

He: Of course. You have Bram.

F: I mean to keep him.

He: Offices up the stairs, my private sitting room also, company Dressing Rooms to the left as one approaches the Coal Store. Then Paint Room, Prop Room, Wig Room, Gas Room, Carpentry, Leading Lady, Chorus, Chief Musician. Some mumblecrust or another is running about with a map. Can't remember his name, little bow-legged chappie, dandruff, Welsh, always looks as though he's coming at you through a snowstorm. Delicious old maze but you'll soon work it out. Now if you'll excuse me, I must return to this wretched sitting, if I can find it, and I'm to have a strychnine injection in my throat beforehand—asthma, you know. You'll start tomorrow morning? I thought "General Manager" as your title?

I: You are joking I assume.

He: Joking is for schoolgirls.

I: But I couldn't manage a theatre. I have no experience of such matters.

He (*with a shrug*): How difficult can it be? Let *it* manage *you*.

I: Look here, with respect, that was not the understanding. You mentioned part time secretarial work and that alone. I have my writing to consider. The time—

He: Oh don't be such a fustilugs, you have managed yourself, have you not, and I daresay no one has died? You appear to be a going concern. And with a wife, no less. Don't talk such a royal lot of rubbish.

I: No but you will want someone who has performed the General Manager's role in a large theatre previously. There is a great lot of work to be done here.

He: You fear new experience? Then how can you hope to be an artist?

I: I hope to be an artist by devoting proper time to that aim. False pretences are a dashed poor foundation for anything.

He (*suddenly angry, tight mirthless smile*): I say, Stoker, let me apprise you as to how much I care about your judgements: somewhere between almost zero and zero. But you will not calumniate me in my own theatre, sir, while I stand here and nod. Do you mind what I say, sir? Or shall we step out the door?

Silence for a time. He lit a cigarette.

He: Apologies, Mrs. Stoker. I should not have spoken uncouthly in your presence. It seems, alas, that your husband and I have had a misunderstanding. My hope was to offer a foothold here in a working, professional theatre, a well-paid position where he might learn and absorb and in time do something worthwhile. Evidently I misread. Perhaps so did he. If he would rather return to clerking in Dublin, then go, with my blessing and only a little of my disappointment. See Walter with your expenses. Here's my hand to you both.

F: Might we take an hour or two to discuss your proposal, my husband and I?

He: Of course. Again, forgive me. I can give you one hour. After that, I must find a replacement.

I: When do you open?

He: In six weeks, with *Hamlet*.

I: For Christ's sake, six weeks. There are holes in the roof!

He (*stone-faced*): Then give the audience umbrellas.

I: I would need to make a study of the principal assets of the company.

He: You're looking at them.

I: I mean the accounts, the books, your deed on the lease.

He (*a sudden, disconcerting laugh and a clap on my back*): You perplex me a little, you beetle-headed old mary. Such *litt*leness in a lumping great ox of your size. The deed is with the lawyers, Braithwaite, Lowrey and Klopstock, 19, the Strand. You will find the ledgers in the office immediately to the right as one exits Stage Left. Cheerless reading, I'm afraid. Like an essay by Bernard Shaw. Here are the keys. Make yourself cosy. Oh, I took the liberty of having some drudge or another put your nameplate on the door.

I: Look here I shall need to speak with you later today, there will be questions, arrangements—

He: *I go, I go; look how I go, swifter than arrow from the Tartar's bow.*

* * *

Pushing open the filthy window, he looks down into Exeter

Street and watches his wife hail a cab for her appointment at the Museum. He wishes that he had not lost his temper, not spoken so abruptly. She has rarely seen him in that mode. He'd hoped to hide it or kill it.

A ballad singer down in the street is working a marionette of a witch. Children gather about him, laughing, clapping; one little boy waving a streamer.

> *The wind she blew*
> *The wicked hag*
> *Wrapped her baby in the bag*
> *The bag she threw*
> *All in the sea*
> *The wind she blew*
> *For thee and me.*

Lunch hour has coaxed crowds out of offices and shops, the narrow pavements overflowing, the beggars hard at work.

Suddenly, across the street, in the doorway of an apothecary's, he notices the young girl who opened the Stage Door to them earlier. Something sickly and kicked-down about her, all in black, like a waif, shuffling her bare feet from side to side, a ghastly dance. She holds her hand out to passers-by but nobody stops. Not right, to see a child of that tender age in beggary. For a girl, it is worse, can only lead to one thing.

In Regent Street, the dolls slowly blink.

If she works here in the theatre, she should be paid, protected. If she doesn't, she should be assisted somehow. Slowly, she raises her gaze, as though sensing his observance. Her smile is cold, freezingly violent. What has he done wrong? Does she mistake him for someone else? She turns and limps away down the street.

He is a strong man but it takes effort to haul open the rusted, creaking wallsafe. He takes out the heavy legal ledger, the thick packets of time-stiffened, wax-sealed documents, places them on the desk, clears a space for his notebook. For an hour, he works a careful way through the columns of figures, a correction here, a small adjustment there, until his temples are pounding with tension. But no matter how he comes at them, the numbers will not tally. He begins the work over, this time speaking the figures aloud to himself. The gap is narrowed but still it exists.

We will dement you, say the figures. *We will chew out your mind. Run, while you still have the chance.*

From time to time, a workman or scrubwoman happens past his open door. He asks if they might know how many seats the theatre contains, is there a map of the stalls and circles, a plan? How much should the tickets cost? Where do we advertise? Are the players paid ready cash? Where is the Box Office? Where are the lavatories? Who is the leader of the orchestra? How do things *work* here?

Nobody knows anything. Some scarcely pause as they pass. It's like being the uninteresting exhibit in a freak show, or acting in a play no one would want to see performed.

That evening, over a simple supper in their boarding-house flat, Florence is pale, seems absent, full of silences. He brings the ledger to the dining table, keeps up his calculations and rebalancings all through the meal, cursing quietly at the stubbornness of the numbers. She stares into her coffee cup. There is something she wishes to ask.

"Did he get around to mentioning your salary?"

"Not in person but he sent me round a note late this afternoon. Three guineas a week to start, rising to four in a year."

"But that's wonderful, Bram, we shall be able to take a little house, maybe in Chelsea or Pimlico?"

"Think it's better we stay close to the theatre, if you don't mind."

"I do mind, rather."

"Let's discuss it at another time?"

From somewhere the yelp of a dog, then the bells tolling nine in St. Mary le Strand.

"I had an interesting day at the library," she says. "The assistants are kindly and knowledgeable."

"Good."

"You might spend some time there yourself, Bram. The Celtic literature collection is fascinating. Better than anything one's come across in Dublin."

"I must."

"One of the librarians showed me through a manuscript about a fellow called Averock. Lopping off people's heads, doing hunnish things to virgins. They had a jolly good go at killing him but of course he couldn't die."

"Do you realise what he's done?"

"Averock?"

"Borrowed from one bank in order to pay the rent on the lease, then borrowed from three more using the same loan as collateral. Then the costumes, the carpentry, the upholsterers, it's eye watering. New music has been commissioned. Venetian chandeliers. The stage *curtains* cost seven thousand guineas."

"Can I help in some way?"

"This extravagance—it's insane. I'm quite up a tree trying to understand."

"I might go to bed now."

"For curtains."

"Why don't you come, Bram?"

"I'll just finish up this. Be along in a minute."

Close to eight the following morning he awakens on the sofa. There's a note from her to say she's gone to the library. The fire in the grate is lighted but the room is cold. Raindrops on the windows cause strange shadows down the walls.

An hour later, returned from his swim at the Jermyn Street

baths, he is making through the hallway when he sees that a letter has arrived for him. He recognises his mother's small, careful copperplate. Opening the envelope, he realises that the landlady has come out of her room and is peering at him worriedly as she wipes her hands on her apron.

"*Come sta, signore?* All is good?"

"Yes, ma'am. Thank you."

"We might please have a brief little talk one moment?"

"Is anything the matter?"

"The *Signora*, she is well and happy today?"

"Very well indeed. She has gone out on an errand."

"I wish and ask you one question, sir. About the Signor Irving."

"Yes?"

"How is it done?"

"Forgive me?"

"In my village—at home—the old people say, there is reason the Lord give us two ears and one mouth, sir, so's we'd listen twice as much as we'd speak, sir, *è vero?* But rumours. Many actor lodge in this house down the years and their stories of him? *Santo Cielo!*"

"I'm afraid I'm not much of a one for listening to tittle-tattle."

"*Sì, sì. Certo.* I say nothing, you understand. But here is an actor, *signore*. Sometime work, sometime no. Like all the actor. But he live in a five-room apartment on Duke Street Saint James, no? Go to auctions. Buy the paintings. The peacock's clothes and the hand-stitched boots. Ellen Terry she the greatest actress of England, *signore*, but she don't live like that, she live modest. This man spend on suit of clothes what another eat with for one year. Tell me—how is it done?"

"If you will excuse me, I am a little late for my work."

"*Sì*, one of the other, he often late. And so"—she draws a finger across her throat—"*arrivederci.*"

"The others?"

"The Signor Irving have four secretary before you. All young man. They no last."

"I don't think that is correct."

"*Stai attento, signore.*" She touches her fingertips in the bowl of holy water she keeps on the hall stand, blesses herself quickly, traces the sign of the cross on his forehead. "*Dio ti benedica.*"

The street is cold, the air smells of rain. As he hurries past the windows of the shops in Covent Garden, he catches occasional glimpses in reflection of a self he would like to inhabit. Purposeful, solid, bowler-hatted, sober, under exigent demands, no time for peasant foolishness. The Man Who Doesn't Believe Rumours.

What's troubling is that sometimes there are other reflections, too. Dolls with human hair. Their delft feet clicking. But when he stops to look again, they're not there.

* * *

VI

In which a newspaper cutting arrives in the morning mail and a character with an important name is encountered

From the *NEW YORK TRIBUNE*
November 30th, 1878
Portrait of an Actor
by G. GRANTLEY DIXON

On the wall of his large but surprisingly shabby office at the Lyceum Theatre in London hangs a framed sampler of needlework, of the sort which readers will have seen in numerous homes. Often completed by girls on the verge of womanhood, as an exercise in the matronly gifts, customarily these primers offer biblical quotations, couplets of improving poetry or commonsense phrases.

The motto on his wall strikes a chillier note: "Sweet, a good friend's failure."

The face is grave, stern, possessed of saturnine depth, somewhat reminiscent of Michelangelo's David. The black hair is worn long, like a poet's. He is jowly, has prominent lips, a massy head and long nose; his brows are heavy, the complexion oddly Mediterranean for an Englishman. A large, granitic, good-looking man, like a mariner or farmer, an out-of-doors person, he is by times curiously graceful in his movements, at other moments clumsy, speaking with exhausting rapidity but sitting stock still for lengthy periods while doing so.

When asked his most treasured possession, he showed this reporter a silver-framed photograph of Sarah Bernhardt asleep in her coffin.

I asked if he did not think it a queer picture for Miss Bernhardt's publicity managers to have circulated, given that she is alive and, presumably, well. "She may be well," he responded, "but no actor is truly alive. To me, that is the meaning of the photograph."

His large, grey eyes can seem bistre-coloured in lamplight. He suffers considerable short-sightedness and is given to odd, sudden squints, as though seeing some apparition no one else has noticed. He reads German and Dutch and collects "in a small way" works of art and medieval books "on necromancy and alchemy."

"But I am not a wealthy man. Nor should I wish to be. One can imagine no heavier curse."

"Than wealth?"

"Than wealth of that sort where its possessor need not work. After trinkets I should think it would buy only one thing, an evil thing I should never like to have, which is too much time to think. That is not good for a man. He begins to imagine slights."

On his desk, when we met, was a collection of the folkloric tales of Italy. "I began my life as a puppet," he assured this reporter inscrutably. "Then I became a real boy."

He smokes without cease, or forgetfully abandons a cigarette to burn out in the ashtray while he expands on some point or amusingly defames some important personage, in a purry, felty voice that slightly over-pronounces its esses. The tip of his left thumb is missing. "The result of an accident. I stuck it in Shaw's eye."

Mr. George Bernard Shaw is disliked (and nicknamed "Dreary O'Leary") by Mr. Irving because of that writer's insistence on stories of ordinary persons and their lives. "Like going along to Royal Ascot in the expectation of seeing thoroughbreds," Irving says, "only to find two flea-bitten mules butting heads in a ditch."

This reporter has heard it whispered that Irving is in favour of giving the vote to women?

"I am certainly in favour of taking it away from men."

Like many actors in England, he speaks in the clipped cut-glass accent that one suspects he was not born with, and like all actors, everywhere, his modesty is a form of boasting. One feels he has learned that the most efficacious way of prolonging the ovation is to fall to one's knees, head bowed.

To observe him pull on a glove or turn slowly downstage during rehearsal is to watch an artist at work who knows he is being watched. His recently employed factotum, an Irishman, is rarely far away and busies himself about his master as any new wife about her husband, occasionally completing the other's sentences or fetching in glasses of the hot lemon and paprika tea to which this Lord of the Stage is addict. The Dubliner speaks but rarely in company, having the stoical hauteur of a patriot on the gallows. Fitting, for his employer bears a striking resemblance to the once-famed Robert Emmet, various parts of whom were sundered from various others, on England's most ubiquitous export, the gibbet.

One curious thing is that, when this reporter consulted his notes of an interview that had lasted two pleasant hours, a conversation most engrossing and wide in its purview at the time, they seemed to contain much that was trifling and disjointed and many non sequiturs, almost nothing at all worth saying. It was as though one's notes had been written in invisible ink. But one passage stood out and is given verbatim:

"Playing is my trade, the butter on my bread. But artistry is also a spirit, a secret room in the soul. Where it is or the key that unlocks it is difficult to find, so that sometimes the door must be broken down by a sort of force. That is what is meant by having a style. One's force. Once inside one's own style, proportion changes. The room becomes an anywhere: a forest, an ocean, a prison cell, a fairyland, a number of spheres revolving inside each other, all at once, each on an axis the others know nothing about. At least, that is how one pictures it oneself. To be an artist is to know there are ghosts."

He is the talk of theatrical London for his extravagant plans. Many would like to see this ghost fail.

* * *

Manager's office
Lyceum Theatre
Stage door, Exeter Street,
London 11th December, 1878

Dear Mother,
Thank you for your letter, much appreciated, and for the article about my employer which you enclosed, although much of it is ridiculously fanciful. I did not know the American newspapers were to be had in Brussels. One of the unheralded surprises of London life is finding the odd copy of the *New York Times* or *Chicago Tribune*, which one does surprisingly often, on a park bench, say, or left on a tram, as though a fleet of ghost-postmen from America roamed London. One sees the world quite differently through American eyes. Please excuse this hurried response, I will write more when there is time.

I am glad to know that Brussels continues to be good to you. Yes, my wife and I are settled now here and all is coming well. I was sorry that you and my sisters were not able to attend our wedding but I do understand that funds are short. I feel certain that when you meet Florence you will like her very much and come to regard her as a daughter.

She is a thoughtful, watchful, funny, shrewd girl, of generous and optimistic nature and high intelligence. She is compassionate, too, and feels things deeply. I will say that not every single moment between us has been happy of late, particularly since we came to London, but I expect, at least I hope, that this is not an entirely unusual occurrence among new-married people who do not yet know one another all that well. There is also the unsettlement of the change. I am afraid I have grown rather fixed in my ways down the years and am perhaps too accustomed to my own company. My wife is understanding and tolerant but I will say that there have been moments of difficulty, all caused by me. I should like to be a better husband and hope I can be.

My duties here at the theatre are proving more toilsome than I had anticipated but I am hoping that this will ease with time and acclimatisation. Thank God, our opening night has been postponed a few weeks, otherwise I should have ended in the madhouse. For now, I must often write upward of 50 letters daily and see to all manner of tasks about which I have had to learn hurriedly. I seem to talk all day long and come home fagged to death. My employer moves in strange ways, a phenomenon not unknown among artistic people, who in my experience can have particular eccentricities and grandiosities, but then, who has not. I expect everyone has peculiarities of his own, be he barber, plumber, or king. One has heard it often contended that women are the unpredictable sex. That does not seem true, to me.

Our situation here is pleasant, although we haven't much room as yet. The plan is that we shall move in a bit, once things settle. I do appreciate what you say about the dangers to morality of theatrical life but you are not to worry yourself. My position, essentially, is managerial.

As part of my agreement with my employer, he will look at pieces I might write or adapt for the stage and so I am ardently hopeful for success on that front, at some point. I have been thinking that there might be a play in the American Civil War, perhaps "The Assassination of

President Lincoln" (which barbarous outrage itself took place in a theatre, as you know, and was perpetrated by a disappointed actor), or the struggle of brother against brother and so on, but we shall see. It might be too recent for decency.

Well, then, Mother, that is all my news. I am a little uneasy in myself of late, I don't know why. Pray for me.

I enclose two pounds.

Forgive my untidy scrawl. It seems worse since we came to London.

In haste but with my respectful love to you and my sisters.

* * *

THE VOICE OF ELLEN TERRY

Oddly—you wouldn't have a cigarette, darling?—thank you—no, oddly, I have very few distinct memories of the building itself . . . (*inaudible*) . . . One has spent so much time in theatres, you know, they rather all come to seem the same. But I know dear old Harry spent a ransom on doing it up. So they said at any rate. Probably he exaggerated, shouldn't wonder. He enjoyed making you feel he was hiding something a bit shocking.

Do you know, I can never remember exactly when I met Harry, he was just always there, like the sky. We did *Romeo and Juliet*, I seem to recall, in Cirencester or somewhere, when I was nineteen or twenty. He was kindly, a personable cove. Shatteringly handsome. And he had a sort of softness towards the older actors, which I always found touching, spoke to them with great respect and goodfellowship, even though some were long past their best nights. Which in honesty might not have been all that starlit to begin with. Journeymen actors—may

God bless every one of them. But he'd take them out walking the morning after a show, sit with them a while in the park. Make a little fuss of them, listen to their stories of the profession. He'd be careful to address them as Sir or Ma'am. Those small things count, with me.

I always think it important to say, about Harry, that he had once been very poor. A young actor starting out on the road—at that time, you'd know hunger. Harry knew what it was to be exhausted and cold, maybe to walk sixty miles between towns for a job, not to have had a proper bed or a place to wash. There was a winter when he was too poor to afford underwear and was sleeping in fields and doorways. So, the old actors were his heroes. He'd walked their roads.

We'd bump into each other now and again afterwards, in some awful "digs" in the provinces. He was amusing and charming, had the good flirt's trick of making you feel you were the only person in the room, which, even when you know the trick, is fun to see done well.

His party piece was a satirical impersonation of himself playing Lady Macbeth. "Look at me, I don't take myself tremendously seriously," that type of fellow. Which is always a sign that they do.

Another tactic, the poor booby, was that he'd flatter your hair. "Oh, your beautiful russet ringlets, Angel, is *russet* the correct word?" You see, he knew that every other chap in the room, if he flattered you at all, would burble on about your eyes because that's what chaps did. So, it was always your hair with Harry.

That way, you were supposed to notice he was different from the rest. Tremendously full of feeling and sensitivity and refinement. I saw him do it five hundred times. Mr. Russet. It could be early in the morning, it might be after a First Night party, you could be looking like the portrait in Dorian Gray's attic, it was still "Dolling, your beautiful hair." (*Laughs.*)

Oh of course he was in love with one, just ardently, immensely, and going to shoot himself if he couldn't have you, and in love with someone else three minutes later. By the time you'd boil an egg, he'd have pledged undying devotion elsewhere and be about to leap off London Bridge if rejected. One admired his energy.

He enjoyed when the Westminster Public Gasworks opened, whatever year that was. Gave him a new way of threatening to do away with himself if refused.

Keep thwacking the golf balls, one of them's bound to go in. That sort of chap. A bit scattergun in his approach to wooing.

It was simply the way with Harry, like waiting for sunrise. But once you made clear that you wouldn't be going to bed with him, he'd look oddly relieved and calm down. And the matter once raised would not be revisited, I will say that for him. He didn't make a nuisance of himself. Funny old skellum. Never dull. There are men whom it is important not to take the slightest notice of when they're talking, if it's after ten o'clock at night and they've had a glass of beer. Harry was one such mammal.

They really and truly don't mean to be idiots. But it's like a Roman Catholic person not wanting to feel guilt. Might as well ask water to run uphill. Except that *might* conceivably be contrived. With a pump.

Once, he asked my sister to run away with him, to Rotterdam I think it was. She said no and he asked my brother. That was the most important thing to understand about Harry. Essentially, what he wanted—darling, who wouldn't—was someone to run away with him to Rotterdam.

It's what all of us want, isn't it? Of course, nobody gets it. Probably not even those misfortunates who are in Rotterdam already. One wonders where *they* want to run away to. Crouch End?

But he'd grown up and taken on a bit of sensibleness—is that a word?—by the time he opened the Lyceum. What age? Oh, in his middle thirties I should guess, darling, no one counts these things too carefully in our profession. 36-ish, perhaps? He was 36 a long time. (*Laughs.*) And by the time he was 36, he had acquired all the maturity of an only sometimes irksome schoolboy who needs cuffing about the head just once a term. Early developer, our Harry. For a man.

I should think the best feature of the old Lyceum was where it was located, slap in the middle of London. One's played a frightful lot of cities up and down and abroad. Cologne. Berlin. Paris. Sydney. Wonderful theatres, my heavens, and then there is New York. But I do sort of feel London is where a playhouse belongs, dashed if I know why. Something to do with the weather.

And Shakespeare. When one knows he might have walked the selfsame street, it rather puts a fizz in one's blood. You see the Thames, and you feel, golly, the Globe was just yonder. He might have got the idea for *Macbeth* on Southwark Row or the Embankment. Pepys. Kit Marlowe. Those ghosts are all about. That's what I found, at any rate, as a young actress coming up. But it was thirty centuries ago, darling. One was so full of— what is the word?

No, I wasn't there when Bram came, although, queerly, I often think I was. Somehow he was always there, like that rainy light coming in the windows. He was a darling man, rather obsessive, exquisitely serious. He could be absentminded, too, the sort of fellow who goes out in unmatched shoes. One used often to think he would have made a wonderful monk.

He didn't at all seem the sort one would employ as a manager. Head in the clouds sort of chap, not a clue about the things that really matter in a theatre, like money and tickets and making sure the gutters have been cleared and someone's sweeping the foyer and the actors aren't poisoning each other.

A little of that is all right, it keeps up morale. Too much of it and the audience starts noticing.

Harry was ruddy useless, felt management to be beneath him, and so Bram wouldn't have had, what's the word, say a mentor of any sort. A bit imperious, was Harry. Knew he was Harry.

"King Henry the Ninth', I used to call him, as a tease.

But an ingénue can grow into a role, after all. One supposes Bram must have done. God knows how.

* * *

In the Upper Circle, he is trying to make an accurate count of the seats, but his hangover is making it difficult. The total keeps slipping, the numbers swap and shimmer. Three times, he has had to recommence from scratch, the floor plan he has found is inaccurate, forty years out of date, and the ruckus from down in the auditorium keeps crashing through the bulwarks of his solitude.

A trumpeter is quarrelling with a Liverpudlian ticket-taker, the noise is like an aria from Hell. Teams of plasterers are caterwauling and joking as they work, moulding putti and gilded angels and escutcheons to the fronts of the curved new boxes. It is as though the seats rearrange themselves the moment he turns his back, like school brats disconcerting a new teacher.

We are uncountable, say the rows of velvet seats. *You think the dust falls on us. In fact, we create it. We creak when you raise us, we moan when lowered. We are Manhattans of woodwork and we reek of damp britches. We shall punish you for the long centuries of seatly servitude when the lowest parts of your race were pressed into our velvet flip-down faces. But our day is approaching. We shall sit upon you. If you prick us, do we not bleed?*

He walks to the edge of the balcony. Peers down into the parterre. The swimmy-headed compulsion to jump.

Teams of workmen are sprinkling shreds of lemon peel and

handfuls of cinnamon—someone reckoned these odours repel wild cats—while scrubwomen on their knees trowel up the never-ending pellets of cat dirt. Meanwhile, three large and ugly tabbies sit watching from the stage, occasionally licking their paws. There is no doubting which species is the audience, which the show.

Now a slim, fox-faced fellow in a too-tight suit appears behind him at the top of the Upper Circle stairs.

"Mr. Stoker, sir?"

"The same."

The young man descends.

"Name of Jonathan Harker." His cockney accent is music. "I wonder if you've received my note?"

"I am new here, Mr. Harker. Catching up, as it were."

"I've took the liberty of writing to Mr. Irving, sir, about a position as apprentice scene-painter? Got a portfolio of my sketches here, should you care to take a look?"

Forests, deserts, beautiful portraits of soldiers, carefully inked mazes, seascapes, Turkish bazaars.

"This is fine work, Mr. Harker. Where did you train?"

"Paris now and again, sir, whenever I could afford it. But self-taught, really, I suppose you might say."

"Been at it long?"

"Since a boy, sir."

"You're a little too good for the theatre, this level of detail is better than we need. Had you thought of seeking something at the *Illustrated London News*?"

"The theatre's what I love, sir. Proper determined on that. I don't care to work in no newspaper."

"Why not, lad?"

"Too sad, sir. All explosions and earthquakes and wars no one wanted. Chum of mine went to Zululand, sir, for the *News*, doing pictures once a week. Went into himself, no lie, never really come out."

"I'm not sure we have anything at the moment. Perhaps come back in a few months once we're up on our feet?"

"I do clean work, fast, sir. You wouldn't regret it."

"I don't doubt you. You seem a nice, bright boy. What age are you?"

"Twenty, sir, next birthday. I'd work every hour of day and night, sir, so help me I would."

"I don't know. I don't know. What sort of terms were you looking for?"

"Whatever you think is fair, sir, what I want is experience. I ain't looking for no fortune, just a start and a bit of beer money."

"Can you count, Mr. Harker?"

He laughs. "I believe so, sir, yes."

"Count every seat in this theatre. Consider yourself employed."

* * *

Three o'clock of the morning. Decent London lies abed.

The hour when the city's statues commence to twitch and creak, descend their lichened pedestals in powderclouds of rust.

A bronze Lord Lieutenant with a death mask for a face. A cracked marble Viscount with eerie blanks for eyes. A General on his horse, ruined by time and London gullshit, they clank through Hyde Park to drown babies in the Serpentine that oozes through the city's nightmares.

No cruelty is beyond the statues. They live in the corroding rain of indifference, have endured being walked past by millions.

Gargoyles peel from a belfry, Death-Angels from mausoleums, tiny Christs from ten thousand gravestones. Dead Earls and their dowagers from coffin lids of granite. Stone imperial eagles from stern pillars outside palaces flap graven, etched wings over Whitechapel.

In deathbeds from Kent to Camden, a crashing weight is slammed. Doctors call it a stroke, a heart attack, a collapse. The statues have struck again.

* * *

His wife enters the breakfast room with a packet sent her by a cousin who works at the British Consulate in Berlin. A pirated copy in German of an anthology, *Best English Ghost Tales*, containing an early story of his own.

"Rather flattering surprise," he says.

"In what way?"

"Well, that anyone would bother to translate one's work. Or to read it at all, come to that."

"You don't feel it to be wrong that your permission wasn't sought? And I assume you won't be paid."

"Copyright is a form of hubris, even selfishness in a way. How can something of the imagination be owned? May as well copyright birdsong. Or dawn."

"The author of birdsong and dawn is acknowledged hundreds of millions of times every day."

"This is different, my darling, it is not worth the bother."

"How can you say so?"

"Most books die young. Sad but true, I'm afraid. In literature the rate of infant mortality is high."

"Every birth is worth recording, Bram."

"Nice idea. Doesn't happen."

"But a book could have an afterlife about which the author knows nothing."

"How so?"

"It might find readers years later, even after the novelist has died."

"I have never heard of such a case."

"What of that? It could happen."

"Theoretically yes, but—"

"There is also right and wrong, Bram. Or doesn't that matter?"

"I must go to my work. Don't upset yourself."

* * *

Shortly after eleven, he attends the meeting he has called of the house staff. Boxkeepers, ushers, stagehands, fitters, scenery-movers, painters, musicians, 87 people in all. He distributes the rosters, answers the employees" questions, most of which have to do with overdue wages, although some have to do with cats. "All you want to do, sir, is lay your hands on a couple of gallons of fox piss. That's the stuff will drive 'em out." Reasons why a theatre manager might not want to sprinkle his premises with vulpine urine are expounded, as are the likely difficulties of sourcing several gallons of same.

He had hoped Irving would attend but there's no sign of him, no message. "The Chief stays in bed until nightfall," someone jokes.

At lunchtime, head throbbing, Stoker takes a cab to Green Park, cools his face at the fountains, scribbles a few notes on his cuffs.

That elderly gentleman in the bath chair, being pushed by a maidservant. Two schoolboys rattling a stick through the grating of a fence. That shoeless man beneath the wych elm, dozing in the cold sunshine. What are their stories? Where are they going?

He pictures his Florence in the sepulchral silence of the Museum, surrounded by her books and papers. Then his Florence stepping out of her nightgown, letting it pool about her ankles, coming to him. So strange, marriage. Does everyone feel the same? Like music you can't quite read.

Returned to the office, a packet is waiting on his desk with a note. "Look this over, if you would, and see if there's a play here. If so, you might run up a treatment. Yours, Henry. P.S.: I assume you read French. You seem the type."

The book is a collection of feverish stories by an American writer new to him, published by a small house in Paris. Eerie, sick yarns that would give you the shakes. People walled up in cellars, dead hearts that still beat, men harrowed by doppel-gängers who haunt them. There might be stage possibilities in one or two of the tales—but roughing them out into scenes seems to burn them down, somehow—yet an idea of his own arises out of the ashes like an odour, a ghost story set not in the past but now, in Piccadilly.

How terrifying that would be for the audience, to see their own city on the stage but stalked by a monstrous evil. His ghoul would dress like an aristocrat, in finest Savile Row, would have a box at the opera, a carriage, membership of a Mayfair club, a teddibly English accent. At night he'd climb the hundred steps that lead to his townhouse's turret, where he'd sit in a glass room glaring down on High Holborn through perpetual storms of heartache. Then he'd take to the streets, razor hidden in his waistcoat. And o, my dears, the revenge.

For a twist—yes—the monster is not a man but a woman in men's attire, wronged by men all her life. First she steals away their wives. Then, late at night, she strikes.

Would it work? Might it upset people, cause unrest, unhelpful questionings? Never enough time to think a story *through*. Never enough money to stop thinking. Money is everything. He didn't know it before. What a writer thirsts for is time, the permission to fail if needs be, the removal of the thumbscrews brought by having to pay the rent. Money is a work of fiction but it is needed all the same. The only kind of fiction that is.

The Costume Designer insists on speaking with him, the Orchestra Conductor is upset because a Second Violist has still not been hired, the actors are threatening mutiny because many of the wigs have lice. Two of the windows in the Quickchange Room are broken. The printer doing the programme has absconded with the money. It's like standing on a pier in a storm of circling winds, wondering which of them will carry you away.

He buys a referee's whistle and brings it to production meetings. When they threaten to get out of hand, as invariably they do, he blows it as hard as he can. Nothing can be accomplished if they shout each other down, he explains. Here is my hat. You will place it on your head. Only the person hatted has permission to speak. All other members of the company will *listen* in respectful silence.

". . . Mr. Stoker, Mr. Stoker, I was here first . . ."

"One at a time! Let us not be *unruly* . . ."

The hat is accepted resentfully by the Chief Cloakroom Attendant who announces her immediate resignation.

He dreams of being in a cathedral-sized theatre carved out of ice, glacially quiet, a translucent basilica. Irving is seated in the Dress Circle peeling a pomegranate with a dagger, feeding handfuls of its bloody beads to his dog.

* * *

VII

The reader of respectable moral character will wish to pass over this chapter, in which pages from a diary kept in Pitman shorthand are offered, unclean expressions included.

5th January, 1879

Today my first book arrived in the mail from Dublin, having been commissioned by my former masters at the Castle while I was still in their employ.

The Duties of Clerks of Petty Sessions in Ireland.

It is every bit as enthralling a read as it sounds.

But Florrie was lovely about it. We had champagne.

6th January, 1879

Told H.I. that I had been examining ways of making economies. One measure was that we might not beeswax the actors' shoes before every performance, as he wishes to be done, but once or twice a week, the principal players only, and use common household polish, which is many times cheaper.

H.I.: All shoes will be beeswaxed daily, twice on matinee days.

Self: There is surely no need?

H.I.: Yes there is.

Self (*reluctantly*): As you wish.

H.I.: All swords, crowns and armour will be silvered before a performance, all costumes laundered and pressed, the players fined a night's pay if they stain them. There is never to be so much as a speck of grime on my stage. The people want to see magic. They had better see it.

This, while behind him, on that same stage, a filthy grey cat hopped from packing crate to upturned cello-case to head of a prop Grecian statue, where it sat, regarding me coldly through the reams of ashen dust before loosening its mess over Athena.
An image which I think shall remain with me awhile.
Placed order for thirty pounds of beeswax.

7th January, 1879

This afternoon after luncheon I stepped out of rehearsal (which was very fractious indeed) and went to Hatchard's book shop on Piccadilly to enquire as to the whereabouts of the work I had ordered some time ago but was irritated to be informed, in a somewhat lofty manner, that it had not yet arrived from the United States or was detained by HM Customs at Southampton. One would have imagined that, here in the capital of the civilised world, such relatively small requirements would be easy to supply. Damned frustrating.

But, then, surprisingly, as I made to leave, the young man (impudent mouth, lustrous black hair) called me back to the counter and said, *mirabile dictu*, that the parcel he had opened the very moment following my departure in fact contained the book.

It is *The Principles and Science of Modern Theatrical Effects and How They Are Contrived* by Edward Helsing and Edmund Lagrange. On the cursory overview that I was able to give, it appears poorly written—these colonials approach English as though blaming it for a murder—but contains a series of fascinating and detailed illustrations on the modern way of achieving such effects as authentic lightning, the roar of storms, the rushing of rivers, battle charges, cannon fire, earthquakes, tornadoes, typhoons, billows of smoke, ghosts, so on. Many of these would be shatteringly expensive—a matter no American impresario worries himself too much about, of course, the book is written as though money were rain—but some are intriguing and might be achievable even for a non-millionaire theatre.

The chapter on make-up is especially rewarding and gives direction on achieving such usable appearances as "Moroccan," "Arab," "ape-like Irish," "Mediterranean (swarthy)," "criminal," "Spaniard," "nobleman," "murderer," "low morals (male)," "low morals (female)" and "innocent girl ruined by duke." There is in addition a most fascinating and serviceable chapter on the conveying of "sundown" and "dawn with birdsong," this latter a marvel, what sounds a truly fiendish and awe-inspiring trick by which a player appears to disappear (as it were) before the audience's eyes. It is done with precisely triangulated mirrors set behind a procession of scrims.

I mean to make an intent and long study of this and similar works for I believe that the theatre-going public will soon tire of old fashioned ways. In London this decomposition has already begun to occur. New sensations are wanted, modern, of our own world. If we can but steal a march on our rivals in this regard, we might triumph. "A lot is accomplished by distracting attention or by hiding in the open," as Helsing states in his sometimes almost literate preface. As though we didn't know.

On the way back to the theatre I found Piccadilly Circus closed by the police because of an incident of public disorder—a woman had thrown paint at a passing cab containing the Prime Minister—and detoured across Leicester Square but was sorry to have done so. An army of poor people had congregated there, in pitiable and heart-breaking condition, very emaciated and in a terrible way. To see the men with their dignity taken away from them is a dreadful sight, many the worse for drink or given over to opium, and to see the women and children is appalling. Many of these misfortunate people were from Ireland, as I heard from their supplications. Gave what I could. Wished I had more.

How can such want be permitted in a wealthy, a generous kingdom? Why do we think that these people have different feelings, needs, from our own?

One small moment unmanned me to tears. A pigeon was hopping along on a patch of dirty grass having sustained some sort of injury making the use of one wing impossible and was flapping and piteously leaping. A feral little dog scampered from the rubbish heap and went to have at it, snarling. One of the ragged children leapt out shouting wildly "hie, hie, away" and waving his arms until the mongrel slunk off, and the poor disarmed pigeon toddled on towards God knows whatever set of metropolitan jaws. But it moved me to my core to see that, in even a tiny child who can have known little enough of mercy or fairness in this world, there is at least the desire that matters should be evened up.

Intending to continue my return to the theatre, I turned down Charing Cross Road and went by St.-Martin-in-the-Fields Church Path onto the Strand, when I happened to notice, through the window of the French Café on the corner of Villiers Street, the unmistakable figure of the Chief. He was seated alone and reading the *Manchester Guardian*. Glancing up, he saw me and, with a warm smile, beckoned.

"And how is our princely Mr. Stoker this fine morning, bedad?"

I said I was well.

"So I see," he said. "Like stout Cortez when with eagle eye he gazed upon the Pacific."

He asked if I would take a cup of civet coffee with him.

I answered that I had a full plate of tasks to deal with at the theatre but he insisted, saying the place had dealt with itself for two hundred years and could struggle on another half an hour without our interference.

"You shall be a welcome relief from the cussed newspaper," he said pleasantly. "I don't know why I buy it. There is never anything one *wants* to read, don't you find? Only the things one is told one *should* read by way of improvement."

I found him in breezier mode than on previous occasions, amiable, likeable, affectionate. He was having a dish of porridge, onto which he poured a dram from a hipflask. "Bourbon County whiskey," he explained. "Nunc est bibendum, *mon brave*."

There was a morningtime sleepfulness in his manner, which can be charming in men.

"Had a rough old time last night," he said with a rueful grin. "Fell in with bad company, down in the underworld. Place where a fellow can find whatever sort of fun he prefers. Head's thumping. I don't usually use alcohol."

"Why is that?"

"I become unimpressive."

I said he must be the only gentleman of the theatre not to be a devotee of the grape.

"Well, let's see," he answered, "I can reckon my account. In the mornings, as you've witnessed, I have a measure of Bourbon with my mash, like a good old horse. Then a glass or two of hock and seltzer around eleven, for pep. A bottle of claret with luncheon, a Beaumes de Venise afterwards, a flute of iced champagne around three to keep the old boilers fuelled, a good glass of beer or two immediately before I play—they like to see you sweat for them—then no grog at all until after the show. I have a snifter or two then, all right. I regard myself as practically teetotal."

I laughed, and then it occurred to me that this was the first time I had ever seen him truly off the stage. He was like a different man.

"You have a gentle face when you laugh," he said. "You should do it more often. It gives the old boat-race a holiday."

By now my coffee had arrived and a plateful of blood puddings.

"How are you settling in, so, my good Bram?"

"It is not without its challenges. But we're getting there, at least I think so."

"Rehearsals coming along?"

"I believe so, yes."

We spoke briefly of an innovation he is making to *Hamlet*, a play which contains only two parts for women. He wishes us to be bold, to greatly swell the court of Elsinore, "fill it with lasses as well as lads, as many as we can. Nothing drearier than a lot of blokes striding about the stage slapping their thighs. One might as well be at a football match."

I said I would arrange it as soon as was practicable.

"I was thinking," he continued, "your burden is heavy. You must let me know how you may be assisted, if a secretary or so on would help. Your enthusiasm is valuable, I would not want to lose it. In the meantime, we should have a natter about the root of all evil."

I looked at him.

"I mean gelt," he said. "I want to raise you, say, to four guineas a week. I can't do it just yet but I shall be able to, soon."

"Thank you, my wage is more than adequate, it is generous."

"You must permit me to insist. The labourer is worthy of his hire."

"Let us see how matters stand in a while."

"Good-oh. Any difficulties I should know about? Actors murdering each other? Give 'em a kick up the cooler if so."

I said I did have one thing I might say to him about the players, a question he might wish to look at from their point of view.

"I doubt I should want to do that. It's never happened before."

He is one of those men who rather enjoy being inscrutable.

We spoke for a while about his habitual practice, which to me is odd, of not attending rehearsals but of having the players manage without him, indeed of being so often absent from the theatre. His feeling is that over-familiarity should be avoided, that "the spark" he wishes his productions to evince comes from "freshness and danger." What did I think? I ventured that, whilst I understood and respected his policy as the product of long experience, I did feel that the younger players in particular would benefit from his presence among them and perhaps were in need of an anchor, a guide light, a sort of father. He nodded.

"I dislike this bloody English mania for preparation," he said. "The best things are never prepared, they unroll, they merely *happen*. But you'd know that, of course, being my fellow Celt."

"Your fellow?"

"You are looking at no Saxon. I have Cornish blood from my mother. We have our own ancient Celtic language and lore, our customs."

"I had not been aware of that."

We seemed by now to have steered ourselves into some sort of blind alley. There was silence but for the tinkling of teaspoons on china, before he began again, "Mrs. Stoker is well, I hope? It will be an adjustment for her, London life and so on. You mustn't give us all your time, you know."

"I shan't."

"A spouse can lose courage when left too often alone. I have seen it happen many times in the profession. You don't want that."

"No."

"Can't tell you what it means to me, old love, having you

join the adventure. One feels the danger of trying is lessened when one does so with good friends."

"I am honoured," I said, somewhat flummoxed, "that you should see me as a friend."

And then he said a curious thing.

"Friendship, for me, is a matter of recognition. A kind of homecoming if you will. One can't explain it. Yet every human alive has had this experience once or twice. When we met, I recognised you. That is all I can say. Do you feel what I mean?"

"Of course."

"At night, I go into myself. This is rather a confession. I drink a bit of laudanum now and again for an old complaint, tore my back as a lad. Find it brings me to a realm where there are souls, not bodies. I have met people there. I have even met myself. It will make you uneasy when I say that I have met you, also. We were in fact married in some previous world, you and I, our other selves. Or perhaps in the next one. Who knows?"

I laughed. "Which of us was the bride and which the groom, one wonders?"

He smiled back. "How dull you are, sometimes, you earth-bound clodding ninny. Well, here we are mooning and prattling like a couple of spoony schoolgirls. Back in harness, say I. Chop chop."

On the street outside, he whistled up a cab, which was to take him to an appointment at the bank. For some reason, there came into my mind the vision of the poor people I had seen earlier in Leicester Square.

I said to him: "May I ask you something?"

"Anything."

"The first morning my wife and I arrived at the theatre, the Exeter Street door was opened to us by a girl of perhaps twelve or thirteen. She looked hungry and mistreated. Who is she?"

"There is no girl, old hog."

"But we saw her plain as day."

He shook his head. "Children are forbidden to work in a theatre, it is a strict condition of the lease."

"How strange. I could have sworn."

"I don't know who or what you saw. But there wasn't a girl."

Up came the cab and away he went with a wave.

I decided to alter my route and redirected through Soho. Went to find a certain "song cellar," The Drakes, in a lane off Dean Street, which I have heard some of the boys at the theatre mention to each other, a private club where men meet late at night for companionship and singing. But perhaps had got the address wrong for could not locate it.

A pity. I should like to be under the ground, singing with a lot of fellows, while London sleeps.

Perhaps I shall look again.

* * *

12th January, 1879

This morning my Harker came in, despite it being a Sunday. I am ever more impressed by him and wish I could have an army of Harkers. But having one of him is nice enough to be going along with.

He and I ran a little experiment out of the book and attempted the production of chemical smoke but without success apart from the blackening of our neckties. We shall adjust the proportions and try again presently. In the meantime, he is proving a great help, a good-humoured, pretty, calm boy. We spent an hour in the Under-stage together, covered in dust and oil, fixing the gears on the hydraulic trapdoor and repairing its badly rusted crank. Gratified to say we succeeded eventually. I found using the hammer enjoyable and vivifying. There is nothing quite so bracing as good honest sweat between men.

There is about Harker, which I like, a most admirable curiosity, a keen willingness to learn.

I suspect he also has things to teach.

13th January, 1879

My own Harker has drawn me up a most attractive and detailed plan of the theatre, with every seat marked, Stalls, Dress Circle and Upper. By these means, we may know on any given date how full or not the house shall be. All we need do is to place a waistcoat button marked "x" on every sold seat. Another capital innovation of his has been to set an ordinary schoolhouse blackboard up in the flies so that the riggers may have a written record of every cue. He is a font of bright notions.

On an impulse, I asked if he himself had ever been to the singing club at The Drakes. Eyes not meeting mine, he said that he had not but knew fellows that had. I said I had gone looking for it the other day but had seen no sign or board. "There ain't none, sir," he told me, still averting his gaze. "Those as wants The Drakes seems to find it."

"The clientele in the main would be bachelors, Harker, would you say?"

"I'd say gentlemen what prefers the company of gentlemen, sir. In a manner of speaking."

"Like every other club in London, then," I said, attempting a joke.

"In some ways, sir," he replied.

"What sort of singing do they do there?" I tactfully enquired.

"Molly Cockleshells does a turn on Tuesdays, round three in the morning. Comic songs, I'm told."

"Has she a pleasant voice?"

"She's an 'e, sir."

"Ah."

"There ain't all that much singing goes on, in truth, sir," he continued. "It's only when the police comes to raid, the fellows starts singing, that's the cover."

"I see."

"Yes," he replied. "The Drakes ain't a place no gentleman wants to get nicked, sir. There's other establishments where a better sort of gentleman goes what's safer."

"From the police, do you mean?"

"And from blackmailers."

"The more careful sort of gentleman. Where would he go?"

"I've heard tell of an establishment, sir, near Portland Place. But it's invites only and a thousand guineas a year. Dunno how a body would join."

"I am speaking from curiosity only, you understand."

"Course, sir. I've already forgot we've spoke."

On the debit side of Lyceum life, it would appear that my suggestion to the Chief that he attend the rehearsals for *Hamlet* (which he began to do this afternoon) has not met with universal enthusiasm.

I was standing in the wings with young Harker, the both of us uncoiling a new set of hempen ropes together and sharing a joke, when this unedifying exchange ensued on the stage, between the holder of the title role and the spirit of his deceased father.

The Chief: You are playing the king of Denmark risen from his tomb, not a drunken chimney-sweep interfering with himself behind a hedge. Again, you dotard! And *frighten* us this time. God's nightdress, you are about as otherworldly as a knocking-shop spittoon.

Mr. Dunstable (*as the Ghost*): "My hour is almost come, when I to sulphurous and tormenting flames must render up myself."

*

The Chief (*impatient*): "Alas, poor ghost!"

Mr. Dunstable: "Pity me not, but lend thy serious hearing to what I shall unfold."

Silence for a long moment. It became uncomfortably evident that the Ghost had forgotten his lines.

The Chief: UNFOLD, for the love of Christ, what are you waiting for, a bloody telegram?

Mr. Dunstable: Sir, I am sorry, if I could have a short break.

The Chief in high rage kicked over an expensive chair.

He: Five minutes, you donkey. Go and have a feed of oats! Come back here not knowing every single syllable of your words and I will slice out your heart and stuff it up your transom. You bracket-faced, sexless old ponce, GET OUT!

At this point, I told Harker to busy himself elsewhere and went tactfully onto the stage. There were resentful glances at the Chief from some of the younger company in particular. It does not do for the general to lose his composure before the troops. If he does, they begin to wonder what a general is for.

He was by now downstage left, cursing to himself in an unrepeatably obscene manner and quaffing from a bottle of whiskey which his dresser had brought. His dog padded on, trailing a lead of chain, and nuzzled at his thigh in a manner that seemed piteous, like a man dressed as a dog. Seeing me, the Chief nodded in a way I have come to recognise. It is neither an invitation nor a rejection. What to do?

A curious little fact had come to my notice during the day. It had amused me, and now I hoped it might divert him, too, and suck the poison out of the moment. That done, I would find some place to spit it.

I asked if he and I might have a brief word about some small matters.

"Such as?"

"Your wife has written," I told him, "to say that she and certain members of her family would like to have tickets for the first night."

"Give them."

"I notice that Mrs. Irving, like my own espoused saint, is named Florence."

"What of it?"

"I—Nothing, of course. Merely the coincidence."

His face was thunderous dark. "We are estranged. If that is any of your business. Was there something else on what I suppose must be referred to as your mind?"

I was thrown by this abrupt dismissiveness and had to look about. "I believe we need more carpenters," was the best I could do.

"Then find them."

"We appear to be a little short of ready funds just at present. A cheque was declined this morning. Perhaps you might arrange for a further subvention from the bank?"

He repeated my last sentence in a derisory cawing sneer of an Irish accent, which I did not like, and then he continued: "It does not occur to you that I might have more urgent difficulties on my hands than getting out my begging bowl for you again?"

"For me?"

"For all of you! *All of you!* Must you bother me incessantly with these petty vulgarities? Cannot you see that I am busy, must you all drain me dry? You are paid to be a *manager*. Then do a little managing. Stop *wringing me out* like a bloody dish-cloth, can't you."

The hound on its chain lunged at me, its filthy jaws dripping. Some of the players were frightened, and I was, too. The Chief snapped a finger and the dog wilted back.

"I have done my best," I said, upset, "in difficult circumstances. I will continue to do so, of course, as long as you wish. If my services are not what you require —"

He resumed, riding over me. "You call this arse-about your best, sir. I should like to see your worst. We open in a week and the scenery isn't even painted. I suppose that is because I have not done it myself."

Stung, I turned and called out "Mr. Harker, if you please, are you ready?"

"Thank you, Mr. Stoker, sir," came the cry from up in the flies, and in a heavy thunderous rustle, the great backdrop was unfurled.

Dust from the floor rose slowly around it and the canvas rippled a moment before tautening. Never has a more gorgeous Elsinore been seen than young friend Harker's, the jet-black battlements and lofty crenellations and ranks of culverins' mouths, the high lamplit windows, the black and silver gargoyles, the sky a silvered grey against which the limelight will glow in a sumptuous, unforgettable lustre. Fifty-seven feet high and eighty-two across, it seemed to zing and pulse with a vivacity so electrical that one could almost hear it. The players, the carpenters, the workmen in the auditorium fell silent in awed admiration, and then, from every corner of the house, applause began to ring, from the women cleaning the stalls, the lamplighters up in the chandelier, the plasterers, the gas-boys, the furnace-men in the Under-stage, the violinists tapping their bows on their instruments. "Bravo, that man! A cheer for the painter! Hurrah for the Lyceum Theatre!"

All but one.

I could see that he was impressed as any sane witness would be, but, like a miffed schoolchild, he could not bear to be seen admitting it. He did not join in the appreciation but stalked into the wings pursued by the dog and made directly for the narrow staircase that leads to his private sitting room. Hurrying after him, I said that a word of encouragement to the men and Harker would go across well.

"I pay their wages," he replied coldly from the stairhead. "I am not their mother, thank Christ. They may suck elsewhere for their milk."

With that, he entered his quarters and slammed the door behind him, so hard that the call-noticeboard on my side of the wall fell down.

There was no further rehearsal today.

Curiously, the cats seem to have emigrated en masse, as though some overlord commanded them to leave.

17th January, 1879

4.33 A.M.

Took a sleeping-draught, two drachms of powdered morphine and camphor, but it gave me a frightful dream. The Chief was breathing out fog, in filthy, yellow wisps, which wreathed about him like cigar smoke but seemed alive. It thickened and dispersed, oozing horribly through the windows. Those who breathed it fell down dead or clawed at each other. Awoke, drenched in sweat. Alone in the house.

Florence returned to Dublin last night for her nephew's christening at St. Ann's Dawson Street, the church where we were married, as she reminded me coldly.

We had quarrelled before she left and there was not time to make it up.

She has got a bee in her bonnet again about something that does not matter, the question of the pirating of my writings, this time in Hungary. Always I point out that they would earn only pennies and are not worth bothering about but my saying so seems to frustrate her. In any case, as I tell her ad nauseam, it is exceedingly difficult to copyright a book.

She countered that she had studied up on the matter at the British Library and had even consulted a notary. The solution was for me to make a stage-play rendition of every story and have it performed just once, and in this way the work would acquire the legal copyright protection that stage plays enjoy. I said it was a ridiculous notion and that she should not have engaged any lawyer without my permission. She continued, "An inventor patents ideas, as surely you know. Is not a book an invention, like the spinning jenny or a weighing scales?" I said "Not as useful, I'm afraid." Angrily, she left the room, saying "Grow up, can't you," and only returned when she was packed. Asked if I minded her going to Dublin. I said that I did not (although I did). It was as though we were seeking permission of one another for something else or asking some other question in disguise. Then felt as if I had said the wrong thing. Then missed her.

Walked until late, over to the East End, Shadwell stair. Stood and looked at the river a long time.

Had thought all of that was over, would end with married life.

Perhaps never thought that. Dissembling.

Thoughts chirruping and cawing. Do not like the dawn. If dolls walk, now is the hour.

18th January, 1879

Half past midnight

Yesterday morning I was on the Strand with Harker and

some of the apprentice players (who were in costume) handing out playbills for *Hamlet*, the run starts tomorrow night, God help us, when I noticed, in the window of Atkinson's stationers, one of those new and portable machines about which so many have been rabbiting excitedly. After we had finished our efforts at advertisement, which were rather jolly and good-hearted bantering fellowship—I doubt we sold many tickets but the happiness bonded us—I went in to ask a closer look. Cupid's arrow pierced me hard.

Mr. Atkinson has let me take it with me here to the theatre on approbation and I am writing on it now. Bust me, it is capital fun. I find the chunking sounds it makes most pleasant, when one operates the keys. By the use of carbon paper inserted between the leaves on which one is type-writing, a perfect copy is produced. What larks.

Just a moment ago I type wrote a note for the company noticeboard saying

THANK YOU FOR YOUR DEDICATED WORK IN RECENT TIMES, GOD BLESS AND KEEP YOU ALL, THE CHIEF.

But it is time-consuming to make the letters and so I return to pen for the moment.

With this machine, one could be anyone.

* * *

VIII

19th January, 1879

An extraordinary day and night. I shall never forget it.

The feeling backstage was one of high excitation, the manly players in their finery and paints and armour, the lovely ingénue actresses all tripping about in their gorgeous silken robes and scarlet slippers, a delightful sight, like a summer-besotted garden, or a jeweller's window conjured into life by a wizard, although I did have to stop our Ophelia spilling cigarette ash on herself and uttering words of a decidedly sailorly stamp. At one point as I passed, she was laughingly in conversation with the actress playing our Gertrude: "Oh it's medicine, darling, going to bed with a fellow. The best way to get over a man is to get under another one." But when dealing with young people it is sometimes best to go a little deaf. It is only innocent sauciness.

Up until 19:00 the fleets of painters and varnishers were still toiling like Egyptians, finishing here, touching there, the devil knows what. The whole auditorium reeked of fresh paint and new carpet so that I had Harker burn incense on the stage.

At 29 minutes past seven precisely—I checked on my fob watch—I began calling out to the chief ushers, whom I had stationed carefully about the circles, boxes, and stalls. Each man returned the call to me, "Ready, sir, thank you." On the precise moment the bells rang for 19:30 in St. Mary le Strand, I called out "Seven-thirty, gentlemen, curtain is thirty-two minutes precisely. Thank you. You may open the doors."

Even as the audience began to stream in like a tide, I noticed a patch of damp on the wall of the box nearest the prompter's desk, and, there being no one else at hand, hurriedly found a brush and patched it up myself.

First to arrive were the poor, many of whom were drunk and ragged in old cords and moleskins and peacoats and rather abusive to the boxkeepers but in a goodhearted way. One of them glowered at me as he passed and said "Oy, windy-wallets, what you lookin at then?" I told him to be off with himself and we traded banterings for a while. He and some two hundred rabble were ushered into a separate area at the rear of the stalls, behind the new cast-iron fencing, which I must say looks exceeding handsome. We gave them beer (and, at Harker's suggestion, empty bottles, for a certain purpose). Mob in place and contentedly spitting and fighting with itself, the respectable audience was admitted.

Seat by creaking seat, row upon row, the auditorium quickly filled, the boxes, the parterre, the rows up to the gods. The hubbub of the audience chattering, laughing, crying out seemed to suffuse the whole building—it was as though poor old Lady Lyceum's lifeblood had been transfused back. Some of the actors and I peeped out through the curtain. It was like no excitement I ever felt in my life. Dizzy, giddy, I could have wept for joy but had to keep my formality and not be unmanned. "Oh, Auntie Bram"—this is how some of them have taken to addressing me—"isn't it wonderful?" And they were teasing me, "Auntie, put on a costume, come into the scene with us, do, it shall be ever such larks."

At seven minutes to eight I spoke to the flymen before they ascended their ladders, reminding them that there are seventy-nine speech cues in our version of *Hamlet*, so they must listen hard and do their work, and that I loved and trusted them. They cried "three cheers for Auntie!" Then the flower girls and apprentice stagehands, most of whom are very young and from the poorer parts of this neighbourhood (it being the Chief's wish, as well as my own, that these people be taken on here and offered a path to self-betterment). I often think that these youngsters, who have been given almost nothing by way of education or chances, are my favourite people in the theatre if not indeed the whole world.

I said we were embarked on noble work together, that each and every one of us was a representative of the Lyceum Theatre. They must go about with decorum and hold their heads high, as good hard-working girls and boys, for their parents should be proud of them, as I was. Then I shook them by the hand and gave a hansel of two shillings each and a copy of the thank-you letter I had made on my type writing machine. I am moved by these young people and their simple matter-of-fact friendliness with each other.

It pleases me deeply, the Chief's order that all proceeds of our first night be given to a fund for the needy of the parish. He in person has given a hundred guineas.

Lightning flashed outside, through our tall high windows, throwing shadows about the auditorium and over the splendid dark drapes, and the audience gasped in a laughing way, cheering each flash. It was as though Mother Nature wished to help us set the Gothic. At five minutes to eight I gave the signal for the musicians to come into the pit, which they did to a tremendous and sustained ovation from the whole house. They commenced with a couple of light-hearted arrangements, which had the cheap seats caterwauling along, then "God Save the Queen," for which a (mostly) reverent silence (mostly) was observed, then "Lilliburlero" and "The Harp That Once Through Tara's Halls." I was about to give the order for the house lights to be extinguished when the Prop Captain hurried in and said there was an urgent difficulty.

Torpedoed, I was not able to move while I listened. Then I uttered many obscene words, in truth the same fricative monosyllable over and over, which somehow helped me to think. I commanded the Prop Captain to keep his voice to himself, we must not spread unease among the company, for once that particular genie is out of the bottle it will not be coaxed back in again. I sent a note into the pit that the orchestra was to repeat its overture programme until further orders, no matter the audience, no matter the appearance of Jesus Christ himself in the stalls should that happen, then I followed the Prop Captain and his apprentice to Dressing Room Number One, ordering them to wait outside.

There he stood, by the window, naked but for a robe, a long-handled dagger in his hand. Rain pelted the glass like a weird simulacrum of applause and the lightning flickered strange chiaroscuro. Hearing me enter, he turned, face haggard and lifeless, as a tree whose every leaf has been stripped in a gale.

"I have been vomiting," he murmured. "Cancel the performance."

I told him it was a minute to curtain, that what he asked was impossible.

"We are not ready," he said. "I tell you. Call it off."

He looked frightened, shocked, as a child shuddering from a nightmare or a sleepwalker awakening in a moonlit park. And I could see that this was no prima-donna pose, no seeking of attention, but that some darker animus had attacked him.

"The house is full to the gunnels," I ventured. "They love you. Can you not hear them call out?"

For by now, the audience were chanting his name.

"Poor fools. Give them back their money. You can say I am indisposed."

"How?"

"Unwell. Asthmatic. Whatever you wish. Only please don't mention my pigeon-livered cowardice to the company. Couldn't bear them knowing their Chief is a bottler."

"I do not understand. What is there to fear?"

He said nothing, only crumpled before me, wordlessly thumbing away tears. I had never seen this before in him nor could have imagined it in my wildest fantasies. In plain truth, I did not know what to say.

"You may trust me as a friend," was the best I could do.

"You shan't mock me?"

"Speak to me with trust, we are both men."

"You know my eyesight is bad."

"What of that?"

"It is worse than I thought. It has worsened of late. Tonight, as I sat to do my paint, I could scarcely see my face in the glass."

"I can imagine that that would be disconcerting but we can find an oculist in the morning. The important thing, for the moment—"

"Sometimes on the stage I look out and see the darkness. Not their faces. Been with me since childhood. Afraid of the monsters."

It was then I noticed that, on his dressing table, among the bouquets and telegrams, was a bottle of Scotch whisky, in which a nice hole had been made. I think of that spirit as disappointment-in-a-glass and could see he was in a somewhat Caledonian condition, indeed the full Hebrides were looming into view through the mists. On the basis that probably we were lost already, I poured a measure for him and a larger one for me.

"As a boy, I used to stammer," he said. "The masters beat me viciously. Sometimes—irrational thing—I think they're waiting in the darkness. Willing me to fail. So that everyone will forget me. Jumped-up little son of a travelling salesman. Never amount to anything. So my demons say."

"Every sensitive person has demons."

"You don't seem to have any."

"I have plenty."

"I see none."

"My father and mother left me. They emigrated some years ago. I had been very sick as a child, I never attended school. I missed them."

"I lack your courage."

"I've no courage at all. I'm a dull clerk from Dublin, nothing more."

"You have a core in your heart. Anyone meeting you for two minutes feels its presence. Do you know what I have in mine? Nothing."

"Don't talk rot."

"Nights I have sailed, old thing. Into myself. Through storms you couldn't imagine. Evil apparitions. If you could see the thoughts in my head you would murder me out of pity."

By now the lightning was flickering away like a bastard's ingratitude and he looked appropriately skeletal and ghoulish, an effect to which he added by periodically stabbing the point of the dagger into the cork-lined wall. And I did not doubt the truth of what he was saying. At the same time, I have been around enough actors to know that they are capable of uttering gibberish of this sort, especially on a bellyful of malt.

"Go out to the stage," I said. "Fight *back* at the demons."

"I can't."

"I shall stand in the wings for the entire performance. Look over in my direction from time to time. And say out the words."

"No."

"*Screw your courage to the sticking-place.* It is your destiny. It is waiting. The men and women working yonder have given you everything they have. Will you tell them that their everything isn't enough?"

"You can tell them I am unwell."

"I'm damned if I will. Bloody *tell them yourself.*"

He nodded. And now, he did a curious thing. On the third

finger of his left hand, he has long worn an opal signet said once to have belonged to Edmund Kean, presented to him some years ago by an admirer. He wrung it off, with some effort, and insisted on placing it in my hand.

"That's for luck," he said. "A first night token."

I said I could not accept anything of such value from him.

"It is an old belief among my sort that a gift from one of us to another may not be refused on a first night. But you may offer me something in return. I must take it."

"What have I that you want?"

"Oh, Auntie." He chuckled and his face brightened a little. "You tearing old flirt."

On my own hand, I had a little tin Claddagh ring that had been worn by my father. These are not expensive, are sold in the seaside villages of Galway for a couple of shillings to "trippers" and the like. I took it off and gave it. Eyes filling, he slid it onto his finger.

"Death or glory," he whispered. "Help me into my dress."

By now, my anxious fob watch was telling twenty past eight and ticking a hole through my waistcoat. The house was rowdy and restless, there was jeering from beyond. I got him clad, as best I could, while he muttered away in some weird language I had never heard in my life but which turned out, so he said, to be Cornish, although it might as well have been Watusi for all one knew or cared.

He scribbled a note and commanded me to have it delivered to the box in which his wife and her party were seated, then he tugged the dagger out of the wall and kissed it three times. Collinson and the Prop Captain came in to lead him down to the wings. Off he swayed, tottering drunk, like a tart towards the magistrate. Nerve-exhausted, utterly strained, I stopped behind for a long while. I heard the roar as he took the stage, the blaring of trumpets.

How I yearned to be back in Dublin Castle, among the

ledgers, the soothing dust, the lullabying breeze of Mr. Meates's disapproval, the nothing-to-be-doneness, the restful ever-sameness, the luxuriant irrelevance, the all-consoling dismalness, the peaceful postprandial burps of the clerks.

Man's doom is that he can never sit easy where Fate has placed him.

There was no whisky remaining in that bottle when I left the room.

* * *

By the time Stoker entered the wings, the police had been summoned, constables stationed about the house, arms folded or truncheons drawn. In a single, brilliant light, Irving stalked the boards regally, gesturing at the immensity of his shadow on Harker's backdrop. But his voice was still hoarse, too faint, uncertain, as it had been since the top of the show. His diffidence was confusing the other players. Seven cues had been skipped in three minutes.

"Can't hear you, mate," came a yell from the back of the stalls.

The laughter appeared to throw him. He wiped his brow. Stuttered. Gulped.

"To d-d-die, to s-s-sleep . . . No more, p-perchance . . ."

Stoker turned to Harker.

"Was that note delivered to Mrs. Irving?"

"Sir, I've brung it up to the box myself but Mrs. Irving wasn't there, sir. Her sister and some friends was."

"What did she say?"

"Just told me to go along, sir."

The hissing began. Irving stared at the boards. It was as though some vast serpent had slithered its way up from the sewers.

"What do we do, sir?"

"Be patient. Let him fight."

"But he's losing."

"Steady nerves. He shall win."

Now the Prompter's Assistant hurried in from the backstage dock, accompanied by a little boy with a serious, wrinkle-eyed face.

"This is he?"

"Yes, Mr. Stoker, sir."

"Stand beside me, lad," Stoker said. "There now. Don't be afraid. It's rather exciting when one thinks about it. Stand up big and strong, there's a mighty broth of a boy. Be sure Daddy can see you out there. Harker, bring me a lemonade."

Ten feet away, in the light, Irving turned and saw his son. The boy waved shyly. His father nodded back, swallowing hard, face dripping, walked downstage, hand on hip, stared up at the backdrop. A slow handclap had commenced and was growing around the auditorium, whistles, stamping of boots, howls, jeers.

A call came from the gods: "Irving, you stuttering fool!"

He turned like a gunfighter challenged.

"And by a sleep"—he spat the words—"to say we END the heartache. And the thousand natural SHOCKS that flesh is heir to. "'Tis a c-consummation devoutly to be wished. To die, to sleep, to sleep perchance to dream—ay, there's the rub, for in that s-s-s-sleep—"

"Sir," Harker said. "Do we drop the curtain?"

Irving walked to the lip of the stage, into the gale of mockery. He stared at the audience. Ripped open his shirt. The demonic glare lit his eyes.

"WHAT DREAMS MAY COME," he roared. They rose to their feet. "*When we have shuffled off this mortal coil, must give us pause,*" and now nobody could hear his voice, for the thunder of the crowd. He let it rain on him, shook his locks, held his hands above his head. And then, as they wailed and cackled and screamed, he did something no actor had done in the history of the world.

He stepped down into the auditorium before them.

Through the aisles of astonished watchers.

Down the stunned parterre, towards the cast-iron fence.

Pulled the dagger from his sleeve as he clambered up the railing. Snarling into their faces, as the vanquished clawed out to touch him.

"To GRUNT and SWEAT under a weary life. But that the DREAD of something after death . . . puzzles the will . . . Thus conscience does make COWARDS of us all."

They bellowed. They howled his name. In the wings, Stoker wept. As the ovation shook the chandeliers, Harker nudged him. A young woman in a shimmering ivory evening-robe had come into backstage and was silently greeting some of the crew, embracing, shaking hands. There was something tomboyish in how she held herself but also a strange grace. She seemed at ease in her body, was fluent in quiet laughter, and she moved through the shadows as one born in them. Ungloving, she kissed the upturned face of Irving's child, ruffled his unruly curls.

She plucked a cigarette from the lips of the Prompter, took a puff, then popped it back in his mouth and with a smile refused the chair the actor playing Rosencrantz had brought for her.

"I say," she whispered to Harker, now offering her hand. "Gorgeous backdrops. I am Ellen Terry."

* * *

IX

*In which an eerie interlude is offered, a wondrous country
discovered, and the question of nudity considered*

At the post-show celebration, held on the stage, Irving is
quiet, seems withdrawn and exhausted.

"What do you mean, she didn't stay?"

"As I told you, she left after only a moment or two in the
wings."

"She didn't wish to see me?"

"She remained thirty seconds, if that."

"Any message?"

"Just this calling card."

"Read it out to me, can't you? I haven't my spectacles."

"'Darling, well done. Your Ellen.'"

"That's all?"

"I have let the newspapers know she attended. Come, a
glass of champagne. Congratulations."

But the fizz doesn't spark him. Scowling for the photographer, peremptorily accepting handshakes and embraces from
the players, sulking as he watches the beckonings and flirtations. Chefs have set up stoves to fry sausages and boil crayfish,
furnishers have draped the pillars with lengths of crêpe de
Chine. Minstrels in domino, strumming lutes and plucking
dulcimers. A bucket of lobsters overturns and its denizens
escape, inching across the boards towards the wings.

"Best cooked alive," he mutters. "Like critics."

"I must leave," Stoker says. "I am completely bunched and
hope to get a little writing done before sunrise, now we're up
on our feet."

"You are not permitted to leave. If you do, I shall curse you. I see by your chuckle that you do not believe in curses."

"I believe in science."

"The religion of fools."

"Science is measurable truth. Curses are fiction."

"Read your Darwin, old hog. Even a fool is occasionally correct. There was a time in earthly history when the apes could not speak. Then some found the power"—he quaffs his glass—"whilst others disbelieved."

"And?"

"And so, in every generation, a small number possess powers that the rest of the apes do not have or believe in. That elite is what brings about whatever small progress there is."

"I find the notion fanciful. I am a democrat."

"Find it what you wish." With his dagger he stabs morosely at a dish of ribs and rare liver, the unctuous bloody juices running down his chin and staining his collar. "Thrice in my life I have sincerely wished harm on an enemy. I uttered his name nineteen times, a black-magical number. In each case, he died within the month."

His dog slinks to him from the wings. He feeds it a dripping steak. Three laughing young actresses approach with a salver of grapes. "Auntie, you look famished, let us feed you."

"Careful there, ladies," Irving chuckles. "Your aunt is a respectable girl who is on her way home to the nunnery."

"Oh no, Auntie, don't go! . . . Really you mustn't, it's too bad of you . . . Auntie, will you dance with me, I shall be the boy?"

"Waiter," Irving calls. "More fizz for my aunt."

"I suppose I can stay for just one."

* * *

Tottering homeward after dawn, through crowds of

workers and schoolchildren, he remembers to buy the news-papers at the stand on Tavistock Street. Fumbling for his keys, he enters the house. From her seat at the communal breakfast table, the signora regards him, a vision of florid sternness among the porridge plates.

Upstairs in his sitting room, he lights the fire, puts on a kettle and seats himself in the window banquette. Outside on the windowsill a mangy London crow is staring in at him like a cornerboy. The sky is yellowish grey with smog, as though the gods have vomited.

TRIUMPH FOR IRVING
LYCEUM BROUGHT BACK TO LIFE
GALA REOPENING OF LYCEUM ATTENDED
BY MISS TERRY IRVING RISES AGAIN

As he reads, his hands tremble, and his eyes begin to hurt, and he realises he is not alone in the room.

"Florence. My dearest heart."

Her hair long and loose, her dressing-robe gull's-egg blue.

"Is everything well, Bram? I was a little alarmed."

"We had—a celebration after the show. It rather ran on. I'm afraid I am somewhat drunk."

"All went as you hoped?"

"One or two hiccups. Only to be expected with so little time for preparation. Ellen Terry was there. I shook her hand."

"You didn't get my note? I sent a boy with it last night."

"Things were so busy, you see, I didn't open it. But thank you."

"For what?"

"For sending the luck note. It was thoughtful of you."

"It wasn't a luck note. I went to the doctor yesterday."

"My love. Is everything—"

She seats herself by the fire, her face pale as salt.

"He says I'm expecting a baby."

* * *

20th January, 1879

At noon I went to the theatre only to find it locked up and shuttered. Empty bottles, cigar butts on the steps, dubious puddles. Looked very poor indeed. Got a mop and bucket. Cleaned up the piss.

The innumerable excitements of the thespian life.

One detail disturbed me though of course a mere coincidence: on the sill of one of the portico noticeboards, a doll's shoe.

In the foyer, the silk sofa was torn and three of the large French mirrors stained with I think red wine. Disappointing, disheartening to see such evidence of unruliness among the players. I suppose one should be grateful the bastards didn't break into the Box Office and rifle the takings. Thankfully, being actors, they would be too stupid to contrive such a deed. Most actors couldn't find a hole in a ladder.

The entire floor of the Box Office anteroom was covered in pound notes. As I bundled them and counted the receipts, I was taken by the intense silence around me, which seemed remarkable, eerie. No street sounds, but sepulchral stillness, like being inside the deadest most aortic inner chamber of a Pyramid. Never have I noticed before, must be the thickness of the walls. I could actually hear the scamper of the mice in the ceiling above me. Apart from them, I was alone. So I thought.

Entering the auditorium, I was startled to see the figure of a man on the stage. Tall, broad, in a cape, with his back to me.

When he turned, I saw it was the Chief, last night's dagger again in hand.

When I greeted him, he made no reply. It was as though he had not seen me or was in a trance. The approach I made was cautious, in case he was dreamwalking, which Collinson and some of the older players say he does when under a strain. They must not be awakened quickly, those who night-roam.

"Chief," I said. "It is I."

Now he seemed to swim up to the surface of himself, to become aware of where he was. There was a sore on his lower lip and it appeared to be suppurating badly. I noticed his feet were bare.

"Did you see her?" he asked.

"Who?"

"The girl-child. In the balcony."

"There is nobody here but we two. Take a moment to compose yourself."

He beckoned me up, but, by the time I had gained the stage, he had hurried away into the wings. Now I saw the light from his office at the top of the stairs.

His face was white and waxen, his hands trembling badly. The room smelt stale and turgidly oppressive, as though someone had slept in it, which perhaps he had. On his desk-blotter was a syringe and a small bottle containing a clear liquid.

I knew what it was and wished he would not resort to it, but its use (and overuse) is not unknown among people who work at night or are given to nervousness. I went to open the curtains and window.

"Close them."

"But it's a crisp healthy morning, I only thought to—"

"I said CLOSE them. Are you deaf as well as ignorant?"

I was shocked to be spoken to in this manner. Gruffness I have seen in him, but I had not myself received the treatment he sometimes metes out to the actors. Nevertheless I did as he asked. To every dog his first bite. It occurred to me that he was losing his mind, was under some kind of mental or nervous attack brought upon him by the exhaustion of these past weeks of preparation, for his whole face looked distorted, like that of an entirely different man. Even the voice seemed different, quite emptied of manliness or feeling, as the voice of a mechanical dog.

"Get on with whatever you are here for," it said.

"I came in to see to the correspondence. That was all."

"Then see to it."

"There is a letter of congratulations from Tennyson, a note from Wilde, one from Beerbohm Tree, one from Shaw."

"Shitting hypocrite."

"Requests for interviews from *The Times* and the *Illustrated News*. But perhaps those might wait a day or two. Until you have had a chance to rest yourself."

"Nothing from the palace?"

I looked at him.

"Thought the queen might have written," he said, now staring hard at his hands as though he had never seen them before. "One would think she might want to encourage excellence for once in her idle stupid life. Vulgar middleclass trollop."

By now, I was truly frightened and could see that a doctor was needed. But having no other choice for the moment, I did my best to humour him.

"You were happy with the evening?"

He uttered a tight, bitter laugh. "You ask Christ if he was happy with the crucifixion. I will never forget the shame. I've seen a better play done by drunken beggars in the street."

"There were naturally First Night nerves. But the audience was more than satisfied. I expect you haven't yet seen the notices this morning?"

He tapped his head. "I do not need to see them. I see them in here. Before any of those whores' curs writes a line it is visible to me. Nothing scalds me like the praise of a fool."

I (*reading aloud*): "A Masterpiece Performance."

He (*snapping*): "Burn it."

I: "For Heaven's sake."

He (*louder*): "Dare you talk to me of Heaven when you have put me in Hell? You and the other mediocrities who stain this place by your presence. The thought that Ellen Terry was here to endure it makes me sick to the stomach."

I (*standing up to him despite his approach*): "The company's performance in my view was of a singularly high level given the difficult conditions under which we have been operating."

His rage was now so extreme that it caused him to stammer and drool. "You are not in M-M-Mickland now. I do not accept your grubby standards. It must be flawless! Every night. Nothing less than perfection will do."

"That is a noble aspiration," I said, "but not practicable. Please calm yourself."

Now he roared from the pit of his lungs, his whole face ragingly scarlet and engorged. "It is *not* an aspiration! It is how it shall be."

"Again, I appeal to you—"

"Anyone who doesn't wish to join me, there is the door, only mark you I shall have my pound of flesh before he goes." He pointed the dagger towards me as he spewed these ugly words and I was afraid that I soon must have no option but to strike him and knock him down, which I had rather not, for I have never struck a man less than my height and weight. But it was good to know that if I must, I could fell him.

By now, he had shouted himself into a new moon of the anger, a quiet, cold, bitter phase. I said nothing, for it is better to let a man rant and bubble when his blood has run away with him, for the sooner rage spills, the faster he calms. He snatched a cigarette from a silver case on the desk and lit it and seemed to smoke away the entire thing in three or four dredger-like sucks. I poured a tumbler of absinthe from his decanter and took a small sip for I needed something merciless to drown down the nerve. And now we came to the true meat of his rage.

From a drawer in the desk he pulled out a copy of *Belgravia* magazine and tossed it contemptuously on the rug between us as though it was some piece of vilest obscenity.

"I suppose you know what that is," he said without looking at me.

"Of course."

"Do you deny that this rag contains a so-called story under your name?"

"It is a well-thought-of journal among literary men. Why would I deny it?"

"'Literary men.' An oxymoron if ever there were."

"You may banter if you wish."

"*You* are employed—and remunerated well—to assist me in my work. Not to compose witless yarns for bitches that have recently learned to walk on their hind legs. I am entitled to every shred of your attention and support. You did not give it. You betrayed me. What is more, you associated this theatre with the trash appearing in that publication. What have you to say for yourself?"

"I write a little in what minuscule spare time my position here affords. I am sorry if that does not suit you. I shan't be stopping."

"You shall do precisely as I say, when I say it, without question."

"On this point, no."

"You will defy your superior?"

"If needs be."

By now, I could hear voices and laughter from the stage downstairs, and the thud of the trapdoors opening. Some of the flymen and players must have come in for the rehearsal of *Macbeth*. His dog appeared in the doorway and regarded us, long tongue hanging. In the wings, someone was playing a jig on a violin.

I have seen many expressions on the face of the Chief but never one quite as resolvedly charged with raw hatred.

"Get out of my sight," he said. "Before I harm you."

* * *

THE VOICE OF ELLEN TERRY

At the time, I loved attending a London First Night. And I did adore a tragedy.

Darling, who wouldn't?

Adultery, vengeance, cruelty, lust, betrayal.

That was before one got through the foyer.

I was hoping you wouldn't ask. Must we? Oh I see . . . Well I suppose it's so very long ago that probably it doesn't matter. But yes, I toddled along to the opening night of Harry's Lyceum.

Didn't like it much, I'll be honest.

Harry could be a dreadful old stomper, a scenery-chewer, as we say. It came out like that when he was nervous, he'd take a bite out of a goblet. Stamping like an ostrich. Sweat and spit flying. Darling, if you were seated in the front row of the stalls, you'd want a sou'wester.

There are people whose cup of tea it is, but I wasn't one of them, I'm afraid. If I want to hear a fellow roaring, I'll get married.

Make no mistake, he was a peerless actor. The greatest I'll

ever see. Majestic, powerful, like an animal not a man. You couldn't look away, not even for a second, it was as though your neck was in a vice and your eyes on the stage. Couldn't *blink*, damn near. Couldn't move. There was only one Harry, on a good night he was untouchable. And most of his nights were good.

I never saw anyone more able to get out of his skin. Like a snake, we used to laugh. But we knew he was the greatest. What Harry had was unearthly. That's the word I would use. I swear to the Dickens, he actually changed before one's eyes. Gave one collywobbles to see it. Magnificent.

Trouble is, he adored the applause and that gets in the way. There's a certain sort of actor—a clap-hound, I term them— who'll do anything for the applause, set himself on fire if he needs to. And Harry was king of the clap-hounds.

In a lesser player, one wouldn't mind, might even sort of admire it. One does what one can, after all.

But it irked me when Harry did it. He did it too often. It was like watching the world's greatest concert pianist juggling coconuts in a booth on Southend Pier. Fine, so far as it goes. But there's a Steinway behind you, darling. Give us a ruddy tune while you're up there?

That was what one felt about the night. "Stop clap-hounding, idiot. Don't be such a tart. Be Harry."

You see, acting is not a matter of pretending to be someone else but of finding the other person in oneself and then putting her on view. It's nothing mystifying, it's what children do; you'll have seen them when they play. It isn't letting on, it's *being*. I learned it when I was a little girl myself, my father ran a travelling pantomime. He never told me "Pretend to be a fairy." He'd say "Today you're a fairy, Len. Fly."

So, I don't like seeing the acting, I like seeing the fairies fly.

But one doesn't say it, of course. Well, one can't. And one mustn't. What's done in a performance is done, there'll be another tomorrow night, and you must *never* put your sister or brother player in a funk. Cardinal rule. The eleventh commandment. You'll have an off night yourself. It happens to everyone, often enough on a First Night, when people are anxious. And you wouldn't want them doing that to *you*.

The way of saying it gently is, you don't go to the party. So I didn't. Bit stubborn. There we are.

One was young enough to think high principle is important. Nowadays, I'd pootle along and get squiffy as hell and lie a ruddy hole through a bucket.

The best acting at a First Night is never on the stage. It's always at the party afterwards.

* * *

2nd February, 1879

It is difficult to know quite how to manage a particular and notable aspect of backstage life without either giving offence or causing self-conscious feelings among the young. One wishes there was a confidante one might ask.

The fact is that, during performances and sometimes even rehearsals, a certain amount of "quick change" is required, for the Chief wishes us at the Lyceum to pride ourselves on the gorgeousness of our costumes and the dexterity with which they are deployed. It is his habit to inform us with no little frequency that the response he wishes to evoke in the audience is not the statement "that is wondrous" but the question "how the ****ing **** do they do it?"

What this means, in effect, is that many of the younger players are in the habit of wandering about gaily in a state of not inconsiderable déshabillé, the girls in undergarments and sometimes rather revealing bodices, the muscular boys in hosiery or waist-wrapped towels, without shirts. And, since a certain amount of pulchritude is expected in a theatre, the backstage has a particular atmosphere, like a hothouse.

What is odd is that none of the orchids seem to notice the steam but blithely saunter about the wings, or in and out of each other's dressing rooms or the Green Room for a smoke, whistling, jabbering, eating sandwiches, mullarking, modesty protected by only the flimsiest of robes. In addition, they are in the custom of administering massages to each other, some-times with oils or unguents, and of helping each other with stretching and bending exercises.

"Be not righteous overmuch," Ecclesiastes counsels. Wisely.

It is not that these youngsters' innocence is not delightful, in its way, but even in Eden there were limits. And we do have such a frequency of visitors to backstage—locksmiths, delivery boys, master joiners, so on—and they are not accustomed to unselfconscious eccentricity in the middle of the day, although one boiler cleaner quipped that he was, "having worked in the House of Lords." This afternoon, for example, Miss Bowe, Miss Hughes, and Miss Blennerhassett were onstage running through the opening scene of the three witches—"when shall we three meet again, in thunder lightning, or in rain"—the wardrobe mistress on her knees measuring them for their expensive and somewhat scanty costumes as they did so. Her measuring-tape was attracting a number of envious looks from a Mancunian upholsterer who had come in to fix the Royal Box and almost stabbed himself through the hand with his needle. I myself was thinking a different but not unrelated thought: So much money for so little silk.

Young Harker was stood upstage, his pink face rapt. He looked like an accordion someone had recently played hard. I believe he has eyes for Miss Blennerhassett. I wandered over to him and attempted tactfully to distract his attention by show-ing him a conjuring trick I have learned with playing cards and a sixpence, but he did not seem to be as interested in my conjuring as he was in Miss Blennerhasset's. I remarked that while she was undoubtedly a pleasant and sprightly girl, I myself did not reckon her among the leading players we have in the company.

"I believe she has hidden qualities, sir," he said, with a stressed smile.

She was not quite hiding them at that moment.

It is good to be of an age when these silly distractions come and go but do not preoccupy one at all.

* * *

16th February, 1879

Have resolved to stop scribbling notes on the frontispieces of books. Bad, slovenly habit.

Awoke in a mood of great joy, breakfasted with Flo. Read to her, Petrarch's sonnet *Aura che quelle chiome bionde et crespe.* My Dubbalin Italian made her laugh. Walked to work flooded with a strange magnanimity of spirit, wished there was some acquaintance that had done me a wrong and needed forgiveness. But I could not think of anyone.

Good hard day. *Macbeth* coming well. The Chief utterly enthralling at rehearsal.

Afterwards he asked to see me a moment. Offered congratulations about Flo, said he wished to pay all doctoring expenses, his man was the best in London. I said I could not accept this offer, generous though it was, and he said Flo and I were to bear it in mind all the same. I said we would.

This evening I was in my office writing letters for our forthcoming New York tour, when Patrick "Pigeon" O'Shaughnessy, the Stagehand Captain, came in like a bad smell from a drain in August. He is not a sort I like, indeed I should wish to be rid of him, for he drinks and I suspect steals and makes a nuisance of himself with some of the girls, but one must be careful as to what one shows. When Pigeon is in the room, one would need eyes in one's arse.

Asked me if I had done anything about "that other matter, sor" and I said that I had not as yet. He meant the fact that we have an urgent requirement for more storage rooms for our scenery. He is one of those Irishmen who enjoy making you reach conclusions.

An hour later, I was smoking a cigarette in the street behind the dock and looking up at the stars when along came young Harker, a pleasant sight. He was wearing his blue suit, which I always like to see him in, and a rakish cap like a pretend fisherman's. We passed the time together with my pointing out Orion and the Great Bear to him—he said to me, a little flirtatiously, "you are a great bear yourself, sir," and I said I should have to put him across my knee and give him a paddling if he spoke to me so naughtily and we shared a brief laugh and a manly clap about the shoulders—and then I said we would have to think in a more purposeful manner on how to solve the storage conundrum.

I asked how he was coming along with a task I had given him, which is to sort out and systemise the keys. The Lyceum has, by my reckoning, approximately one hundred and fifty doors, and the score or so of massive iron rings we possess, each of several dozen keys, long, short, thick, rusted, make no sense that I can see, if ever they did. Easier to unravel the Gordian knot. But my Harks is a determined boy.

He led me into the nook backstage that he has made his own, a little L-shaped cubbyhole that he has shelved and fitted out ingeniously with all his paints, sketchbooks, fabrics, so on, even a hammock, and there, on his workbench, I was delighted to see the fruits of his toiling. He has labelled every last key and bought new hoops, one for each floor, and so now we may see what we have.

As he went through them, explaining, he came to an uncommonly large black cast-iron key, approximately nine inches long, which, he said, was for "Mina's Lair." I did not know to what his queer phrase adverted, and he smiled at me puckishly. There is something quite kissable about him at such moments.

"Mina's Lair" was the name given by the older stagehands to an ancient warren of cellars located beneath the north-eastern end of the dock. I asked if this might provide a solution to our difficulty, if the cellar-system might be cleaned out and employed as the scenery store. Even if it took some considerable work to do it, the site would have the twin advantages of adjacency and inexpensiveness. He shook his head with great gravity and said the men would not go down there.

I asked why not.

"Mina was a maidservant what was murdered there, Mr. Stoker, sir, in the old queen's time. Was once a row of fine mansions where the docks is now, see, but they burned. Scottish girl, in service, fell in with a viscount and then a baby come along and he strangled the both of them and walled 'em up in the cellar. Bad luck to disturb her."

"Superstitious ruddy nonsense," I chuckled. "Hand me that key, you silly flapdoodle."

"I should really rather not, sir."

"Oh, rot me, lad, do it now."

He did as I had requested but looked so apprehensive that he made me laugh. Indeed he grew green as an old pork pie. He was a man of the world, he insisted (which made me chuckle, he being so young), but the backstage lads *would* have their stories. It was said that, last time the door had been opened, thirty years ago now, the charwoman who turned the key had burst into flame and run screaming through a closed window. An upside-down cross had been daubed on her tombstone. Weird cries, whimpers and "scratchings" had been reported from behind the door, not by any of the lads themselves but by others who delivered to us intermittently or were on the premises to perform some service or another. A Roman Catholic priest from St. Patrick's, Soho Square, had once come in to attend an actor who had fallen ill and was approaching his end. The good Father had pleaded with the stagehands to take the man out of "this accursed place" and had been seen to sprinkle the door with holy water, uttering the rite of exorcism as he did so. I told Harker not to be ridiculous but he would not be commanded. Indeed, he made an excuse when I asked him to accompany me, pleading an appointment with the curtain-makers (which I know he did not have). So, off I moseyed alone.

It took a while to locate the door to which he was referring—truly we ought to number them all—but finally, after some error and trial, there it was: small, of black-stained oak, one would need to stoop to go through it, in a narrow brick corridor at the very back of the loading-dock, a gap one would pass without noticing. It amused me to see, when I looked closely at the spy-hole, that some wag had carved a capital "M" and a skull-and-crossbones into one of the planks, many years ago, presumably.

It was clear to me, as I ventured to turn the long key without snapping it, that the door had indeed not been opened in quite some time. Spiders had nested in the architrave. The door itself felt massively heavy. But then I saw that it had slipped its top hinges and was in fact resting on the floor slates. With strenuous effort I managed to lift it back on to its bolts, pushing it open at the same time.

The source of the infamous scrabbling was soon revealed. Our old London friend, *Rattus norvegicus*, was much in evidence. We, his fellow citizens, always seem so afraid of this nuzzler, and disgusted by his rummaging, rapacious curiosity, but, while I would not claim to love him and crave his guest-hood in my house, I am content enough to share the world with him. He must do as he must and did not ask to be here. Unlike Man, he does not murder the females of his race, nor ever is he cruel to his own.

Before me I had expected to see a staircase descending into the cellars but what I discerned through the murk was in fact the precise opposite. In a small vestibule, a simple, unvar-nished, steep wooden stairs without banister led not down-ward but *up*. Like an idiot, I found myself calling out "hello up there?" Unsurprisingly (indeed happily), no reply came back. Lighting my lamp, I began to climb.

This soon led to a second flight, then a third and fourth, each course reversing over the one preceding it. The wood-work was rudimentary, here and there quite splintery, and the odour of old dust, while not unpleasant, was intense, even though (strange) it did not interfere with my breathing, in fact the air tasted cold and vivifying. At ten flights, I lost count. Several times during my climb I was but inches from the old roof-slates and could hear, from as it seemed very far below me, the cries of a glue boiler and a berry seller down in the street, and the warble of nesting pigeons on the ledges and gut-ters outside.

O strange and magical country! One felt a veritable Gulliver-on-the-Strand. Spread before me were a number of lengthy connected attics, perhaps two hundred yards long in total, divided here and there by chimney-stacks and pillars, illuminated by shafts of dull daylight from dirty windows in the roof. Here and about lay old trunks, broken caskets, lengths of carpet, and everywhere great curtain-like sheaths of inch-thick spider-web which I had to employ my penknife to slash through as I made my way along. It was evident that no human had set foot here in decades.

Many alcoves of crumbling masonry gave the eyrie the

atmosphere of a queer sort of catacomb and, in some of these, boxes of old mildewed books and other trash had been dumped. The effect of my lamp's red-yellow flame refracted in the curtains of spider-web was remarkable, seeming to spread itself like a miasma of dancing silhouettes and penumbras. Near a chimney-stack I happened across the ruins of what I presently recognised as a large harp, wrenched, as it seemed, into three distinct parts but its rusted thicket of strings yet knotting the poor trinity together. It made me sad to see that. I said a prayer of my own sort for fallen brother harp, the emblem of my country, after all is said and done, and for who-ever's hands had long ago made him sing.

Onward I pressed into the strange-lit murk, through the cooing of the pigeons and the drip of ancient pipes, treading with no small caution for, here and about, there were holes or loose boards in the floor so that one could see the skeletal cross-beams and joists underfoot. Again, one heard many scut-tlings and sudden scratchings from the darkness as I disturbed it, but those did not bother me much.

From a rafter dangled a family of leering marionettes, the king, queen and one-eyed jack of spades, but so splattered with bird dirt that I did not want to cut them down, every part of their paint faded and powdered away, leaving them pale as the ash or willow from which they were hewn but for their cheeks still red as the cold.

More trunks, then, in stacks, and oh—macabre sound—a string of jester's bells twisting dully in the breeze. An over-turned old throne was my next discovery, its cushions and backrest quite gnawed away to tatters. I set it up on its legs and it seemed to peer at me forlornly, but not without a smidgeon of regal grace, as I pushed on. Rain was making its pleasant sussuration on the ancient slates above me but then suddenly it stopped. My Lilliput fell silent.

I had by then made my way to the furthest end of what I

had thought the main attic's extent, but now, to my surprise, I saw that it turned a corner. Into the short limb of the capital L, I pressed.

Here it was darker, for there were no roof windows or mullions. The odour was different, like old straw, but my lamp found out nicely made stone walls—small, black stones like little cobbles or pieces of anthracite—which admitted no moisture I could see.

Near me, I noticed a length of yard-knotted hemp-rope dangling from what appeared to be a hatch-door in the ceiling. Placing my lamp on a crate, I tried the line with my hands. My tugs told me it was fast and, in probability, sound. It took little enough effort (though I was glad of my gymnasium days) to shin-and-knee up its length, and when I pushed at the hatch door it opened backwards with a slam.

Out I clambered. Down a short length of fixed iron ladder and—marvellous!—I found myself standing on the breeze-blown roof of the theatre, with the most splendid and inspiriting vista imaginable before me, of London and the river, all the way south-easterly to the domes of what I think must be the naval college at Greenwich, beyond that the farmlands and forests of north Kent.

Wind-slapped, still not satisfied, I eased my way gingerly up the slates of the very apex of the nearest point and perched there a while, exhausted, happy, the Lyceum Theatre between my thighs as it might be, the weathercocks spinning on many a rooftop around me, gusts of river breeze smacking vivacity back into my face, the stern, magisterial beauty of the steeples and chimney pots in the smoky distance and the mountainous turrets of black and russet clouds.

Already a crescent moon like a phantom's grin was visible thousands of miles above Piccadilly. Below me, in the windows of offices, I could see clerks and other poor drudges at their work, hurrying to and fro, but none of them knew I was there.

It occurred to me that, at this moment, not one solitary person on this planet was aware of where I was, an odd thought but for some reason intensely pleasing. Indeed I found myself overcome, tearful for the joy of such a solitude. I do not know why that should be.

Presently, I must descend from my roost. This I did going slowly, with care, across the dampened mossy slates and down through the hatch-door, closing it after me. The light of the attic seemed somehow to have changed, refreshed by the air, or perhaps it was merely that now I saw it differently.

On the raked floor of a narrow alcove or declivity sat a long wooden box, in some ways resembling a coffin but longer, wider, of humbler wood than we use for that purpose. Say a packing chest. It was nothing extraordinary yet there was some aura the object transmitted, a queer magnetism that refused to let me leave. On the lid, strange figures were carved, with proportion and precision, so that they must mean something, but I did not know what.

I made a note of them.

Alas, poor humankind. The wellspring of all troubles is that, once seen, a box must be opened.

But my schoolyard spooks were misplaced. There had been no need for alarm. The box contained nothing but earth—rich, loamy and black—which clearly had been employed at one time as ballast.

I sank my fingers in and as quickly recoiled, seeing the dirt was wriggling with pale white slugs, fat as Weymouth oysters and almost as horrid. But then I reflected that these, too, like Friend Rat, must live. We can cross the oceans by steam, build tremendous bridges, dredge tunnels, construct terrible machines of war, cure sicknesses, crush ignorance, and we can redden the map of the world with the scarlet of royal England, but we cannot make life. Except on the page.

It was at this moment, or soon thereafter, that I happened to glance at my watch, assuming forty minutes or so to have passed. To my astonishment, I had been in the upperworld more than three and a half hours. Far below me, the play was about to begin.

* * *

THE VOICE OF ELLEN TERRY

. . . But a dreadful lot has been made of how changeable Harry could be. It's true, he had moods and dark humours by the bucketload. To be fair to him, which people who didn't know him sometimes aren't, he was actually rather human in that way. Just wasn't as good at hiding it.

What's that?

No, Harry wasn't discourteous, dear, I don't think that's quite fair. In some ways he was uncommonly decent and fair-minded. Small thing: it was always the case in London theatre that the backstage was governed by the Chief Stagehand, it was he who set the rules and generally ran how everyday things were done and employed the casuals and so on. Home Rule, if you like. It's an important tradition. Well, the men working backstage would pin up postcards of a certain sort, you know, from Paris. Some were innocent enough, I suppose one might term them a little risqué, but others were too frank, like something out of a ruddy medical textbook. Tiresome, but it was permitted in every theatre in England. You looked the other way or got used to it.

Wouldn't put up with it nowadays, darling. Burn their theatre down for them first. It's in every contract I sign, "the backstage will be suitable, by Miss Terry's standards." Well, you have to let them know who's the talent.

They're not paying to see *you*, chum. They are paying to see me. So I'd better not be inconvenienced. Or it's curtains.

To his credit, Harry wouldn't have it at the Lyceum, he let it be known. Famously, he said to the Chief Stagehand or someone: "What they look at on their own shilling is none of my affair, but my backstage is a workplace, not a gin-shop, and we have women working here. The men may pin up anything that would not upset my mother. And my mother is a damn sensitive lady, I warn you."

When the Chief Stagehand tried to insist, Harry countermanded him in a line that became legendary throughout London theatre. "We have sixteen-year-old girls here as cleaners, we have seamstresses and actresses. They should not have to walk through a whorehouse in order to do their work."

He enforced it, too. He'd fine infractors a day's wages. Home Rule was all very well but the emperor stepped in sometimes. That takes courage, the natives don't like it.

So, Harry could be a brick. But he wasn't always.

It's just that everyone has a Mr. Hyde, another version of the self. A direction not taken, perhaps. A road we didn't know existed, or had no name for. We each of us carry our choices about, don't we, darling? And every choice is a rejection, when you think.

But there is, too, a kind of shadowland where the Other always lives. Or at least, never dies. Just goes on. Hard to stumble into happiness if you don't leave your shadowland behind. Harry never did, quite. Neither did Bram. Theatre people don't, as a rule. Goes with the job. Everything is so precarious, almost all of the time. Makes it hard to settle. One gets fidgety. And when you're someone else, every night, and twice on a Saturday, you can forget what it's like being you.

I always felt, you know, two hands are needed here. One to

wave farewell, the other to close the heart. Some ancient poet has an ode about it, can't think of his name. But easier said than done. I don't know that anyone succeeds.

Questionings. Dawn-thoughts. Mind ticking like a watch. Four in the morning but you're staring out a window. What if I had married that other person? Or remained unmarried? What if I had accepted that job, or emigrated or stayed, or lived my life in a different way, a way that was truer to me, perhaps, but I was afraid of what people might think or say?

You see, part of you *did* do those things. To imagine is to do.

And there are moments when you feel a murderous envy of that part. The self that escaped. The self that chose freedom.

So, out comes the rage. But already too late.

It's the only thing one's learned. We're in shadowland.

* * *

17th February, 1879

2.15 A.M.

All night, since my ascent to "Mina's Lair," I was unable to concentrate on my preparatory work for the American tour. Descending, I realised that I had a notion for a story. It was as though I had stumbled into it, above in the shadows, and it had adhered itself like dander to my clothes, beard, and eyebrows.

The story would be in ten or a dozen monthly parts, told in the form of letters and entries in a private journal, the one to be at odds with the other. That is to say, the narrator in the letters is dissembling, or, as in a pantomime, does not realise what is happening to him, but the audience does and wishes to cry out "Look behind you, Chump!"

Part the First. A young man of facts, perhaps a scientist or mathematician, journeys to a distant land he does not know. Persia? Africa? An island off Connemara? Some place beyond the mapped world.

Say a lecturer in Medicine, but not an important professor. He must have that slight grain of stupidity all effective protagonists require, that quality of not getting the point at once. Say a junior in surgery at Dublin University or the Sorbonne, so besotted by his studies that common sense has never been valued or acquired. The sort of man who sees but does not see.

He is in search of a precious elixir, a potion that gives eternal life, which springs from a long-lost well or cleft in a rock. Drink it and one never dies.

Make him an orphan. No mother or father means his moral compass is askew, no guide, he must struggle on alone.

Arrived in the unknown country, he finds all the inns are full. In the midst of a violent storm he is taken in by an elderly nobleman, the lord of a stark and forbidding palace. At first the host is icily hospitable, if eccentric, which the young doctor ascribes to loneliness and the depredations of old age. Or to a discontented marriage.

The nobleman has all the queerness of unstintingly perfect hospitality. Plentiful food but always the same dish, a strange meat.

Unending wine, from his vineyards, but the lord will not partake of it himself. Is never witnessed eating. "I breakfasted late and do not sup." Heavy doors perpetually locked. Bars on every window. "You may leave in the morning," but morning never comes. Every night he falls into soporific, annihilating sleep but awakens in darkness, his host telling him he slept too long, the day has passed and with it the opportunity to depart.

Later

Quarter past five in the morning. Have just awakened from a terrible nightmare.

Was working at an anvil, bashing iron with a hammer. The spear-tipped black gates of an ancient cathedral torn down and being smelted in a furnace.

Then walking some city to which I have been, part Rotterdam, part Munich, maybe Prague, but none of those, or a composite of all. Gloomy streets, hungry doorways, skeletally thin tall houses overlooking canals. Strange figures hurrying through the desuetude, wolfish grunts, blue flames for eyes.

Wore a suit of armour so heavy I could scarcely move. This was what I had fashioned on the anvil. Droplets of my sweat hissing as they fell on the red iron.

Then, somehow, in a sumptuous chamber, bound, in a throne, hands and ankles tied.

Before me, the three innocent girls from the theatre, but now transformed by some wormlike sinfulness dredged from my imagination to lasciviousness, obscenity, and mockery. They made me watch as they cavorted, one with the others, their mouths now about my face, their fingers in my hair, their lewd acts—I cannot write it.

"O he is young and strong," one murmured, "there are kisses for us all," as she knelt before me, unfastening my shirt. Soon her lips were upon me no matter how I writhed.

Now a hooded figure either came in or was seen to be there. Diamond crown on its hood, sceptre and orb in gauntleted hands.

"Back to your tombs," it cried. "This man belongs to *me*."

But "cried" is too weak. Hideously more than a cry.

It was a scream, like a woman's. But a man's.

CLOSE OF ACT I

X

Entr'acte. In which we return to the train journey which opened our adventure, a pause now being taken by the travellers.

October 12th, 1905, Sheffield Station, 2.17 P.M.

Assisted by the conductor, Stoker descends from the train.

A howl of autumn leaves swirls dustily along the platform, moistening his weary eyes. Early afternoon but the sky is shroud-grey and cast-iron cold. Soot from the town's factories on the air.

Stiff from the seven hours in a seat since King's Cross, he turns and helps Irving down. The older man, frail, is shivering, weary. Stoker fastens the large buttons on his charge's cloak.

"Must be careful," he says. "They say there's a hurricane about to blow up."

"Nonsense," Irving replies, holding a kerchief over his mouth to stop the dust. "I've had worse wind from an egg."

The kohl around his eyes gives him an Egyptian stare. He taps his cane on the platform impatiently. Stoker whistles for a porter. The pigeon-toed man approaches, begins loading their luggage onto a handcart.

"Bradford, is it, gentlemen? Tha'll be wanting platform six at half after three."

"Thank you," Stoker says. "Would you happen to have a tearoom?"

He and Irving link arms in the flail of breeze as they follow the porter along the station. In the park across the street, scabby elms bend and groan. The floor of the underpass is slippery with dirty puddles—the latrine has overflowed, the porter confides tactfully, result of this morning's rainstorm. More on the way.

"Bloody Yorkshire," Irving mutters. "The island of the damned."

"Do shut up, will you."

"Give me my throat-spray."

"Can't it wait a few moments?"

The porter is finding it difficult not to look at the show. You don't often see a man wearing rouge in Sheffield.

Southerner, of course. Spot 'em a mile off. Imagine having to *live* down there among all the other jessies. With pitying incomprehension, he leads them into the tea room, which, thankfully, is almost empty.

Irving seats himself at the most prominent table, opens his mouth in what appears to be the widest yawn he can perform and squirts himself, gargling, with the throat-spray. Behind the dirty counter, Big Jean the tea lady is staring, stern as Boadicea in a cardie. She's drying that glass with white-eyed ferocity. She once slapped an orphan for crying.

"Do you think," Stoker murmurs to Irving, "that you might be a little less ostentatious?"

"Why are there no reporters?"

"Please don't start."

"Is the arrival of Sir Henry Irving in a godforsaken armpit of a town so insignificant now?"

"I didn't think you'd want the press. I know you value your privacy. Now for pity's sake look at the menu."

"In truth it is the same with Northerners all over the world, had you noticed? People who live in the north of countries always inbreed and are mean. Darwin or someone explains it."

"I beseech you—"

"And Darwin or someone is right as the mail. Peasants. Lummoxes. Whippet-training dolts. Wouldn't know an artist if one gnawed off their arse. Which isn't about to happen."

Tongue sandwiches are brought, with a large pot of tea. Time passes.

Irving begins biting, then paring, his fingernails, whistling through his teeth as he does so. Now and again he snatches at the air in an attempt to catch a bluebottle, but like everyone who has ever attempted it, he fails.

"Have we heard back from Chicago?" he asks.

"Not yet. I'm sure we shall."

"For Christ's sake, my farewell American tour. What are they waiting for? Where precisely are we booked and confirmed for the summer?"

"I have told you already."

"Tell me again."

"Philadelphia, Boston, Detroit, Baltimore, Washington, Des Moines, then over to San Francisco, then Helena, Montana, the new playhouse."

"Not Chicago or New York?"

"As I said."

"It is a ruddy poor American tour if it doesn't include Chicago or New York."

"That is why I am working on including them."

"What is that you're reading?"

"It doesn't matter."

"Obviously, it doesn't matter, darling, nothing you do *matters*. I thought we might go mad and indulge ourselves in a little social intercourse."

"You know that I am reading Walt Whitman, you can see it on the cover."

"Auntie *loves* refusing to argue, it makes her feel proper superior, don't it?"

"That's right."

"Loves everything tightening up inside and refusing to give in. Holding onto her ladylike dignity."

"Have you finished?"

"You larger girls do tend to love old Wally Whitman, it is odd."

"Many people the world over care deeply for Whitman's poetry. He was a nurse in the American Civil War."

"So was my cock."

"Splendid."

"He reminds one of one of those fat German nudists one bumps into from time to time, you know at spa towns. Hands on hips like a tea-urn, and everything jiggling about. Terribly proud of himself and manly and lacking in bourgeois shame and so on, and you sort of wonder why. Makes one pine for a bit of reserve."

"If you are feeling at all reserved, please surrender to that feeling."

"Thank you, darling. Another tongue sandwich?"

"I am ignoring you."

"It is the finest tongue in Yorkshire."

The day-mail for London roars through.

It's birching they want, big Jean reflects. Mind you, being Southerners, they'd like it.

"What year did we play New Orleans?" Irving asks. "'86 or '87?"

"'88. Our seventh American tour. We started there."

"I don't think so."

"Our crossing was Southampton to New Orleans. We took on supplies at Philadelphia."

"That's right, I remember now. We started in New Orleans. And we ended in Washington, wasn't it, Bramzie?"

"No, we ended in New York. Washington DC was the penultimate show."

"Are you certain?"

"Positive."

"Could have sworn it was Washington."

"We played four nights in Washington, then finished with a week in New York. The final performance was *Faust*, August the twentieth, 1888. It started late because of a streetcar accident. You had a cold."

"I don't think that's right."

"It is."

Nothing is said, they sit silent in the window. The older with a crocodile's ability not to move, nor even blink, his assistant rarely turning a page.

He cannot be reading. Why is he pretending? As though awaiting permission, some cue from the teacups. Some sign that their story will be permitted to continue, the arrival of a train they doubt is coming.

ACT II
DO WE NOT BLEED?

XI

A letter

27 Cheyne Walk,
Chelsea,
London.
13th August, 1888

My dearest own husband, my much missed Bram.

I am sending this to the hotel in Washington DC and hope it arrives there before you do.

I trust that the American tour is coming out as you hoped and that you are looking after yourself and not too tired as the end peeps over the horizon. Nolly is on top form but misses his dada. Six months without you is a significant portion of a nine-year-old life. But he has been cock-a-hoop at your weekly parcels of toys, which always seem to arrive just as he is feeling mopey.

I have pinned the tour schedule and a large map of the United States to his bedroom wall so that he can follow your progress. What we do is to push a large needle into each city as you arrive there, and then the next, and so on, and we join the needles by lengths of draper's black thread. The web is become an extraordinary knot, stretching westerly as far as Portland, Oregon, and San Francisco, northerly to Chicago, down to Charlotte and Lynchburg and Richmond, criss-crossing and retracing so that it looks like the lair of some monstrous Lord of Spiders. In addition, Nolly has begun a funny game with me, where he will say "Tonight my daddy is in the city containing the Liberty Bell," and I must pretend not to know that that is Philadelphia, or "Tonight my daddy is at latitude 41.6, longitude 93.6," and Nanny or I must attempt to guess where that is. (Des Moines.)

He is getting big and very strong for a boy of his age—you shan't believe the size of him—and is able to chop wood, which I would prefer him not to do since that new axe is still so sharp, but he wraps me around his finger. I shall probably take him to Dublin on a little holiday next week for his birthday since my parents are quite in love with him. He is a little slow at his letters but will come along in time. I said to him a moment ago, "Noel Irving Stoker, you shall write to your father." So, you may expect an epistle from him soon.

I have a funny story to tell you, oh Bee, I wished you were here to see it. Some time ago—did I tell you—the Mechanics' Institute decided my classes in reading and writing over the years had been such a success that they wished to take on a person to administer further schemes of the sort. I suggested, more accurately insisted, that I be one of the adjudicators, and after much grumbling and huffing, they agreed.

We received a couple of dozen applications and sifted them down to three, a task requiring much Christian forbearance on my part, as my colleagues tried to insist on jemmying in their own friends or favourites, sometimes with wearying directness. On a number of occasions I stepped outside the committee room, pleading the need for fresh air, and took the name of Our Lord in vain, which was revivifying.

The Tuesday arrived when our trio presented themselves for consideration. Our jury of interview comprised four. Mr. Masterson, Mr. Madison, Mr. Mowbray, and myself. One would not have wanted to stammer on the sound "M."

In came the three candidates each to give an account. We spent twenty minutes conversing with them and took notes as they answered. I will show you the notes when you come home.

When I tell you that one of the applicants was a pleasant, intelligent woman of thirty, working currently as a governess at Blackheath, speaking French, German and Italian fluently, the second a young man, also pleasant, a good-looking almost-halfwit who could not stop folding and unfolding his arms, the third a scrofulous old bore who staggered in reeking of whiskey and mediocrity (but was a great friend and comrade of Messrs Mowbray and Madison), you will know which contender was preferred by my colleagues, but they played their cards close for a time.

The young halfwit we eliminated quickly, for differing reasons. My fellow jurors, being oldfellows, did not like that he was young. I did not like that he was a halfwit.

He was breathtakingly handsome, as I say, but not to be entrusted with anything more demanding than counting the buttons on his waistcoat. I was given the task of breaking the news to him, he was waiting in the anteroom. He appeared relieved at being rejected and went away pleasantly, folding and unfolding his arms, tripping over his laces in the corridor and in general being completely adorable.

We came then to consider the governess, and I spoke ardently in her favour. If anything, I said, she was excessively qualified and experienced, we were fortunate to have attracted a person of such gifts. She had impressed me, during our conversation, by her calm, measured voice (which reminded me of your own mode of speaking).

Teaching children was rewarding, she had said, but was perhaps not for everyone. There was honesty in her manner and a likeable straight-forwardness. She wished to make a change in her life. In addition, she had been the only one of the three aspirants to have given any thought at all to the position, suggesting that the classes might be expanded to take in such matters as hygiene and household budgeting, which would be of interest to the wives of our members.

"Gentlemen," I said, "let us afford her this chance. Such an outcome would be beneficial to all."

Well, the silence that descended, Bee! It was like being on the moon. They smoked and thought and considered and smoked and looked at their thumbs and smoked. If knighthoods were awarded for the ability to smoke and say nothing, the queen would have been busy that Tuesday.

Finally, Mr. Madison roused himself to utterance. "A governess, you know, is not always quite the thing, Mrs. Stoker."

I asked if he would care to expand.

"There is sometimes a reason a woman is not married," he said gravely.

Looking at him, I could think of several.

"Every governess has a story," he added. "That is the plain fact. Often there has been scandal or hushed-up unpleasantness in a governess's past. We have our membership to consider. Many of them are young men."

"I concur," announced Mr. Mowbray, a large brute with no neck. "Governesses are not wanted at the Mechanics" Institute. We have difficulties aplenty as we are."

"And you, Mr. Masterson?" I said, more in hope than expectation. "Will you ride to my rescue, good knight?"

Mr. Masterson is a Yorkshireman of the blunt-speaking sort and on this occasion he conformed to type.

"Governesses be oars," he said.

"You mean the implement one rows a boat with?" I asked.

"Governesses, Mrs. Stoker, be damaged goods. Ah speak as Ah find. There tha art. An Ah'll tell 'ee good an' plain why she don't 'ave an 'usband. She don't need 'un, that's why. Why 'ud she bother? The woman next door's got 'un that'll do just as well."

I actually laughed aloud, which was rather embarrassing. They looked at me like a triumvirate of troglodytes.

"And I don't care for the idea of hygiene," said Mr. Mowbray with a shudder. Which anyone ever standing downwind of him would have gathered.

"Indeed," agreed Mr. Madison, shaking his head. "We don't want that kind of thing starting up, not on our watch. We couldn't be sure where it would end."

They then went in to bat for the drunken comrade, who was proclaimed a mightily fine fellow and a man of the world "like ourselves." He was asserted to have addressed the four of us on the committee with good humour and fellowship.

"He thought there were eight of us," I said.

On we wended another hour, his alleged qualities being trumpeted, his almost incapacitating incoherence put down to the anxiety of being conversed with by a group, an experience that most teachers do have to face, I pointed out, since classrooms rarely comprise one student.

Puffing like grampuses, they smoked and evaded. Finally I reached the buffers.

"Gentlemen," I said. "I have fifty pounds a year from my dowry, as you know, which for some years I have donated to the Institute. I will write to the bank tomorrow morning and cancel the arrangement if you continue in your refusal to see sense. And I will write to every newspaper in London and to every one of your members, explaining the reason for my decision. They may agree with you. They may not. I am willing to take the chance. Gentlemen, good afternoon, I wish you well."

"Look here, Madam," said Mr. Mowbray, which was fuel on the fire.

"I am not a Madam," I said, as I gathered my coat and handbag. "And Mr. Mowbray, you are not a mechanic." This is the worst thing one can say to anyone at the Institute. It's like calling a Frenchman a Belgian.

Happy to say, the governess was offered and has accepted the position. But dearest Bee, it was like a play, a ridiculous comedy. Perhaps you will write it one day.

Well, Nolly is calling me now and wants feeding like an ogre.

Thank you for the books you sent from Chicago. If you have time, could you see if you can find me a collected Louisa May Alcott over there? But don't go to trouble, it's only if you find yourself in a bookshop. I mean a fine edition, it would be lovely to have on our shelves if so.

I miss you and love you madly and am sorry we quarrelled so horridly in the weeks before you left. Come home safe, my dear husband. Let us start out again. I have a feeling our better days are at hand.

Your Flo

* * *

XII

*In which a mummy of Dublin's St. Michan's church
is encountered and an odd manliness about the purchaser
of a book is noted*

Hurrying the north quays of the Liffey, the lanes behind the Four Courts, Mary's Abbey, and the alleyways near the slaughterhouse and the markets, dawn-lit gutters, mouldering cauliflowers, cows' skulls. On Coppinger Row he pauses, is suddenly a snuffling worm, corkscrewing with savage force through the entrails of the earth, poddles and nooks, declivities and culverts, sewer pipes, silver-seams, secretly buried children, crushed granite and schist, banks of clay and Vikings' teeth, through the cobbles of St. Michan's crypt.

Above him is evensong. *Tantum Ergo, Amen.* Down here the reek of chalk and rotted coffin. A ghoul the height of the capstone clambers wearily from his box, hair floor-long, raven's nest in his ribcage, patches of ragged chainmail dangling from his femur as he dons the shield he was wearing at the siege of Jerusalem and bawls for the other mercenaries to fall in.

Stoker awakens in his cabin. The Atlantic roils hard.

Around him, the creaks and groans of the ship, beyond the porthole the shrieking night.

The Crusader is still here or in the land behind eyes, axe through his helmet but flailing on at the sands. But the crash of a breaker shudders him back to the nothingness. Stoker listens to the drumbeats but soon they fade, too.

The sour heavy taste of ship's wine.

In red candlelight he sees with irritation that his fob watch has stopped.

Pulling on his dressing robe, he makes his way hand-by-hand along the guy-roped galley, through its eye-watering odour of vomit and spilled beer, up the steps, and in through the glass doors of the Maindeck Saloon. The lanterns are burning, some of the actors at a baize table are noisily playing poker with the props-lads. At the bar, he orders a double port-and-brandy.

Harker in a corner is sketching the scene. He approaches. She looks up at him smiling.

"Bad night, sir," she says. "Captain says it's calming."

"Hope he's right, my good Harks."

"You quite well, sir?"

"Just a nightmare. Rich dinner. Had you a chance to finish counting the takings from Boston?"

"Seven thousand two hundred and thirty-three dollars, sir. The lot's in the strongbox down in the purser's office. He's arranged for an armed guard like you said."

"Thanks for helping me with that, Harks, I was butchered and bushed."

"How much'd we take in all, sir? Thirty-two?"

"I reckon it thirty-three thousand dollars over the whole tour, after costs. San Francisco was nine thousand, but they can't all be so good."

"Not a bad season's poaching, sir. Care for another swizzle? Put lead in your pencil."

"Thank you, Harks, no. Chief about anywhere?"

"Ain't seen him this three hours or so. I believe he offed to bed, a bit shickery."

"What time is it, do you know?"

"Coming on for five of the morning, sir, Greenwich time. We're approaching your homeland, as it happens."

On deck, he walks for a while in the not unpleasant lonesomeness of the sea-traveller. Cold, but the roiling ocean has its consolations to impart. In a dawn where you are nothing, not even a drop, all things will be washed away.

He watches the islands off Kerry loom slowly into view as, behind him, the sun gilds the sky's edges. Wisps of smoke can be seen from the distant chimneys of cottages, coracles are setting out from the coves trailing nets. By some odd trick of the water, a chapel bell is heard tolling, but he can't see the church no matter how hard he stares, and now he realises it's the bell on the upper deck.

In the coracles, men with lanterns, hefting long harpoons. What can their lives be like, the people who live in such a nowhere? To exist one tide from death. Why don't they emigrate?

Avaunt, the Crusader whispers. *Jerusalem is lost.*

The skullish starkness of Skellig Michael jutting up from the breakers like a mountain fallen from the sky. Monks and penitents lived there once. All men. Who could endure it? What was their conception of God, that their loneliness would appease Him?

At the time of an ancient plague, one of the hermits came to believe he was the last alive in all the world, carved his farewell into that wilderness basilica of granite, thinking none but the avenging angels would ever read it. A thousand years before Chaucer, before *English*. Mother told me the story, one evening by the fire. The callipers so heavy, my legs weak as water. But Father said none of it was true.

Stoker pictures his mother. Seven years since he's seen Dublin. Never seems to be time any more.

Six months away on tour, a fortnight since his wife and their son left for their holiday in Dublin. What shall it be like, to live with them again?

Out of the hiss of churning sea and the cry of the gulls arises an afterpresence of their arrival in New Orleans. The sultry heat, the hauteur and strange beauty of the people, their stories of the "zonbi," the vudú, the living corpse, Barón Samedi, in his stovepipe hat. Some Louisianans were former slaves, others wore diamonds and silks. All, to Stoker, had a dignity, a calm; they held themselves like aristocrats come into an inheritance. The women were mockingly handsome.

The tomb of Marie Laveau, said by some to have been a witch. Why were those thousands of nails hammered into her wooden grave-marker? It was how you cursed an enemy, the custodian explained. Other ways were the black-cat bone and the mojo hand, the dark power of the crucifix and the sanctified Host. Tales of vicious retribution, bubbling like a gumbo in which a fingerpinch of gunpowder had been dropped.

The spices. The perfumes. The flash of eyes from a doorway. The smell of okra, the Spanish moss in the trees. A morning when he and some of the actors went out to see the bayous. Alligator hunters, Cajuns, in their "junkanoos" and culottes. Lake Ponchartrain. The knightly courtesy of everyday speech. The roar of the Mississippi entering the bay. He had never felt further from Dublin.

Then, 72 cities in 25 weeks. 122 shows. The exhaustion, the trains. The Niagara Falls of paperwork. The receipts and lost passports, the cancelled hotels, the actors suffering diarrhoea and toothache and fevers, needing doctors in the middle of the night, losing their wages at cards, falling in love with attractive Midwesterners and not wanting to move on to the next city, getting rolled by finaglers, robbed by ladies of the street, being arrested, arraigned, jailed, bailed, bitten by mosquitoes, stung by hornets or roasting slowly on the flames of American success, everyone wanting to touch them and asking them to talk "in that accent," the impresarios arguing out every clause of the contract, bargaining, hectoring, in several cities weeping, not wanting to pay, pleading bankruptcy or a dying relative, scenery going missing, an actress absconding with a cowboy, the stagehands wanting more money, five broken limbs, three impregnations, one surgical procedure ("extraction of bullet from actor's thigh following misunderstanding at barn dance, $80"), the theatre destroyed by a tornado in Detroit.

The closing night in New York. Stagehands sweating, shirtless, down in the pit, to pump the gas along the half-mile of tubing from 8th Street and Astor Square, up through the theatre's trapdoors. The billowed gush of flames, the screams of the audience, the skreek-skreek of the orchestra's strings.

A hundred slum children from Orchard Street in the Lower East Side, hired as demons, were wailing and clawing the air in their black sacking hoods, as the ten-foot-high wooden skull was lowered from the flies, Irving as Mephistopheles in the hole of its left eye, red and silver cape and the horns of a stag, come to drag wretched Faust down to Hell.

Stilt-shoes had been cobbled for him, with yard-high heels. He towered above the gibbering house, squeezed blood from the air, beckoned, cackled, quivered in a frenzy, pointed at the wife of the corrupt mayor in the front row, and at the climactic scene, thanks to a mouthful of gasoline oil and a match, spat fire half the length of the parterre.

The police had been summoned, the whole company threatened with arrest if such an irresponsible stunt were undertaken again. Mark Twain came backstage to offer congratulations, the Chief genuflected before him, kissed his hands. At the end of the night the theatre manager begged Irving to extend, cancel the trip home to England. A crowd of ten thousand had gathered in Astor Place, chanting his name, fighting the police for the chance to see him, touch him. Touts were already selling forged tickets for a newly added run, every printer south of 14th Street was cranking out fake handbills. The Chief said no. "Leave them wanting more." The complaints of blasphemy would help next time.

Past Cape Clear, the fjords of Kerry, the inlets of West Cork, Sherkin, Ballyferriter, Skibbereen. Near Kinsale the ship stops and there comes the heavy splash of the anchor dropping.

Weariness enfolds him as he watches the little supply boats breasting out from the town, laden to the gunwales with food and fresh water. The lighthouse glimmers bravely, spreading its yellow beam over the surf. He becomes aware that he is not alone.

"Good morning, Bram."

"Chief."

"The old country, what? I was watching the seals just now. Remarkable faces.

Like humans, don't you think?"

"Some say so."

"Get the receipts done all right?"

"Harks gave me a lot of help."

"Thirty-two thou?"

"Thirty-three."

They stand together at the rail watching lights come on in the distant town, the tug-men roping packages and boxes up the lines to the waiting stewards. The sky behind Kinsale is a rich red and gold.

"Odd," Irving says. "All this time since little Harks let us in on her secret, one still can't quite think of her as a girl. Or quite forgive the lie."

Stoker accepts an American cigarette from the offered silver case. "She was afraid. One can't blame her. Women found it impossible to find her sort of employment. Her lie was an innocent one and we gained by it."

"Couldn't concur more. All the same, bit odd. Dressing up as a chap and going about so-attired. Still does, as you know, rather dandyish too. I said to her the other week in Seattle, 'Jenny, my dear, you are the Beau Brummell of the company. Do you know what she said?"

"'Second only to yourself, sir.'"

"Ha. She told you?"

"And everyone."

"Sweet girl. Many gifts. Rather mashed on her, in truth. Chap in the picture, do you know?"

"My understanding—not that we've discussed it much—is that our Miss Harker does not see herself as the marriageable sort."

"Ah. Quite. Well, that's all right too, you know."

"Indeed."

"Never met anyone who really *was* the marriageable sort, if I'm honest."

"Never?"

"Perhaps a couple of Catholic priests."

"Shall you go up to London from Southampton as soon as we dock?"

"Better do, to get the gelt banked? You'll follow with the company?"

"Of course."

"Oh, thanks for your help, old Bram. Should have said it before. Thrilled the old tour came off quite so well in the close. Wouldn't have done without you."

"A pleasure."

"You'll find in your cabin a polished wooden box about so high. Little gift for you inside. Got it in Philadelphia."

"There was no need."

"And triple everyone's wages, would you. And run up a letter of gratitude from me, the usual wording, heartfelt, so on? I'm a little tired now, off to doze."

* * *

PHONOGRAPHIC TRANSCRIPT

This is Stoker speaking.

Today is what. The first of September, 1888.

I am sorry to say that it has happened again. I was not in

through the door fifteen minutes from Southampton, had barely unbuttoned my coat and embraced Nolly and Flo and given them their gifts, when an old enemy came in and ruined what might have been a happy homecoming. It was Florence that introduced him.

Copyright.

"I have made an appointment with a notary," she said, "for tomorrow at eleven. He shall take us to the War Office. That is where patents are registered."

I explained that I was busy.

She said that she would change it.

I said, "I am always busy."

"Why so curt?"

I said it had not been intended as curtness, that I was probably a little tired after the voyage.

"Do you know what I hate, Bram? How you make me the scolding wife. The shrew. The termagant. The pantomime harridan. Your obstinacy writes the lines I have no choice but to say."

"There is always a choice."

"Silent acquiescence, do you mean?"

"Wifely supportiveness might be a better way of terming it."

"In whatever her husband wishes, great or small or indifferent."

"I seem to remember you taking vows not a million miles from those."

"Do you dare to lecture me, Bram, on the vows I entered into? After six months away from us, you might take one minuscule instant to reflect upon your own."

"I stand corrected."

"You bloody do, sir. That's right."

"Have you finished?"

"I will not tolerate your condescension, Bram. You will not cut me down to size. Do not say to me things you wish to say elsewhere. Wifely supportiveness is something you are quite capable of giving. Just not to your wife, it would seem."

"My writing is my own. The only thing that is. I shall reach all decisions about it by myself."

"There is no yours and mine between lovers."

"Is that right?"

"There is a better you than this, Bram. Where has he gone?"

"To the War Office to have himself bloody patented."

I left the house in rotten funk and walked for a long time, the four miles over to Bow and back. Felt very low after what had happened, very lost, self-pitiful. Confused as to how we have come to this pass. It is as though, faced with the prospect of living with one another again, we see a chart of some sea we do not know how to read.

Terrible day for London. News came this morning of the savage murder of another poor girl, one Mary Ann Nichols, body found near Blackwall Mansions in Whitechapel, having been subjected to unspeakable mutilations. The third such girl in five months to meet such a dreadful death. Now we know we have a monster at large in London.

As this evening I walked, I saw many women hurry through Leicester Square looking frightened, in threes and fours, arm in arm, eyes darting about. Hundreds of police on duty but that is not assuaging the dread. Newsboys outside Charing Cross, wildness in their eyes, crying up the murders. Men I overheard beneath the streetlamps spoke of little else but the crimes and the forming of armed gangs to patrol the East End. Battalions of rumours. The killer is a nobleman, goes about disguised as a Catholic priest, is a Russian, is a surgeon, is a soldier, is in fact two quite different men, or three. Is dressed as a woman.

Add to this that London's fog is poisonously thick and filthy at the moment, with horrid black smuts and noxious-smelling dust, so that some ladies had on veils and some of the men wore hoods or kerchiefs, and the atmosphere was disconcerting.

Also, an extraordinary number of drunken people in the streets, and many unfortunate girls of that sort who have met such unspeakable ends. One would think they would be terrified away. The city seemed a perverse carnival with its ringmaster the murderer, conducting us in some grotesque masque of pretending not to see.

On Exeter Street, I happened into Harks, in men's clothes, looked pale and sick like a bad watercolour of herself. She was with her brother, whose name I think is Frank, who appeared craze-eyed and a bit absent with shock or perhaps had been drinking. We talked for a moment or two and then they went away.

Stories of the poor girls' degradations and mutilations circulating like a fever, a delirium that feeds on fear. Like many kinds of poison, that sort is an addiction.

Went to a cellar club off Frith Street for an hour or two but did not like it, there were boys there too young and lecher-eyed old men. Said to one of the boys I wanted nothing, had come for companionship only. He cursed me. "What you doing here then, grandad?" God knows I should like to stop frequenting such places. But then night falls and I go out, as though looking for someone. Or myself.

Afterwards, having nowhere else to go—I had somehow mislaid my billfold or I might have gone to an hotel—I made my way here to the Lyceum and let myself in.

There was nobody to be seen. That was—let me look—about three hours ago now.

Found a blanket in the Props Room and came here to the Crush Bar, where I have put two armchairs together and have passed the time by investigating how this ingenious machine works—a gift from Himself, a memento of America—and I believe I have now mastered it enough to get [*indecipherable*].

Well, then, it is now four minutes past eleven o'clock at night. We are dark this evening. No one is here.

An uneasy room to attempt sleep in, perhaps because of all the mirrors.

Imagination is playing up. Keep thinking I hear footsteps on the stage.

Conscience makes cowards of us all.

To bed.

* * *

Slept poorly and awoke half an hour ago. Very cold, monstrous thirsty.

It is almost five o'clock of the morning. Headache. I have been searching about the place looking for a kettle or some other means to make tea but can't find one.

Terrible dreams. Dreadful. Worst I ever had.

The things I have done that no one knows.

7th September, 1888

Since conditions at home are turbulent at the moment, to state it mildly, and since every bothersome ruddy nuisance in London makes his way to my office at the Lyceum all day and all night, I have acted on an odd fantasy and taken my type writing machine and a few essentials up here to Mina's Lair.

Am glad I did so.

I should think that anxieties of a silly kind would prevent one actually living or sleeping here (alas). But, for work, or simply as a place to be alone from time to time, I find my newfound retreat among the spiders suits me well. Quite apart from the privacy, which is its most inestimable treasure, it is well lighted, quiet, and not overly comfortable, which latter fact keeps one alert and going.

Always, when I have lived in a room affording a view, I have turned my desk from the window.

Doubtless it shall be bracingly cold in the wintertime but a blanket or two shall prevent extremes. A kettle and even a camp-stove would not be impossible.

If my friend the roof wishes to leak, why, he may, and more luck. I shall move my position and thus remain dry. There is no table or desk—at least I have not yet found one among the lumber—on which my word machine may be set but an upended couple of boxes have been press-ganged into service as my escritoire and the old throne in which some Lear or Hamlet once fumed is a comfortable enough working chair. Yes, I mean to get a little stove on which I may brew a tea or heat a mug of stew, I saw one in the window of the Army and Navy.

So then. Idea for a story: a type writing machine is haunted. Clacks out its own macabre tales, which horrify its owner, an unsuccessful and untalented author who lives alone in the stark humble house he has inherited from his parents, somewhere dismal and thief-ridden like Deptford, and whose literary efforts are rejected without fail. Each morning he comes into his study and finds a new and ever more bloodcurdling tale having been written by the machine overnight. He locks his house, dismisses the servant, causes bars to be put on every window, but still the queer stories are there every morning, in neat piles beside his machine.

Maddened by his failures, envious of the successes of others, he begins sending these tales out to magazines. They are published beneath his name and have an immense success. Great riches and fame come, beauties surround him, he purchases a town house on Piccadilly which he fills with quattrocento pictures and precious bibelots, but his own writings continue pallid and forceless; always he must turn back to the haunted machine and its eerie spewings.

All night he sweats in bed listening to the hideous yacketing tap of its own keys, until finally he reads a story in which his own gruesome death is predicted. He destroys the machine with a hatchet but, as he does so, the police break down his door and arrest him. The evidence, mailed to Scotland Yard the previous evening, is his written confession of the murder of an unfortunate girl of the streets. It was made on his type writing machine. He is hanged.

This morning, about eleven, after the crew came in to commence building the set for *Dr. Jekyll and Mr. Hyde*, I went to Hatchards on a private sort of mission, having donned a pair of spectacles and a heavy cap, in case I should encounter anyone. It proved an interesting adventure but not in the manner I had imagined.

What happened most queer. Still seems so.

I entered and was pleased to see that the young assistant on duty did not know me, so that I need not have bothered with my little subterfuge. In any event I was careful to mix in with those who were browsing. Indeed, I happened on an old book that rather intrigued me, Rymer's *Varney the Vampire*, a great thick slab of a tome that I have heard amusingly described by Himself as "the worst book ever written in England, which is quite the claim." Out of curiosity, I purchased it. Perhaps might make a play. A bad book often will.

At one point, happening to look out into Piccadilly, where many boys of a certain sort were hanging about looking for trade, I noticed, through the window, a stately figure in a long gown, all in black, with a thick brocade veil that had a motif of silver starfish. There was some quality of the statuesque, as though she were someone not quite present, indeed the sight brought to mind the "aisling" poems my mother used to sing, in which a swain encounters a ghostly woman in the sky or by a lake. Emboldened by this muse, I took my intended purchase to the counter and, as I paid for it, embarked covertly on my true purpose.

"I was wondering," I said to the assistant, blushing to the

roots of my being, "if you happened to have in stock the debut novel of a certain author, a Dubliner I believe—I cannot think of his name at the minute—but the title of his book is *The Snake's Pass*? It was noticed approvingly in a recent number of *The Spectator*."

Dante's ninth circle of Hell, the inferno's deepest pit, is reserved for the wickedest sinners, Traitors to their Benefactors, who in the fieriest, filthiest dungeons of Hades suffer the eternal degradation of the ingrate. Were there a tenth circle, it would be reserved for the only creature yet more debased and unforgivable: an author promoting his book.

"I do not think I have heard of it, sir," the assistant said in his sing-song Welsh voice. "Permit me to consult the catalogue if you will."

"I believe it received an admiring notice the other week in the *Hampstead Tribune* also," I shamelessly said. "You might want to stock a book such as this, I am sure there would be demand."

"We cannot stock everything, sir, but let me take a look for you now."

I remained unsmitten by lightning as I stood at the counter and the lad of Harlech ran a finger through his lists.

"I don't see anything at all by that title, sir, what sort of work is it, do you know?"

"I believe it is a supernatural tale," I said. "*The Spectator* pronounced it 'in places chilling' and 'winningly readable'."

"Mr. Huntley?" the young man now called courteously to an older colleague. "Thing called *The Snake's Pass*? Do we have it?"

"By an Irish johnny, that one," the senior man called back. "I staggered through the proofs, dreadful piece of tosh. Didn't order it."

Now came a strange voice from immediately behind me in the line. "It is a fine work."

I turned. The speaker was the black-veiled vision I had seen outside. "Thank you, ma'am," said the young assistant, with no small degree of embarrassment. "Our difficulty is that there are so many books to keep track of and not all of them last."

"This one shall," was the blunt reply.

I paid for my purchase and exited the shop, startled. A couple of minutes later, she left.

Curious, I followed as she crossed Piccadilly hurriedly, the sudden, hard breeze blowing the skirts of the long black gown. Workmen were plastering posters as we entered the Strand: "Wanted for Savage Murder. Man in Leather Apron."

My quarry turned into a tiny side street whose name I do not recall, one of the lanes leading down to the Thames. At a distance I followed, but by the time I had entered the alleyway there was no trace. Swim-headed, I paced, but nothing. As I turned to go back towards the Strand, a tall, bullet-headed man emerged from the rear-kitchen doorway of a café and regarded me.

"Matters on your mind, sir?"

I said no, I was merely going about my business.

"What line of business would that be?"

"A line that is no concern of anyone else."

Here he approached and took from his pocket a badge of credential. He was one Landry, a Detective of the Metropolitan Police.

I told him I was General Manager at the Lyceum Theatre. His features betrayed no expression, but that in itself was expressive. I felt suddenly hot and afraid.

"Only I formed the impression you was pursuing that lady, sir. All the way dahn from Piccadilly Circus."

"I wasn't."

"Oh wasn't you?"

"May I go?"

"Raise your hands above your head for me a moment, sir, if you'd be so kind."

I felt there was no reason not to comply and so I did as he requested, trembling a little while he searched my pockets and my general person. He took some papers from my overcoat— a scene from a play I had been trying to sketch—looked over them, scowling, before putting them back where he had found them.

"You're from where would it be, sir?"

"I am a Londoner."

"You don't sound like no Londoner. Over here a moment, sir, turn to the wall, part your feet."

"I was born in Dublin. I have lived here some years."

"Old Ireland. Troubleful place. Brings its troubles over here to the mainland every now and again, in't that right? Pat likes his dynamite and porter."

By now he had finished searching me. He watched while I turned to him.

"I have seen you before," he said. "Where would that be, I wonder?"

"I haven't an idea, I'm sure."

"Frequenter of Soho after dark, sir?"

"No."

"Odd, that, Mr. Stoker. Soho's where I seen you. In the alleyway outside The Drakes one midnight, only you didn't go in. You was thinking about it. Looking over your shoulder. You wanted to, I believe."

"You have mistaken me for someone else, I know of no such establishment."

"Close cut, Mr. Stoker. We raided that night. Everyone 'found on' got six months."

I said nothing.

"Little piece of advice, sir. Have a care where you stroll. And following ladies? Not wise."

"I assure you, Detective, I was following no lady."

"I only hope I don't have to visit you at home one evening,

sir, to follow up on this matter and take an official statement. Mrs. Stoker might find it distressing."

"I should not like that," I said.

He nodded. "When I was searching your pockets, I noted two pound notes in your billfold. I am collecting for the Police Benevolent Society at the minute. P'raps you'd like to make a donation, sir."

"Of course."

"Most generous of you, Mr. Stoker. I think we'll make it three. Be seeing you about, I daresay."

Returned to the theatre, I came here to my upperworld. Wrote for a time. Then slept.

Dreamed that I was falling from a great height into London. The scream of the wind. Red moon.

* * *

XIII

In which the veiled apparition is seen again in Piccadilly and a letter to a Father Figure in the United States is written

This afternoon I had a meeting with Himself which proved upsetting and in certain respects disturbing.

He was in his office being fitted for a wig when I arrived and was wearing a Shylock nose. We went over some business matters pertaining to difficulties with the lease on the Southwark warehouse but it was evident to me that he was paying even less attention than usual. I formed the view that he had lunched well and was somewhat in the grip of German viniculture and Scottish distilling. Presently he sent the Wardrobe Mistress away and said there was a question he wished to raise with me.

"These murders," he said. "What do you think?"

I said I was as shocked as was everyone else.

"That is not what I meant," he interrupted. "Reckon there's a play in them? I think it could make a splendidly frightening show. We'd pack out the house for a year."

I was so floored that for a moment I did not know what to reply. Then I said—a bad joke—that I doubted it was possible to purchase the performance rights to a murder.

"Shame," he said. Then, taking out a copy of this morning's *Times*, he scissored a portion of the front page away and pinned it to his wall. The headline was: another grisly slaughter in east end.

"My hero," he said. "The prince of impresarios. Got the whole of London talking about him. For free."

The Chief has been long in the tiresome habit of disconcerting the gullible for no reason but his own amusement or to observe their reactions. But we were entering new country here.

"People love to be disgusted," he said. "Human nature, that's all. Fear is money, my dear aunt. As Shakespeare knew."

I said I could not for the life of me see what Shakespeare had to do with these dreadful events. More fool me for biting. I should have remained silent. "Got everything to do with it, Auntie, look at the plays. Poisonings, suicides, mothers eating their children. Makes this killer seem a naughty schoolboy peppering the vicar's jam."

"Good," I said. "If our meeting has quite finished?"

"Pity and terror," he continued. "That's what the Greeks said. The secret of drama. They knew their onions."

Again, I found myself, against all better judgement, sliding down the slipway and into the swirling sea of his cunning. "The depravities of the world are no matter for art," I said, hating myself the moment I did so, for the use of the word "art" by anyone who is not a painter always betrays the user as a posturer who deserves a good kicking.

Here he detonated the mocking laugh towards which he had been building all the while, perhaps since he rose this morning.

"You breathtaking, cocking hypocrite, Auntie. You are drawn to filth and horror as a worm to the shit. Pootle home to little wifey, where you perform your uxorious duty, but you always suspect there's more, don't you, my love?"

"You are drunk," I said. "Go lie down in some hole."

Grinning bleakly, he reached into his robe and from it pulled a copy of my book.

"*De Shnake's Pass*, by gorrah," he sneered. "Excites you, doesn't it, Auntie? To lift up the stone. See the maggots wriggle and gorge on the muck of your lust. A pity you lack the finesse with which to express it. Must drive you quite insane with frustration."

I approached and snatched the book from him, which, given his condition, was not hard. The sour-apple reek from his breath would have felled a racehorse.

"Stroked your nerve, have I, Auntie? Always knew how to find it."

"Let me make one thing plain and clear to you," I said. "We are not presenting a play 'inspired' by these murders."

He shook his dewlaps and imitated my accent and as I turned to depart he reeled me in again.

"By the way, I know who it is."

I stopped in the doorway.

"You quiet types can be savage," he said, "in your furious little hearts. You are far more cruel than the show-offs."

"I leave cruelty to those who specialise in it," I said.

"Oh it was nice that they put your picture in *Punch*," he went on. "Had you seen?" He pointed me towards his desk, on which lay a folded-open page of that journal displaying a cartoon. It depicted a simian, slack-jawed, monkeylike face but with the nose of a pig and filthy dripping fangs, on its head a leprechaun's hat emblazed with a shamrock, around its neck a set of rosary beads with dangling crucifix.

The slogan was: THE IRISH VAMPIRE.

There have been instances in my life when I was glad not to be carrying a loaded Winchester. This was one such moment.

* * *

THE VOICE OF ELLEN TERRY

. . . And well, that was the time of the Ripper, you see. Dreadful time for London. Never quite recovered. I don't know if you have ever lived in a city where a murderer was loose and keeping on and bloody on at it, but it has a way of infecting everything, like a poison in the reservoir or filth in the air.

One looks at the neighbours differently. Starts remembering things that didn't happen. That chap down the road who glanced at me in a funny way in the library the other week, or that queer little cove in his tobacconist's shop. Wonder if it's him doing the killings. Has he chopped up his wife, walled her up in the cellar? For a day or two, I thought it was our vicar, a fellow who never looked you in the eye when you spoke to him. That's what happens, you see. You start suspecting everyone.

There was gossip that he was a foreigner, stands to reason, people said. "No Englishman could ever carry out such hideous things." Filthy rubbish about the Jews painted up on the walls. A lot of bunkum gets talked when you're living with something like that. People want to reassure themselves. Must be one of "The Others." England's funny that way. Probably everywhere is.

No, I wouldn't say I felt afraid. That's not quite the word.

Darling, I've played the late show at the Liverpool Apollo on a Saturday night. Hell itself holds no fears for me.

I should say I felt more resentment and anger than fear. Small thing: I was living in Surrey at the time, in the countryside near Richmond, which is ten or a dozen miles from the West End, and I would drive myself home in my own pony-and-trap, every night after a show. It was something one loved doing, it kept one sane, upstairs. Extinguished the fire one gets from being onstage. Never wanted or needed a driver. Preferred one's own company. Midnight or one o'clock, sometimes sunrise, no matter. I drove myself home unaccompanied.

Very calming and settling, to leave the theatre at maybe two in the morning following the after-show talk and an hour and a half to clop homeward. Rinses the applause out of your ears. Kills the roars. Slow trot along Oxford Street, nobody about.

Along by Park Lane, Bayswater Road, Maida Vale, out towards Acton. I had a sweet pony at the time, Firefly, coquettish but an oak-hearted girl. We must have taken one another home a thousand times.

The different birds one heard as one came to the outskirts of the city and then the meadows beyond, tiny linnets and tits and wood pigeons and finches, no more bully-boy London gulls. Being able to hear the river. That coconut smell of the gorse. If it was later, coming on for five, say, on a warm spring morning, that orchestra of the dawn chorus could move one to tears of joy. The golden sky above. The alleluia of the linnets. Firefly and me, and a night of good hard work behind us. No feeling like that in the world.

We'd stop on a stone bridge, over a meander of the Thames, and I'd give her an apple or a carrot and I'd have a last cigarette. I'd tell her "Well, we got through another one, love, that's another night survived. There's Richmond in the distance, we're nearly home, girl."

The Ripper took that from me.

A small private reason to despise him.

He took everything from others, I know. From me, he took England. Because one had to be sensible, those nights had to stop. So they stopped. But I would not grant him the importance of my fear.

Still, one felt for the younger girls, you're pretty vulnerable on a stage. Even at the best of times, there is always a sort of element hanging around the Stage Door wanting to give you trouble. Men can take a notion about an actress, always have, don't know why. And it's a one-way mirror, isn't it, when you think. He can see you up there in the light but you can't see him back. Women attending a play are better at realising it's just made up. We don't get so carried away.

It was obvious that this Ripper coward had it in for a certain sort of girl, whoever he was. I don't like to use the word that's often employed to describe them. As an actress, one gets called that a lot. Oh yes, it's quite true, there was still that idea. A woman in a theatre was only one step removed from the street corner. Do you know, I'll be honest, I'm not quite certain that idea's ever died out, quite.

As for me, once the murderer got into the swing of things, I took certain precautions of my own.

Probably better not say. Oh well. Since you insist.

On tour to Baltimore in '86, I'd bought just the dishiest little Smith & Wesson revolver, about the size of a lady's purse. Actually, now that I remember, I won it in a charity Tombola, for war widows or orphans or something. Or amputees, perhaps it was. You know the Americans, they're always having a war.

You could buy a gun in Baltimore as easily as people buy candyfloss or apples-on-sticks in England. Well, I took it back on the ship to Southampton with me, just thought, you know, unusual souvenir. No, I didn't mention it to the Customs chappie, flounced through the barrier, best minxy smile. Oh, I tell a lie. He asked for an autograph. Which I gave. The ruddy gun was in my garter. Honestly, the folly of youth.

Well, when the Ripper got himself going, I took it down from the shelf. Brought it up to Hampstead Heath one night. Shot a yew tree. Rather fun. Shot a dustbin on the way home, in the Earls Court Road. Mischievous, I admit. Good lark, though.

I just thought: Mr. Ripper, you'd better not make my acquaintance. Step out of the fog at me and you won't step much further. You might do Len in, but I'll blow your ruddy teeth through the back of your skull as I go.

This girl wasn't for ripping. Not without a fight.

I thought, come here to pretty Len, dear, and see what she's got. I'll make puddles of you, darling. Rip that.

I still have it somewhere at home. I used to keep it in a

hatbox under the stairs. I remember once showing it to Shaw, the Smith & Wesson, not the hatbox. He asked me to let him shoot it—all pacifists are terribly excited and obsessed with weaponry, one's found. But I wouldn't. Give an Irishman a gun, angel? You must think I'm off my chump.

Anyhow. Where was I? Yes, the time of the Ripper. I still wonder who he was. Do you?

* * *

28th September, 1888

We have located a site that, with a modicum of modification, may be employed from here on as our scenery store. It is a disused pair of large railway bridges, side by side, near a quarter called Buck's Row, a somewhat desolate and hungry neighbourhood of the East End. The structures are dry, of good granite blockwork, ninety foot high and will be defended by barbedwire *chevaux-de-frise* and by the cast-iron gates I have ordered from the Sun foundry at Glasgow.

Today Harks and I went to the site to take copious measurements and to attend to the paperwork with the Railway Company, whose people appear relieved to be rid of the responsibility and, what is more, to receive a handsome rent for casting it away. Contract signed, they fled like phantoms from dawn, the ink on the parchment still tacky.

Harks seems less convinced than I am about the venture. She had been doing one or two calculations in her ledger— this is never good news—and pointed out to me in the hansom that there will be seventy thousand pounds worth of scenery stored there within a matter of a few weeks, many individual pieces immeasurably valuable and impossible to replace, the sets for thirty-one of the thirty-four shows in our repertoire. She spoke of damp, theft, wreckers, dust. Also, she is worried about rats.

I think she is inclined to fret, not always for good reason, but I could see a sort of merit in at least one respect, which is that we should arrange immediately for a rota of watchmen. I told her that local fellows would do well, who might be trusted and will not want more than a few shillings. If I know anything about cockneys it is that they will always relish easy money, especially when accompanied by the opportunity to do violence. In addition to guarding the store they might regularly set out traps and cages so that any quadruped guests might be prevented from nibbling on Elsinore.

"Thank you, sir, I'll see to it," she said, staring at the upper arches of the bridges in an odd way, as though she had seen someone suspicious there.

"How did you find this place, sir?" she asked me, then.

I told her the truth, which is that I walk a bit at night.

"You don't want to be doing that, sir, with what's occurring in the East End. One of the girls, they found her only a couple of streets away."

"So I saw in *The Times*."

"Cousin of mine works at the mortuary, sir, where they brung the girl after. Said you wouldn't credit the things he done to her. Man's a monster."

I said nothing to that. The belief that wickedness is the province of monsters, not men, is consoling to those who are young.

She began to enumerate the dire butcheries perpetrated on the body of this girl but I implored her to stop, I could soon bear no more. Hearing such things spoken was in some way to defile the girl again.

"Know what they're saying, sir? That he dresses as a woman."

"I don't think you should pay too much attention to rumours, Harks, old thing."

"Queer to think we might walk past him in the street at any moment, sir, all the same."

"Quite."

Back at the Lyceum, I found that I could not concentrate on the receipts. Came up here to the attics. In strange mood.

Was thinking of the poor girls. How they must have suffered.

Headache, a bit breathless, weepy.

Went out onto the roof and looked down at the city a long while. My mind seemed to picture the tens of thousands of rooms, all empty, as though some plague or terrible curse had purged them. The great nave of St. Paul's, the Mall, the Palace, the rookeries and hovels and grog shops, empty, the gaols without prisoners, the workplaces burning, the Zoo's cages opened, the beasts roaming Paddington. And only one man left in London.

Seemed to glimpse myself, then, as through a curtain in time. What came was a day when I was aged seven or eight, in bed, as ever, unable to walk or even to move my withered legs, and this particular afternoon feeling mighty low in my spirit, as a lonesome and sick child can. Some schoolgirls had seen me through the window and teased me horribly, in that gesturing, face-pulling imitative manner that is merciless because accurate.

Mother could do nothing for me, I wept all day. Father came home from his work. Still I wept. It was a golden summer honeylike evening, I could hear the other boys kicking a ball about in the lane, the neighbour-girls skipping and singing their little songs. Father, who was not strong, nevertheless picked me up, gathered me into his greatcoat and carried me across the tramlines to Fairview Park.

On the bandstand, the people were dancing quadrilles. A puppeteer—from memory an Italian—was wooing the strollers, the screeches of Punchinello at Judy coaxing whoops from those who stopped. A lady at an easel was sketching with chalks. The parish priest, a gloomy Derryman who always smelt of peppermint, was reading his breviary beneath an oak. I asked Father what did Roman Catholics believe that was different from what we ourselves believed and why should we not befriend them? He said we Protestants were in a boat, were crossing a great river, our safety was assured by Truth and God's Grace but that we should always pray for those of our unfortunate papist neighbours who could only swim. Some might cross. Most would not. Bread was bread and could never be blood.

Mother shushed him. She was gentle. The night's warmth had made her mellow.

There we remained, my parents and I, until nine or ten o'clock, whatever time the park was locked. Mother had brought cushions and a hastily assembled, simple picnic, Father his meerschaum pipe and an old book of the Connaught fairy tales, from which he read while I lay on the grass, gazing up at the sky. At one point, a balladeer was singing a queer song. "There once was a woman and she lived in the woods, weela, weela, waulyeh." That is all that happened. Written down, it does not seem to amount to much. But were I to live a thousand years, I should never know a happier few hours.

When I came down from the rooftop, I foostered for a time on the wretched type writing machine but nothing of even the faintest worth would come. A remark of Dickens that I had read in a preface unfurled in my mind and it occurred to me to put certain events of the day into the Third Person, change the details. But I was exhausted by then, and still in strange mood, haunted by the killings, by the faces of those girls.

I type wrote and copied a slip for Harks to pin in all the backstage dressing rooms and women's lavatories.

ATTENTION
UNTIL FURTHER NOTICE, NO FEMALE EMPLOYEE OF THE LYCEUM THEATRE IS TO GO

HOME UNACCOMPANIED AFTER DARK. THE COMPANY SHALL ARRANGE & PAY FOR CABS, WHICH SHALL BE ORDERED FROM A REPUTABLE FIRM & TOLD TO WAIT AT THE STAGE DOOR. YOU SHALL BE CONVEYED HOME IN GROUPS OF THREE & THE DRIVER WILL WAIT TO SEE YOU IN. THIS IS NOT A REQUEST BUT AN INSTRUCTION & WILL BE OBEYED.

BY ORDER—THE CHIEF

But it was too wordy and it annoyed me.
So I tore it.

* * *

Emerging from the Army & Navy Stores, parcel in hand, he is startled by the apparition that meets him.

Across the street. In cold sunlight. Outside Hillenbrand the jeweller's. The black-veiled figure from Hatchard's.

His gaze follows her like a spot-lamp as she moves along the pavement.

She pauses to look in shop windows, a dressmaker's, a milliner's. She seems to be taking notes. Scribbling in a book? An oddness in how she holds herself, the way she moves in her clothes.

She crosses Southampton Street, hastens into Grantchester Alley. He keeps his distance a moment too long and by the time he enters the filthy lane, there is no sign of her. Some instinct sends him leftward at the corner, and there, a hundred yards from him, he sees the long black coat, the hurrying gait.

Unwomanly.

Is it true? Can this be happening? Sweating, he pursues.

She turns right. Now left. Along the Strand. Crosses Exeter Street. Up the steps. Through the Lyceum stage door.

Stoker runs. The corridors of the theatre. Where has everyone gone?

The coat sweeping through the stalls, down the aisle, up the
steps to the stage, towards the staircase to the Chief 's office,
Stoker gasping and tripping as he follows.

"Ho, stop there," he calls. "This is—"

"Bram," says the Chief. "You look ghastly. Why so breathless?"

The veiled figure is standing in the window, peering down
at the street.

"Now you're here," the Chief continues, with an odd, tight
smile, "may I present to you the salvation of the world, the finest
actress in England? Please meet my great friend, Ellen Terry."

She turns slowly and lowers the veil. Her violet eyes take in
light.

"We met briefly once, Mr. Stoker. Backstage some years
ago."

"What's the matter, Bram old thing? Shake Ellen's hand, for
pity's sake. You look as though you've seen a ghost."

"I . . ."

"Cat's got his tongue, Len. Poor Bramzie's lost for words."

"I would rather you did not tease Mr. Stoker on my
account, Henry, darling. The first time you and I met, you were
a little lost for words yourself."

"I hardly think so."

"Incorrigible faker, you were and you know it. God's truth,
Mr. Stoker, your Chief sat there tapping his fingertips on the
restaurant table and glancing at himself in the soup spoons."

"Bram's the manager and head bottle-washer about the
place, Len, damned fine one too. Answers eighty letters a day
for me. Devil with the pen. He's a relatively well evolved mammal, you'll find him approachable."

"I am aware—but thank you, darling—of Mr. Stoker's skill
with the pen."

"You are?"

"I have read Mr. Stoker's novel *The Snake's Pass* and found it very fine. Some of his earlier tales in the magazines were recommended to me by Shaw himself. I adore your storytelling, Mr. Stoker. You have quite kept me up all night."

"O, bit of good news, Bram. Miss Terry is joining the company with immediate effect. She has signed her contract. Here it is for the files."

"You didn't mention to me that Miss Terry would be joining the company."

"Did I not?"

"No you didn't."

"Well, the sun arose this morning and will be setting tonight. Perhaps I didn't mention that to you either."

She laughs lightly. "I feel I am rather interrupting a marital spat."

"Not at all, darling," Irving replies, "we just do it to warm ourselves up."

"Nevertheless," she says, "I must along, forgive me for calling so briefly. Adieu, sweet prince." She holds out a gloved hand for Irving to kiss. "And nice to see you again, Mr. Stoker, I shall look forward to some agreeable chats about writing."

A handshake and she is gone. As though she was never there. Irving leans on his desk, pretending to read a script.

"Edible, ain't she?" he says. "Rather stirs the old lava."

"She is the highest-paid actress in England. How are we to afford her wages? We are already in dangerous debt."

"Perhaps you could sell your body? By the pound, not the hour."

"May I insist that you answer?"

"Only you're getting a little chubby lately. Wifey feeding you up?"

"Levity will not run this theatre."

"A little of it might help."

"I am supposed to be General Manager here, to share in the decisions—"

"Odd you say it, darling, you seem rather more interested in scribbling these tiresome stories of yours that nobody wants. Barring that idiot Shaw, of course. Might have known."

"That is unfair."

"You demand a share in my decisions while I play no part in yours? Nice bargain, Auntie."

"For once in your life, stop manipulating, can't you."

"If it is your view as General Manager or Imperial ruddy Warlock or whatever it *is* you term yourself, that having the greatest leading lady in the world is a mistake, I shall be happy to cancel her contract, of course. Perhaps you would prefer to play Ophelia yourself ? You would do well as a madwoman."

"I tell you, we cannot afford an addition such as this to the wages bill. One can't get blood from a stone."

"Oh one can, darling. If one knows how to squeeze."

"You are being disingenuous."

"Pot and kettle, methinks. Shut the door on your way, there's a love."

* * *

27 Cheyne Walk,
Chelsea,
London.
2nd October, 1888

My dearest and most excellent good man, Walt Whitman,

Thank you for the postcard of the Brooklyn Naval Yard, which I have pinned above my desk at the Lyceum. I am gratified to know that you are keeping well and rallying after your recent cold. Some of the actors here at the theatre (who must keep infections at bay so as not to lose their voices) swear by the consumption of garlic. In wintertime it is their custom to hang the white flowers of that plant about the windows and doors of their dressing rooms.

My own method of warding off illnesses is to lift the dumb-bells every morning, which I do at the Jermyn Street bathhouse near Covent Garden. A half-hour of vigorous lifting and squatting followed by a plunge in the frigidarium seems to set me up for the day, then I stand under a 56-gallon douche and I use the time to think.

I hold warm memories of meeting you at Brooklyn during our American tour last summer, of the pleasant afternoon we spent together, of your golden hospitality.

It had long been a hope of mine, as you know, to some day shake the hand that brought *Leaves of Grass* into the world. Your work has been sacred all my life as a man, but even as a child I believe I was waiting for it, as one waits for a sort of holiness, as the seed waits for sunlight.

Little did I dream we might also sit together a few hours on the veranda at your home and talk in such a free and unguarded fashion of so many private things.

For one of my sort, what was so frightening as a boy was to think one was alone, unfriendable, an outcast—and always would be—but then your verses quietly sang that there were others, many others, whose secret hearts were the same. No solitude is so terrible that it cannot be borne together.

Happy the day I laid eyes on the wise, kind face of my lighthouse. In these dark times for London, one must fix on one's consolations.

My beloved adopted city quakes in chains of dread. You will no doubt have read of the spate of murders. Two misfortunate poor women were slaughtered on one night last week, the first in Berner Street, not thirty minutes from my place of work, the second in Mitre Square—both again with the most hideous mutilations imaginable. It is whispered—horrid thought—that cannibalism was done, and other acts too obscene to write. One poor girl had been brutalised with a wooden stake.

The newspapers yesterday morning published excerpts from a terrifying note purporting to have been sent to police detectives by the author of these monstrous bloody deeds. It was signed "Jack the Ripper."

I enclose a copy.

It is eerie to walk about at night, as I sometimes do for a few hours after the audience has gone home and the theatre has closed, since the air clears my mind and calms the sometime over-anxiousness I have suffered all my life.

To know the killer is nearby, might be as close as one's own shadow, has moved through the same air. It is polluting us.

I see this church, that gallery, that street, this train station, and I say "he has walked here" or "so he might." I look out at the audience through a crack in the curtains and think "perhaps he is sitting in the balcony." A bloodstained box was left on the Lyceum's steps one morning when I was coming in to work. I swear, I was afraid to open it, was trembling as I did so. (It contained beefsteaks my employer had ordered.)

This fear drains goodness and mercy. The map is splashed with gore. We feel joined to the brute as a twin, the something within that wants to kill. I do not know that I can ever see my London again.

The great streets and avenues are deserted after nightfall. The people sorely frightened, the newspapers screaming. The other midnight I took a cab to Kensington and from there walked across Hyde Park to Porchester Square near Bayswater, and counted less than ten souls on my way, all of them police constables.

In the East End, to which my walking often takes me,

nightfall brings a miasma of terror, like an infestation of wasps. Many of the tenements have had improvised barricades put up outside, of old carts, scrap iron, broken furniture, whatever the poor can find. One macabre sight was that they had broken into an undertaker's premises and stolen out the coffins. These they had stacked across the filthy entrance to their street, as a wall, if you will.

One hears the people behind their flimsy curtains as one steals past in the darkness. But one may walk the three hours after midnight and see nobody.

Matters here on the personal front, too, are troubled, I must own. The plain fact is that, to my great regret, my wife and I are living somewhat separately at present, indeed she and our son have returned to her people at Dublin. I write to her every night or two, and she does write back. Our terms are civil enough. I think we both are aware that, for the happiness of our boy, proprieties must be observed. But hopes have been hurt (on both sides) and there has been a cooling.

As to the causes of the disharmony, they are several, some too complicated to enumerate, others one would shy from committing to paper. From our conversation, yours and mine, at Brooklyn, you will surmise what some of the difficulties are, but there are others no easier to bear, perhaps harder.

My work at the Lyceum has not at all helped. Whilst it has brought security of one sort, in another way it has weakened defences. The hours are long and late, the demands unending, the responsibilities of the position seem to sprout like the tendrils of Jack's beanstalk so that I never quite know what I am supposed to be doing but always know that I am supposed to be doing everything that someone else is not doing and to be doing it quicker, for less money.

I am perpetually under a considerable strain, so that I have forgotten how to be at peace or ease with myself, and a man such as that is a torture to be married to. My employer, like many persons of the theatre, can be mercurial and difficult to please, expecting the most exalted of standards while not always living up to them, particularly in his dealings with subordinates. As with all sensitive people, or, should I say people who lead with this view of themselves, he can be a martinet with no feeling whatever for the sensitivities of others. At the same time, the remuneration is that much better than anything I could expect for clerking or hackwork. In any case I do not seem fitted for any other sort of employment. I am aged 41 now, as you know. I have left it too late.

Another difficulty, loath though I am to face it square, is the Antarctica of time that I have squandered on my writing. The few shillings this has earned over the years will not be sufficient to pay for a tombstone and have proven costly indeed, not only on the family battlefront—where much harm has been done by my absence—but in other, more private respects. When we are young we do not think that time is a currency. Then we notice the account running low.

Bitterly I regret that I ever saw a book in my life and rue the day I ever permitted that horrid succubus, Ambition, to sharpen my pen.

How I admire your own artistry, which is purer, cleaner, manlier. You write for the winds, uncorrupted by hope and untouched by hope's sibling, despair. That sort of adamantine certitude and refusal to bother with nonsense reminds me of Chaucer, who must have felt, if ever he thought about it, that he should have no readers at all and who nevertheless persisted. But of late my own pilgrimage seems to lead down troubled roads, with no Canterbury at the end that I can see.

One builds up one's fortress as best one can, with bombproof walls no cannonball could burst, but even the tiniest balistraria will admit the occasional bullet. And where is the arrow-slit that will keep out the bees of envy? This book, that play, the other collection of tales—works which in all frankness seem mediocre or unambitious to me, although hand on heart I mean their authors no harm—set London and the world ablaze. One's own efforts, meanwhile, fail to light a tuppenny candle. I feel as one who has cut open his veins only to find they contain sewer water. Perhaps I need garlic at my windows.

There is nothing more contemptible than jealousy in a man who is able-bodied and has food and a bed in which to sleep, but alas, it can be compulsive and cancerous. I find that I am not able to turn to the literary pages of the newspapers any more, nor even to look at my bookshelf. As for the theatre, once my island of consolation, it is turned to a dungeon, for these days if I did not work in one, I could not bear to enter one; any play I commence to write seems mortifyingly worthless and turns to ash before the first soliloquy. You were correct in your gentle admonitions when we were strolling together at Brooklyn, your fatherly-brotherly arm on mine. How often I recollect the moment when your wise face turned to me and your twinkling eyes shone with experience as you told me the theatre is a place of illusions like the mirror-land in a carnival; it will do well for little children, not for men.

There it is, my good Friend. I shall write happier and less self-pitiful words next time.

If you pray, please will you remember me in your prayers so that I can shake myself out of this black and self-pitiful slough of mind? Let me remember those in London tonight who have lost everything they had to such evil.

My loving wishes to you, most excellent oak-hearted man.

WHAN that Aprille with his shoures soote
The song of Whitman hath perced to the roote.

P.S.: I enclose a supernatural tale of mine that was published recently in one of our little magazines. It has no merit
but I suppose one must keep one's hand in. Should there be
a journal in New York silly enough to like it, they may have
it for five or ten dollars, or even for nothing if they will send
me three copies.

It is about an exquisitely corrupt earl who refuses to die.
I loathe almost everything about it.

* * *

XIV

The night-walking

Rumours. Whisperings. Names scribbled on walls. An innocent butcher's-apprentice is beaten by a crowd in Whitechapel.

The ripper is "a Jew," a banker, an Irishman, is being copied by another murderer, is an actor, a Hungarian, is a peer of the realm, is a vagrant. Every night, London closes, but he appears to roam at will, as a man made of fog in a novel.

Walking along the Embankment from the ferry he takes into work, Stoker pauses at a news-stand, reads the headline of the latest atrocity but doesn't buy the paper any more. He pushes on, towards the Strand, where, in a tiny shop on the corner of Southampton Row, an old man sells rare books that are fantastically expensive, but a bargain can sometimes be happened upon in the barrows out front. Anyhow, he can't face the theatre just yet. Soothing to rummage the spines, faded morocco and calfskin, the consolation of greying frontispieces and redundant cartouches.

People talk of the slaughtered women as though they are chapters of a disputed canon. Mary Ann was one of his, Elizabeth got done by another. Mark me, there's two of 'em, you see if I'm wrong. Like a common-room disquisition about Shakespeare and Francis Bacon. How can they be so cold?

"Good morning, Mr. Stoker."

He turns but, for a moment, sees only the crimson sun behind her. After that moment he removes his hat.

"Miss Terry."

"Checking that they have you?"

He gives a short, embarrassed laugh. "It is my wife's birthday soon. I had in mind to find her an old book. Of love poems."

"What a beautiful notion for a gift. You are a romantic beneath your proper exterior, I think."

"Don't know about that. But she appreciates poetry."

"Such as?"

"She has a fondness for Dante. She has read him in the original. Often we have promised one another to visit Florence some day."

"I should like to meet your wife. Does she come to the theatre much?"

"She isn't a night owl, I'm afraid."

"May I join you in the search? You're not too busy?"

"I was just finishing up and about to go to the office. Thence to the bank. I see you are not wearing your veil this morning."

"The people recognise me. Sometimes it's a nuisance. Today I don't seem to mind."

"Are you going to the Lyceum now?"

"I am coming *from* the Lyceum, after a ruckus with the costume designer. She wished to dress me as Cleopatra in what appeared to be a pair of vicarage curtains. Some of the language I used was not ladylike, I'm afraid. She accused me of being vain."

"I am sorry to hear that. I shall have a word with her when I get in."

"Please don't, on my account."

"As you wish, of course."

"Imagine such a thing, Mr. Stoker. An actress, vain."

"Certainly it would be unusual."

Instead of smiling at his acknowledgement of her joke, she pops her eyes like a schoolchild in a magic mirror-maze. "Shall we walk a little if you've time, Mr. Stoker? I was intending to go over the river. There's a cloth merchant's I rather like across by Waterloo."

She offers her arm and he links it.

"A great artist is surely entitled to a moment of vanity," he says. "If that is what it is. Artists go by their own lights."

"Vanity makes women weak. Pride makes them strong. You know of my perfectly scandalous life, I imagine?"

"I don't read the sort of papers that spread gossip and falsehood. These days I don't read any at all."

"No falsehood, I'm afraid. I am rather the fallen woman. Married at seventeen, my children have different fathers."

"I know."

"I always think it better to get my secrets out in the open when I meet a person towards whom I am drawn."

"A reputation is often a work of fiction, I have found."

"Reputation, faugh. I have had several of those, Mr. Stoker, sometimes in the course of one evening."

Crossing the bridge, she looks down at the river and points out the seabirds but he is observing the passers-by elbowing each other as they notice her. A boy approaches, purple-faced, and asks her to sign his cuff with a nub of charcoal. A train-driver presents her with a posy of Sweet Williams he had been intending to give his mother for her birthday. A Scottish nurse in crisp whites actually curtsies. It is only the arrival of a police constable that disperses the gathering crowd and permits the stroll across the bridge to continue.

"Do they often give you flowers?" Stoker asks.

"Quite often, if one lets them. Men in particular. Then the poetry starts coming, I do wish it wouldn't."

"You are very beautiful, of course. I imagine you've been told so."

"Most women have. Usually late at night. I say, forgive me, my eyes are streaming rather, it's this wretched cold sunlight."

"Sensitive people are affected by the weather."

"Do you smoke, Mr. Stoker?"

"Sometimes, yes."

"I like a feller who smokes. Have a snout now if you wish. In point of fact, might you spare one? Another secret vice of mine."

She accepts the cigarette from his case and cups his hands as she lights it. He is trying to rise above the thought *I am smoking with Ellen Terry.*

"What is your own secret, Mr. Stoker? A proper sort like yourself. So polite and so shy and so full of reserve. But your sentences boiling with rage."

"I don't know that I have any secret."

She peers at him. "There is no person alive without a secret."

"I was often ill as a boy," he says. "Some sickness for which nobody seemed to have any name. Until I was seven years old I never knew what it was to walk or even stand."

"Polio?"

"No."

"But you were lame?"

"Whatever it was, my mother used to dose me with patent medications, which in those days were soused with cheap alcohol. I often think I spent most of my childhood drunk. She would read to me, in my bed, the Grimm stories and ghost tales. At other times, they tried leeches or cupping; my parents, I mean. It was a terrible feeling, of losing one's lifeblood."

"Come now, Mr. Stoker. We women endure it every month. My frankness doesn't take you aback I see."

"Sometimes she and my father would pay a local man to carry me to the pantomime with them. I suppose I found it thrilling to be frightened in safety."

"Some of your work has frightened me."

"Me too."

She smiles, crushes out the cigarette, darts it into the Thames. "Harry—The Chief—tells me you took literature as your degree at the university in Dublin?"

"As ever, the Chief is wrong. Mathematics and science. Didn't trouble the professors much. For me it was theatre that opened the door."

"I think you are in love."

"It is unrequited, I'm afraid."

"How so?"

"I had hoped, when I was younger, that writing would be my profession. That I might have had success with it, provided for a family, so on. Made a name. But many are called. Few are chosen."

"You are working on something at present?"

"A notion's churning around. Probably nothing."

"A novel?"

"A play."

"Is there a lead role for a vain actress?"

He is silent. She tries again, less probingly.

"May I ask how it commences?"

"An arrogant aristocrat, preying on his subjects."

"I wonder where you can possibly have found such an idea."

"It is not a portrait of anyone. If that is what you mean."

"Nothing comes of nothing?"

"King Lear was wrong."

"Oh, look at the sky, won't you. Blue as cornflowers today."

For a moment she is silent. The river-song rises. The gurgle of water, the lapping against hulls. She is the only woman he has ever seen blow smoke-rings.

"You blush when you speak of your work," she says. "Like a girl about her boy. I wish you could see yourself. Your face changes."

"To tell a story to another," he says. "To touch another person, someone you never met. That hope—moves me. Someone out in the darkness, near the back of the stalls. Or a lonely young man or woman who couldn't afford a seat so is standing in the gods. And words themselves are so beautiful. Just to play with them. Like music. I feel—when I write—as though I become another person. A stronger and better man. Silly notion."

"I don't see anything silly about it. *Au contraire.*"

"I do."

"Purple or scarlet, do you reckon? With my eyes."

"I'm sorry?"

"My *dress*, nitwit. For Cleopatra."

"I would have thought, if I might, smoke-blue," he says.

"Ah. Smoke-blue. 'Tis a mystery you are, sweet and noble Mr. Stoker. Your beautiful words. I should like to know you better. Would this stronger and better man care to buy a girl a cuppa?"

As they turn towards the teashop, a dark sight takes them.

Ahead, on the street, a police barricade has been set up. Constables are herding male pedestrians into groups to be searched. From time to time a hooded man in a boilermaker's doorway points a gloved finger; the indicated passer-by is dragged, protesting, into the line.

"Mr. Stoker," she says quietly. "Who can that be?"

"An informer, perhaps."

"Do you suppose another poor girl has been found?"

"I hope not," he says. "Shall we go?"

* * *

9th November, 1888

After Miss Terry and I had a cup of coffee and a talk, we went to a little draper's she likes on the southern bank of the

Thames. The shop is in a dark lane whose name I did not notice and is owned by an Indian gentleman and his good lady wife (although run, it would seem to me, by an Indian lady and her husband).

The fabrics were breathtakingly exquisite, mostly silks, but also some finespun cottons, of astonishing radiance, colour and reverberating vividness, the lady explaining to me—Miss Terry knew already—that a "saree" of such high quality can be exceedingly expensive but will last and can be given by the woman as an heirloom.

The ships bearing these garments all the thousands of miles from the East are moored at the dock immediately perpendicular to this laneway, a remarkable thought in itself. The best sarees are made of diaphanous silk so fine that the garment may be passed through a wedding ring.

I waited while Miss Terry selected a few (actually many) (actually *too* many) samples to be delivered by these pleasant and hard-working people to our Costume Shop. From time to time she would go into a private room behind the counter and, with the lady's assistance, don a saree, then emerge and ask my view, wearing the garment in what I am told is the traditional manner, wrapped around the waist, with one end draped over the shoulder, baring the midriff.

I must say, she was a sight of great grace.

After a time, two beautiful-looking English children came down to the shop from an upper room in which, it seemed, they had been playing with an Indian girl, the daughter of the house, whom I should say was fifteen, pretty as a sunflower and full of smiling kindness. They ran to Miss Terry and embraced her, addressing her as "mummie." Imagine my surprise to be told that these were Miss Terry's son, Gordy, and daughter, Edy. She is in the habit of leaving the little ones here to be minded when she is at rehearsal, she explained, a happy arrangement for all parties, as I could see by the delighted faces. I gave the girl of the house five shillings so that cream buns might be enjoyed later by all and was hurrahed in several languages as a result.

Returning to the Lyceum not long after lunchtime, we were met by an unusual scene. Miss Terry and I—I am not comfortable calling her "Len" because Len is the name not of our plumber exactly but of a frequently inebriated Welshman we call upon when the drains overflow—found Harks on the stage with an angry-looking, fish-eyed sort of man in a raincoat and unappealingly crushed homburg.

Harks was a bit consternated and, as is sometimes the way when this happens, flustering her words. The man interrupted her in a manner I felt to be rude but we must not underestimate the great burden that is physical unattractiveness. He introduced himself as one George Orbison, a detective with the Metropolitan Police. He wished, so he said, to speak with the Chief.

When I asked to what purpose, Orbison was again a bit sullen. He was one of those types that enjoys having something he can't possibly tell you, and rather lording it about. It interested me that, seeing Miss Terry, he took her in for a moment but that his face displayed no emotion whatever. One imagined him practising that in a mirror.

At this point, the Chief steamed out of Backstage Right and a queer sort of play then ensued.

Chief: What is the meaning of this interruption to our work?

Orbison: Afternoon, sir. It's about these murders in the East End.

C: What about them?

O: This play you are presenting at the moment, sir. *Doctor Jekyll and Mister Hyde*. We'd like you to take it off, if you'd be so good.

Why so?

We are hunting a savage madman, as must be obvious to anyone. Another girl was found this morning, this time in Dorset Street near Spitalfields. We believe so-called entertainments such as the one you are presenting might set him off. As it were. Or others might be inspired to copy him. If they haven't already.

You are standing in a playhouse. What we do is put on plays.

I've been advised to insist, sir.

By whom?

I'm not at liberty to say.

This is England or hadn't you noticed? The police do not close theatres where freemen live.

I will thank you not to take that tone with me, sir, and to lower your voice. I am not one of your minions to be bullied.

Dare you speak to me in my own theatre like this, you odious pipsqueak?

Here's an envelope for you, sir. It's all copies, you can keep 'em. It's a file on your good self, sir, very thorough you'll find it. Certain interests you enjoy, certain late night companions. Shame if it were ever to fall into the wrong hands.

The Chief paled, growing older, as he looked through the packet. I have rarely seen him silenced, never so quickly, and I found myself wondering what the contents of such a powerful envelope might be. Exaggerations and gossip, no doubt. He likes to pose as a great libertine and spread rumours about his vices, a habit I have for years advised him to put down, unavailingly. *Hamlet*, Act Three, scene four comes to mind. Hoist with one's own petard.

Observing his eyes was like watching a stream into which a stone has been dropped, clouding, blooming with grit, now clearing.

The nasty visitor was now staring at him in a hateful way. I am certain that the glare, like the inscrutability, had been practised in some lonely, ill-smelling room above a pawnshop where they accept deadmen's clothes. "I can close this establishment now," he said. "Or you can comply. The decision is yours."

Orbison's voice had somehow changed, had become husky and piping, as though his throat contained an organ.

At this point, Miss Terry, who had been quiet, stepped forward. "We can play *Othello* tonight," she said with gay excitement. "I know Desdemona back to front, the scenery is similar. Harks, run and see if the dresses are in store, like a love?"

"We'll do no such thing," the Chief snapped. "Over my dead body."

"Mr. Stoker," said Miss Terry, "perhaps you'd call the company for rehearsal at half past two, the opening scene, all attending."

"When broken shells make Christmas bells," said the Chief angrily.

"Thank you, Detective Orbison," said Miss Terry, shaking the nasty man's paw. "The Lyceum shall be delighted to accede to your request. Perhaps you and Mrs. Orbison would like tickets?"

"I shan't play the part," said the Chief. "I warn you. I shan't."

"Shut up, do," she said. "Go get your blackface."

Less than seven hours later, as I watched from Backstage Left, a worried-looking Othello drifted over towards me during a fanfare from the pit. "Where is Len?" he hissed. "For Christ's sake, she's *on in ninety seconds.*"

I hurried out to the corridor and witnessed a memorable sight, a vision seen by no other in the storied history of theatre.

212 · JOSEPH O'CONNOR

Sliding frontward down the banister, pursued by a near-hysterical trio of dressers, came Miss Alice Ellen Terry in all her tousled magnificence, barefoot, grim-faced, ardent. The gown was the glowing indigo of a peacock's neck, the cigarillo between her lips was not lit.

"'Pologies," she whispered. "I was taking a wee. Button me, would you, Auntie?"

She turned, hands held high, the dressers buffed up her paints, hair and kohl, as I attended to the gown's rearward fastenings.

"Buggeration," she said. "Get a move along, ladies. Where in ruddy hell are my dinky doos?"

Shoes donned, she stamped, then did a burst of an Irish jig ("to break 'em in"), then on she strode, *precisely* on cue, to an oceanic roar that seemed to rock the whole house, the ovation lasting fully two minutes. It was like watching a changeling, as though her physical being had altered, become—I have no other way to say it—somehow more intensely itself. Not once did she acknowledge the applause but stared up at the gods, holding the back of her hand to her brow.

Othello trudged over again and glowered at me as they cheered.

"Scene-stealing cow," he muttered.

* * *

14th November, 1888
Coming on to dawn.
Chirrups and caws.
Have been awake all night.

At one o'clock this morning, following a lavish supper (crustaceans, champagne, Tokay wine) that was held on the stage for the company, Harks and I put the Chief, who was weary, to a camp-bed in his office, then lit our lamps and went out to the street so that we might see our ladies into the long line of cabs we had ordered. One by one, they went, last to go being Harks herself who shared with Miss Terry and Patience Harris, our costumier.

Their hansom had not yet rounded the corner of Exeter Street when I found myself beset by the old compulsion.

Stood alone for a time. The feeling would not melt.

How I willed away my visitor. But no.

Rain had fallen earlier in the night and the air was still damp, but a stinking fog was rolling its inexorable way back in from the river, wrapping the filth of its muddied gauze about the gaslights and candlelit windows so that one could scarcely discern the doorways of the shops across the street. Again I attempted to summon the will to wend home but the thought of the empty house was so saddening.

I returned inside the theatre for some minutes, used the lavatory, washed my face in cold water. But what stared back at me from the mirror was no cleansed or soothed soul. I found and donned my heavy frieze overcoat, took a long knife from the Green Room, extinguished the last lamps and left.

As I set out along the Strand, the silence was unearthly. Onward I walked, through the writhing, filthy fog. Every window was darkened, the thoroughfares and alleys empty, feelings tumbling through my mind like rats in a sack. Reaching the riverbank, I made for the East End.

The distance from Exeter Street to Whitechapel is scarcely three miles but something queer happened to time, I was at once fast and slow, and I had the frightful sensation of not being able to blink, of being worked by something other than myself. It is hard to put into words the torrent of thoughts, the fierceness of the isolation, the terrifying passivity. It was as though I was not in control of my steps.

I turned a few blocks from the river and went by my

instincts, into a barren neighbourhood of warehouses, gantries and depots. The few dwellings and tenements were pitiably shabby, doorless, in decrepitude, rags doing duty as curtains. Not a tree nor a single flower, but rank weeds in rusted troughs, here and there a starved dog tearing open a dumped mattress or pile of rotting trash. Every other wall carried the pasted warning:

IT IS FORBIDDEN TO WALK ALONE
IN THIS QUARTER AFTER DARK—BY ORDER,
METROPOLITAN POLICE.

Ahead of me, in a red-lit doorway, I saw the figure of a skeletal young woman awaiting custom. Poor child. How wretched the abjection of one who must ply that trade even on such fearful nights. Now sensing my presence, she moved quickly backwards, into the shadows. Her scarlet lamp was extinguished.

I reached into my pocket to remind myself the knife was still there.

And that was when I saw him.

Before me, in shadow.

There was no mistaking the sight.

The black-cloaked man moved with weird slowness and yet springiness across the gloomy street, glanced up at the icy moon and made away, southerly, in the direction of the docks, with a curious half-trotting sort of gait. I could see that his right fist held a short, heavy cane, say a cudgel, on his head a large-brimmed black hat, like a matador's.

As I followed, I fought the urge to vomit, so strong was the terror. My dress shirt and undergarments were heavy with sweat, my tongue slick and sour, my blood fizzing. I was horribly cognisant of the click of my shoes and wished I could somehow silence them.

Soon my quarry and I reached the riverside. Tall ships were tied-on at the gantries, their bare masts and empty decks giving them a look of death-vessels in a dream.

To fight my fear, I decided I should sing in my mind. But my mind was so ablaze that, ridiculously, I could only think of one song.

> *The boy I loves, is up there in the gallery.*
> *The boy I loves, is smiling dahn at me.*
> *There he is, a-waving of his ankerchief.*
> *Pretty as the robin, wot sits upon the—*

The scream that split the night was bloodcurdling, abject.

It had come from a hundred and twenty yards away, a railway culvert beneath the river. I wanted to run, to pretend I had not heard it. Now came the gruntings and cries of a violent struggle, a volley of hard, dull clunks that brought to mind lead pipes being beaten against brick, a girl's voice in gasping terror, and the most awful guttural echoing snarl, like that of a wolf.

Looking about, I saw no one who might come to my aid.

. . . Help . . . He's killed me . . . Help a poor girl

I took out the knife I had brought for my protection but my palm was so drenched that I could scarcely make a grip on the hilt.

"There are four of us here," I called. "I warn you, come out."

Silence now from the culvert, broken only by the slapping of water.

Again was I tempted to turn and run hard as I could through the streets to my house, not even to look back, never to speak of what I had heard. But cowardice is the cause of every evil in the world. Steeling myself as best I could, I crept onward.

From behind came a sound that froze me: the breathing of a man. That was all it was; the intake, the expulsion. That such a sound, the evidence of life, could strike shafts of abject terror. It is something I shall never forget.

When I turned, he was standing in a pool of silver moonlight, a sacking mask over his head, with eye-holes burnt. In his left glove was the cudgel I had seen him with earlier. In his right was a butcher's cleaver.

I cried out, as loud as I could, in the hope that someone passing even at a distance might hear me, perhaps one of the sailors on the moored ships.

"Shhhhhss," he hissed in a weird simulacrum of gentleness.

Without otherwise moving, he now opened his horrid mouth wide, baring saliva-dripping teeth and dog-like tongue. And then came a snuffling chuckle I recognised.

As he took off and pocketed the hood, I thought my temples would burst.

"So now you know all," he said.

I was unable to speak.

A long moment passed before he crumpled into laughter.

"I *followed* you, idiot," he said. "When I saw you'd left the theatre unaccompanied on one of your insane bloody strolls. You don't think any self-respecting Chief would let you alone to be gobbled by Saucy Jack?"

"You damned. Unspeakable. Wretch," I said. "You are a cur, not a man." And I continued in obscene vein. But all he did was laugh. And point his shaking finger.

"Your face, o dear Auntie, how I wish you could see yourself."

By now he was helpless with mirth but after a couple of moments recovered himself sufficiently to gasp, in finest falsetto, "*Help me, Aunt . . . Oh do . . . I'm a girl in a pickle . . .*"

As I left him, I could hear his cruel glee dying slowly away.

"Hello?" he called out. "I say, you're not leaving me alone here, old man? Don't go!"

I did not stop until I had reached my empty shell of a house.

Now dawn.

Heart racketing.

Brain-boil.

* * *

XV

In which Miss Terry reveals a secret and the theatre's ghost is met

In the Leading Lady's office that Miss Terry has insisted on having installed as part of her contract, she rises from the desk, crosses to the meeting table.

"Where are we with the list, Bram? You were on page four? Can we hurry?"

She has asked him to let her observe his work as a manager, is planning to run her own theatre one day.

"I have paid the wages," says Stoker, reading from his notebook of tasks. "Arranged the auditions, spoken to the bank, ordered the glazier for the new doors to the auditorium, settled the accounts for refurbishing this room."

"That can't have cost much," she says, looking about, "the furniture's off a scrap heap."

"And there is a reporter from *The Times* downstairs, gristly old sort. He would like to speak with you for an hour about the show."

"Have him fed to the Chief's dog, will you? Fussy don't mind a bit of gristle, do you, old fellow?"

The hound utters a grunt from its rug by the fire.

"The publicity would be useful in selling tickets."

"My hat to their tickets, Auntie, let them come or not."

"Without tickets being sold, there is no theatre at all. As you will see when you run a playhouse yourself."

"If you insist."

"I do."

"I surrender."

She returns to the desk, pulls a handkerchief from a drawer and uses it to polish her spectacles.

"It's always the same tedious questions from the reporters," she says dully. "They make one lose the will to live. Vot do you reckon to Shakespeare? Vot is it like being a vumman in ze theatre? Ow does you put togezzer a portrayal?"

This is one of her odder mannerisms, the adopting of what she describes as a Hungarian accent to imitate anyone she finds an irritation.

"Well, how do you?"

"I look at the people around me. How does anyone?"

"You look?"

"A limp? My housemaid. A squint? My aunt. A nice old girl? You. A pompous but likeable bore? The Chief."

Stoker permits himself a laugh. She imitates it back to him with such exactitude that he startles.

"Watching is meat and drink," she says. "People are food. You have surely noticed that the Chief has put your own particular way of reading a book into his Macbeth?"

"I hardly think so."

"You lick your fingertip before turning a page. So does his M. His Iago touches his face when frightened. So do you. There is a gesture you make where you touch the tips of your palms, you do it when you're asking for something—watch carefully, he'll use it."

"A coincidence surely?"

"Nothing is a coincidence."

"This is."

"Pop over and open that drawer in the cabinet for me, would you, Bram? You'll find a bundle of little sketchbooks. Fetch one of them over like a good man. Any at random."

The tome's wrinkled pages are of greying old parchment, every inch of space alive with inked drawings of hands, mouths and eyes, free-flowing lines of footprints, bits of musical notation.

"You drew these?"

"It's the way I go into a part, darling. I look. That is all. Their mannerisms, habits, things about their accent. How a character walks is as important as anything she says. The way she lifts a wineglass. The way she draws a curtain. Whatever words she puts the *weight* on when she's saying a sentence. Most of all her stare. Get that, you get everything."

Stoker riffles the pages. A nun's head turns towards the viewer, smiles, bares its teeth.

"Started doing them as a girl," she says. "Tip I got from my father, an old warhorse, took me on for his panto when I was only seven or eight. 'Always attend to your sketches, they'll stand to you in the end. Your scholar's got his schoolbooks. But a player's got those.' "

"They are beautiful. I didn't know you could draw."

"No no, it's not beauty, it's just *looking*, dear Bram. It's knowing everything contains the opposite of itself. It's the key to playing Ophelia, Desdemona, Lady M. Put something into every lover that wants to be rejected. And something into every villain that wants to be loved. All the evil in the world, it comes from shattered love. Forget that and the audience won't believe you."

"Aren't we straying a little from theatrical management?"

"These wonderful stories you write? That's why they don't sell as well as they might do, darling. Oh, you can scribble a fine sentence but more ginger in 'em, more zhoosh. Because you've not done your sketches. You've not enough to draw from. Now come down with me and watch the Ripper at rehearsals, will you."

"The Chief's new nickname among the players is not something he knows about."

"Oh I should think he'd rather like it, wouldn't you say?"

The Merchant of Venice. They sit together in the wings. People come and go, asking questions, seeking money, but he finds it hard to turn his gaze from the light of the stage, as though a scrim of gauze has been raised, some diaphanousness removed.

There is no costume, no wig, only an ungainly man in a dressing-robe and battered top hat, calling into the darkness as he sucks on a cigar

"Shine the bloody lime, man! It's *me* they'll want to see."

The light adjusts. But the Chief is still unhappy.

"I said BLAZE the blasted things, can't you. And give it some red, you twittering drip, before I come and stick my boot up the highest rafters of your hole!"

The beam reddens down. "Now we're farming. Good lad." The Chief lowers his head heavily, as though its weight has increased. When he raises it again, the face is not Irving's.

It is longer, scrawnier, forty years older. The voice has the quiver of an old man frightened and hurt. There is confusion in the eyes, stony shock in the grimace, disbelief in the curve of the abject mouth which drops occasional stunned question-marks into the text, like ice cubes into a vat of hot blood.

He hath DISGRACED me and HINDERED me half a million? . . . LAUGHED at my losses. MOCKED at my gains? . . . SCORNED my nation? . . . THWARTED my bargains . . . COOLED my friends? . . . HEATED mine enemies. And what is his reason? I AM A JEW.

The scrubwomen working in the stalls pause and turn. He looks at them a long moment before seeming to notice them. He totters towards the footlights. Kneels. In silent tears. Points towards his face, fingers trembling.

Hath not a Jew eyes? Hath not a Jew HANDS? Organs? Dimensions? Senses? Affections, Passions? FED with the same food? HURT with the same weapons? Subject to the same diseases? HEALED by the same means?

He waits. Oh so long. As though trying to force them to answer. His arched eyebrows asking, his features wrenched in pain.

If you prick us—he joins his fingertips as though begging a cruel judge—then the howl of betrayal—*DO WE NOT BLEED?*

Stoker feels her link his arm. "Terrible old ham," she whispers, "but you see, he's done his pictures."

The reporter from *The Times* is waiting. Off Miss Terry goes. There are tickets to be sold, truths to be concealed, suggestions to be hinted at, spotlights to be ducked.

Hot, breathless, Stoker rolls up the left sleeve of his jacket. As though seeing a man on a stage for the first time, or noticing a ghost that has always been there, he watches, scribbling pictures on his cuff.

It will not be too long before he climbs again to Mina's Lair. There was never any choice of destination.

* * *

Since she has not slept in a hundred years, "awakening" is not the word for what happens to Mina. It is akin to the turning of a tide, the fall of a shadow across stone, water becoming steam or ice. A crow stares at nothing. A small flame falters. At such moments Mina notices she is here.

In her attic of dust and spiders, she listens.

Sky-shriek, rat-scuttle, gull-call, heron, the tittuping of squirrels across the ancient roof, then the snore of the oaken rafters. The creak of bony pillars and chimney-stacks and newels, the wheeze of dead pipes, the rumble of an old furnace's long-defeated innards. Not having a body herself—earning nothing but trouble from it when she had—she finds bodies a fascination.

Time is different for Mina. Five years in one second. A month is a hundred years. Her senses come in contours the living don't see. She thinks in the shape of a coffin.

A heavy
crate is not
as heavy if the
crate is well made
Every stagehand
knows it is so
but no one
knows why
It is one of
the things
I know

Sometimes she voyages out, wanders the riverbank, the backstreets. There are hours when she stands in the Stage Door.

She has been glimpsed in the Royal Box, once or twice on the Upper Balcony. Some say she walks Exeter Street on the night of a full moon. There are occasions when she can be seen despite not wishing to be, and others when she would like to be, but can't be.

Out she wraiths across Tobacco Wharf, whirling up among the masts of clippers, swooping low towards the bollards and dreggy waterlines. Trailing comets of story, afterlives of sin. Past portholes and casements, down chimneys, through locks. London has no secrets from Mina.

Some nights, she is a wall of dust moving slowly across Piccadilly, causing passers-by to marvel and to rub at their clothes; others, she is a tolling from St. Mary le Strand that exhumes a long-buried memory of broken love. She has been seen as far away as Deptford, on the waterfront at Gravesend, in the portico of the Royal Opera House, among the street-girls behind Charing Cross station. The sudden *click* behind you in the still and empty hall, the sense of a presence in the room. That time, late at night, when you felt certain you were watched, when you were terrified to raise your eyes from the pages of your ghost story because of what you might see in the mirror.

Awakening is not the word. Here she is in her flaxy roost, her purgatory beneath the slates, this girlchild made of dusk and betrayal. She spins herself slowly along the spine of the roof-beam, tendrils around the ribs of the rafters.

The intruder is here again. Sat hunched at his machine, in a globe of pale candlelight and exhaustion. Whatever can he be doing? For whom?

His own spinnerets cannot be seen, but they exist all the same. Around him, the web of spun words. Onward he weaves, not knowing quite why, through the smogs of self-doubt and the starbursts of rage.

A large man. Portly. In that way like her murderer. The candlelight takes on gold and purple. There is a reservoir of savagery in him, it seeps from his pores, but there is also something stranger, a woman-gentleness. He comes here every evening, this chubby, bearded fire-eyes who thinks himself alone in the attics. Rolls his shoulders, punches the dust, scratches hard at his scalp, unjackets his weird machine.

Mina listens to its clack as her motes come and go. The racketing ching and chunk, its whirr. Her nothingness rearranges herself in harmony with his tapping and the dirty bronze glow from the skylight. She whispers to her sisters, the moonbeams over London. She waves through the broken slating as she counts up the stars, one for every woman was ever murdered by a man, and a constellation of failed, dead books.

His first. His second. His third. His fourth. She has watched as the forlorn twinkle for each of them was added to the night, a pinprick of luminous irrelevance. When he looks at them himself, they have the ferociousness of the sun, but other people don't even notice, and this he knows, too. Still, he comes climbing to her attic.

Tell my *story*, she says. *Give me back my life*. But he can't or won't hear. His tapping is too loud.

She has the feeling that is *why* he makes his words, so he won't have to listen to what happens when the curtains of a silence part.

Her fingers strum the body of the broken harp. He thinks the weird music is made by the breeze.

When her teardrops smudge his words, he tells himself the stain has been caused by the leaky roof.

Weeping? Yes, she weeps. A body is not needed for that. Tears are the part of grief that is visible above the waterline, they are not where the wreckage is done. Nights she has stood in front of him and *screamed* with all her vanished heart, tugged at his hair, slashed at his face. *For pity's sake, storyteller. See me.*

He stares up and sees only three droplets from a rafter, caused to drip by the force of her scream. One night, she tried so hard—agonising, the effort—but when he turned from his machine towards the place where she was kneeling before him in supplication, he saw only a one-eyed cat.

I am not a one-eyed cat. I am not a drop of rain. Why can't you see me? I am here.

Back he swivelled to his machine, podgy fingers playing the keys, his thick brows caterpillars of sweat. Desperate not to lose his thread. Must have been wintertime because the attic's great pipes were roaring, all around the veins of the world. The spider-web smelt queer with the metallic stench of the heat, there was a taste of iron filings where her tongue should be. He had taken off his shirt, was gulping from a flagon of water.

A glue of sweat trickling his back. His face red as months-blood. The tip of his tongue protruding.

On the table, a ledger, his scribbles of runes. He stared at them, translated them, bashed out the sentences, pausing to shout a blasphemy or to light a cigarette on the glowing corpse of another or to howl in abject frustration at the effort of what-ever it was he was attempting, as a man trying to pass a kidney stone.

Up she crept behind him. So close she could see the tiny hairs on his neck. Peered over his shoulder, saw the strange words the machine was making.

The <u>blood</u>. Is the life. I was conscious. Of the presence. As if lapped. In a storm. Of fury.

* * *

"Papa, will you help with my Latin prep?"

A fervent, serious sixteen-year-old boy, eyes shining with intelligence, in his nightshirt, by the fire, playing with a model theatre.

"Not at the moment, old thing."

"Mamma, can't you make him?"

"Bram?"

"I am busy with these papers."

"For heaven's sake, Bram, he's hardly seen you in weeks."

"Mamma, Papa, please don't fight again . . . You prom-ised."

An hour later, the guilty father pads his way up the stairs, tells the nanny to leave the room. The boy's eyes are strained; his face pale as the bedlinen. Yesterday he was a baby. Tomorrow he'll be a man. On the table by the washstand, a model soldier stands sentry, his glossy scarlet livery giving back the candlelight as a music box on the counterpane tinkles "The Star-Spangled Banner."

"Wotcher, there, Nolly."

"Papa."

"Been crying?"

"No."

"Fluff up a chap's pillows shall I?"

"Missed you awfully when we were away in Ireland, Pops."

"Missed you also, old tyke."

"Mama says you've been writing another book."

"We'll see."

The father glances about the room, at the fleets of expensive toys the boy is getting too big for, the hoops and glittered puppets, the swords and suits of armour, the shields and ships-in-bottles. Something macabre in the helplessness of toys, like relics of a lost religion, the strange beauty of creatures becoming extinct.

"Is there a monster in it, Papa?"

"Wouldn't be much of a story if there weren't."

"Oh spiff, I like a monster story. Is he outstandingly horrid?"

A spear of longing pierces the father as he strokes his son's hair.

"He's horrid in his way. But then other times, he's sorrowful and just wants to go to sleep."

The boy chuckles. "I never want that."

"But this feller's been awake a thousand years. He's bushed."

"I don't see why that should make him sad."

"That is why we have stories, Nolly. So we can know what it's like to be someone else."

"Why would we want that?"

"Because sometimes it's beastly tiring being us."

"Are you and Mamma going to fight again?"

"No, pet. Sleep easy."

In the living room, she is seated by the window, looking out at the rain. He opens his briefcase, retrieves papers, sits by the fire.

"Another book, then?" she asks, in a quiet, quavering voice.

"Not certain just yet. Probably nothing."

"You don't feel that we see little enough of you as it is? Out every night of the week and never home before dawn. Four books to your name and none of them what you had hoped—"

"You put my failure tactfully I see, but you put it all the same."

"And now the writing of yet another is to take up whatever minuscule shred of time you do not already give to that—creature."

"I thought I'd have a last go. One final attempt."

"Your writing seems to lead to nothing but hurt feelings for you."

"I suppose a man's feelings are still his own business."

"Then why would he marry?"

"I daresay he wonders."

"I daresay so does his wife."

The flames in the grate crackle as the fizzing coals adjust. A point has been arrived at. The spouses opt for silence. But the magnetism is too strong for peace.

"I have asked Mary to make up the guest room," she says.

"Of course. If you wish. What's brought this on?"

"It wakes me when you come in from the theatre at dawn. And then you seem so restless."

"I see."

"Let's try it for a bit anyhow, see how it works."

"Agreed."

"Very well." She opens her book, an old edition of Dante he bought years ago from a stall on the Embankment.

"Might I read to you a while?" he asks. "If you could tolerate my Italian?"

"That is kind of you, Bram. Maybe in a bit."

"I spoke gruffly earlier, Flo. I am sorry. Don't be angry with me, will you?"

"Not angry. A little afraid."

"Of what?"

"Where do you go, Bram? When you remain out all night?"

"I have told you, there are often important people to entertain at the theatre. It seems to go on and on like the Hundred Years ruddy War. Someone has to do it."

"Like the Hundred Years War."

"And then I—write for a while. In the attics. I have made a sort of workplace. It soothes me. And then, my head is so full that I need to walk."

"Might one ask where?"

"About the city."

"But what is there to be gained from walking Oxford Street or Haymarket in the black-dark dead of night?"

"That is what one gains—the stillness."

"You never feel in danger?"

"Perhaps feeling *a little* in danger for once in one's life is part of the experience."

"I am not up to riddles at the moment, Bram. If you'll excuse me, I'll to bed."

She rises, goes to the bookshelves, runs a finger along the spines.

"Flo," he says. "What is the matter? You sound as though you are not asking the question you wish to ask."

"Do you wish me to ask it?"

"Do you?"

She gazes at the fire as though seeing it for the first time. *Stop this now*, say the flames. *Leave the room. Dim the lights.*

"I have heard it whispered," she says, "that Irving and his wife have not lived together in some years."

"So I am told."

"Why is that?"

"How should I know?"

"The subject has never been mentioned between you?"

"I haven't regarded it as my business or had the effrontery to ask."

"You know what they are saying of Oscar Wilde?"

"Flo, for pity's sake."

"That he goes about with boys. That he flaunts what he is."

"A flamboyant man attracts rumours. People are lazy."

"He has been attracting them a long time. It must be very cruel for Constance and the children."

"I fail to see—"

"Don't humiliate me, Bram. That is all I ask."

"I am not that sort of man. As you surely must know."

"What I know is that there is a hidden part of you. That is where you live. I used to hope you might admit me, that we might live there together one day, we two and Nolly. But I have realised that we never shall."

"This melodramatic way you're going on, it doesn't become you, Flo. I am not a secretive person, no more than anyone else. If I have occasional need for an hour or two of solitude, that is hardly a criminal matter. Anyone listening to you would swear we didn't live in the same house."

"We do not live in the same house, Bram, we make believe we do. For whose benefit or amusement I am not at all sure any more. We do not live in the same *country* most of the time. You emigrated years ago. To the Lyceum."

A sob draws them towards the doorway. Their son is there, watching. "You promised you wouldn't beastly quarrel again," he weeps.

"We're not, pet," says his mother. "Just playacting."

* * *

XVI

*In which a curious household is described
and a star alights on the Lyceum*

One night the following week, the post-show notes
called by Miss Terry run late. Disagreement arises
about schedules for fittings, figures that won't tally,
dates for a projected tour of Germany. By the time things are
thrashed out, it is gone two in the morning. Irving suggests the
three of them adjourn for a nightcap.

His private Sitting Room upstairs, a part of the old Costume
Store, has been renovated, walls papered, good lamps brought
in, thick carpets laid, seascapes and hunting prints hung.

Three respectable old sofas someone found in the cellars
have been rescued and placed in U formation at the fireplace,
broken legs propped up by small stacks of books. The wooden
ceiling is low, as that of a ship's cabin. The view from the little
windows is of rooftops and stars. "A comfortable bachelor
kip," Irving says, beckoning them in. "Nothing fancy. Now, a
brandy I think."

From the doorway, the fly-drops above the stage can be
seen, eerie as a dinosaur's skeleton. From the river the lonesome hooting of tugboats. He pulls a couple of rugs from an
ancient-looking sideboard—black, Elizabethan, heavily
carved—and, kneeling, stokes up the hearth. The stillness, the
warmth of the fire, the heavy goblet of single malt, the low-
ceilinged comfort, the exhaustion. All three fall into sleep,
each sofa cradling its occupant, and the moon looks down on
London's lonely.

In coming times, long years and decades later, the oddness

of what happened over those months will occur to them. Her children were in the countryside with their fathers; she did not like to be alone at night; it was understood that there was a man—several men, perhaps—to whose assistance she did not wish to resort.

Irving had experienced some difficulty in the wake of an incident at his lodgings—he was then living at the Albany, an apartment-building for gentlemen—and, while he had not been asked formally to leave, it had been made clear, in that English way that is so fluent with silences, that now might be the time.

For his own part, Stoker was in one of those snowdrifts that can be encountered at the crossroads of a life, the milestones obscured, kicked down. The fact that the obscuring has been done by the traveller himself is not much consolation. His wife was teaching dockers' children in the slums of Liverpool, their son away at school in Winchester. The empty rooms of the house seemed haunted by loss, a settled sadness. Simply put, there was no one to go home for.

Winter came. He began to write poems. Graceless, clunking efforts but perhaps there was something in poetry that could help him resolve a conflict many people who married hurriedly have met, a rainstorm the vows don't predict. Readers of a literary journal, *Lippincott's Monthly*, in April 1888 were offered a curious rondeau, a fifteen-line verse, signed "Abraham Stokely."

> *Eyes that laugh in leaps of light,*
> *Lilting music, gay and bright*
> *Like sunrise on a lonesome lake.*
> *Ever changing. Ever free.*
> *Never can I be with thee.*
> *East to west, my changeling goes*
> *Like moonlight on an English rose*
> *Late at night in a London lane.*

Evermore, my heart is slain.
Never can I be with thee
Even as I dream to be.
Lovers walk, lost hour by hour
Like actors in a lime-lit bower.
Evermore, I am not free.
Never could I be with thee.

Few of those readers would have noticed the maladroit poem's secret: the name revealed when one read the first letter of each line downwards.

It became the trio's habit to retire to Irving's quarters every night. A dressing screen was fetched. They brought books, changes of clothing. The matter was never discussed, and anyway was understood to be temporary.

There they would go, up the steep, backstage stairs. He would open a bottle of claret, another of brandy, have breads and potted meats, a cheese, jugs of water. The fire would be lit, the gramophone wound. One might read to the other two, or tell a ghost story. After they had supped and played cards or sat in companionable silence, dazed by the blaze that can burn long in the wake of a show, sleep would come into that room.

In all his life, Stoker had never known such merciful sleep: deep, annihilating, peaceful. If dreams came, which happened rarely, they were of that sort in which women quietly sing. To stir and hear the comforting sputter of the logs, the rain. The pleasing heaviness of hefty old blankets.

In the mornings, they would breakfast together and walk to the Jermyn Street baths, returning to the theatre for noon, the commencement of rehearsals. It was a season of driven work, of inhabited silences. No one thought it would be the start of the end.

The conversation arose one morning in a café near the theatre.

"It can be done," Stoker insisted. "All it takes is the will."

Irving scoffed into his toasted muffin, wiped the butter from his lips. "*Electricity*? On the stage? You are living in a dreamworld."

"Isn't that what we are paid to do?" Miss Terry said.

"Darling mine, there is electricity at the Lyceum already," said the Chief. "Its name is Henry Irving."

"Sweet Christ, the third person. Such self-effacing modesty."

"Modesty is for virgins, dear. You should give it a try."

"Shaw admires my modesty and says he wishes a place in my heart."

"What he wishes is a place in another part of you, dearie."

Stoker pressed. "I have made a thorough study of the matter and I *know* how it is done. If we do not patent this effect, someone else will use it, mark my words."

"Let the vulgar do as they please. We are not cheapskates for the gaping."

"I have been told by a reliable informant that Shaw is interested," Miss Terry said slyly. "It would be agreeable to beat him to the pass. Petty of me, I know."

The arrow struck its target.

"How does it work, then?" Irving asked. "If you're so high and mighty about it."

"It is a system of batteries and of metal plates held in the hand. If you study this sketch I have made"—Stoker slid it across the table—"you will see what I mean."

"Ballocks to your bloody sketches, come to the theatre and *show* me."

Back at the Lyceum, Harker was seated in the wings, chalking sketches on the wall before her desk. The bricks seemed alive with butterflies, dragons, unicorns. She glanced up when she heard the trio approach.

"Morning, Harks," Stoker said. "We might run that little

experiment if you've a moment? The Chief here is ready to see the fruits of our scholarship."

Harker nodded, reached into a drawer and removed two saucer-shaped plates of polished steel, handing one to each of the men on the stage. Consulting her textbook a moment, she stared up at the flies, as though making some lastminute calculation.

"Get *on* with it, Harks," snapped Irving. "If you're wasting my time, I'll run you through."

"Chief," she said, "if you'd kindly pick up that sword over there. Mr. Stoker, sir, perhaps you'd be so good as to fetch the other. This little plate thingamum you hold in your left fist. Like so?"

Doing as commanded, each took his position, raised his sword.

"On guard, gentlemen," Harker called. "I am switching up the battery."

"Are we certain this is safe?"

"Have at it."

Stoker stepped forward, left hand on hip, épée held out before him. He had fenced for Trinity College, knew the classical positions, but was not entirely prepared for what was about to occur. Irving, less assured despite his thousands of performances with a stage-sword, was moving with the particular swagger of false confidence.

"Get over here, you ruddy Fenian," he growled with a grin. "I'll stick some English sense up your transom."

As their swords touched, the fountain of sparks shot so high in the air that a workman up in the flies roared in fright. The *zizz* of clashing blades, the gush of silver and bronze stars made Irving fall to his knees. Miss Terry was clapping in delight. Harker cheered and hugged her.

"Again," Stoker said. "Cross my sword."

By now some of the players had come from the darkness of the wings and were gaping in awestruck wordlessness.

Irving rose slowly, wiping his eyes with the hem of his shirt. "Lay on, Macduff," he said.

The hilts clashed and parried, a geyser of crackling scarlet hailstones, spurts of cordite-scorched lightning tore the air.

"*Fight, Chief!*" yelled Harker. "Run him, Auntie," shouted the actresses. "The winner gets my colours," called Miss Terry with a laugh, but the joke seemed to stoke up the contest. Irving swung and blocked, sparks dancing from his blade, Stoker bobbed and ducked, now jabbing, now flailing, his back to the proscenium's right pillar as though attempting to push it down, now fighting his way out, sweating, grunting, through the hissing great wreaths of coppercoloured smoke, the stench of iron filings in flame.

Within a week, they had begun using the effect in performance, in *Hamlet* first, then in *Romeo and Juliet*. The newspapers erupted in praise.

EXTRARDINARY SPECTACLE AT THE LYCEUM
"HOW IS IT DONE?"
IRVING TRIUMPHS AGAIN

Queues for tickets started forming earlier, sometimes from dawn; teams of scalpers roamed Exeter Street and the arcades of Covent Garden, buying and selling passes. It was whispered that the queen herself wished to come and see the Lyceum's miracle. She didn't, but Irving was skilled in the art of making a denial seem a confirmation, and he winkingly sang up her non-attendance in every interview he gave. "No no, Her Majesty will absolutely not be coming. If she were, I could hardly tell you."

He gave Stoker an instruction to have printed on the tickets that the "extraordinary electrical fighting" was so violent and terrifying that "expectant ladies, the elderly, or those of nervous disposition" should not attend. "Trained nurses are on the premises," announced special notices in the foyer. "Should you feel you are about to faint, call an usher." Seven thousand pounds" worth of tickets was sold in one month. The quickest way to frighten people was to tell them they'd be frightened. The desire of an audience to obey.

One Saturday night in February, when the second house was stuffed to the rafters, Stoker got pleasantly drunk watching the show from backstage. Miss Terry as Lady Macbeth would have produced noisy adulation on her own; the addition of the sparks meant cacophonous applause every time they appeared, so loud that it drowned out the orchestra, to Stoker's private disapproval, but the happiness of the house is prime. During one massed prolonged gasp, Lady Macbeth took advantage of the distraction to hurry over to him and whisper that she had noticed someone important in the third row. She was certain, she said. There was no mistaking his clothes.

"Make sure he's invited back afterwards. Send Harks out for fizz."

"Cunning rat bastard," Irving said. "Ruddy typical not to tell us he was coming. He'd love to catch us unawares. We'll fix him."

An hour later, show over, the company filled the stage, awaiting the special visitor. The finest champagne had been hurriedly commanded, flowers and a cold buffet for fifty from Claridge's. Photographers were setting up downstage, getting in everyone's way and attempting to appear knowledgeable and busy.

He came in blinking from the wings, as one rarely seeing the light, a fleshy whiteness about him, Irving leading him by the hand. The britches were dark-red velvet, the cape knee-length sable, his fingers adorned with many rings. He was a little too ample to stand very long, so a trio of stagehands fetched a settee from the prop store.

To Irving's embarrassment, from time to time the guest

addressed him as "Sally," a nickname no one at the Lyceum had heard before.

"Ah Bram," Irving said. "Here is a countryman of yours. You know my very dearest friend, Oscar Wilde."

"Good to see you again, Wilde. It has been a long time."

"Bram, my good covey. You are looking delicious." Here he turned to the Chief. "Your manager and I have a long connection. Of an intimate nature."

"Oh?"

"Wilde and I attended Trinity College together," Stoker said. "It was a long time ago."

"Oh there is a little more than that to our story, old love. Shall you tell our guilty secret or shall I?"

"It is no great matter but Wilde was a friend of my wife's. When they were younger. In Dublin."

"Childhood sweethearts, one might say. Well, Flo was a sweetheart. We were briefly engaged to be married, if you can imagine such a marvel. But she left me for a better man, isn't that right, Bram? One's hair quite curled with grief."

"My wife speaks of you with warm fondness and is proud of your success."

"Yes, these days they pelt one with compliments instead of rotten eggs. But one is always an optimist. They used to throw bricks."

"Perhaps you and Mrs. Wilde would come to supper with my wife and me at the house one evening? She would find it most agreeable to see you again."

"Kind of you, darling, but I don't think it would do. Best to let old flames burn down and putter out, don't you think. Otherwise it can lead to bad blood."

"I say, Wilde," Irving said. "May I present Ellen Terry?"

"Ah." Rising with formal courtesy, kissing her hand. "Our Lady of the Lyceum."

"You are too charming, Mr. Wilde."

"That is why England shall strangle me, Miss Terry. In Ireland, having charm is seen as an accomplishment. Here, it is a shame on the family, like an idiot cousin."

"Pish, Oscar, old thing," said Irving, "you are a little too hard on us. We exported our language to you primitives, after all."

"Indeed you did, darling. Now we can say 'starvation' in English."

"Now, Oscar, you are naughty, but there is a time and a place. Let us not waste the rare pleasure of your visit on a battle of wits."

"Yes, I shouldn't like to fight a battle with an unarmed man."

Around the stage arose the particular laughter of subordinates who are observing the cutting down of their employer and his inability to do anything about it.

"Sally loves to fence," Wilde continued, smiling, lighting a cigarette in a long ivory holder. His teeth were stained almost black. "As we witnessed this evening. What a simply *merveilleuse* consolation for you, darling, all those manly sparks gushing about, it was Venetian, no *Athenian*. My dear, one was quite over*come*."

"You see I've studied electricity," Irving attempted. "Many said it couldn't be done. But I knew better."

"But of course you did, darling, knowing better is your greatest talent; what's more, it's brought you so far you daren't abandon it now. In the fight between Sally and Shakespeare, Sally always wins. She is a trumpet for Shakespeare to blow."

"I say, you are talking like a character in one of your plays."

"Oh I don't think I talk quite as brilliantly as that, *mon petit ange*, but thank you for the attempt. An insincere compliment is the only laurel worth having." Accepting a flute of champagne from a chorus girl, he now turned towards Stoker. "Chin chin," he said, "and how is your writing coming along, old thing? One has such happy memories of when we used to read one another our sestinas over crumpets in the Quad. When shall we see a play from your quill?"

"I've rather given up on that front. But here is a copy of a little book of mine you might look over. It was published by a small house last year."

"Why, how excellent. *The Shoulder of Shasta*. How deliciously evocative. Do you know, my favourite part of your novels is invariably their titles." He quaffed the remains of his drink and rose wincingly to his feet. "But now I must away, I have bad associates to fall in with. Thank you for the book, Bram. I shall enjoy taking you to bed with me this evening. Like old times, what?" Turning to the company, he bowed, tracing a crucifix in the air before him. "Well done, children. Reverend Mother is proud of you."

The applause as he shuffled off in a cloud of self-assuredness and French cologne was perhaps a little uncertain.

More wine was summoned. The celebration ran late. Many of the players—the younger ones in particular—had been thrilled by the guest and the mischief he had loosed. To have shared the same stage as the notorious Wilde. If it never happened again, at least it had happened once. His presence was understood by them as an affirmation of their arrival, the appearance of a star over the Lyceum and her people. They did not know how soon the star would fall.

Perhaps every actor joins the profession out of the desire to one day have a story to tell. Many found theirs that evening. Some of those towards whom he glanced would say he shook their hands. Those few whose hands he shook would say he embraced them. Others would soon deny that he had been there at all.

Ellen waltzed with Harks, with Stoker, with Irving, then Irving and Stoker waltzed, to the delight of the players. Boys reeled with boys, girls jigged with girls, Irving waltzed with his dog. "The Walls of Limerick" was called for, then a strathspey and sailors' hornpipes, the orchestra's violinists joined by several of the stagehands, a Manx fiddler and Cornish piper among them. When the champagne ran dry, a barrel of cider was barrowed in and broken open. Couples were noticed drifting hand-in-hand into the darkness of backstage, or out to the loading dock, even up to the boxes. The night Saint Oscar came to call.

Dawn had begun to rise by the time the stage emptied, players and squiffy musicians squabbling or spooning or helping each other homeward through the cold. Stoker, a little unsteady, returned from the street, where he had been whistling up cabs and handing out stacks of coins for fares. Downstage, near the wings, Harker was on her knees, shakily lighting a candle.

"Still here, Sergeant Harks? It's gone five."

"Doing the ghostlight, sir. Old tradition in the theatre. Always leave one flame burning when it's time to go home so the ghosts can perform their own plays."

"Don't know about that. We don't want to burn the ruddy place down."

"Rather I put it out, sir? I shall, if you say so."

"Oh, dash it all, leave it. We need the ghosts on our side."

"Night then, Mr. Stoker."

"Night, Harks. Safe home."

"My crikey, what a knees-up. Shall never forget it."

"None of us shall. Well done."

"Didn't Miss Terry look a picture, sir? Pretty as an orchard. That gown, blow my eyes, she's like looking at a symphony."

"She was beautiful, indeed."

"You're a little sweet on her, sir, ain't you? You can tell me your secret."

He says nothing.

"I am, too," Harks laughs. "I think everyone is."

"Miss Terry is a remarkable woman. We are blessed to be her friends."

"You know what my old dad used to say about marriage, Mr. Stoker? You can look in the jeweller's window, once you don't smash and grab."

"Wise man, your progenitor."

"Might I ask a favour, sir? I should like to give you something."

"What is it?"

She slid herself over the lip of the stage and down into the front stalls, where he was gathering empty bottles into a sack.

"You're a regular proper diamond, sir. The best I ever met." Now on tiptoe, she kissed him on the cheek. "If gentlemen was my run of country, I should want you for my own. Since they ain't, I'll say thanks for all you done for me."

"My own dearest Harks." He shook her hand, then embraced her. "You were a splendidly beautiful boy, now you are a handsome young woman. Most of us will never be either."

Bright with smiles, she left. He cleared the final bottle, then sat alone in the second row, enjoying a last glass of claret and a fine Louisiana cigar he wasn't quite certain how he'd come by. Ripples of ghostlight played against the dark folds of the heavy curtains, the brass of the kettledrums, the glossy pillars of the proscenium. Soon, he would go out and walk the night-markets of Covent Garden, fetch the morning newspapers from that lad on the Strand. It was certain that at least some of them would report on Wilde's visit. The publicity would be beyond price. A strong night's work.

The musicians. The dancing. Wilde's black teeth. The crackling swords. It would be good to sleep until noon, then to do something honest and manual. There was that trapdoor needing to be fixed, pulleys-and-ropes to be rehung. A tough, sweaty day whanging in nails, tautening bolts. Hard work would wash away the exhaustion.

In the ghostlight, he dozed. A common dream came to him. He was on stage, naked, the lines of his dialogue tantalisingly close, as though butterflies of words were drifting past. Reaching out, his fingers met water. The audience baying and whistling—although he couldn't see their faces, he knew Wilde's was among them. Florence was here, too, he could hear her calling out to him. Suddenly he was falling through space.

He jolted awake, dry-mouthed. The theatre was quiet. The first bells from St. Mary le Strand tolled for seven.

Stiff, sore, he rose to his feet, uncomfortable in the evening suit he had slept in, shoes too tight, hangover coming, pins-and-needles spangling down a rope of sinew in his aching right thigh. The ghostlight had burned out, plumes of candle-sperm hardening on the boards. He found a spoon and began chipping away the cold wax.

An eerie sound took him. He looked up at the chandelier. A tiny bird, perhaps a wren, was flitting from crystal droplet to droplet, now alighting, now flitting, now lighting again, her glassy, tinkling music like a Japanese orchestra. A spew of her droppings fell. The chirps grew shriller. It seemed to Stoker that she would dash against the ceiling or exhaust herself to death. His powerlessness to help was horrible, he found himself urging the terrified creature, chivvying, beckoning. Suddenly, she swooped towards the parterre, but whirled back roofward again, into the one of the upper boxes. The chirping stopped. She must be safe, or dead.

Exhausted, he mounted the steps to the stage. As he gathered the last glasses and oyster-knives and tablecloths, a foolishness loomed up at him from the pit like a phantom violinist. Turning, he faced the house.

Empty velvet tiers subtly gilded in the dawn-light that came streaming from the high dusty windows.

Was it possible that Wilde's question to him about playwriting had been more than mockery? Was mockery, if you could read it, the jester's way of advising? Might he yet stand here one night in the wake of his debut, an audience calling "author" or crying out "more?" His son would be here, so would Florence and her people. Perhaps Ellen would play in it.

Perhaps Ellen . . .

If only . . .

He seemed to see the headlines, the theatrical notices, his surname splashed across posters. O, wouldn't that silence them back in Dublin.

Not Stoker? The little clerkfella? The cripple couldn't walk? Queer kind of owl, used to haunt the town all night? Sure how could he be famous? We know him!

Money would rain. Runs in New York and Chicago. The freedom of money, no more scraping and welcoming, no more arguing with cloakroom attendants and worrying about receipts. A townhouse in Kensington, a library for Florence, a manor in the country with a study overlooking a paddock, the life of a literary gentleman turning down endless invitations in measured, well-fashioned phrases. Forgive me, I am occupied with my forthcoming tour and am declining all distractions, even ones as tempting as yours.

Now he saw in the empty tiers the faces of his parents, the clerks at Dublin Castle—everyone that had ever said no. The crushed hopes, the secrets, the failures would be amended for. That he had ever lived would matter. He would not be forgotten. He would stand on this stage in the furnace of applause, teareyed, magnanimously forgiving.

Come, gentle sleep. Up the staircase he climbed, towards Irving's quarters, drunk on elated weariness. As he opened the door, the scarlet light of the embers changed to purple. He heard the crackle of coals as they shifted in the grate.

The three old chesterfield sofas gleamed in the half-light. It struck him that two were unoccupied.

On the third, in a tangled sheet, Irving and Ellen lay naked, asleep, her head on his chest, their thighs and arms enwrapped, the gloss of his loosed hair spread across a white silken cushion, their clothes strewn like rags on the floor. Firelight the colour of brandy shimmered on her skin.

Seeming to sense his presence, she opened her eyes.

"Oh," she murmured. "Bram. That's to say . . ."

"I am sorry," he whispered as he left.

* * *

XVII

*In which an author murders his books
and Desdemona visits an Asylum*

Unfurling with the dust beneath the rafters of her attic, dead Mina witnesses a strange scene.

Gaunt, weeping, the interloper, on his knees, is ripping up copies of his books. He has a stack of them, the height of his waist, is systematic in the destruction. The covers are jerked back hard, he reefs out the pages.

The Shoulder of Shasta. What can it mean?

Pulling open a dirty skylight, he flings the shreds into the air. She darts out and sees them borne away on the wind towards the Thames, handfuls of torn paper blackened by ink, like a murder of crows over Waterloo Bridge.

In the windows of the theatre at daybreak, she sees red reflections of his dream. The Count pulling a sheet from the heroine's naked body, unfastening his shirt, running a fingernail down his abdomen, from his navel to his moss, opening his flesh like a fruit. He holds the back of her head, forces her lips to the wound, her hands around his torso as she sucks him.

Blinking, he now realises he is at the dining table with his wife. The tall clock in the corner bongs quietly, as though apologetic for interrupting the silence.

"It is pleasant," she attempts, "to have you home for an evening."

"For me, too."

"They're not missing you at the theatre?"

"They can manage one night."

The maid comes in with the soup. Silence falls like an anvil.

Only after she leaves does the conversation force itself to life again, an ember inflamed by the waft of a closing door.

"Is something on your mind, Bram? You seem a little pre-occupied."

"Nothing."

"I saw your *Shasta* this afternoon. In Hatchard's on Piccadilly. The assistant told me they had sold three copies."

"We are rich."

"In some ways we are. There are many ways of being rich."

"There is only one way that matters when the accounts come in."

"You know that is untrue. At another time, you would say so."

"I wish it were another time, then. But it seems to be now."

"To have our son is a great blessing. I see you in him at every moment, in how he laughs when he sings, how he counts on his fingers despite being clever enough not to. And for you and I to have one another, still. I thank God every day. Your kindliness is a great blessing to Nolly and me, your manliness, your hard work. Your decency."

"What's brought this on?"

"I have a confession to make, Bram."

"A confession?"

"I hope you don't mind. You left your notebook on the hallstand the other morning. I read a little of your new idea. The vampire story."

"That story is dead. It turned out to be nothing."

"I hope not."

"I burnt it the other night and am glad to be rid of it. Now let us change the subject if you don't mind."

She nods, opens a drawer in the table, produces a clutch of scorched pages.

"Don't be angry," she says. "I rescued it. Poor creature. A little frayed around the edges. Still here, though. Like us."

His eyes are hot and moist. He accepts the blackened bundle.

"You are the finest, most admirable man I have ever had the honour to know," she says.

When finally he is able to speak, his voice is trembling. "I have never been worthy of you, Flo. I am still not, now. The happiness you have given me. To have a family. A home."

"You are loved the way you are, Bram. I think I understand."

"Thank you. My treasure. I only hope I am not too late."

They return to their starter, the sustenance of many a marriage both in sickness and in health, long spoonfuls of Silence Soup.

* * *

In the darkroom off Bow Street, he and Harks are watching the wizard pour the solution. What happens next is miraculous.

Irving's face appears in ghostly negative, then—incredible—in positive, staring out from the shadowland of plate glass. Next to shimmer into being is the frown of Desdemona, haughty, disdainful, queenly. The chemical stench is so strong that the photographer's eyes are dripping.

The printer accepts the heavy plates like the precious relics they are, wraps them in thick blankets, carries them with motherly gentleness one by one across the alleyway to his works. Hard to believe that the clattering pistons and whirring cogs won't smash them or do some lesser violence, but an hour later, as promised, the playbills begin unrolling from the pressdrum.

"Oh, sir," Harks says. "That's goodnight to the competition."

She has arranged for a fleet of slum-boys to be waiting with buckets and paste. The urchins accept their cargo and payment of pennies, steal off, murmuring Stoker's instructions as they go. "Every billboard, every wall. Plenty more where these came from. Don't stint."

Next morning, a crowd of the awestruck gathers outside the theatre.

In the noticeboards, on the pillars, in the windows of the main doors.

Playbills with photographs of the actors.

Not drawings. Their faces. Twenty inches by ten. Ellen Terry is asking you personally to come to a play. All she wants is five shillings. You'll be in the same room. The stern Chief is staring through the kernel of your soul. Are you able to resist that command?

Across the street, Stoker watches. People cluster and point. A constable burbles up, waves his arms for them to move on, but after a moment removes his helmet and stops shooing. He stands, hands on hips, shaking his head in patriotic amazement. Is there anything Britons cannot conquer?

Stoker crosses, enters the lobby, climbs the brass-railed staircase to the foyer. His bundle of keys is heavy. There is much to be done.

By the drinking-fountain, Desdemona is waiting, in a muslin dress and cartwheel hat.

"I've not seen you in a while, Bram. You are plastering London with me. I am become wallpaper."

He nods, goes to unlock the auditorium doors. "Things have been busy. And I have been spending time at home."

"I have something small for your birthday. It's today, isn't it?"

He had forgotten.

Rising, she approaches, hands him a leather-bound notebook.

"I thought you might fill it with your beautiful words."

"That is all in the past."

"Don't speak like that, Dull. Why so cross?"

"If you will excuse me, I have rather a full plate this morning."

"I went to a seance," she says. "Out of curiosity, nothing more. The medium told me I know a man who will one day write a story that will stop the world on its track. Published in hundreds of languages. Whose hero will be unextinguishable."

"I don't hold with such nonsense."

"Interesting, all the same."

"I imagine she was speaking of Shaw."

"Why would you assume 'she'?"

"I gave the matter no thought."

"Bram, about the night of Wilde's visit—"

"That is none of my affair."

"If I gave you the impression that you and I could be more than a friendship, I am sorry. I didn't mean to. I am so madly fond of you, perhaps I slipped."

"You didn't. And if you had, it would be very wrong of me to have given in to the feelings you describe. I am married."

"Do you think I don't know?"

"So is he."

"So am I."

Harks and three of the younger players hurry through the lobby, making for rehearsal. A crowd is forming at the lattice of the Box Office.

"I should attend to my work," Stoker says.

"Do you hate me?"

"How could I?"

"But *do* you?"

"Never."

"The friendship I have with you will outlast everything else. I knew it the moment we met. And I know it, to this day."

She is clench-lipped as he holds her. The embrace is noted by some in the Box Office queue who nudge one another and point.

"Wretch," she whispers. "You have made me cry and ruined my make-up."

"You are lovelier without it. Dry your eyes. Here's my hand-kerchief."

"I have something difficult to do this morning. Do you think you might come with me? As a favour?"

"I can't."

"Please, won't you?"

"Really no. I mustn't."

On the train from Charing Cross down to Sevenoaks, she falls into a doze. He reads over a bundle of bills, from the silk merchants, the printer, the firm of carpenters who refurbished the pit. She murmurs in her sleep, seems disconsolate, fighting something away. One of her gloves falls from her lap, he picks it up, the ivory lacework still warm. When he replaces it on her blanket, she grasps it without awakening, her long fingers twisting, now tugging at the wrist-button. *Leave me*, she whispers. *I am not for this test.*

Arrived at the station, they find a pony-and-trap by the portico. The driver says he's been sent to collect them.

The leafy lanes dapple. Clean air from the meadows, the mellow grey sky over haycocks. She names every field as they pass, every hillock. He pictures her as a child, dancing these very cart-tracks, brambling and roving and coming the tomboy, wassailing with the carollers at Christmastime.

Through high cast-iron gates, the gloomily solid mansion looms up, the time-blackened chimney-stacks and belfry and turrets giving it the appearance of a birthday cake in a nightmare. The brass plate on the pillar, DR. MANCHESTER'S PRIVATE ASYLUM FOR IDIOTS AND THE INFIRM, is at first the only sign that the house is an institution, but, as they enter the elm-lined, neatly gravelled driveway, they notice teams of inmates at supervised work in the orchards.

"You lived here?" Stoker says. "What in heavens was that like?"

"Rather more peaceful than the Lyceum."

In the porch, the current proprietor, a Dr. Mansfield, is waiting. In his thirties, Hispanically handsome, a bit damp with excitement, he stumbles down the steps, hands clenching and unclenching, as one about to begin a dance number in a show. His is a sort of professional patience, a tendency to over-enunciate, to go slowly. It becomes clear that he has a favourite word.

"Miss Terry, capital to meet you. You are *most* welcome back to Dr. Manchester's."

"Thank you."

"And your mother was the *cook* here, how capital."

"Not certain she always found it so. But it is good of you to see me."

"Oh the honour is mine, Miss Terry, it is mine entirely. I have seen you play many times, it is always so . . . capital. May I dare to venture that you are even more strikingly beautiful off stage, in the daylight?"

"Flattering of you."

"When I proposed to my fiancée, do you know what I said? 'If Ellen Terry won't have me, perhaps you would.' "

"How too divine." He turns to indicate the door. She sticks her tongue out at him. He turns back.

"This gentleman is Mr. Stoker, my great friend," she says.

By now they are walking a stone-flagged corridor lined with barred cells, in which inmates are sewing oakum or mumbling in strait-waistcoats and chains. Orderlies wielding truncheons stand about or pace. The reek of old meat arises through grates in the floor, with a woman's high, broken wail. In one cell, an inmate is pouring water from a jug into an identical jug and back again, over and over, singing gibberish to herself. In another, an old man is standing to attention in long johns, his beard in three plaits, to his navel.

"There was a particular reason for your visit, Miss Terry?"

"I am to play Ophelia again soon."

"So I saw in the *Pall Mall Gazette*. You shall do it capitally, *capitally*."

"For this reason I thought it should be useful for me to see people who are mad."

"We have an abundance of them here, of every condition, as you'll see." He has something of the salesman about him, a grubby pride in the merchandise. "Burners, catatonics. Religious melancholics."

"And what is Ophelia's condition, would you say, Dr. Mansfield?"

"Capital question, there has been a good deal of scholarship on the point. The verdict would appear to be that she is a sufferer of what is called erotomania. Often brought on by an extreme shock, although we're not sure precisely how."

"How would you characterise it?"

"If one may speak frankly?"

"Please do."

"It is an intensely delusional state, the false belief that one is desired sexually."

"I have known a good many middle-aged actors who suffer from this particular ailment."

The doctor looks at her a moment too long.

"Quite," he says. "If you'll follow me through here? Be careful not to approach the cells."

At the end of the passageway, a metal door leads to an anteroom in which stand three large cages, two unoccupied. In the third, on a metal chair, a tall, completely bald man in full evening dress is playing a flute sombrely, large head bobbing, long-lashed eyes shut.

"A gentleman I should like you to meet," says the doctor. "How are we today, Mr. Mulvey?"

The patient shows no sign of noticing the intruders, his long frail fingers nimble on the keys as the melody doubles back on itself like a tern in flight.

"Patrick is what is known as a zoophagous maniac, Miss Terry. This means that he fixates on killing animals and devouring them. We started with insects and spiders, then mice, on to rats. Then I'm afraid we went a good deal further."

"Why would he want to do that?"

"Again forgive my frankness, it is partly that he sexually enjoys seeing them suffer, or has convinced himself that he does, which is not quite the same thing, then there's another aspect to it, too. He believes consuming them will extend his own life, perhaps render it eternal. The higher the creature, the longer the life. Some would say it's a common enough delusion, seen in certain religious practices. Eating the body, drinking the blood, so on."

"Is it usual for a patient here to be dressed in that way?"

"Patrick has an intense dislike of uncleanliness, it distresses him greatly. We arrange that he is given fresh clothing every six hours, without fail. And he is bathed twice daily, which soothes him. He prefers to be attired formally, in the manner you see there. We do our best for his comfort. It is an effort."

"Poor, dear soul. How can any creature making such music be all evil?"

"We find music is of great benefit to many of our patients here, Miss Terry. We are proud of our Lunatic Orchestra, the first in Great Britain. They perform on Saturday evenings, it is rather popular with the local people, the children especially. Unfortunately there is no performance today."

"He is a member of the orchestra?"

"He conducts it."

"Shall he ever be cured and released, do you think?"

"Alas, his condition is of a character that makes it uncontrollably progressive. Spiders to birds, to cats, so on. In the incident which resulted in his coming here some years ago, he stabbed a cab-horse in the throat and killed it. Often fancy he's licking his lips a bit when a guard happens past, eh, Patrick?"

The man ceases playing. Places his flute across his knees. Adjusts the pleats in his trousers. Straightens his necktie. Stares at his hands as though they have only recently been sutured onto his arms and he is not certain what they are or whose they were. Gaze crinkling in confusion, he slackens his neck so that his chin comes to rest on his collarbone. He is so bald that the dome of his head reflects the cold sunlight from the tiny cruciform window across the way. His murmurs are scarcely audible—an enervated lilt, like a spell.

"Patrick, these are important visitors, they have come down from London, will you say good morning? Miss Terry is our most celebrated actress. Mr. Stoker is her colleague at the Lyceum Theatre."

Evincing no sign of having heard the invitation, the patient attempts to stand. They now see that he is chained by his ankles to heavy iron hoops in the floor. He glares up at the roof of the cage, brandishes his flute at it. Whipping around, he glares at the interlopers. When he opens his mouth, the sounds are back-of-the-throat guttural, studded with weird plosives and clucks.

"It appears to calm him," the doctor explains, "to babble away in his babytalk like that. I suppose we'd all do it if we could, must reduce the strain, one imagines. We let him do it at any rate. Perhaps you'd like to follow me this way?"

"Might I shake his hand?" Stoker asks. "Before we go."

"I wouldn't advise that, sir."

"If I am willing to take the risk?"

"Bram, don't. Please?"

"He is my brother human being, I do not feel he shall harm me."

The patient approaches the bars. His knuckles whiten as he grasps them.

"I say, Stoker," the doctor says. "I must insist you stand away. Patrick bit off half a warden's face last October. The man lost his sight. *Patrick, sit.*"

His utterance erupts again, a tumble of strangled syllables. Saliva drips from his mouth and falls on the bars. He thrusts out his bony hand, the skeletal wrist tattooed with anchors, his gaping, tortured face like a map of forgotten islands. Beckoning, yammering, pleading with his eyes.

"I can solve one mystery for you, doctor," Stoker says, being led away, shaking, from the chamber. "What he is speaking is Connemara Gaelic."

* * *

XVIII

A journey

17th March, 1895

St. Patrick's Day.

Last night I resumed work on the story that has been digging into me like a tick. However I attempt to be rid of it, the damn thing returns, so that it haunts my dreams as bloodily as my days.

I am entitling this draft "The Unkillable." Please God let it be the last, I want rid of it, exorcism. Saint of Ireland, if you exist, come drive it away like the snakes.

I should be relieved to see the blasted thing die.

It opens at an asylum in the countryside, near Dublin. The year is 1847, the famine is raging. A peasant has been brought there in desperate condition, by the police. Emaciated, wild-eyed, unable to speak, he scribbles down the frightful experience he has recently lived through at the hands of [*there follows a 79-word paragraph that has proven indecipherable*].

. . . of the nightmares. Heavily sweating.

But today, Sunday, we had a pretty time at the theatre, all the pleasanter for being unexpected. Florence being away at her sister's in Limerick, I brought Noel in with me to see Harks's scene-painting workshop.

Journeyed in by ferry. Wind from off the river blew my terrors away.

The dear girl came in especially, which was good of her on

a Sunday. Theatre people can be remarkable in their kindliness.

She showed N the great brushes, which shipbuilders use, and paint-pots, the giant canvases and how they are unrolled from their spools, told him the pretty names of the colours. Gave him a turn at the tinting on the new Gothic Castle she is doing up, he choosing the silver for the edges of the clouds. A heart-warming surprise was that, presently, E came in with her own children, and then the Chief happened in with his son.

The children, who are all within a few years of each other, enjoyed a wonderfully rowdy and jump-about afternoon, the Chief performing conjuring tricks for them, pulling candies and pennies from their hair, E frying up sausages backstage and teaching them to dance, Harks all the while making funny caricatures and chalking their faces for their delight, then a many-hued gang of soldiers did battle with the grown-ups.

The children announced after a time that they should like to put on "our own play," and so, following a rummage with Harks in the old baskets up in the Dress Department, they did, capering about the Lyceum stage like knickerbockered dervishes. A more amusing sight one never saw, each of the nippers imitating a mortified parent. Noel's "me" was quite hilarious, he puffing out his cheeks and stomping about officiously as he brandished his wooden scimitar and cried "to bed with you all bejaypers!" in his best attempt at a preposterous Dublin brogue. I thought Len would die of laughter.

Her children are clever, careful talkers, well-spoken, considerate, a markedly bright intelligence and seriousness in their way of going on. The boy, Gordy, already knows many of the Shakespeare plots and is able to talk about them structurally. His sister has something of her mother's wisdom and wry watchfulness.

The Chief 's lad is quieter, a little given to over-sensitivity and seeing slights. Worked himself into a funk when he thought the others had teased him, which perhaps they had. But a nice boy. Gentle. Eyes the size of saucers. A couple of candied fruits and all were friends again. Ellen sang "Where E'er You Walk" and "Believe Me if All Those Endearing Young Charms," the Chief gave a recitation of the "Morte d'Arthur." Harks sang an innocently naughty song of the cockneys, learned from her brother, a soldier.

> *"I loves the girls what says they will and them what says*
> *they won't.*
> *I loves the girls what says they does and them what says*
> *they don't.*
> *But of all the girls I ever loved, one girl was heart's delight*
> *And that's the girl what says she don't but looks as though*
> *she might."*

Ellen's boy brought the house down when he remarked with episcopal solemnity, "I do not believe that this song is quite suitable for young people."

At five o'clock, we all sauntered out in a body to Claridge's for high tea on the Chief, which, for four peckish grown-ups and four ravening youngsters, must have cost him a sultan's ransom. Ellen had persuaded Harks into a simple fern-green gown and put her hair in diamanté beads and the dear girl looked quite lovely, turning many a head. She, Harks, adored it there and insisted on sending a postcard to her mother (two miles away in Bow) from the Post Office in the lobby. To see the high-and-mighty waiters having to tolerate our paintstained crew was naughty and jolly. Amazons of lemonade and ginger pop were caused to flow, great peaks of ices and Eton Mess scaled and demolished by our ragged mountaineers, while their guardians enjoyed a bottle of Krug, a Château Latour '42, oysters, a side of venison and hot salmon sandwiches with pickle, then, stuffed to stupefaction, the happy party ended with a huzzah for St. Patrick and a groan of disparagement for the snakes. The maître d' was glad to see us go.

A golden sort of day, to see everyone so happy, like one single noisy family of a different sort than is usual. If only every Sunday could be like that.

18th March, 1895

Alas, yesterday's light-heartedness faded pretty quickly. I came in at about 11 for a meeting regarding next season's costumes, to find no playful battle roiling away on the stage but an unpleasant and difficult scene.

John Stokely, the tailor, a gentleman hailing from Edinburgh and never letting you forget it, was standing at the stage table, sketchbooks and portfolios before him. "Sir,"—he was addressing the Chief—"really, one must protest. There is a long-established way of doing the dresses for *Macbeth*."

"Don't talk such bilge will you," the Chief replied curtly. He appeared in surly humour as he brushed away the contracts I had brought for his signature.

"These costumes have proven most successful in the past, sir," said Stokely. "Changing how it is done would be a grave error."

"Bugger the past. The Lyceum is the future."

"But sir, these tartans are authentic."

"I do not give a tosspot feather for authenticity. Neither does the audience. Bad enough that we must endure real life without paying to see it in a playhouse."

"Sir, I am not accustomed to being spoken to in this manner."

"I imagine you are more accustomed to it than you realise."

At this point, he, the Chief, snapped his fingers a bit imperiously. Harks came onto the stage looking uneasy. Accompanying her were two of the young stagehands whose names I have forgotten. They were all three clad in what I can only term Viking warrior apparel, horned helmets, leather trews, bearskin breastplates, furred leggings. The effect, if I am honest, was somewhat disconcerting.

"I have had these specimens made up," the Chief said briskly. "From my own design. I want Iceland. Thor. The cold north. Slaughter. This is a tale of blood and savagery, a play about *violence*, not a box of damp shortbread in an old maid's drawers."

"But I was told by Mr. Stoker that you would be using the *existing* costumes, modified, for reasons of economy."

"My cock to what you were told by Mr. Stoker. I am telling you now. So whip out your little needles and get stitching like a seamstress, else be gone and toss your caber while you're about it."

Here was where I committed an error. Perhaps I was tired.

Angered at not being consulted, inflamed by a coven of Monday-morning resentments, I found myself questioning him, and in front of the staff.

"Have you any idea what these costumes will cost?"

He turned to me. "Here comes the clerk."

"The clerk that runs this theatre."

In a moment he was on his feet and into my eyes. "You do NOT run this theatre, drill it into your skull, sir. It is my name over that door. Every day. Every night. You are nothing but a surplus population."

The Chief is one of those men who is able to use the word "sir" as an insult. "My point is that I have the responsibility of imposing order on our accounts," I insisted. "If that is not done, we might as well throw our hats at the thing and shut shop. If I have told you the once, I have told you a thousand times. We cannot go on with productions of Napoleonic flamboyance, the bank is at our throat every day."

"Then GO," he roared, stabbing his finger towards the auditorium. "Get out! Or stay! The lukewarm I shall spew from my mouth."

This was apt scripture to be quoting, for by now he was frothing with rage. I could see that some of the players and stagehands were upset. Harks was being held back by a trio of steamfitters. I attempted to keep my composure but would not stand still to be bullied.

"There is no need for you to speak to me—or to anyone here—in that demeaning fashion," I said. "It is a disgrace that you do so at all, but that you do so in front of others is calculated to humiliate. It is unmanly to insult people who may not answer back."

He scoffed. "I think you like it."

"You are insane, then," I said. "And ridiculous."

"Then why are you still here?"

This I ignored. The back-giving of cheap answers is not much of a gift, except in a music-hall comedian putting down a drunk. That is not a role I wish to play.

He threw the question at me again and again, but I would give no reply, and in the end, he stormed from the stage in a fanfare of blasphemies.

"This meeting is over," I announced to the company. "Be about your work. That is all."

They did as they were told but silently, surly. For which one cannot blame them. This cannot continue.

Flo is entirely correct in what she feels about this wretched moneydevouring Lyceum and its arrogant overlord, although she has permitted me to reach the inevitable conclusion alone.

The fact—I have known it and attempted to ignore it—is that I must now begin to seek for a position elsewhere. Otherwise, harm will be done.

* * *

Dear old Bram, my precious thing,

I received your letter of resignation but have torn it. Don't be silly.

Went to your office just now but stoutheart Harks said you had sallied home. I left a couple of sketches on the desk and would value your estimation when you have a moment or two to look them over. Should you reckon them a lot of cock, we can start again, of course.

As well, this note is to apologise for my beastly behaviour towards you this morning at the costume call. It was quite, quite wrong of me. Do forgive me, old love. Lately I have felt drained white.

Before the meet, a wretched reporter from a vulgar little excuse for a newspaper had been irritating me with his questions of almost hackleraising impudence as to my private arrangements. On top of a sleepless night and the usual battalion of worries, I took it out on you, for which I am sorry.

Let us give it cannons roaring; that was all I meant. I regret that I did not discuss my ideas for the dresses with you in advance, as I know I should have done. You were correct to remind me that I gave you that promise. I shall endeavour to do better in future.

And I shall rein in the spending, I swear on my soul. I can never let something as filthy as money come between us, you and I. What you say is wise and proper, there is no need for extravagance. I shall make myself a veritable old maid of frugality whom you may address as Prudence Irving.

I find, when I make the mistake of allowing myself to become strained, that it comes out in these filthy rages I can't seem to grow out of. At these moments, which I hate,

264 · JOSEPH O'CONNOR

I seem to become a spectator, as a tramp encircled by moonlit wolves, at a brazier in which his own clothes are burning. The venomous things I shout at people, particularly at you, are the things I want to shout at my stupid, ugly, graceless, witless, obnoxious, ungrateful self.

Your friendship is of such value to me that the word "friendship" cannot describe it. In some space between words, this is where we live, you and I. You are my rock, old fellow. I lean on you too hard. You are the water I drink, the man I wish I were.

I would never know the poetry to put my thankfulness into. But it will give some idea if I say that I love you as my companion and loyal true comrade, as my encouragement and hope, as the counsel I turn to whenever I am afraid. As the source of all courage and any dignity I possess.

At one time I would not have thought it possible for two men to become so close as we two. Now I know that it is. You are my mirror, the other half of my self.

I am ashamed to have taken you for granted and sometimes to have spoiled the happy peacefulness you have built at the Lyceum, for all of us.

You are so highly thought of here. Len adores you, as do I. Given the hectic busyness of the everyday and the incessant demands on all our time, these things sometimes go unsaid but you must never think them unfelt.

No theatre, no enterprise of any sort, could have a nobler or more admirable ambassador. The younger people here see in you an example of how to comport themselves, the older know you as a respecting friend, a gentle but strong protector, so full of common sense, always, but never too busy to spare a kindly word. These things are noticed and appreciated, not only by those who most benefit. The best of the Lyceum is no play we have ever presented. It is the way we have tried to do things. It is you.

God knows I do not deserve your forgiveness, but heart in hand I ask it.

I have been thinking that we—all of us—have been too long in filthy, foul, fallen-out-of-love-with-itself London. I should like to take the whole company on a trip, a little holiday, somewhere quiet where we might sit about and read and build ourselves back up and get a bit of good simple country food and peace for a day or two, far from prying eyes. And swim in the sea. And not think about Edinburgh tailors.

To that end, I have been revolving a scheme, which I would like to discuss with you, perhaps over breakfast or a cuppa. Or might you let me give you luncheon at the Garrick tomorrow? The hot scoff is muck there but the cold table is not too bad and the Johnny who looks after the wines keeps a tolerable Mouton Rothschild up his apron for me. One must avoid the legions of baying bores there, of course, but with a little subterfuge and sitting with one's back to the room it can be done.

What might you think? I am sorry, my dearest love. Give me another chance, can you?

Ever yours,

Thane of Glamis and Cawdor

* * *

Beneath the vast iron roof of King's Cross station, the newspaper reporters are waiting. The morning being cold, they stand clustered together. Ignoring them, the Lyceum stagehands stack the packed gear for loading, Harks ticking off items in her notebook.

Cases, hatboxes, haversacks, and carpet bags, a large oaken wardrobe-trunk with iron clasps and thick ropes, its heavy lid plastered with labels from the American tour—Boston, Philadelphia, New Orleans.

Fifty yards away, in the main entrance, Stoker and Irving are watching. A compromise of sorts has been negotiated. Irving's dog on a length of chain cocks his back leg against a wall.

"Fourth Estate, my royal arse," Irving mutters.

"If you give them a word or two," Stoker says, patiently, "they have promised to leave. Let us not antagonise them at any rate."

Irving nods. "Into the valley of death."

Crossing the station, they see the reporters nudge and turn to face them. The dog gives a slavering snarl.

"Gentlemen of the press," the Chief says. "The bastard children of Blood and Remorse. You hunt in a pack, I see."

"Why are you going to Scotland, Mr. Irving, sir?"

"In the coming season, we intend to give London a production of *Macbeth*. That is a piece by a playwright you won't have heard of, a glove-maker's son from Birmingham." He pauses to light one of his Parisian cigarettes. "The like of this production will never before have been seen. It shall be ambitious, spectacular, entirely without precedent, and a danger to public morality."

"Mr. Irving is joking on the last point," Stoker interrupts.

"Starring in the main role—naturally—my unassuming self. The zestful Miss Ellen Terry shall appear as Ophelia."

"How do you spell Ophelia, sir?"

"With two effs."

"Again Mr. Irving is joshing," Stoker says quickly. "Ophelia does not appear in *Macbeth*."

"Ah, Bram, you are spoiling my fun."

"What has any of this got to do with Scotland, Mr. Irving?"

"I have always found the Scottish people amenable and admirable. They are bookish and cultured, interested in science, progressive in their laws. I am leading my company to Inverness, from there into the Highlands, so that we may rinse London and its so-called civilisation out of our hair."

"Why would you want to do that, sir?"

"Because *Macbeth* is not set in a public lavatory in the Earls Court Road, my little love, familiar as you might be with such a locus."

"Costing a bob or two I expect, sir, this production of yours?"

"If the cost of the scenery alone were to be expressed as a stack of shillings, the stack would be the height of the moon from the earth. Add the price of Miss Terry's costumes and the number becomes actually frightening."

"Blimey."

"As you say."

"Any chance of a word with Miss Terry, sir? We'd be awfully appreciative."

"That, my dear gentles, you must ask her yourselves. You will find her at the Lyceum, she is not accompanying us on the quest, but is posing this afternoon for a portrait by Mr. Whistler, nude but for some judiciously placed oak leaves. Miss Terry, I mean, not Whistler, thank Christ. Now if you'll excuse Mr. Stoker and me, we have young minds to corrupt."

As they board, a hail of yelled questions is thrown after them but King's Cross station has already begun to recede. The engine spews a gloomy hoot.

Irving stands in the aisle, the whole company assembled before him, filling this carriage and the connected one beyond it. Harks and a stagehand unclasp the large oaken trunk. Out of it clambers the most celebrated actress of her generation, a little ruffled as she accepts Stoker's help.

"Rot me," she says, "someone get me a ruddy beer."

"Right," says the Chief. "We can let down our drawers. Thanks to all for your patient assistance with the little play we've been performing this morning. That coven of rats will be scuttling back to the Lyceum and from there to the night mail for Inverness. By then we'll have arrived at our true destination."

"Where's that, Chief?" Harks asks. "Do tell."

"O a gloomy little dump. But we'll liven it up, never fear. Now, who'll start the sing-song? 'Rule Britannia'? 'Danny Boy'?"

Groans of protest at his teasing come back at him like a wave.

"Would you like to tell them where we're bound, Bram? One feels they'll mutiny otherwise."

"We shall see," Stoker says. With a smile.

* * *

PAGE TORN FROM *MITHRINGTON'S PLAINSPEAKING GAZETTEER*

Whitby, North Yorkshire, at 54.4863° N, 0.6133° W, a pleasant and healthful resort, lies in the borough of Scarborough, part of the North Riding. What at first appears a village is in fact a commodious port, with vessels from many lands seen regularly in the harbour and the tongues of many visitors, some from faraway nations, to be heard in the little cobbled streets.

As with all ports, it must be owned with candour that the occasional "roughneck" incident has occurred at Whitby. Not every public establishment is quite what one would wish. But the preponderant atmosphere, we are happy to report, is safe, of Christian character, and suitable for ladies.

Fancies, jewellery, combs, frames and other keepsakes are offered by a goodly number of the small shops. Jet is mined at Bilsdale, Snotterdale, and Stokesley. Articles of scrimshaw and nautical trinkets may also be had. Many an old fisherman of Whitby, seated on a stone bench in the somewhat eerie graveyard, regales those who will listen with stories of smugglers, whaling and shipwrecks, a certain number of these yarns containing more adjectives than veracity and all of them a good bucket of sea-spray.

Since the railway reached Whitby the locale has attracted

"trippers." The town boasts a number of evocative ruins, including those of the 13th-century church of the Benedictine abbey whose lonesome desolate hulk, perched high on a cliff "that beetles o'er its base," gives a melancholic stir to the viewer. It is said by local persons to be haunted by "poor Constance de Beverley," a nun who broke her rule of chastity and, as punishment, was walled up alive. The ghost of St. Hilda, too, has been witnessed, staring down from one of the Abbey's high windows. While we give no credence to unchristian stories, our duty is to report them. Indeed, on a misty, starlit night, the Abbey seems to evince otherworldliness.

The "Barguest Hound," another of Whitby's parliament of spooks, is a red-eyed, Satanic dog. One of the port's two lighthouses is haunted by a keeper who fell to his death on the rocks below. Add to this the spectral stagecoach whispered to carry drowned sailors about from their resting place in St. Mary's churchyard and the sceptic may come to feel that Whitby is bounteously supplied with tall tales, as Newcastle with coal, Texas with oil, Ireland with papist superstition.

[The chapter ends here, on the upper recto of a page. Beneath the printed text and overleaf, the following passage appears, in pencilled Pitman shorthand.]

3rd April, 1895

The libel action taken by Wilde against Lord Queensberry began this morning. Am relieved to be away from London.

Tonight had a crayfish supper but I think its meat was a day too old. Gave me frightful dreams. Awoke three hours ago here in boarding house—it was just before two in the morning—terribly shaken by nightmare of being locked in a box. Dreadful, dredger-like, hellish thirst. Palpitations of the heart. Should not have taken whiskey on top of champagne.

Crept downstairs in search of water but whole house had retired. In the darkness could not find the kitchen.

Went into the hall lavatory but nothing so much as the tiniest droplet left in the tap, tank must have been emptied, house being so full. Returned to my room, dressed hurriedly, went out.

Bitingly cold night, many thousands of brilliant stars, half-moon high behind the Abbey. Everywhere in the town closed and shuttered up, every curtain in every street pulled. Walked about in search of fountain or pump for animals, could find none, which was queer, for I had noticed several as we went about in the course of the afternoon. By now, the thirst so terrible that my tongue felt made of salt. Agonising headache, I was trembling.

Made my way down to the harbour, thinking a sailor or watchman might help me, but no boats tied up at the quay, only larger vessels at anchor further out in the bay. Saw lights on their decks and in some of the portholes. Had a rowboat been at the pier, I should have gone out to one of the vessels, there to beg for a sup. But nothing.

Sat down on a bollard, wretched, very weak, red visions and flashings that stung my eyes. Before long, my supper came up. Felt a little better then, in stomach and head. But still destroyed with thirst, all the more for having vomited.

Strange, all I could think on, damned story.

Returning through the streets, dizzy, somehow sundered from myself, as though my mind were following or going ahead of my body, about to be sick again, and went into the gateway of a church, having no other resort. The violence inside my bowels and stomach was racking. Afterwards tried to clean myself with grass. Noticed, nearby on the footpath, a bottle some reveller had abandoned.

Mercy gods, it had once been full of mild ale and had a few swallows remaining. These I got down with the humblest thanks to providence. It was the sweetest coldest drink I ever had.

Came back here to the boarding house. Harks now was awake, with some of the other girls in the downstairs parlour, all speaking together quietly, playing rummy for buttons, the noise of my going out having disturbed them. They were talking of Wilde, will he win his action. She found me a pitcher of water and a blanket, for I was shivering uncontrollably, teeth chattering, sat with me a while, held my hands. Her womanly, simple good-heartedness began to calm me, it was like the return of light. "There there, my poor Auntie, you've had a bad 'un, don't be frightened so."

Had I seen on my moonlit expedition the monstrous dog?

I had not.

The party of drowned mariners?

Not even those damp gentlemen.

She laughed and made us up a cigarette and told me a saying of her mother's, "ain't the lucky dead but the living we should fear." Asked my private opinion on Wilde's chances. Said I felt certain he would win but feared it a great pity the action were ever taken at all, for, between she and I, Lord Queensberry was a bullying, ice-hearted brute who would always wreak vengeance, though it take him ten years. Such leeches are creatures of violence, the infliction of agony is their drug. There are slurs better borne than contested.

Did I think it possible that a man could fall in true love with a man, or a girl have a proper sweetheart another girl? Not "a passing crush or spooning," she said—"everyone has those"— but the marital sort of love that might have longevity and be the heart of a house where happiness would flower.

I said it was late at night to go into the discussion but that I had heard of cases.

"It's all sorts in the world, sir," the dear girl said.

I answered that she was right, that everyone can hope for the mercy of providence, and I asked if I might speak to her in a frank manner and she indicated that I might.

"What I am about to say, Jenny, could have me jailed," I said. "It could destroy my wife and family and take me away from them in handcuffs. I want you to understand that."

"I've already disremembered you saying it, sir."

I told her that when God made time He made a ruddy great lot of it, and, when He made people, his artistry was not limited to This Sort and None Other, that Love is not a matter of who puts what where but of wanting only goodness and respectful kindliness for the loved one. There is no sort of love that can never find its home. Life has its cruelties but it is not as cruel as that.

I felt that this settled and reassured her, sweet child. Said that I would always be her friend. She replied she would always be mine. Then we sat in silence for a time.

"You still look a little peaked, Auntie," she said, then, bathing my forehead, "you shall sleep in with me and the other girls."

Thanked her but said that it would not be quite proper.

"I should think you and I would be quite safe from one another, sir," she said, with a light laugh, "given God and so on." I made no answer for a bit.

"Still," I said. "One must give an example."

After she had retired, with all my thanks, I came up here to my bed. That was an hour ago. Sunrise is coming.

Still unable to sleep, I read in a book I borrowed from the public library here in Whitby a few years ago and forgot to return. Brought it along this time in order to give it back, for a book thief is a bad sort and brings ill luck on himself. Bloody old yarn, quite the half of it made up. Removed a page of notes I had scribbled. Wilkinson's *Account of the Principalities of Wallachia and Moldavia*. Must get a copy of my own when we return to London. Try Hatchard's. Chapter entitled "Vlad D."

His snarling, vicious, mineral eyes. His way of coming in through the locks.

* * *

Late at night, when the theatre is closed, and the ghostlight lit, Mina comes down from her loft and blows about the aisles, a draught in an empty playhouse. She is present in the dust that appears on the seats, in the scrabble of mice, the whistling of loose slates, in the muskiness you might think is traces of expensive perfume remaining in the Dress Circle boxes when the duchesses have gone home.

She is present in the glow of the ghostlight itself, a flickering, ardent, goldyellow-gold the colour of August apricots.

Time is different for her sort. A second can last a century. A decade might pass in one breath. Every night she sees every play that was ever performed on that stage and every play that will ever grace it in the future. The fools, the lovers, the harlequins and monsters, the queens and kings laid low.

The wraiths and costumed animals, the thundering prophets. The magnificent armies and their blood-soaked banners. Among them, the storyteller walks.

The same man, the lonely one, who used to come to her attic, worn low by his secrets, a part played too long, who toiled at his word-machine as though it were a cathedral organ and he must play an impossible cantata. He stands quietly downstage, candle in a glass, staring at the hundreds of Lady Macbeths who seethe at the empty darkness. "I would," they chorus, "while it was smiling in my face, have plucked my nipples from his boneless gums . . ."

She is able to go into his veins, to rove the meadows of his mind, to see the volcano of molten hopes. She feels pity for all his species, they are so lost, so unknowing. The bleats they call language can say nothing worth saying, it is like trying to pour the Atlantic into a thimble made of steam. And still the chimps persist.

Sweat dripping onto pages. The weird runes he scrawls. His

heroine in a coffin, writhing in bliss, stake penetrating her heart.

Harder. Slower. O gentler. I die.

Now his overlord, his chief, comes processing from backstage, with a woman who is the queen of England. The chief kneels on a cushion, the queen touches his shoulder with a sword; the audience pretends something magical has happened.

The pretender is the first of his profession on whom the honour has been bestowed, although everyone who has ever received it, or ever will, is an actor, as is the woman bestowing it, who never asked for her role, whose costume includes a crown, whose part was written by another, and whose props include an Empire where the sun is afraid to set.

"Queen Victoria" is her role. "Sir Knight" is now his.

From this tragicomedy the word-miner turns his apelike gaze. Candle burning in a bottle. His nights run long. He stands, paces, sounding the words to himself, as though reading them aloud could anger their embers, which it does. From below he hears the applause, but he pays no attention.

The castle. Of Dracula. Stood out. Against. The sun. As we looked. Came an explosion. A terrible. Convulsion. That brought us. Weeping. To our knees.

In the streets, words are gathering, blazed in black on front pages. The storybooks called newspapers shriek at the storm.

WILDE GUILTY OF INDECENCY
'WORST CASE I EVER TRIED,' JUSTICE WILLS.
PLAYWRIGHT IMPRISONED AT HARD LABOUR

Now the smoke of ten thousand fires starts to rise, as all over London the caches of letters are burnt, from Islington to Greenwich, from Richmond to Bethnal Green, a crucifix of compass points over the spider of the city, the binding-ribbons fraying and purpling in the flame, the scorched leaves wilting away.

New letters, old letters, notes unseen in forty years, stashed between the pages of a volume of Baudelaire's poems or stowed in a secret drawer in Papa's study. Silver cigarette-cases are tossed into the Thames; their private inscriptions darken as they succumb to the ooze. The night-train to Paris is crammed to the gunwales. Marriages are hurriedly arranged.

Mina watches it all. How can it have happened? Once the city was a forest, a knot of shadowed pathways, backwoods everyone knew about and nobody minded all that much; if they did, they could always look the other way. In one night, that is over. A moat is dug around London. How they stare, the flint-eyed crocodiles.

* * *

XIX

In which notice of legal summons is served

Attention of Bram Stoker, criminal libeller.
Lyceum Theatre.
London.

Sir,
I must address you on a matter which, with no small
urgency, shall have grave legal implications for you.

Some time ago there arrived here at my mountain home
in Transylvania a set of galley proofs of your recent compo-
sition about my person, Exhibit A, a book entitled *The
Undead or Dracula.*

How these came the thousand miles from London to my
hand is of little import. Suffice to say, when one has a
colony of bats and the ghost of a headless postman in one's
employ, matters are expedited with efficiency.

I was surprised, indeed taken aback, that you would
compose a piece about my humble personage, especially
that you would do so *sans* my agreement. I am not sure
what I can have done to have wronged you so severely that
I deserve this libellous retort.

I do not care for the proposed binding (as mentioned in
the cover letter). Yellow? Holy hellfire. You wrap me in
mustard. But it is agreeable, at least, to see you attempt to
appeal to a colour-blind readership.

Turning, if I may, to the contents of your book, I must
say that I was saddened and, presently, outraged. The evo-

cation of my homeland is vivid, the dialogue is toothsome, but you have been harsh and unsympathetic in your portrayal of me and have been unstinting in your efforts to rob me of my name. In plain truth, I found it difficult to recognise myself.

As the embodiment of evil bloodlust, I do understand that the challenges of capturing me on the page are not inconsiderable. But ought you to have stressed the negative?

I will have you know, sir, that being a vampire is not easy. The hours are unsociable. The clothes are old-fashioned. Opportunities to meet girls are limited.

If one is at all a gregarious type, the vocation can be burdensome, since, when misunderstood, it can have the effect of making people give one a wide berth. One does not receive invitations to many house parties or picnics, for example. Last summer I purchased (at not inconsiderable expense, even for a gentleman of my uncontrollable wealth) a set of the wonderful new "roller skates" but they remain in their box, unused, for no one has asked me to accompany him to the rink and one doesn't like to stick out by tootling along alone. People can be insensitive. I shan't lie, it hurts one's feelings.

If I may say so, the clouds of prejudice and disapproval in which we, the undead, must try to rub along as best we can are not at all dissipated by books such as yours. Sir, a little tolerance of others goes a long way. One wonders if your mother never told you that manners cost nothing. Do you not feel it would be a better use of the talents G*d gave you if you wrote a good old girl-meets-chap sort of story?

In particular, I was upset by the joke you make on page 37, that "the Count would have made a good lawyer."

I hope that I am a good sport, but that is a horrid thing to say about anyone.

You have left me with no recourse but to engage the firm of Messrs Klopstock, Leutner, and Billreuth, a trio not to be tangled with. (If you doubt me, try pronouncing the firm's name after a third glass of claret.) I have instructed them to sue the britches off you.

When first you and I met—how long ago was that?—I suppose that I liked you well enough, with your wondrous beard and your twinkly Irish eyes. But soon you became—I shall be frank, sir—a persistent nuisance. Calling on me without notice any hour of the night or day, interrupting my leisure, remarking on my appearance, constantly poking about at me and refusing to let me alone, *looking* at me in a queer manner and writing down my every utterance. In short, you had little respect for my privacy. How would you like it had I written a book about YOU? Perhaps one day I shall.

During all the many hundreds of hours that you and I have spent together (a good number of which I found exhausting and detrimental to my skin), I was forming the impression that at least you and I were friends and understood one another's little ways. But now I see that your opinion of me is low. The fact that a chap commands wolves and knocks about with lascivious ghouls does not mean that he is a bad egg. Have a heart, can't you. It is not easy for those of us who work at night.

You will by now have noticed that this letter is in the handwriting of my assistant and amanuensis, Miss Ellen Terry. She is terrifically fond of you and proud of you for having written this wondrous book, which scared the skirts off her so much that she had to sit up all night in bed.

She sends you her deepest love and her fondest embraces. Indeed she says you are a genius as well as an utter darling who should be shouldered, strewn with garlands, through the streets.

I, on the other hand, am not so easily impressed.
Sir, Yours,
Disappointed of Transylvania

* * *

The Chief, in the Royal Box, is watching rehearsals for *Twelfth Night*, dog at his boots, bottle of rough gin on an ottoman. In the months since Wilde's sentencing, a pallor has greyed him. He has been absent from meetings, preoccupied, dishevelled, sleeping on a shakedown mattress kept in an old outbuilding for the understudies. His fingernails, untended, are becoming an embarrassment.

He doesn't turn when Stoker speaks but pours himself a measure, hand shaking.

"You've written what?" he says, at last.

"A supernatural tale."

"Christ, not another. What is this one called?"

"The Un-Dead."

He utters a quiet scoff. "The Un-Read, more like."

"I have made a play of it so that it can be performed and the copyright protected."

"You foresee torrents of interest in the copyright of this masterpiece, do you? Great hordes of the unscrupulous bent on pirating your characters?"

"One can never be too careful."

"One can." He drains his glass, gives a wince, with his teeth unfastens a cuff. "Tell me, where did you intend performing this towering masterwork?"

"Here, I had supposed. I am a little taken aback by your question. And your attitude."

"I cannot permit amateur works by part-timers to be performed at the Lyceum. We are not a bloody Music Hall, we have standards."

"Obviously I am aware of that, since I have striven to raise them."

"Then you see the position. There is no need for further discussion."

"There is need for you to be reasonable. I will insist."

"This latest efflorescence of your artistry, what is it about?"

"It is a vampire story."

"Christ help us."

"Why would that be a difficulty?"

"Vampires have been done to death. As it were."

"It includes what I hope is a strong male lead. Would you read it, perhaps?"

"You expect Sir Henry Irving to play a bogeyman in a pot-boiler? Shouldn't think so, old love."

"As a favour."

"Use the Lyceum, if you must. Me, you don't use."

"That is your last word?"

"You are meddling with matters you do not understand."

"It is a story. That is all. Will you at least watch the performance?"

"I am busy, can you leave? Make certain I am not disturbed again today."

* * *

ROYAL LYCEUM THEATRE
Sole Lessee and Manager: Sir Henry Irving
18th May, 1897
DRACULA
~~Or~~
~~THE UN-DEAD~~
10.15 A.M.
One performance only

* * *

The morning is fine, London's air sweetened by drifts of apple blossom from the parks. A new flower-market has opened at Covent Garden. Workmen on turrets of scaffolding are whitewashing the frontage of the Opera House. A great tenor is coming from Italy, a soprano from Chicago. Banners flourish from palaces; guards parade up the Mall. Shop windows gleam like lake water in sun.

Boys dawdling late to school would scarcely notice the overcoated man who is suffering an unseasonal head cold as he hands out a stock of badly printed playbills. He goes back into the lobby and waits.

Early summertime in London. Butterflies in Piccadilly. A morning when hope is hard to kill.

He thinks of Wilde in prison. Tries to send him a thought. He thinks of the women who were murdered by the Ripper. What he himself is facing this morning is small, almost nothing. It doesn't deserve this fear.

For a staging to qualify as a copyright performance at least one ticket must be sold; money needs to change hands. He waits an hour, watching the street. The exchange is not going to happen.

Harks comes quietly from the auditorium and says the time has come to start, the players are making their way down from the Green Room. There will be no music, no make-up, no costumes, no scenery, the curtain will remain up, for safety. She crosses to the Box Office, buys a ha'penny seat in the gods.

"Done," she says. "We're legal."

"Dear girl, thank you. I'll smoke one cigarette and come in."

"Right you be, Auntie," she says, letting him alone.

Outside, the light changes, a flock of swifts comes swooping down Exeter Street and a woman's silhouette has darkened the doorway.

"Florrie," he says, surprised. "My love."

"You don't mind?"

"Heaven sake, how could I mind? You're not too busy? I didn't expect you."

She comes to him, looking a bit lost, as though intimidated by the gilt and crystal of the foyer, the strangeness of being in a theatre in daylight. Their brief and spousal kiss is noted by the portraits on the walls.

"I'm afraid it shall be something of an intimate performance," he says.

"That can be the best kind. Break your legs."

He leads her up the staircase, through the heavy doors to the back of the stalls. The house lights are up and will remain so. On the stage, the players have gathered in a ragged attempt at a circle. Their scripts are bundles of pages torn from galleys of the book, marked up in coloured pencil, glued hastily together. There is a confusion about who is meant to start; the actors exchange quiet laughs.

Seated on a beer-crate in Stage Left, the prompter calls "beginners." Dracula puts aside the *Times* crossword and clears his throat. Quietness comes down. "Curtain," announces the prompter, out of habit. But no curtain rises or falls. The words are uttered into the air.

Dracula is hungover, scarcely knows where he is. He is reading, not playing, the lines. No voice in the history of stage-craft has transmitted less feeling; he's like a bookie naming the horses that fell at the fourth, a priest rushing through Monday morning early Mass. "Yes I am the count, my curious friend. Never invite a visitor to cross my threshold." Harks provides the wolf-howl, reducing the younger players to gulps and mutual elbowings as the trilby-wearing, raincoated Count drones on through his yawns, "the children of the night, what beautiful music they make."

From time to time, the stagehands and flymen pause a

moment to watch, availing of the opportunity to light pipes or chomp sandwiches. An upholsterer glances up from the stalls. Behind the actors, mechanics are attempting to install the new hydraulic gantry; throughout the performance they jemmy open the crates that the cogs and chains came in, discuss the schematic drawings, disagree, mutter curses. Mop-women are swabbing the stepway down to the pit, which is empty but for a blind piano-tuner who is impatient for the nonsensical distraction to cease.

"My master is coming," squawks the actor playing the lunatic, Renfield. "I shall catch him all the flies. I do only my master's bidding."

As the embarrassment creaks to a close, a messenger boy arrives from the publishers with two twined-up parcels of books. Each player receives a copy of the inelegant tome, cholera-yellow cover, title printed in blurry red. Platitudes and pretended thanks are offered to the author, whose mortified wife has already returned home.

Ablaze with the special shame of the playwright who has watched his work fail, the burden of having to keep the hot face straight, he cracks jokes and pucks shoulders, accepts unmeant congratulations, lost in the maelstroms of false glee. All the ardour that the players didn't bother putting into their performances, he ardently puts into his own.

The show must go on. You must not let them see when you are hurt. And none of it matters, because what's happening is only an observance of decency, a wake at which it would be bad form to speak ill of the deceased. In a little while it will be forgotten, the poor thing will be permitted to die. As though it had never been born.

It is Harks who comes to take him by the elbow, put an end to the agony. As she leads him backstage they see the Chief, smoking beneath the staircase. The wise thing, the only course, would be to ignore him, keep walking. Do not offer the sword.

It will be used. But there are those whose childhoods bequeath them an addiction to pain.

"Then you watched the performance after all?" Stoker asks. "What did you think?"

There is silence. He smokes. The dog appears behind him. Still not too late to go, to hurry out into the street, to find a room in which to weep alone ten years.

"I see you brought our old friend the Ripper into your work after all," Irving says. "Your one-time moral scruples notwithstanding."

"The piece has nothing to do with the Ripper. What are you talking about?"

"Coincidence, you will tell me, those elements of the piece. The preying on young women, the sick obsession with their blood. Of course everything is grist to your mill. Isn't that right, Bram?"

"How so?"

"I should rather not discuss it at the moment. I have work that needs doing." He drops the cigarette to the floor, mashes it out with his foot.

"I would value your opinion."

"I do not think so."

"That is for me to judge."

"Very well." He sighs, stares up at the stair-head. "I thought it filth and tedious rubbish from first to last. A bucket of piss and schoolboy vulgarity."

"I see."

"This is what you have learnt from your years at the Lyceum? Where Shakespeare was god? Where beauty was our aim?"

"The script, such as it was, was culled together hastily. If perhaps you were to read the novel and base your final judgement on that."

"Damn you and your 'novel'. A cheap, fetid, piece of lavatory trash. Choked full of arch glances and cowardly hints, you sly little hack. Things you don't have the nerve to spit out like a grown-up. A penny dreadful reeking of sex-weirdness and pimples. Confidences I imparted to you, man to so-called man, now quoted like daubings on the wall of a jakes. A phonograph where your heart should be, that is what you have. And the gall to mention the name of *Ellen Terry* in this sordid gutbucket? How dare you look your reflection in the face?"

"Enough."

"But your sort *has* no reflection. You are vampiritude itself. You take all and give nothing, but gorge on those around you. Then, enjoy your miserable self-portrait, you bloated, talentless slug, you are the only one in the world who ever shall."

Harks now steps between them, voice shaking. "Chief, I'll thank you to step upstairs and calm yourself down."

"*Shut* your impudent mouth, woman, and don't get above your station."

"You thick-headed, posturing ponce," she says. "You bullying low bastard, you'll talk of my station? You're due a razoring but I wouldn't dirty my blade on you. Come over here, Chavvy, say that to my face. I'm a London-born girl, you remember that, Tosspot, else I'll beat you to Brixton and back, you bitch's leavings."

"Get out of my theatre."

She spits at his shoes. "Stick your playhouse up your frock, John. I never liked you."

The Chief strides onto the stage and bellows at the stagehands, "Get any shit that belonged to that pantomime out of my sight. We have a play to perform this evening."

"We was just talking a moment to Miss Terry, sir. Hold your horses if you would."

"In case you had failed to note it, Miss Terry is not your employer and neither is the author of that abortion. *Get it out.*"

Now she is crossing the stage, her face a mask of fury.

"Could you comport yourself with the tiniest *shred* of dignity," she says. "You might be down yourself one day, don't kick another when *he* is."

"He is a little Irish clerk, Ellen. That is all he ever was. These pretensions to so-called literature are the curse of all his countrymen, I never met one of them didn't think himself a bloody poet, as does every other savage on the face of Christ's earth."

"Stop it, can't you. He is listening."

"My theatre is almost penniless and he's puking his stupid stories. Wish to Christ I'd never laid eyes on him if you want to know the state of it. He's held me back, that's truth."

"You would be nothing without him. This place would be a ruin. He has given you nothing but loyalty and love all this time and this is how you reward him?"

"Some were born to serve. It's all they're bloody good for."

"You filthy arrogant pig. How dare you speak of any friend of mine in that way? He is many times the man you will ever be."

"THEN GO TO HIM. God knows you have never been selective before."

The few steps from the wings seem to take Stoker twenty years, and the punch that has been building in him every second of that time fells the Chief like a punctured sack. He sprawls, lips bleeding. No one moves to help him.

"You cur," Stoker says. "Get up."

But he doesn't.

"Enjoy your revenge, Bram. I hope it soothes your envy."

It is like the unleashing of a poison gas, this sight of the Chief laid low. It will never be put back in the vial. He elbows up, gapes about, blood spilling from his mouth and nose, wipes his lips with the back of his wrist, begs a handkerchief but nobody has one. There is no script for this scene. Even the dog looks afraid.

The felled Chief manages to stand, leans against the

proscenium pillar, wheezing, the florid red map on his white linen chemise like a splattered Africa. He bends, picks something tiny from a crack in the floor, undrapes his cravat, wraps the tooth in it, gasps racking him. One of the costume girls brings a towel and a pitcher of water. He keeps brokenly whispering the same word . . . "violence . . . violence" . . . as the girl, now weeping, attempts to help him.

A police sergeant is here, calling out from the main aisle. He needs to see the proprietor, it is an emergency, he says. There is no time, they must hurry. It must be now.

Outside a fleet of hansoms has been hurriedly summoned. Every player, every stagehand, every carpenter tumbles to find a place, the ticket-girls, the ushers, the box-boys, the mechanics. As the convoy makes its glacial progress across thronged Waterloo Bridge, prayers arise from the passengers, as steam from a train. God help us. Don't let it be true.

Some are weeping or trying to console, others sit glass-eyed, silent. In the distance arise the spires of south-east London, beyond them the hilltops of Kent. The drivers are whipping their horses, "on, boy, *on*." Now the mountains of thickening smoke, rising over where Deptford must be, coaxed by the wind into a vast spiralling corkscrew.

On the Mile End Road, three fire-wagons appear, bells clanging, axe-men at the ready, and a division of the Horse Police thunders from its barracks, but the smoke is so chokingly black and the sky so dark that those who have seen these things before know it is already too late

They hear the fire before they see it, a bellowing, churning crackle, which grows louder as they round the barricades into Tobacco Dock Yard and the horses whinny up in terror. The railway bridges are burning, the scenery store is ablaze. The sight is not possible. How can stone burn?

Ropes and pulleys on fire, a roaring conflagration, black and purple flames licking viciously at old masonry, smoke streaming ever upwards, flaps of burning canvas rip themselves away and float into the wind, others whip themselves like flagellants. Elsinore and Venice. Birnam Wood and Caesar's Rome. The Forest of Arden, the storm-tossed sea, all of them burn, their ancient oils in smoulders, now melting, now smoking, collapsing in on themselves, now bursting into globes of orange-black flame. Lines of men passing buckets but nothing can be saved. The fire-wagoners, the Lyceum people, rush forward to help, high cries echoing around the upper caverns of the scorch-blackened arches. The moss on the walls burning, the wild flowers among the bricks, the abandoned rail-tracks up on the summit, the little sheds and work-shacks. And now the bricks themselves.

The backdrops pop and burn, one by one the vats of paint explode, the hanging-racks collapse and sunder. A moving, squealing, scrabbling flood as a hundred thousand rats flee their metropolis among the stones, scuttling over the boots of the carpenters, swarming over each other, over their own blind young.

In the high unseen nooks, wrens" nests are burning and a sparrowhawk on fire falls through her final agony. Hosepipes have been connected to a culvert from the canal but in the face of the bellowing furnace-like heat, their puny spurts turn to steam. Soon the hoses themselves are burning and must be sacrificed. As the first of the bridges starts to totter—impossible sight—those fighting its flames rush back.

It shudders, this mountain of blockwork, lowing groans split the sky, boards and gutterings from its upper level rain down, broken pipes and manhole covers, rusted bolts, warped planks, showers of mortar, then the heaviest blocks themselves, the vast capstone and voussoirs, which seem to fall with strange slowness and shake the earth when they hit, the sound so sickening, the clouds of red-black dust.

Like some terrible giant of stone attempting to uproot

himself from a captor's chains, the second bridge shudders, incensed by the death of his brother. "Fall *back*," call the captains. "Christ's sake, fall back!"

The galleon on which Faust was sailed into Hell, the battlements trodden by Banquo's ghost, the balcony from which poor Juliet asked the reason for names, all inside the angered arch is now vomiting flame and utters a bilious roar. Burning innards flail and spill, a cataract of falling sewage spills down the soaked and tottering walls in a hail of filthy gravel and burning railway sleepers. The stench of tar and cordite, the spumes of crashing sparks. As though in trance Irving totters, magnetised towards the monster. His stagehands drag him back.

"My life's work. My plays. *My children* . . . I am ruined."

As the second bridge collapses, bent trees on its summit ablaze, the avalanche of broken blocks sends a tremoring roar so far through south-east London that it is measured by the Royal Observatory at Greenwich.

"Stoker," Irving rages, being led away through the dust cloud, his trembling hands singed, shocked face blackened like a sideshow Othello's. "You vengeful Irish parasite. You cursed me this day. I will never forgive you. My murderer."

* * *

XX

The Fall

Fog spreads across Mina's windows like an evicted child's breath.

She is a pentagram drawn in blood.

An upside-down crucifix.

All's well that ends well.

No.

Mina knows all languages, has inherited all dictionaries, has counted up to the number where infinity stops.

But these creatures she will never understand.

When first came the apes, they began their custom of naming everything they saw, like a conqueror putting a stamp on his colony: prompt table, forestage, paintcloth, cyclorama, greenroom, stalls, vomitorium. But why name the things that will all end in dust and leave nameless the things that shall live?

A salt-shake of stars across the blackcloth of the sky.

The kind of praise that makes the waves dance. Why have they no word for that?

She screams her name at him nineteen times, a black-magical number. He thinks it's just the wind in the eaves.

Mina
Mina
Mina
Mina
Mina
Mina
Mina
Mina Mina Mina Mina Mina
Mina Mina Mina Mina Mina
Mina
Mina

A shadow among the purlins, the weary oaken skeleton, she watches the man with the word-machine, he is weeping.

"Stoker," his name. One who burns fires. Everything in him dried up and smouldered out by anger, an arid Arizona of the heart.

The greatest actor here is none of the players on the stage but the man come to haunt her attic every night. All these years he has played himself, he knows the role well, is often convincing as he plays it.

But then there are the othertimes. They all have their othertimes.

Times when he carries his lantern into the fog of himself. Through realms of flames and whispers, forests of shadowed memories, caves where the daubs on the walls are of monsters, made with a bloodstained palm.

He is not breathing air. He's breathing Mina.

He inhales her with the dander. She roams his fevered bloodstream, the canyons of his heart, his jellyfish lungs, the vats and pumps and valves that keep him living, in the world he makebelieves is the real one.

He
believes
in his senses
when even a dog
hears more and the bat sees
more and a fox has keener smell
and the fishes talk by touch
and the hummingbirds
by taste and the lowliest
earthly vermin know
more of their rock
than this ape
who refuses
to know
it

Light in at the window, through a gap in the curtain of sacking. He listens to the plash of the rain.

An actor remembers every part ever played. There are times when he wonders why.

Mina knows.

What they call life is a ghost-ship. On the ship are many rooms. Small. Others grand. Some princely. Some poor. An uncountable number. There is always another. This is how they escape the prison of the self. To see the world through the windows of someone else's room.

There is only one way. He tried to build a room. Poor scatter-heart. Now the ship has been burnt.

* * *

30th May, 1897

At dawn this morning, took the ferry down the river to work. Cold, blowy day. Felt feverish, a chill coming on. Wheezing, hard to breathe. Black phlegm when I coughed. Took a half grain of arsenic and a dose of chloral.

Unlocked the building—no one in—went directly up to my office. Of late find myself unable to look at the stage.

Commenced to empty the desk and shelves, tie my books into parcels. Much work in the task, shall take four or five days. From down in the auditorium and backstage I heard people coming in. But I did not go down.

Stepped out into the corridor for a smoke when I noticed E coming up the stairs. She looked bad. Asked me what I was doing there. I said lately I have preferred to smoke out the big bay window there, on the landing, don't like the stench in the office. Could see there was something she wished to ask me. Felt I knew what it was, but, since might be wrong, did not prompt.

Would I see him?

I said no.

Nodded, said she understood. Followed me back to the office, shut the door behind.

As a favour to her, in honour of friendship, might I reconsider my stance? He had suffered such a bad shock, she feared for his sanity.

I said that his sanity, in my own view, had gone several leagues past the point of any normal person fearing for it, his behaviour to me at the staging had surely made that clear. As for what she termed my stance, it was nothing so worked-out. All I had remaining to me was an instinct for survival. No more would I grovel for my dignity.

I must surely know what he was like? Headstrong, mercurial. Saying things he didn't mean and soon came to regret. It was hard for him, being stubborn, burden of genius. The usual claptrap and balderdash.

I said I had no interest in what was hard for him, would no longer give consideration to the agglomeration of self-regard and cruelty that too often calls itself genius.

How so?

Had hoped to come to the matter more gradually with her but suddenly it was there between us like an unwelcome acquaintance who comes in and sits down at the table. The bard is correct. If 'twere done, it were better done soon.

Told her I am leaving the Lyceum, have written and sent my letter of resignation. This morning put the house for sale or lease, whichever proves the quicker, shall be returning to Dublin with the boy and Flo as soon as is practicable.

You shall kill him if you do, she said. He would not last a year.

Good, I said.

You do not mean that, I know.

At this point, I don't know why—tiredness and strain, I must suppose—my feelings began to spill over and overcome me. She listened as I spewed my litany. To have failed so long was painful enough, to have done it this publicly had left wounds from which no friendship could recover.

"Love survives all," she said.

A remark I ignored and a demonstrable falsehood. If there is one thing I have had my fill of by now, it is actorly trash.

One endures them bleating away like spoilt ninnies at rehearsal, *would* my character do that, *should* she wear this. One wishes the misfortunate author would rise from the tomb and tell them *do what you are bloodywell told*.

God knows how fond of her I am and the high regard in which I hold her own artistry but these people who dress up for a living all have something amiss with them, some hollowness where sense or ordinary morality should be. This they seek to

fill by spouting emotionally evocative but substantively mean-
ingless gobbledegook, followed by a deft half-turn-away as the
lights fade. I should rather listen to any raving idiot in the street
than an actor. At least he doesn't expect you to applaud.

Back again she flew to the subject of the Chief like a mater-
nity-crazed bird to its nest among dragons. She wrung her
hands and insisted. I stood my line.

Added to his personal slight was his professional arrogance.
He had never listened, had met my every plea with gainsaying
and mockery, had ignored my counsel with metronomic regu-
larity. When I asked him to quit insisting on productions of
such ludicrous flamboyance, every word I uttered he ignored.

Our backdrops were burnt. We were led by a madman. For
this I had left my country? Ruined my marriage? My happiness? Missed the hours better spent with my child at home?

No, I said. No more.

You are saying to me what you would like to say to him, she
said.

That much was true, one supposed.

Then she did something I wished she had not. Reaching
into her cloak she pulled out a copy of that accursed book that
I wish I had never seen or begun to contrive. When I bring to
mind the thousands of wasted hours it represents, the mau-
soleum made of paper, the hundreds of miles I walked in its
wretched company, I hate myself for ever having been born
with the storytelling disease and having squandered, in its service, whatever life I was intended to live.

"This work is your country," she said. "Is it no consolation?"

It took every famished fibre of the little manliness I have
remaining not to seize the book from her hands and hurl it out
the window. Followed by her. And me.

"No," I said. "It is not."

"Forgive him?" she said. "For me, if no one else?"

"Not even for you," I said.

A coughing fit beset me, and I shooed her away. Racked, eyes streaming, I coughed half an hour. Took more arsenic. Chest felt on fire.

* * *

5th June, 1897

This evening, boxes packed, after the performance had started and I knew that everyone would be occupied, I made my last journey up to the attics to fetch my notebooks and type writing machine. Ribs aching badly. Sore to move.

My lamp's wick was damp and would not light but there was enough of the quarter-moon through the windows so that I could make a cautious way. As I moved through the murk, I could sometimes hear the applause from far below. It occurred to me, how little I have ever liked that sound. Always it makes me resentful.

I placed my machine into its jacket, made a great pile of my notes and drafts and spent a not entirely unhappy half hour cutting them up into little pieces, scattering them from the rooftop and watching them drift away on the wind. As must be so with any murderer, the work in itself was not pleasant, but it felt a liberation to be rid of the evidence.

The filthy air was at least cold, which gave some sort of respite. Took another grain of arsenic, determined not to cough. I tried to send my mind to my lungs.

Returned inside, I dismantled the little desk I had contrived from old packing crates for I wished to obliterate all signs that I had ever roosted in this accursed eyrie. If I were unfortunate enough to see it in my mind's eye from time to time, as I hoped I never should again in my life, it would at least be as when I saw it first, which would mean that I had never been there.

It was at some point during this labour of moving the boxes and crates that I heard a clomp, which seemed to me a footfall. Below me, the performance was by now in full spate, *Twelfth Night*, but this sound had seemed to come from behind me, in the attic.

Reassuring myself that the mind can work mischief in a lonesome place, I went back to my task, but again came the footfall, heavier than before. When I turned, I saw—thirty yards from me in the shadows—a now unmoving but unmistakable shape.

"What do you want?" I said.

He came closer.

"So this is where you lurk," he said. "Often wondered."

His presence had startled me but I would not give him the satisfaction of my saying so. Ignoring him, I resumed my task.

"I thought you should know," he said, "that I have sold on the lease. I am closing the Lyceum for ever at the end of the season."

Now I had little true alternative but to speak, although my every wiser instinct begged me not to. Why is it so difficult to nod and turn away?

I asked how he dared to do such a thing without consulting me or anybody else. Was this to be an absolute monarchy?

"What else would it be?"

Told him he had no right to trade the lease without at least a discussion of the matter but that his audacious selfishness would hardly surprise me any more.

"Perhaps," he said with a shrug. "What is done is done."

"And the players? And the others who work here and need a livelihood? And Ellen?"

"They will find other work."

"Have you had the decency or courtesy to tell them? It is quite clear from your demeanour that you haven't."

"I have been a little preoccupied of late and worried about things."

Anger, by now, was fuming in me like a lust. Did his arrogance and insensitivity know no bounds whatever? What was it in him that must always destroy?

But presently I was sorry I had uttered harsh words.

"I have cancer of the throat," he said. "The surgeons are certain. My voice will go first. To a gasp, I am told. Then it will disappear. Before the inevitable."

He glanced up towards the skylights. A blear of rain was falling.

We were quiet for a time together, in that dismal, dusty place. Then I asked when he had received the news.

"Couple of months ago," he said. "They weren't sure at first. Had me scuttling about to so-called specialists, nasty men most of them, but I've never minded a charlatan, long being one. Was certain myself of course, had been for a bit. Quite painful all the time, been worsening for a few years. Spitting up blood. Should have pootled along earlier."

"Surely something can be done?"

"There's this Harley Street panjandrum says he can make the pain tolerable. Thirty guineas a visit. It would be cheaper to die. But an actor without a voice, you know, is a year without winter. No point, I'm afraid. There it is."

I was silent, not because I felt nothing, but because I did not know the words to say. His composure was striking and seemed to flow from some spirit of stoicism that I had never once seen in him or suspected him of having. Felt a reluctant admiration for him, for this trait at least. If only one had seen more of it down the years.

He was glancing about the attic now, with an expression of sad affability.

"I should like to live my last up here," he said, "with the rats and the spiders. Ain't it queer that spiders don't have a voice either but that folks are so afraid of them? Well, perhaps that's why. Their silence?"

I said I had never given the matter much consideration.

"And you could find me a coffin to sleep in," he pressed.

It was his way of raising for discussion the most recent quarrel between us but I did not find his approach adept and did not want to reopen the scar. There are situations best brought quietly to a close.

"So this is where you wrote it?" he asked.

He took my silence as affirmative.

"Normal chap wouldn't find it conducive," he continued, "a rum haunt like this. But I can see where you would, being the queer oddity you are. And I would, myself, too. Something delicious about being above the world of shit and malice, nobody knowing one was here."

Told him it was simply a matter of convenience, nothing more.

"Ever see her, old thing?"

"Who?"

"Poor Mina."

"No."

"She feels close," he said. "Do you think she is watching us?"

"Can you leave? I have work to do here."

"Saw her three times myself, at least I thought so, down the years. Twice during a show, she was standing at the back of the stalls. The third time on Exeter Street one midnight."

The sound of the audience applauding came up through the floor.

"I shall be with her soon," he said.

"Don't talk like that."

"It shall be a very great success, you know. Your vampire book. I have seen it." He tapped his temple. "In here. When you and I are long gone, your thirsty Count shall be famous all over the world. Like Judas."

I said he must be taking leave of whatever was left of his senses.

"Occasionally taking leave of one's senses is medicinal," he said. "They always seem to be there when one returns."

From the pocket of his dressing-robe he pulled a bottle of Hungarian Tokay whose loosened cork he pulled out with his teeth, then spat it away.

"I shall not ask you to shake my hand," he said. "We should neither of us like that. But will you have a parting drink with me, man to man? For old times" sake?"

From a second pocket, he produced two goblets, one inside the other, half filling each with the rich and heavy-scented liquor. To get matters over with, I accepted. He raised his glass and chinked mine.

"*King Lear*, Act One, scene two," he said. "'Now gods, stand up for bastards.'"

Through the floorboards the orchestra gave the closing fanfare of trumpets and timpani. He smiled at the absurdity. I did not.

"The play is over," I said.

"Let's hide here a while."

"There will be guests to be entertained. I imagine they shall want to see you."

"Can you picture it?" He chuckled. "The symphony of Englishness they'll all have to perform, the glib and oily art to speak and purpose not." He took a deep, final swig and crushed the glass beneath his boot. "Like a pack of rats giving you a bath before gnawing out your eyes."

"You should go," I said. "It is not fair on Ellen to have to entertain them alone. I shall see you as far as the stairladder."

"Ever the gent. Lay on, Macduff."

"Tread carefully, the floor between the joists is old and very frail."

"Like myself," he replied. Predictably.

The moon through the upper windows was yellow and vast, seeming closer than I had ever seen it, as though it was observing our progress along the lofts, indeed so close that I almost fancied I could make out the features many say it has, the cliffs, the great gorges, the dead riverbeds and canyons. Below us, the audience gave out its final cry of "huzzah." Through the crevices in the floorboards, the house lights came slivering.

"One thing I have learnt, old man," his voice croaked from behind me.

"What is that?"

"All things considered—one's had time to think it over—there was no greater Shylock than I."

I stopped, astounded. "That is all you have learnt?"

"What else did you think?"

"Doesn't matter."

He took a small step forward. Suddenly he was gone. From below me I heard the fall and the screams.

* * *

From THE TIMES, June 6th, 1897, late edition

The immediate closure of the Lyceum Theatre, the Strand, London, has been announced, following an accident suffered last evening by Sir Henry Irving, proprietor.

Sir Henry, who holds the distinction of being the first member of his profession to be knighted, fell through the ceiling above the stage, a distance of some fifty feet, to the immense shock of the audience, players, and orchestra. A performance of *Twelfth Night* was approaching conclusion.

A doctor and his brother, a guardsman, were present among the house and were able to attend him. Sir Henry sustained broken ribs and a fractured leg, and for a brief time lost consciousness. "A fall such as this would have killed a lesser man," the doctor remarked to our reporter. "Sir Henry would appear indestructible."

Refunds will be furnished for cancelled performances.

CLOSE OF ACT II

ACT III
ARRIVING AT BRADFORD

XXI

In which midnight brings Friday the thirteenth

They leave their bags with the porter at the Midland Hotel, walk from Duke Street to Manningham Lane. Irving is tired, leaning into his walking stick. Mill girls hurry by, doffers and pressers, their wimples giving them a look of postulant nuns.

Down Darley Street and Victoria Street, ragged children are playing football. A rhubarb pedlar is going from door to door. Weary carthorses clop, pulling wagons of wool.

Posters in the theatre's noticeboards announce:

STIRRING SCENES FROM SHAPESPEARE'S
TRAGEDIES & "THE BELLS."
GOOD SEATS AVIALABLE.
TONIHGT THE BRADFORD ROYAL BIDS IT'S
FAREWELL TO SIR HENRY IRVING.

"Christ," he mutters. "I wasn't worth a proof-read."

"I shall have a word with them about a correction," Stoker says.

"Shouldn't bother if I were you. No one else will have noticed."

"That isn't the point. Shall we go in?"

"Aren't we early?"

"I thought you'd like to settle yourself. Take a look about the stage as usual. We'll send out for a meal in a bit, play a hand or two of cards? Is something wrong?"

Irving gazes, looking lost, as though seeing a northern English street for the first time.

"Stomach's a bit buggered, if I'm honest. You shouldn't have let me sleep on the train like that. Hate waking up twice on the same day, like a waterfront tart."

"Would you prefer to go back to the hotel and rest a while?"

"Buggeration to you and your hotel. Ruddy kip."

"I merely thought—"

"You know what I'd like, old pet? Mouthful of fresh air up on the moors. But no time, I expect, on this slave-driven schedule you have me on."

"You agreed to the schedule."

"The slave must agree with the overseer."

"We have a couple of hours if you wish."

"How would we get there?"

At that moment, as though preordained, a hansom appears at the end of the hilly street, the heavy-coated driver nodding to himself as if sleeping. It turns and trundles towards them, slowly, heftily, the piebald between the shafts whinnying at a passing duo of miners. The driver awakens, mumbles yes, he can take them up to the moors. But what part would they like to start from?

Since neither of them knows, he suggests Hardcastle Crags, a few miles short of Top Withens.

Through the town, past the factories, into brambled lanes and hedge-row-lined cart tracks, under arches formed by leaning oaks. Poachers and tinkers stare. Oaks turn to sycamores. The sky over Bradford pale as ice.

Meadowsweet and forget-me-not in the overgrown ditches, the incense of distant woodsmoke and wetted bog garlic. A wooden bridge over a stream. At a waterhole in a distant copse, deer are nuzzling, drinking. From the middle distance, the whistle of a train and the tolling of chapel bells in the town, then the four o'clock siren from the colliery.

Now birdsong and fox-bark, the gurgle of water over rocks. Clouds roam the sky like white-bearded warlocks. The stunted milestone for Hardcastle Crags.

The driver helps them out, points a route marked by standing stones, agrees to wait an hour. "Tek tha time, gentlemen. No 'urry."

Heathers sway on the seeping heath. Birds whirl from blasted whins. Grouse, owl, skylark, snipe. In the distance a ruined manse-house cowers beneath a cliff.

They follow the streamlet down, cross on moss-speckled stepping-stones, face into the oncoming hillcrest, and the iron light grows creamy. In a patch of tussocked bog, a donkey regards them as they pass, his glossy black eyes like overcoat buttons.

"Yonder's Haworth," Irving says. "Where the Brontës lived, you know. They were Paddies, like you, misfortunate wretches."

"I daresay you'll find they were English as apple sauce."

"No, the mother was Cornish but Papa Brontë was born a Mick. Scuttled out of there soon as he could, poor jollocks. Isle of sentimental murderers and God-crazed old maids."

"You're certain? It's not a surname I ever heard in Ireland."

"They were 'Prunty' over there. Daddy P changed his moniker at Cambridge. Added the umlaut as an aftertouch, rather stylish disguise don't you feel. Of course every Irishman ever born is a fraud."

Stoker shades his eyes. Irving swigs from a hip flask. Years ago, he lost consciousness for three minutes, following an accident at the theatre. His joke was that he had awakened at the doors of Hell but been sent back by the devil. "Full House. Too many actors here already."

"Always thought it would make a cracking play," he says. "*Wuthering Heights*, you know. The violence. The graves. The suffo*cation*. What a thing, with me as old Heathcliff.

Monstrous tearing bastard. And Len as Catherine. That fire and ice she does. 'Nelly, I *am* Heathcliff.' Never got around to it. Should have."

"Perhaps it isn't too late?"

A cheerless laugh is coughed back. "Heathcliff on a walking cane, with his cocoa before bed. Withered grey balls and a nightshirt."

"It's many years since I read the book. I shall take a glance if you wish?"

"Shouldn't bother. Be nice if Len were here. Good old times, eh?"

"Good old times."

"One's been given so much. One can't complain. But it wasn't given me to have something I'd have liked, a happy little marriage. Nor to Len. Sometimes wonder, old chuck, if it was given to you."

"What's brought this on?"

"You are so loyal to your wife that you never discuss it. But I hope you've had happiness, old duck. Really I do. Of course, every marriage looks a little strange from the outside. Even ours."

Stoker laughs.

"I suppose Florrie and I married hurriedly," he says. "Our courtship hadn't been long. In all truth we didn't know one another well."

"Remained together for the sake of the boy, was it mainly?"

"Oh, I wouldn't leave my Florrie. As well leave myself. She is the mother of my child, for which I could never repay her. But there is something more between us. It is hard to explain."

"Do tell."

"I remember—not long after we married—coming to London, the excitement. I think it was in Green Park, it doesn't matter where. We were looking at a little boy flying a kite near the bandstand. The expression on Florrie's face, the good-naturedness and joy. I said to myself, 'Stoker, old thing, you're not much of a fellow. Not much of a writer, not much of a man. But she gave you her word. The noblest person you ever met.' And no one had ever given me that before. Rather floored me."

"For me the only family was at the Lyceum," Irving says wheezily. "You, Lenny, our children when they'd come in. Queer, it's those hours one remembers lately, not the performances or the applause. Of course, so much of everyday life is performance, don't you feel. Can we pause a moment or two? I'm a bit breathless, old love."

"Of course. Sit and rest. Over here near the trees?"

"I wasn't kind to you, Bram. About your scribbling, I mean. Most contemptible weakness in any man, envy. I'm sorry your ruddy old Drac fell so flat on his arse."

"He'd be flabbergasted by your generosity, I'm sure."

"Love to have written something myself. Never had the courage. To be revealed like that, it frightened me."

"You reveal yourself every night of your life on the stage."

"Kind of you, but no. That happens very rarely. It happens with Len, it's her gift, extraordinary thing. Len is always Len, no matter who she's playing. That's why they love her. Never saw anyone better at telling the bastards the truth. Suck it down and come back for more. Remarkable."

In the distance, the waterfall. He looks without seeing it.

"When I was a young'un, you know, starting out in the game, I didn't even have to *try* tremendously hard. It just came to me, somehow. Like being able to sing. Used to wish some ruddy barometer had been invented that could measure the pressure in my head. The morning of a performance, I'd *boil*. Like a cauldron. Up and up, all day, until I could barely stick the steam. Couldn't speak, couldn't think, feel it fizzing out my eyes damn near. Then I'd walk on the stage and let it blow. O my dears. Didn't give a damn for the audience or the playwright. Or myself. But these days—love a duck—I'm afraid I don't boil. Like some ballsed-up old teapot kicked down an alley. But *you* boil, old thing. It's there in your writing. All you needed was to find a way of letting it out. A pity you never did."

"It's getting on. Shall we make back? You can rest a bit before the show?"

"This was wonderful. Thank you. I think a sherry and a little lie-down."

An hour later he is in bed at the hotel, the heavy drapes shut. He awakens to find Stoker lighting the lamp, putting together the washbowl and jug.

"Buggeration," Irving murmurs. "It's not already time? I was having *such* a pleasant dream. Rather naughty, in truth."

"I have a surprise for you."

"I hate surprises."

"You'll make an exception. Hold still."

"What in hell are you doing?"

"Brushing your hair before I shave you."

"Leave off, you handsy ponce. Get yourself a dilly-boy."

The door opens quietly and she enters the room.

"Who is there?" Irving says. "Come forward. I can't see."

"I was playing in Harrogate last night," she says. "Our friend sent a message that you were here."

"Darling Len? Is that—?"

"Yes it is."

"But soft, what light through yonder window breaks. How marvellous of you to come, my darling, how simply too divine. Bram, you *unspeakable bastard* not to tell me."

"I can only stay a moment or two."

"Wish I'd known you were coming, would have cleaned myself up a bit. Well, how have you been, my dearest angel? Sit you down, for Christ's sake."

"Surviving, old pet. Doing one-night stands at my time of

life, can you imagine? I'm in Uddersfield this evening in the most execrable piece of Music Hall tosh and at the Prince of Wales Birmingham tomorrow in a dreadful old panto by a Welshman with three boyfriends if you can imagine such a thing. Still, it keeps me in bonnets and gin."

"Let me get out of this rotten bed and we'll punish a glass of fizz together."

"Stay there, you old miscreant. I haven't the time, really."

"Hop in with me if you like? Bram won't mind, would you, Auntie? Matter of fact, she'd like to join us."

"Incorrigible devil you are. You look so galoptious, I'm rather tempted."

"My sweetest old minx, you tell such pretty lies."

"What's this nonsense I hear from a little bird about you not looking after yourself properly? That won't do, you know."

"Find it hard to bloody sleep, that's the curse of it all. Shagged to buggery with tiredness all day but awake in the night. Thinking, you know. Going over the old days. What I'd give to close the peepers and know that peacefulness again. Strange what we end up longing for, no?"

"It's getting on for seven," Stoker says. "We should make a start on your paint."

"Oh, let me help," Ellen says. "Fetch me over the stuff, Bram, and a towel? Do shut up, Harry, I'd like to."

Stoker brings the tray of pots and brushes, the powders, the rouge.

"Your farewell tour," she says, massaging the base-pan into Irving's chin, "I don't believe it for an instant. Another ruse for rustling up punters, you irredeemable fraud. Pout your lips for us, can't you? *Pout.* Make an O."

Stoker applies the lip-stain, ochre mixed with violet, while she paints around the eyes, delicately lengthening their lines. "The people shall never allow you to retire, poor old workhorse," she says with a smile, licking her fingertips and smoothing his brows with them, "but even if you did, what a wonderful career you've had, haven't you, darling?"

"Oh yes, a wonderful life of work."

"Just some blush on his right cheek, Bram, why, yes, you're an old master. What have you got out of it all, Harry, do you think? You and I are getting on, as they say. Do you ever think sometimes, as I do, what have you got out of life? Look in the mirror here."

"A good cigar, a glass of wine and some merciful friends."

She laughs.

"Oh, and a tiny little slice of immortality of course."

"How so?"

"My dear Len, pay attention. You are talking to the Un-dead."

"This nonsense again," Stoker sighs, combing out a wig's fringe. "Here's an old bugger can't appear to credit that a scribbler simply makes the stuff up. Vanity, thy name is Irving."

"Oh I never thought that," she says. "Dracula is too gentlemanly to be Harry. What are you playing tonight, darling?"

"I reckoned *Thomas à Becket*. They wanted me to do the wretched *Bells* but then I rather changed my mind. Stubborn old queen. I like to make 'em dance."

"Perfect," she says. "Better shove along in a tick."

"Yes, you mustn't miss your train."

"There was always a ruddy train to catch, wasn't there, my Romeo?" She caresses his face, thumbs the talc and glitter into his cheekbones. "I believe I've spent more time on trains down the years than I ever did on a stage."

"I missed one or two of them."

"This one, you caught."

"My Angel. Our Len. Get thee to a nunnery."

"Good night, sweet prince. Break your legs."

* * *

Backstage, Royal Theatre, three minutes to curtain

A doctor is sent for and examines him by candlelight. The coughing fit is bad, the nosebleed a concern. His blood pressure is falling, pulse is erratic.

"Best not continue, Sir Henry. It might weaken you considerably. The performance must be cancelled or postponed."

"Rubbish. I am an Irving. We Cornishmen don't funk."

"If you'll permit me to insist, sir, really it would be wise."

"Someone get me an ale, I want it cold as the Celtic hell. And shut the house doors now before the bastards start escaping, will you."

"Again, as a physician—"

"Doctor," Stoker says. "I know him as well as it is given any man to know another. There is no point in talking sense. Let him on."

"Boy, here! Bring me that bottle. What kept you?"

The beer is handed over. He takes a deep, annihilating glug.

"The ale makes me sweat, Bram. They like to see you sweat for them in the north." He drains it to its dregs. Turns to the other players. "Know your lines, chaps? Good. Beginners' positions, keep it crisp. Anyone upstages me, I'll boot him up the hoop. Champagne on me later. Cut along."

The house lights are extinguished to an explosion of cheers. The actors hurry on to their opening places. From the pit arises the out-of-tune piano's attempt at a fanfare.

"Bram? A kindness?"

"Of course."

"Go for a stroll about the town. Don't watch."

"Why ever not?"

"It's what I'd prefer, feeling a bit flat tonight. Want you to remember me at my best. See you at curtain down? Crack along."

"You're quite certain?"

"Yes I am. Nancy off."

Outside on the greasy street, Stoker is trudging past the theatre's frontage when the sleet comes. Rows of soggy posters read FAREWELL ƧIR HENRY IRVING. He steps into an ironmonger's doorway to avoid the downpour. Lights a cigarette. In the window is a daguerreotype of King Edward.

That night of fame and glory.

Young Irving striding offstage at the close of *The Merchant of Venice*, fleets of carpenters and builders waiting in the dock. Before the last of the audience have departed the auditorium, the workmen are flooding in, tearing out seats, painting the walls royal purple and silver, unfurling Persian carpets and spools of plush over every inch of the floor. A silken banner is undraped from the apex of the proscenium. CORONATION OF KING EDWARD. ROYAL GALA PERFORMANCE

Gilded carriages on Exeter Street, steam rising from the horses. Princes, rajahs, tribal chieftains, potentates, lairds in rich tartans, sultans in tiger skin, royalty from every unpronounceable corner of Empire, processing through the foyer, along the aisle and to the stage. Archdukes and Magistrates, lords-Lieutenant and Admirals, Contessas in gem-studded gowns. Gold dust and glitter-light twinkling on the air. A confetti of red and yellow rose petals, wine trickling from fountains. In the halo of his fame, newly knighted Irving. He summons Stoker from the wings. Hand in hand, they bow.

The crowd as one chanting "Long Live the King" and the frisson of ambiguity about whom they mean. Irving indicating with his eyes to an apprehensive-looking King Edward that it is he who should step forward and acknowledge the applause.

The steamships to America. The luxury of the staterooms. The tours to San Francisco, New Orleans, Chicago. Ellen in Central Park, ice-cream by the lake. Irving genuflecting before kind-eyed Mark Twain. Did all of it happen? Did any?

He climbs the shabby steps to the Stage Door, past the dressing rooms and Prop Shop. Past the reek from the players' lavatory, past the row of buckets standing sentry to catch the leaks from the ceiling, past the posters for old plays no one remembers any more, descends the Jacob's-Ladder into the wings.

The Chief looks rheum-eyed, sick, has torn his episcopal collar loose, is wrestling with the play's closing moments, which might best him. Stoker glances down at the Prompter's script.

Becket: "My counsel is already taken, John. I am prepared to die."

Salisbury: "We are sinners all. The best of all is not prepared to die."

Becket: "God is my judge. Into thy hands, O Lord. Into thy hands."

As the shabby drape is lowered, he stumbles, the audience rises, cheering. Assisted by two of the bit-players, he steps out and takes his curtain-call, nodding, defiantly pouting, like a highwayman on the gallows. A pagegirl comes from the wings with a bundle of lilies. He kisses her hand, flings the flowers into the crowd.

"*Yorkshire for ever,*" he calls.

In the Dressing Room, he stares at the worn-out ghost in the mirror.

"Let us speak of the root of all evil," he sighs. "Choke the money out of them, did you Auntie, old girl?"

"Are you hungry?"

"How did we do?"

"Four pounds, give or take. The weather will have put some people off."

"Bastard northern tightwads. Barely pay for the hotel."

"Not every performance can sell out."

"If only one were Prime Minister, one could rain cannon-balls on Yorkshire and cull the whole bloody lot of the indigenes in one fell swoop. The average intelligence of Britons would be raised by a mile."

"It will be better tomorrow night. Leeds is a good showtown."

"To think I was once handsome. Look at me, Bramzles. Face like a vandalised cake."

"You've been feeling the taking up of your work again, that's all, after your illness. Now you're back in your stride it will be easier."

"Give us over a bowl of water would you, till Mother gets off her slap."

"Do you want help?"

"I'll do it myself. Don't want your shovel-mitts all over me, I'm not that sort of girl. Have we cold cream in the bag?"

"Here."

"How long are we together?"

"Seven hundred years."

"Sweet Christ. I shall have a special crown in heaven for having worked with a Pat all that time. My first performance was in Dublin, you know."

"You told me."

"Bastards hissed me. Like thisssssssss."

"You told me."

"Never forgot it," Irving says, wiping the paint from his eyelids. "Dublin audience, harshest bastards in the world, never give you a chance. But you have made it up to me, Auntie, for your countrymen's treachery. Perhaps I've done the same for you, eh?"

"How are you feeling?"

"Right as the mail."

"I thought you looked pretty unwell. Near the end."

"Oh I hammed it up a bit, darling, don't worry about that. Mother always knows what she's doing."

"You're certain?"

"They'd love us to drop dead for them, give 'em a story to tell. 'By gum I were at iz last performance, bugger died with iz boots on, never seen nowt like it.' That's what my sort is for. To bloody die for them."

"There is a note from a Mrs. Lauderdale, a cousin of the manager. She requests a lock of your hair and an autograph."

"Tell her no, impudent bitch. Pluck a hair off her husband's arse."

"It's for a charitable fund she is getting up for elderly actors out of work."

"The critics have often taken the whole damned head. I suppose I can spare the interfering old biddy a tuft of its grass. There's a manicure scissors in my purse there, if you'll fetch it."

He bows his head while Stoker cuts. The scissors are blunt, it's necessary to saw, until the curl comes away, a frail grey feather. There is a moment when his left hand is resting on the make-up table.

Stoker reaches down and touches it. Their fingers interleave.

Everything is quiet but for the sleet on the Dressing-Room window.

"Muffle up your throat, old chap," Irving whispers. "Bitter cold night. Must take care of you."

* * *

The lobby is busy, guests coming and going, waiters fetching trays to a wedding party. A fire has been lit in the grate near the dining-room doors.

Now the post-show weariness is coming. He is breathless, coughing.

"Let me sit a moment, Auntie. Bit fagged out."

The stately armchair in an alcove has about it something of a throne. He limps to it, seats himself, plucks a menu from the table. "Oh that's better, that's better, now a glass of champagne, little kidney-rinse."

"You know what the doctor said about drinking late at night."

"But Bradford is *known* for its champagne, old girl. Tiny wee sip. To scorn the devil."

"I will have a glass brought up to your rooms once you retire."

"Is not a wedding the loveliest spectacle in all the world? The charm of the young for the old, I expect. Get the booze in and we'll watch the dancing."

"No."

"Dearest *Jesus*, you are such an incurable mumsy. Sher yeh droive a stake through me heart so you do."

"It is midnight. We have an early start. Be reasonable."

"A mouthful of fizz won't kill Harry Irving. I'll drink a docker under the table, then get up and do *Hamlet*. Oh and ask if they have a nice bit of cold lobster too, would you, or a chicken leg or something?"

"Christ, come on then, you nuisance, take my arm."

"Go and fetch it for me, Auntie? I like to sit and watch the people. It's research don't you know. People are food."

In the bar he happens to notice the doctor from the theatre's backstage, now at a billiard table in a circle of cigar-smoking men. The doctor waves amiably, clenches a fist in the air, mouths the words "well done." Stoker nods back, orders the flute of champagne, changes his mind, asks for a half-bottle. Oh, and dash it, two cigars. Yes, Turkish Latakia if you have them.

A strange moment. In the bar mirror, above the optics, he sees, behind his shoulder, Irving's face weeping. But when he turns, shocked, no one is there.

Hail swooshes on the glass roof, causing everyone to glance upward. The pianist starts playing an old Northumbrian ballad, "The Lass of Byker Hill." He isn't very good but he plays with great feeling. Some of the drinkers join in.

If I had / another penny
I would have / another gill.
I would make the piper play
The Bonny Lass of Byker Hill.
Byker Hill and Walker Shore,
Collier lads for ever more.
Byker Hill and Walker Shore
Collier lads for ever more.

In the lobby, Irving is on the floor, face down, there is blood. Waiters are turning him, pumping his chest, calling out. The doctor hurries from the bar, billiard cue still in hand. Two policemen rush in from the street.

The ice-bucket falls.

The bridesmaid is weeping.
The revolving door turns in the wind.
Someone brings a bed sheet, they drape it over his face while they wait for the priest to come.

* * *

CODA
FRIDAY 12TH APRIL, 1912

SMALLHYTHE HOUSE, TENTERDEN, KENT

6.31 A.M.

The elderly cook is poorly this morning so the lady of the house makes breakfast for her and carries it carefully up the servants' back stairs and along the landing, fresh eggs, tea, two slices of toasted loaf, with a small glass of orange juice and a hot-water bottle. Having plumped the pillows and helped the dear old love brush her hair and tidy herself, she settles her with a jug of fresh lemonade and a stack of back copies of *The Stage* and *Woman's Realm*. Good to have a bit of nonsense to read when we're ill.

Not long before dawn, the lady closes the heavy hall-door behind her and hastens down the steps, their granite slippery in the dew, then across the gravel driveway, past the henhouses and the gate to the pear orchards, through the pleasingly narrow stone passageway that leads to the stable yard. The rooster's raucous call is answered by the bawling donkey down in the waterfield. Steam rises from the dew-laden wellhead.

She love the odours of the stable, their earthiness and plain truth. Daybreak around horses is moving. Leather, saddle soap, straw, the grassy smell of dung. The stern dignity of the massive anvil, cast when Cromwell was a boy, the pincers and horseshoes mounted above the stalls like the icons of some long-forgotten cult. The groom has prepared her pony and trap. She tells him to come along with her, but she'll drive.

"Certain sure, Miss Terry?"

"Certain sure, John, thank you."

Ordinarily she would take out the motor car but the morning is still a little gloomy, and the servants fret when she takes out the motor, even on a journey as short as this one. Anyhow, the clop of the pony on the lanes is comforting as they set out from Smallhythe House.

The lock bridge over the canal, the green mild water; behind the dawn-lit mountain a gold and red sky.

The groom is a little sleepy and smells faintly of cider and feet, but that doesn't bother her, he's a loyal old man, been with her many years. She likes his country silences, his keeping to himself. In the mornings there's a lot to be silent about.

Painted barges sleeping. The long-necked swan in the rushes. The bridge coyly admiring itself in the water. Chaucer's pilgrims walked these rutted lanes on their progress down to Canterbury, whose spire can be seen from that hill-top beyond Amos Blake's Farm when the day is less hazy. Sometimes, late at night, she fancies she hears them from her window, the slow, wry scarves of their tales in the breeze, their mockery of the passing world. So lovely. *Whan that Aprille with his shoures soote.* Would have made a spiffing play. Why did no one ever do that? Bit naughty here and there. Things that can't be said in a theatre. Go gently, good ghosts, down the towpath.

Nearing the village, the sleepy dairymaids hurry with yokes and churns. A pipsqueak of a farmer's lad hefts a wonky wheelbarrow piled high with turnips, cursing at them to dissuade them from toppling. Market day is come, the first after Easter. The gypsies will be trading strong horses and hare-hounds, slapping spitty palms, shouting, boasting, their women quiet and serious, bosoms full of banknotes. The dowser will come from Biddenden with his switch of white hazel, the signboard around his neck, wells found. A potion man will be hawking his bottles near the troughs—"*unguents and ointments, elixirs of love"*—a fiddler by the gates of the church. In this part of the countryside, Lent is still observed. The weeks afterwards seem to burst with release.

Ahead of her, walking, the bonny new schoolmaster but she can't remember his name despite having met him several times. The purple-green of sycamores, the chartreuse of Dog's Mercury, the sneezy tang of forget-me-not pollen. The horse snorts and whinnies at the mayflies. Bright, blowsy buttercups in the ditches, on the banks, flirting with the gloomy weeds. She stops to offer the young schoolmaster the high seat beside her in the trap but he's too shy to accept, says he's on an errand that will take him in the other direction, towards Woodchurch. His pimples shining brighter with every innocent untruth.

Everyone is acting, almost all of the time.

A sweet-faced sow peers from behind a thicket, her many children still asleep in the side-turned old bathtub that does duty as their sty. The blacksmith's blind daughter in the doorway of the forge idly plays "Sally Racket" on her melodeon. She will never see how pretty she is, how all the boys in from the country stare long at her with such serious, lovable foolishness, like Englishmen on the verge of saying something in another language. In the middle distance, from below the mill meadow, she hears the shush-and-chug of the London train, which now utters its tootling hoot as though excited by the dew.

Still too early for church bells, they won't ring before nine. But who would need them on a morning like this?

The day spills its light into the heart of itself.

Clicking at the pony, she moves on.

> *Little Sally Racket*
> *Haul her away.*
> *Earlie in the morning.*

* * *

A NURSING HOME IN LONDON

7.14 A.M.

In the top floor window of the derelict townhouse across the terrace, the lamp is lighted every night.

This morning, he wheels himself to his window and looks.

The coming day purples the rooftops and chimneypots and lattices. He wonders what can be the story of that tall, ghostly townhouse with its long-shuttered windows and bricked-up front doorway, its weed-wreathed pillars and half-collapsed architraves. Who lights the lamp? A street person? A runaway?

Even the ragmen don't come to ransack any more. Anything of value long gone. The gracious dwellings on either side, freshly whitewashed every springtime, their doorknobs and polished windows shining like stars, stare resolutely ahead, refusing a sidelong glance of pity, embarrassed by this shabby squatter in the ranks.

He has asked the nurses, the cheery servants, the cleaning women. They change the subject. The dead house has been empty for decades, they assure him. The owner died abroad—on his slave plantation in Jamaica—there was a long dispute about the will, every last shilling of the fortune was swallowed up by the lawyers, like something out of that Dickens novel, you know the one, Mr. Stoker, which starts with the awfully long court case? *Bleak House*.

The lamplight is only a reflection, they tell him, an optical illusion. A trick of the eye, nothing more.

Some years since a fellow resident, a likeable, religiously disturbed Irishwoman, confided her own theory. That's the ghost of a broken-hearted actor. He called to the door during an elegant dinner hosted by his lover and her husband, Lord Cashel, persuaded the maid that he was on the invitation list, mounted the staircase, entered the dining room, recited a couplet from Dante and shot himself in the mouth with a revolver she had given him. What was his name again? Memory fickle.

Maybe there is a play or a novella in the house. Perhaps *that's* what the light means. Fanciful thought.

Today will bring difficulties but they must be borne. He has determined to bear them alone.

On the table near his narrow bed sits the manuscript of a play he has been trying to write, some thousand handwritten pages. The piece needs the kind of savage cutting he hasn't been able to face, and despite its horrible bulk it contains so little—too many things left unsaid, dropped hints, slippy assertions. He has a strange sense of the play's author being some other man, of having to break the bad news to him; he's not sure how he will take the verdict. Perhaps best for the play not to be published or performed at all. But he can't bring himself to burn it. Not yet.

Through the walls, from the house next door, where a young piano teacher has her flat, comes the blessing of a Chopin polonaise. He listens to the fragility, the melancholic grace. It seems to sanctify the windows of his room, the street below, the policeman on his round, the children making for school, the servants leaving the basement areas and hurrying off to do their marketing. Even the old drayhorse pulling the milk-cart looks nobler. An April morning in London with Chopin.

The music eases itself into a turning point of spangling chords. Somewhere in his room is a book about Chopin and his lover George Sand—at one point their love story had seemed to him another possibility for a play—but those times are over and he is glad to be rid of them. He is too old to look on the world and everything in it as grist. So exhausting, so wasteful of experience. The world is as it is, as it is ever going to be. Raw material rarely improves with the cooking.

He reads for an hour, Whitman's *Leaves of Grass*, so consoling ("I do not want the constellations any nearer, I know they are very well where they are"), as the piano teacher's music drifts like a rumour through the wall. Beethoven's sonata in G, Rachmaninov's 2, Schumann's *Kinderszenen*, Liszt's B minor. He wonders about her, the young teacher; what is her life like?

Sometimes he has seen her leaving the house in the evenings; she looks sad for a young woman, always wears dark clothes. One night it was raining hard and she walked hatless in the rain, down the street to the lamp post, where she appeared to wait for someone. But the person never came. After a while she returned to the house, her black clothes drenched. There was no music for a couple of days.

He has the idea that she needs a friend, perhaps comes from some place far from London, maybe even another country, as so many Londoners do. She might be Hungarian or Russian, her particular sort of beauty is dark. Something Baltic, mournful, in the downturn of her mouth. Should he try to speak with her, offer a kindly word—perhaps sign up for a course of lessons? Ridiculous notion at this stage of the innings.

At eight o'clock the breakfast gong sounds in the hall below, and as usual he ignores it, while wishing the sounder well. He has nothing against his fellow residents individually or collectively, indeed many of them he likes, but, as with almost any human situation, the addition of communal food makes things worse.

One has to wait for it, or one gets too much of it, or not quite enough, or the wrong sort, or someone else's, and then there is the business of having to talk to people or being talked to or having to watch them eat. The recitation of what is wrong with them, the adjusting of false teeth, the spilling of sugar, the mistaking of sugar for salt, the frowning at the pepper-pot as though it were some relic retrieved from a Pyramid, the scrutinising of every tine of the fork for dirt. Some behave as though they own the place, others are silent and seem afraid of the cutlery. Old age is wasted on the old. They're too old to enjoy it.

He puts a hunk of bread saved from last night's supper on the stove to warm up, brews tea in a little metal teapot he borrowed from the kitchens a few weeks ago and which they seem to have forgotten. Soon it will be nine o'clock. He begins a letter to his wife but can't settle.

At nine he rings the bell for the orderly, a gently affable young cockney, a black man in his middle twenties, who comes up in the mornings to help him use the lavatory, then shave and get ready.

By the time he is dressed and out of the bath chair today, the Chopin has become a Field nocturne before melding into the *Moonlight Sonata*, the steady, placating sombreness of the descending left hand. Soon the piano teacher's students will start to arrive and it will be time to go out. There is a limit to the number of times one can face *Für Elise* played by a child.

"That's a chilly one, Mr. Stoker, you ain't going roving? I've a fire lit down in the dayroom, proper strong tea on the go. Cuppa you could trot a mouse on."

"Indeed and I am, Tom. Don't fuss."

"Seen the papers this morning, sir? Lumme, that's a mighty ship."

"Built in Ireland, you know."

"Like yourself, sir."

"They launched me a good many years ago, dear lad."

"Still sailing proud, sir."

"Don't know about that. Still chugging along at least."

"So what you at today, sir? Up to no good I expect?"

"Oh a terribly old friend of mine, the writer Hall Caine, is giving me lunch at the Garrick Club in town."

"There's fancy."

"Yes, I'm advising him on his autobiography. Couple of small points here and there. Know his work at all?"

"Can't say as I do, sir."

"Gifted writer, old Caine, but he *will* go on. And then he doesn't tell us things we want to ruddy know. I shall be advising him to slow down, take his time."

"You'll enjoy that, sir."

"Family all well at home, Tom?"

"The best, sir. Sit still for me a tick, I'll just comb your barnet."

He enjoys listening to Tom tell funny stories about his parents, the mimicries and gesturings, the affectionate mockery. It has become a sort of serial for him, a Dickens novel writ small, and he finds himself looking forward to the daily instalment, perhaps more than he ought—but today no stories are forthcoming. He wonders if everything is quite well, in Tom's life away from this place.

There is never any mention of a girl.

"Now then, sir, you'll pass muster. You've had a bit of breakfast brung up to you, I expect?"

"I did, Tom, thanks, a nice bowl of stirabout."

"That's the stuff to put lead in your pencil, sir. Starter's orders, so?"

"Starter's orders. Thank you."

Tom picks him up pietà-style, nudges open the door with a knee, and carries him down the two flights of rickety staircase. In the hallway, the wheelchair is waiting.

"Certain you'll manage, sir?"

"Right as the mail, Tom. If you'd just open the door."

"Very good, sir. Here's your brolly. Have a lovely morning. Chin-chin."

* * *

A TRAIN FROM RURAL KENT TO LONDON

9.11 A.M.

As the 8.02 from Ashford chunters towards New Cross Gate it slows, and she stirs awake.

A blowy, bright morning. Men on their allotments. A murmuration of starlings, wheeling through a cloud over the gasworks.

She notices that she is gripping her walking-cane tightly, across her knees. For a moment the dream won't let her surface.

Irving on Warnemünder beach in northern Germany, beckoning through the shimmer, the wispy plumes of sand, clusters of wild rhododendrons, his evening suit white—but the lowing of the whistle drives the spectre away, back into the clacking truckle of steel on track. Suddenly she is thirsty and hot.

A gust of wind buffets up to look at her through the windows. *Oh*, says the wind. *Look who it is. Old girl used to be famous.*

From her carpet-bag she takes a flask of Italian tisane and two of her orchard's apples, greenly crisp and cold. The taste brings the house to her, its gracious rooms and mullioned windows, the long, shaded gardens, the conservatories, the library; the rope-swing beneath the sycamores where her grandchildren play.

To have Smallhythe, still, to have held onto it all these years. Rare for an elderly actress to be blessed with a comfortable home, to have anything to bequeath when she goes. A silly thought occurs to her. My gracious, I own three staircases. How in the name of glory did that happen?

Today she will collect the typescript for her forthcoming lecture series, her tour to the United States. The girl at the typewriting service in Covent Garden will smile. Pretty thing, good figure, came to London to be an opera singer, speaks in that lovely Welsh way, so lilting. Angharad?

The April meadows beyond the windows, neat and pleasing to see, the ditches full of wildflowers as Ophelia's dreams. The steeples of the villages, the slow-turning mills, the still and lovely greenness of canal water. Cows bow their heavy heads or shake them at the midges. A foal staggers towards the hedgerow where he stops and gapes at the lambs.

It is like looking at a Constable come somehow to life, the mellowness a retaliation to Turner's passion. Drovers at a campfire, sweethearts canoodling on a stile, a milkman collecting eggs from a coop built on stilts, farm boys and their fathers heading out with mattocks and sickles. Something joyful-sad floods her blood, why is there no English word for that? It is not "bittersweet" but something heavier, more substantial, like claret. Her spectacles mist as she watches.

An image presses at her consciousness, black horses in water, surf in their manes, sea froth all around them, the joy of their whinnying above the surge of pebbled waves. Suddenly the horses are gone, as extinguished lamplight, but pulsing on some retina of the mind.

He tries to come to her again, she feels him hover close. Oh my darling, she thinks, please not now, I'm not able. Why today, after so long? The day is so busy; another time if we must?

He is waiting in the wings of the morning, wants to come on, steal the scene. To prevent it, she opens her bag, takes out a copy of *Les Modes*, but now she hears his shy smile, which isn't possible, she knows. Nobody can hear a smile.

But I hear yours.

For some minutes she tries to read, but the words bring no

quietness. She wishes she had brought something denser, more substantial and demanding, one of those Russian novels as well sprung as an old sofa. This fluff about hats and fashions—*mon dieu*, look at those shorter skirts. Had I dared to go out with my ankles on plain view like that, Mummie would have reddened my behind! But the young must have their way, it's the nature of things to change. If they didn't, wherever should we be? A pity people become old trouts and forget their nights of fun. But maybe that's nature, too.

The carriage is empty but she knows she is being watched. She feels herself blush like a schoolgirl.

All right then, she thinks. Come in for a moment. Only don't make a habit of it, don't go stirring things up. You nuisance.

She feels him drift into her, out of some place of interstellar coldness. Silly old darling. Come closer. The breath of his sigh, his gratefulness. Feels him peering out through her eyes at the mild fields unrolling, at the turrets of frothy cloud, at her reflection in the window. His loneliness receding like a tide.

This is what I look like now, she says. Beauty fades, if ever it were there.

There is no conversation, only a stillness together. As though they are watching a play. That is all he asks this morning, which truly is just as well, because it is all she is able to give. And there is nothing she wants to have out with him any more. Hasn't wanted that for years, no point. Most things between a woman and a man cannot be understood, it's why people invented love poems, a way of filling in the silence.

She listens to his heartbeat as it melds with her own, hears the pulses of his body, its rhythms. Would you like to read *Les Modes* with me, of course you wouldn't, I shan't. It is nice to tease him, a little lovegame, there is gentleness in that. The quiet music of his bloodstream, the aftertaste of his tears. So lonesome wherever he is.

They sit on a train together, and the train approaches a great city, crosses meadows and bridges, passes grey little suburbs, and she wonders if everyone, on every journey, anywhere in the world this morning, is carrying someone else or the wound that person left.

She cannot be the only one. That would be too hard. But then everyone is the only one. Which is also too hard.

Be still, she thinks. This is what mercy feels like.

It's why we have love poems. Because nothing can be said.

* * *

THE PORCHESTER BATHHOUSE FOR GENTLEMEN, MAIDA VALE

10.16 A.M.

Steam hits his face in a scald of wet cloud. As he limps through the atrium, careful on his stick, easing a measured way towards the damp wooden bench by the wall, the mist-wreathed figures of the other men seem like statues, totems in a dream of the East.

Wet tiles drip. Hot coals hiss. Eucalyptus in the air, an aroma of sandalwood and spruce. Ten men are in the room, all naked, most conversing, but this being England the conversation is of the weather, which, it is agreed, might well be worse. The weather is working hard this morning.

Beyond the tiles, out in the world, there are hurricanes, bombs, and strikes, but it is understood, without anyone ever making it clear, that those subjects are generally better avoided by the naked, like the split infinitive by careful writers. The fat masseur waddles in, bath-sheet around his astonishing midriff, bundle of twigs at the ready. He is so obese that his belly looks like a deployed parachute; his Rubenesque hips and breasts glint with oil. Would anyone care for a schmeiss?

Why not, one gentleman says, as though this possibility has arisen unexpectedly, is a pleasant surprise, now laying himself face down on the wet, hot bench like a recently caught salmon on a slab.

Water is splashed on the stones, the mist gushes hard. The masseur begins spanking him smartly with the bundle of tied twigs, now with the wrapped-up towel, now again with the twigs, while the muttering about the possibility of April showers continues and is peaceably passed about the cell like a hookah. The moans of the City gentleman arise from time to time, as the masseur subjects him to surely painful kneading. At one point the groanings become hard to be inscrutable about. "If it's worth doing at all," another gentleman, an insurance agent, says, "a thing is worth doing thoroughly." Watchword of an Empire on which the sun never sets.

Next it is the turn of the author of several forgotten novels, elderly fellow who trundles about in a wheelchair and rarely says much, funny sort of Arish-English accent. Lives in a charity home around the corner. Used to work in the West End. Must have a story or two to tell but keeps to himself. They say he knew Wilde and Ellen Terry.

Poor old cove's in a bad way, body going to ruin. Suffered a stroke in February, his fourth. Bit shaky. Forgets the odd word. Gets mixed up. But must be acknowledged he's a tough bird, here every morning, shine or rain. Can't be easy but he doesn't like to be offered assistance. Stubborn sort of coot. That's a Pat for you, of course.

After the schmeiss, a sit in the frigidarium, and he dresses again, which these days takes time and concentration. He gives a tip—it's never much but he gives it every day—to the young man on duty at the Front Desk and wheels himself out of the Porchester Bathhouse. So wonderful to feel properly clean.

His forearms are aching as he turns onto Queensway but that is only to be expected, he has fallen out of the habit of exercise lately. Today will go some way towards rectification. And the morning, if chilly, is fresh.

O, the little patisseries, the perfumed steam from the Turkish baths still hanging hotly about his clothes. A gang of rough navvies flailing at the road with their picks, while the foreman, cig in mouth, bawls blasphemies. That street-girl on the corner. The peal of the bells from St. Stephen's. The mope-faced Greek barber in his dirty little shop. A nun jingling a collection box for the hungry.

The sight of the street-girl stirs memories of the Ripper times. Terrible that they never caught him, he is probably still alive, could be anyone. The little Greek barber, the foreman of the navvies, one of those naked men back in the bathhouse. Might have struck again afterwards, almost certainly did before. As a Londoner of that season, you carry these things. There will never be anywhere to put them down.

Passing Whiteley's, he is careful to glance away from the windows of the bookstore. He doesn't like to be reminded, too many hurts, disappointments. It is important to remain afloat, eyes on the horizon, always. The past is a drowning madman; throw him a rope, he'll pull you in.

Startled. He brakes.

Ahead of him on the pavement, in a shelter at a bus stop, the piano teacher, her long, black, old-fashioned coat, a filigree of sunshine around her. But when he blinks and looks again, she is an old man with an umbrella. Strange. Just a trick of the light.

Sweating a bit now. Strange prickles in the scalp. The grey light of London, so restful. He pictures himself and the other residents having supper together tonight, all bemoaning their failing livers, kidneys, hearts. "The organ recital," Tom calls it.

Ahead is Hyde Park. He crosses near Moscow Road. A

young woman helps him, takes the wheelchair's handles, pushing. While he isn't ungrateful, he would rather she didn't. If she must, he would rather be asked.

It doesn't do to be a baby. He doesn't require assistance. At the same time, what can one say? The road to hell may indeed be paved with good intentions but, at this age, any paving is a consolation.

Elegant cavalry horses parading on the Row, flanks sleek and moist. Lovers in the bowers of the rose gardens. Little boys on their way to school in their bat-like robes. A pretty guardsman standing sentry in his pretty wooden box, like a toy made large in a dream.

A brass band gathering beneath a trades-union banner. Two schoolgirls dawdling by the fountain. O it would do a body good, a morning like this, to be alive, in the zhoosh of London.

Ellen's word. Zhoosh. A funny part of her charm, those words she'd invent to fill gaps. Gullyfluff: the debris accumulating in the bottom of a lady's handbag. Bippy: an attractive-looking young man of even more than average stupidity. Foozler: a person not to be trusted.

Dear old Len. Whatever happened? Lost touch, don't know why. Wonder if she's still working, if she ever thinks of the old days. Heard she was living in Somerset.

He stops beneath a plane tree, smokes half of one of the four cigarettes he can afford to have today. Would be pleasant to have a newspaper now, why didn't he bring one? Next time he will. And a hip flask.

Keats and gin in Hyde Park, and the soothe of throaty smoke. A consummation devoutly to be wished.

He waits. Time to kill. But it doesn't want to die. Still an hour before the picture-house opens.

He wonders what will be showing today, maybe a newsreel or a Greek tragedy. Perhaps he'll truckle down to Speakers' Corner, listen a while to the extremists? But no, it's too early, there'll be nobody there. They'll still be in bed with their fervencies. He finds it a token of England's mellowness that lunatics are tolerated in public, given places in parks, like fountains.

Tired, a bit abstracted by the steam and the hard massage, he can't face the magazine of crossword puzzles in his overcoat pocket. He looks at his watch. Only seven minutes have passed. Feels a year. Strange hunger and thirst. A cold breeze blows across from Kensington, raising an aroma from the trees, from the grass, from the sedge of the lake. He takes a sheet of filched notepaper from his inside jacket pocket—

THE WILLOUGHBY HOME FOR GENTLEFOLK
OF ABRIDGED MEANS
15 & 16 Brickfields Terrace, London W2

—and begins to write.

~~Dearest mouse~~
~~My darling Flo~~
~~Dear Florence~~

Old girl,
Please forgive my spidery scrawl of more than usual ghastliness. Find I can't manage at the ruddy machine this morning, fingers a bit stiff and pins-and-needles, but nothing to be concerned about, just the cold weather. You may utter hard words at my calligraphy, dear poppet, but in a way it is not a bad thing to write by hand because one has to think about it and go more slowly don't you find? There. Now. I am pausing. For breath.

I was thinking about sponges the other day, how they live in the sea. Do you think the sea would be far higher if they didn't?

Lovely to have received your thumpingly long and newsy letter. Hope all continues well for you in Dublin and that you are feeling a little better and over your chill. It is a damp old town of drears and old maids and foozlers but you are correct, they celebrate Easter with more intensity over there, with perhaps a residual *je ne sais quoi* of the druidic?

I used to love hearing those very forlorn bells you mention from the Roman Catholic church in Fairview, they were cast in Italy, isn't their musicality just wonderful, so orotund and sonorous. It (the RC church) was consecrated in the year I turned eighteen. I remember, on my way home from a shatteringly dull lecture that evening, seeing the great procession, like something out of Chaucer, an exultation of bishops and choristers in their stiff, heavy robes, monks solemnly swinging thuribles, deacons carrying statues of the saints and virgins. Isn't it queer? Everything is there for ever if one knows which room to look in—or opens the door in error while searching for something else. Why then, you go into the room and a whole world is there. Like diving under the sea.

One elderly Czar-looking fellow, I suppose an archbishop or other holy wiz, was holding aloft a golden book with a jewel-encrusted cover, another carried an ostensorium or what I think the Roman Catholics call a monstrance, you know, the circular vessel in which the Eucharistic host is displayed for veneration. A plump cardinal (he might have been?) with an exquisitely corrupt face was being hefted along on a bier. And the glorious clouds of incense. And a veritable army of rather terrifying axe-faced nuns. Quite wonderful.

Given that the whole gaudy had been got up to celebrate the coming back to life of a chap that had been dead, the feeling was somewhat austere, delightfully so. I liked that.

Along the streets the local people had congregated and were singing a hymn, the men doffing their hats as the holy persons and holy objects processed past, the women kneeling, heads lowered:

Faith of our fathers, living still,
In spite of dungeon, fire and sword.

It being Dublin, there was a great throng of poor people from the slums, many of the children and even some of the men barefoot, their feet actually bleeding, so that one couldn't help but reflect on the contrasts of the occasion. I remember mentioning it to poor Father that evening at suppertime. His reply comprised one spat word. "Papists."

A good man in many ways but eaten into by hate. Always sad to see.

I'm glad you went over, old girl, especially since, as you say, neither of your great-aunts may last long now. It is important to make a good effort with elderly relatives. For you to be there at the end will bring great comfort.

Heard a good joke the other day and meant to store it up for you, but now I have forgotten it. Bother. Mind like a jellyfish this morning. It will come back to me.

Saw a splendid moving-picture at the Scala on Thursday last, about the royal tour, entitled "Our King and Queen in India." Outside the theatre some disrespectful person had inserted a "Y" before the title. I liked seeing the Indians' faces. They reminded me of Dubliners.

Otherwise a quiet month here. But all well as can be expected. I am sitting in a cosy rug by a nice warm fire in the dayroom as I write these words, and am being plied with buns and steaming cups of strong tea. The table is groaning with ices, apples and biscuits, lemon pie, jugs of hot chocolate. Everyone here is very warm-hearted and kindly. I feel at home and want for nothing.

Many old chums from theatre days and other idlers have been calling to see me. Hart Crane visited last evening and we had a good old chat about the glory times, and later today I am meeting Shaw. He is giving me luncheon at the Pen Club in the Strand. (There's fancy, I hear you say.) He does rather bore on at one about socialism and all the rest of it and, since taking up ardent vegetarianism has become more violent. But he means well.

So, you are not to worry about me at all, everything is rosy o'grady. I do not like to think of you being in any way concerned, as you were in your last letter. I am feeling right as the mail and am happily going about without the wheelchair these days and generally chipper and hearty. I don't know myself.

What else to tell you, old girl? Let me see. Oh, the pitmen's strike has ended, I am glad to say that they got what they wanted. Imagine having to strike for the right to be paid for working two miles beneath the ground. Isn't it wonderful to think of the great ship arriving in the Cove of Cork from Southampton, what a hooley they shall have, be the hokey. It will be a special mischief and delight to all Corkonians that the mightiest vessel the oceans have ever seen did not call to Dublin but proceeded instead to what they feel is the true capital. Their self-regard, like the ship, is unsinkable.

Matron is talking darkly of inflicting a cellmate on me but I don't know if she shall. I should be happy to shove up a bit in the stalls for another old carthorse, but my room is mighty small so his would need to be a leprechaun's bed. But perhaps jolly to have the company, someone to bore? What do you think?

I long to see you again, my dearest. Let me know when you are coming back.

A Romanian girl who teaches piano has been coming in now and again to play for us old duffers in the evenings, she is uncommonly good. Field. Beethoven. Chopin, so on, the melancholy end of the forest, perhaps. But sad music is cheering in its way. It has been agreeable to befriend her a little, she seems lonesome and somewhat withdrawn, in need of a friend. She and I sometimes have a nice talk by the fire or she comes in to read to me. I tell her not to look back, but forward, always. Loneliness is a terrible thing.

Well, dear girl, the ladies are saying it is time for morning coffee, so I shall bid you adieu and be in touch again soon. In the meantime, your ever loving—

"I say, you old nuisance, what idleness are you at?"

When he looks up towards the voice, he is amazed to see a smiling, thinfaced young man in the tight-fitting tweeds of a dapper fellow-about-town. So like Florence, the shy grin, the animal grace. For a moment he wonders if he is dreaming.

"As I live and breathe. Noel—my dearest boy."

"*Guten Morgen*, honoured Pops of the charioteers. You are looking ruddy royal. Like Boadicea in a bowler."

"But, heavens, what are you doing here and at this hour of the day? Why are you not at your work? Is something wrong?"

"The mighty overlords of the Triple Shield Assurance Company can spare one of their toiling minions for an hour or two. Wanted to see my old Popsicle, spend a little time."

"But how did you know where I was? You look wonderfully bright-eyed."

"That was detective work if you like, regular Sherlock Holmes caper. I calls to the Willoughby, they sends me round to the bathhouse. Cove at the bathhouse saw you trundling towards Queensway. Which made muggins here reckon you were planning one of your interminable sits in the park, no doubt giving yourself pneumonia as blumming usual. So I jumped a hansom to the Kensington side and hiked it back on Shanks's pony."

"What a lovely surprise to see you."

"They told me you hadn't been eating again. The coves at the Willoughby."

"They exaggerate."

"'Appetite of a sparrow and he's up all night.'"

"Nonsense."

"'Won't associate wiv the other residents, keep to 'isself, never leaves 'is room.'"

"Balderdash."

"We are going to proceed, you and I, to a place of repast, and I am going to feed you up like a foie gras goose."

"No you're not."

"So jolly to see your frown. Didn't want you to be alone today, old Pops."

"I don't know what you mean. There is nothing special about today."

"You know well what I mean. I saw it mentioned in *The Times*. Difficult business this afternoon, don't say it won't be, there's a love." He approaches, kisses his father's forehead, tucks in the blanket. "I have a very fair idea of what course you're plotting, *mein Vater*, a certain event commencing at three of the clock this aft? Thought you could stand a little companionship, that's all."

"What news, then, dear lad? Yes, push me a while would you, my arms are tired."

"Wonderful news, Father, I am in love."

"You are in love every time I see you. With a different girl."

"Searching for the right one, that's all."

"You are searching with notable extensiveness."

"One does one's duty."

"Heard from your mother since? She is still with Great-Aunt Lucy in Dublin. Yes, the path through the rose gardens."

"Her last letter made me howl, such an operetta of complaints about Dublin life. The dirt, the impudence, the rudeness of porters. Some chappie name of Larkin has the dockers riled up. No manners any more, no one knowing his place. Do you know, I often think that's why Mummie goes to Ireland at all? To apply the perfect brake to her happiness."

"It's so long since I have been there, I remember very little."

"Great-Aunt Lucy says no good will come of allowing the natives selfgovernment."

"Great-Aunt Lucy has been saying that since about 1732."

"She says spite is as plentiful in Dublin as are the spa-waters in Switzerland."

"Push a little harder, can't you, Nolly? You are a third my ruddy age."

"But I am more beautiful than you, Father. That saps an *awful* lot of my strength. I say, look at that saucy girl over there, what an absolute masher."

"I am a little long in the tooth for that sort of sightseeing, if you'd be so good."

"Shall we see if she has an older sister? Or a Great-Aunt?"

"Push on."

* * *

CHARING CROSS STATION

10.43 A.M.

Arrived at the platform, she makes her way through the welcoming committee of scrawny pigeons, and takes the long spiral staircase down for the Underground to Knightsbridge. She doesn't much care for the Underground but always feels one should use it when up in town, like climbing the Eiffel Tower in Paris or being seduced by a gondolier when in Venice. It's nothing all that wonderful but the servants love hearing about it.

In Knightsbridge, she has a strong coffee in the café on

Carshalton Street. Statues of the Holy Virgin and St. Christopher glare sternly from the shelves, guarding fat bags of rice, boxes of Italian flour, straw-wrapped flasks of wine. An icon of the Sacred Heart, his ripped-open chest, droplets of blood the size of golf balls.

At a table behind the counter the owner is dozing, head down. His beautiful daughter, Elisabetta, is kneading dough. After a while, her father awakens and, noticing the café's only current customer, comes forward in greeting, wiping his hands on his apron.

"*Ah, bellissima Signora Terry, benvenuta e buon giorno, come sta?*"

"*Sto bene, Signor Rusca, grazie tante, e tu ?*"

Thankfully, that is almost all the Italian she knows, apart from bits of Puccini arias like *che gelida manina* but who in her right mind would speak those in real life? Admittedly, there might arise occasions when one's tiny hand *was* frozen but you wouldn't want to be bloody *sung at* if so. Especially by a bohemian. Her few words of guidebook *Italiano* have served her well on her visits to Rusca's down the years. We get on famously with people whose language we don't speak. Unhelpful things like nuance and meaning are eliminated. Smiles and gestures of re-enactment are better forms of communication. Eating together is best of all.

Delicious, Rusca's coffee, a *hint* of bitter in the sweetness. Good coffee is not to be had in any establishment she knows about in Kent, and she can no longer bring herself to make the elderly cook grind it, the poor old girl resenting coffee for its foreignness. Tea leaves grown in Ceylon are somehow exempt from such disapproval, acquiring Englishness or acceptability on their voyage towards the motherland, in that respect like Irishmen. Nothing quite as English as a cup of tea, the cook often remarks. Well, yes. But also no.

Miss Terry has good coffee and a Pall Mall cigarette. The taste of a Day Up in Town.

Blessed relief to savour a bit of time-not-allotted. To feel the lived grit of the city, the splash of accents against one's face, the exhilaration of shutters opening and closing like expectations. The plain stillness of the countryside can be so tiring when one isn't in the mood. Like wanting Beethoven but being forced to endure Morris dancers.

She watches the motor cars and tradesmen's vans trundle by, the open top buses on their way towards Hyde Park or Kensington Gardens, upper decks loaded with trippers. One boy waves and doffs his cap as they pass. She waves back and blows him a kiss. Funny little flirt. He'll be trouble.

Dr. Vasiliev's waiting room is lined with hunting prints, framed old cartoons, theatre posters, like the lounge of a gentlemen's club. Pampas grass in tall pots. A drinks tray with heavy crystal goblets. Shelves of exquisitely bound books, from which she chooses a volume of poetry. Overstuffed creaky armchairs, a thousand times more comfortable to sit in than you'd imagine. An ornate brass samovar squats mock-pompously on a sideboard. She is a little early, pours a sherry, settles down to read. Yeats takes her to Sligo, the call of the moorhens, the pale light, the bitterness of the people. The doctor's girl enters and says he is ready.

A kindly widower, scholarly, a bust of Montaigne on his desk, often a book of poems or a piano score on the chaise longue in his bay window, through which the tall cedars in the park across the Crescent can be seen. Cedars always make her think of his eyebrows.

Serious, frown-filled, laconic Dr. Vasiliev. Even his habit of sucking cloves, which in someone else would be disconcerting, is forgivable. He has lived in London forty years but there is still the music of Moscow in his voice, not the accent alone, but a velvet melancholy. She congratulates him—"*mazel tov*"—on the birth of his most recent grandchild, a girl. ("Ilyana," he says, "for my mother, may she rest.") He offers chai, as he always does. She declines, as she always does.

In the two decades they have known one another she has never taken chai with him but has almost always regretted it on the way home afterwards. Sometimes, thinking about him, she blushes.

He asks with his eyes. She begins explaining the difficulty.

Lately she has been forgetful, prone to stumbles, wrong turnings. Misplacing the odd key or pair of spectacles. There was a minor embarrassment a fortnight ago at the post office in Tenterden when she couldn't remember how many stamps she had set out to buy or in which denominations. She put a letter from her broker in the airing cupboard, a playscript in the sideboard. She neglected to bring a bag of shot when she went out shooting the other day. She has forgotten how many trees are in the apple orchard. There is something else she can't remember but she remembers she has forgotten it. Really, Dr. Vasiliev, it is a bother.

Being a man, he takes a long time explaining what she already knows, that this sort of little nuisance is not unusual at the age they have both reached, that every chapter of life presents the body with surprises which, even if we have read of them or heard them whispered about by confidantes, we somehow never believe will happen to us. She loves to listen to him talk, the marvellous Russian intonation. ("I am khepi to see you, my old fryend.") Often, she tries to arrange an appointment on a Wednesday afternoon, for the sheer joy of the number of syllables he puts into "Vednyesdei."

He is a good man, moves with pleasing slowness, takes her blood pressure, examines her tongue and ears, listens to her heart, asks many questions about her body. It has never ceased to strike her as odd, when one stands away and looks at it, the permission we grant doctors to make enquiries of such intimacy, a licence few would grant even a spouse. There is nothing *wrong*, he says, as though weighing the word on a scale made of air, but perhaps a blood-tonic might be wise, he could administer a vitamin injection now if she would like. She might make a habit of eating a little more of fresh eggs and red meat. Keep up the daily walking.

"And sleep with weendow open. And exercise your lyeft lyeg. Also a glass of good red wine is now and again not a bad thing at our age, not at all. A good beeg burgundy. For the stomach."

As he re-washes his hands and looks in his desk drawer for the syringe, she realises she has forgotten his name.

* * *

Passing the consulting rooms of Nikolai Vasiliev MD, they cross the street to the warmer side and continue towards Chelsea.

Spring has charged London's air, tinctured it with that particular fervent sweetness of very old cities in sunlight, but, since his last stroke he feels the cold like a mortal enemy. Even the hottest days have him blanketed and gloved. There are times when he cannot remember what warmth feels like any more, like trying to recollect the eye colour of a first sweetheart and realising you never knew it.

"All right, Pops?" his son asks.

"In the pink, my Nolly."

"Want to stop for a wizz or anything?"

"No, lad, push on."

He watches the motor cars and tradesmen's vans trundle by, the open top buses on their way towards Hyde Park or Kensington Gardens, upper decks loaded with trippers. One boy waves and doffs his cap as they pass. Funny little fellow. He'll be something.

* * *

In Harrods, which is oddly empty, she takes the walking-escalator up to Jewellery, where she has made an appointment to leave in a bracelet for remaking. A gold bangle inset with forty small diamonds and thirty emeralds, it spent ten years in a velvet bag on the floor of a broken wardrobe in the lumber room, under a pile of old programmes and cuttings. Forgot about it, in truth. Cook happened across it last Christmastime, searching for place mats.

Felt heavy, astonishingly cold to the touch.

"A most fine early Georgian piece," says the chief jeweller, admiring it through his loupe. "Might be a pity to dismember it, Madam? The detail is exquisite, one doesn't see this minuscule craftsmanship any more I'm afraid, one hasn't in years. In all duty, I must apprise Madam that the value should be significantly lessened by alteration."

"Oh the style is too old fashioned and, anyway, I never truly liked it. Great bauble of a thing. Like something a pantomime dame would wear."

"One wouldn't wish to be impertinent but might Madam perhaps be interested in selling? I could offer four thousand guineas? Or it would fetch a pretty sum at auction?"

"You're a darling but no, I'd simply like it remade. Could you do it along the lines of this little sketch I've brought along for you? It would be a gift for my daughter, Edy."

Pleasant, standing beside him while they look over the sketch. He smells faintly of a cathedral in summertime. His cufflinks are tiny portcullises, his tiepin an opal. He rests the tip of his rather splendid pen between his rather splendid teeth. His cow-brown eyes are—there is no other word—*dishy* when he turns to ask his questions. Manicured fingernails. Good firm knuckles. Touch of brilliantine in the ever-so-slightly greying hair. High-polished shoes. Trouser crease that would cut you.

Always had a little weakness for a properly turned out chap. Not that there are many of that species in the theatre, God knows. Most of them look as though they slept in a hedge.

"As to the initials engraved on the clasp, Madam? "To E from H with love." Madam is quite certain she wishes them to be erased?"

"My daughter is also an E, so perhaps you can leave that one. Could you alter the H to an M for Mummie?"

"It would add to the cost."

"I don't mind."

"Madam knows what Madam likes. If one might make so bold."

Oh, if only you knew, she doesn't say.

Afterwards, she wanders a while through the glinting wonderland of Kitchenware and China, buys a silver egg-whisk for Cook and a pretty cotton apron, a pewter tankard for John the groomsman in the shape of a horse's head. Their birthdays are coming soon; something from Harrods will please and surprise them.

I note that you didn't buy anything for me.

She ignores his gentle teasing. But he persists, like a shadow, following her out of China, past Hosiery, through Gentlemen's Outfitters and Hunting, scurrying in her wake down the walking-elevator, his laughter somehow ringing from the tills.

Don't I deserve a gift, too? You ungenerous old bag.

"I am hardly going to buy a bloody saucepan for a fellow who's dead."

A chauffeur is staring at her. He nods and touches his cap. She realises, alas, that her last remark was spoken aloud.

The silvered doors are opened to her by a pair of liveried pages and she finds herself in the magical cave that is the Ladies' Hall of Harrods.

A trio of harpists strum Strauss to a flock of paper doves.

Ceiling-high pyramids of scented soaps, seashell pink, apricot yellow, night-starry blue. An army of lipsticks, standing to attention, scarlets to indigos to mauves to cerise, silver all the way over to black. Jars of rouge and French talc, bath salts and blush. Glass cases of black waxen hands, on which the almond-shaped fingernails have been reddened, or purpled, or greened or gilded, or encrusted with diamanté starbursts. Oils, kohl, henna, lip-glitter, *eau de toilette*, myrtle leaves, eyeshadow, lip gloss the colour of champagne. Bottles of crème, tubes of unguents, carved urns of shampoo. Powders and puffballs, compacts and lash-combs, brushes of painterly fineness. The chandeliers are Montgolfier, the vast carpet is Persian. They say the *wrapping paper* is imported from Milan. And the girl-assistants like living sculptures, dark-eyed, all knowing, tight-clothed, metallic, of lionly allure, as the spritzes of *parfum* incense the air around them and the secrets of pulchritude they guard. If such a thing were possible, it's like inhaling Tchaikovsky.

Now the shock of the window shattering, women scream.

One of the assistants lurches backwards, into a pyramid of beautiful soaps. The shocked girl tries to gather them but it's impossible, there are too many, they roll from her grasp and bounce off the alabaster staircase, felling a rank of lipsticks and splattering the fine shampoos.

The assistants hide beneath counters, others run, white with fear. As though pulled by magnetism, she walks to the star-shaped shatter, looks out at the furious street.

Two policemen dragging a young woman towards a van. She is shouting "votes for all!" They clamp leather-gloved hands over her mouth. Passers-by yell "shame" or "prison's too good"; one elderly Chelsea Pensioner goes to strike her and must be restrained by the constables, who hold him hard by the shoulders while he bawls himself purple. "Suffragette scum. *It's a caning you want. And I'll be the one to give it you! You dirty little Suff. A caning do you hear me, a caning . . .*"

Miss Terry hurries out. The girl's nose is bleeding, her dress has been torn. She is trying to look defiant but is weeping with fear, holding closed her tattered dress, trembling like a foal with the staggers. She cannot be more than sixteen.

Three older women arrive, try to pull her away with them, remonstrating with the policemen and shouting at the girl, as the crowd in the ragged circle grows larger and angrier and the male store-assistants in their elegant suits hurry out looking stunned and a chef on his way to work stops to gape at the drama, a clutch of glinting knives in his belt.

"Constable," Miss Terry says. "You have made a mistake."

"I'll thank you to mind your business, Madam. Go along if you please."

"I saw the entire incident from first to last. That is not the girl who broke the window."

He looks at her measuringly.

"The woman who threw the brick was older," she says, "by twenty years at least, of paler complexion and with long auburn hair. She was accompanied by another, who was keeping careful watch. They ran away in separate directions. I saw the whole scene from first to last, I tell you. The girl you have seized was passing and is entirely innocent. She may have been shouting slogans but she did not do the damage. I insist you let her go."

"You're not . . . who I think you are?"

"I doubt anyone is that."

"But I mean to say . . . Is it . . . Miss Terry?"

"You are observant, but don't make a galloptious fuss about it will you, I am going about privately today."

"You're quite certain we're in the wrong?"

"Quite positive. So much so that I am willing to pay for the damage myself. I shall go to the manager and explain to him what happened. I shall of course commend you and your colleagues for your remarkable expeditiousness in the face of such egregious yahooism."

One thing poor Bram used to say when talking of the Chief. Confronting authority, one has only two choices: Surrender, or try to confuse it.

The policeman tugs at his cuffs. "Let her go, lads. There's been a mistake."

"Thank you, dear constable," says Miss Terry.

As the young woman who threw the brick is hauled away by her raging aunts, her eyes meet those of her protectress. The Chelsea Pensioner is still screaming, being held back by the constables. Cane her. Strip her. Beat her.

When the woman dies, in a hotel fire, in February 1971, she will remember that morning outside Harrods, when enough became enough, and the underground rivers of flame and defiance bubbled out, and a woman she did not know stepped out of a lynch mob.

The stern face of mercy.

The face of solidarity.

A starburst of broken glass on the pavement.

It will seem that life was not nothing, that we were not a race of apes and rippers; that there was a reason for remaining in the world.

J. DOWLING'S CINEMATOGRAPHIC HALL, CALE STREET, CHELSEA

12.01 P.M.

"Called *The Tempest*," the counter-girl says. "Dunno who's in it."

His son pays at the makeshift booth—a couple of halfpennies—and the bored-looking Maltese doorman indicates the shoddy curtain at the back of the foyer.

Once through, they are in a low-ceilinged, airless room that might once have been a rehearsal theatre or the Examinations Hall of a school. Long benches have been fetched in, the windows hung with heavy black drapes, a bedsheet pinned to the wall.

There is no one else here. A draught raises dust.

As he waits, he looks around. Never been to this one before.

He wonders if it will be like the others, if he'll be able to contain himself before his son.

The gaslight is extinguished. Two more punters drift in, tramps getting out of the rain.

As he watches from the darkness, he feels his eyes moisten.

There is nothing more miraculous. Everything conquerable has been conquered. The stuff of alchemy, of wizardry. Photographs that move.

A piece of newsreel is shown first. The vast ship, indestructible, terrible, like some dream-vessel from a legend of sea-rulers. The docks of Belfast Harbour. Tiny people waving Union Jacks. She glides with haughty slowness, three of her four funnels smoking but even the smoke looks polished.

This is the age. Our photographs shall move. Our ships shall not sink. Our hopes have no limits. As the principal film commences, he is touched by the simple elegance of the stage direction that flickeringly appears on the makeshift screen, words written by a man of the London theatre 250 years ago: "A tempestuous noise/of thunder and lightning heard."

At one time, he would have found himself pondering how best to interpret, to mimic, to blast that noise from the wings. Now, in a silence broken only by the racking coughs of the tramps, he *hears* it, clear as a gasp.

Across the wall hurry the drenched captain and his terrified boatswain. You can taste the filth of the waves, feel pitch vomiting from the sky. Wondrous. Impossible. He feels his tears start to spill.

All the savagery of man, the foolish cruelty of sect, the hypocrisy, the disingenuousness, the turning away from hunger—all of it seems somehow atoned for in this innocence and astonishment. That a beast could make such a wonder. That he would bother to try. That, having made it, he would not keep it for some high Emperor alone, for some sultan of illimitable wealth, with a city made of rubies, but would open his tent of marvels for a halfpenny a time so that even the lowest pauper may be made to grasp that he is *not* alone, that his planet is not a cold rock spinning heartlessly through nothingness, that a healing is possible, it is only a matter of opening one's eyes.

They writhe and scuttle on the screen, faces white as blank paper, eyes startlingly wide open, as though warding off death, uneasy in their element, lips moving but silent. If we could see them, this is what ghosts would look like. Sometimes, in other places, a pianist has come in, vamped along to the story, glancing up now and again at what is happening on the bedsheet, the spectacle of humans playing as they have since they crawled from their caves—crawling from their caves was perhaps *itself* a sort of play, a dare born of boredom on a wintry afternoon— but the best accompaniment is silent stillness, just the clicking whirr of the projector, like now, and the occasional awed sigh from an audience member at a sword fight, a promise, a kiss.

In silence it becomes possible to hear what subsists beyond the noise, what has been there all along, the truths that are drifting on the air, often drenched out of recognition but not quite drowned. At such moments you don't need the dialogue—words get in the way—but they project it for you anyway, on ornately decorated slides, with laurels and harps in their corners.

> *Be not afeard; the isle is full of noises,*
> *Sounds and sweet airs, that give delight and hurt not . . .*

that, when I waked,
I cried to dream again.

In the darkness, he feels his son reach across and take his hand. Both of them quietly weeping. A curious thing. Back in headache-bringing daylight, neither of them will mention it.

"Pops," says his son. "Let's not go where you're going."

"I'm going. You needn't come with me."

"But why, Pates?"

"Don't matter. I'm going, that's all."

For half an hour they say little. A sandwich, a cigarette. But they are bonded by having been in the room with the ghosts. Gentleness, mildness, but something else, too, for not all of the airs are sweet.

* * *

A FASHIONABLE THEATRICAL RESTAURANT

1.18 P.M.

Smile, old girl. Someone here will know you. It's the Savoy, after all. Full of actors, impresarios, showpeople. You don't want to let them see you looking restlessly at your watch, it would bring them to the table and then there'd be talk you don't want to be having. Not that there is any sort you do want.

A gin, perhaps? Not alone.

O where on earth can he be? Twenty past already. *Typical* Shaw. *Always* bloody late. Does it on purpose, his power, he's so busy. His time matters more than poor yours.

Pompous twit.

Pompous bloody twit.

Pompous bloody bearded bloody self-regarding *twit*.

Mercy Christ, look at that miserable string quartet over there on the dais, sawing and plucking away like the four horsemen of the Apocalypse, not a smidgeon of musicality or attractiveness among the lot of them. To think Haydn agonised to drag such beauty of himself. Had he ever heard this collection of cummerbund-toting ghouls he'd have burnt his fiddle and become a barber.

Imagine being married to one of them. Or to anyone.

Men, if carefully cast, are so marvellous in so many of life's roles, wonderful friends, lovers, lion-tamers, popes, explorers of waterless or unmapped regions, coal miners, shooters, drinking pals. They have admirable simplicity, their predictability is so soothing. Know a man for fifteen minutes and you know him for life, he will never surprise you again, he wouldn't know how to; asking would only frighten him. But they're simply, alas, not good at being husbands. Almost any woman you'd meet by chance, in a grocery queue, say, or sitting beside you on a train, would make a better husband than almost any man ever born.

Often she remembers an evening twelve or fourteen years ago when she ate a bad oyster at one of the tenants' christenings, with the calamitous results that ensued. For three days she had been wretchedly, vesuvianly ill. Cold, hot, sweating, in agonies, things happening inside her body that made her wish she had never been born in one, raving, burning, weeping, heaving, roaring at the servants to get out of the house so that the indignity of her tortures would not be witnessed or, worse, overheard. For three days her blasphemies scared the rooks off the chimney pots, her innards were the cauldron in *Macbeth*. When all of it was over, she realised one thing. At no point was it worse than being married.

Having to listen to them, talk to them, endure their weird angers, their misdirection of rages better targeted elsewhere, if anywhere at all, which was debatable. Having to watch them

358 · JOSEPH O'CONNOR

suck soup, cut their toenails, sniff their shirts, put their feet up on the ottoman while telling you what things like elections and continents are, because, being a woman, you wouldn't know.

Being told what to wear, who he met at the station, why the indigenes of such and such a protectorate are congenitally ungovernable, being nudged and commanded brightly to *smile, it's not so bad* (rrrr). Having to look riveted while they enumerate the fascinating differences between Liberals and Tories (yawn) or reveal to you that tigers live in India, not Africa (ah!) or prove what jolly sports they are by telling an amusing anecdote against themselves or let you know the bliss- ful tidings of how remarkably quickly they finished the cross- word this morning on the train up to town, faster than any other boy in the kindergarten.

Their nostril-hair. Their odours. Their wet feet on floor- boards. Their reenactment of misunderstandings they had with others of their sex, in which they "do" all the voices. What a microscope is. How to spell "parallel." Their exhausting need to be admired, to be built back up. And that is before we approach what happens in the marital bed—why are they *so* much nicer at it when they are not married to you?—on which rare but sadly not rare enough occasions one recalls the verdict of Hobbes on life: Nasty. Brutish. Short.

The manager approaches tactfully, in a suit so crisply pressed that it must surely be uncomfortable to sit down in.

"Good afternoon, Miss Terry, an honour to see you with us again. You have everything you wish, I hope?"

"Thank you, Paul, good afternoon. How have you been?"

"Keeping well, thank you, Miss Terry."

"Family in the pink?"

"Three little ones now, Miss Terry, thank you for asking."

"Excellent. Your wife's hands are full."

"There is a matter to bring to your attention. Mr. Shaw has just telephoned to our office upstairs with a message."

"A message?"

"He regrets to say that he is detained at rehearsals at the Prince of Wales and will not be able to see you at one as planned. He asks if you will be good enough to wait here for him until half past. Two o'clock at the very latest. I am instructed to look after you well."

"I see."

"May I get you . . . ? Perhaps a glass of something crisp? Anything you wish."

"Will you give that Irish nuisance a plain and simple message for me when he arrives?"

"Of course, Miss Terry."

The next words to come out of her mouth take about sixty seconds to say. Many of them are heard only rarely in the dining room at the Savoy. Some of them, she didn't know she knew.

"On second thoughts, don't bother. Fetch my coat for me, would you, Paul?"

He appears mildly relieved as he nods.

* * *

AN AUCTIONEER'S SALEROOMS

2.15 P.M.

They watch from across Foley Street as the steaming motor cars and hansoms pull up and the people step out in the rain. From the doorway of the auction house come attendants with umbrellas. An overhead canopy is pulled out. More buyers arrive. It is as though an audience is gathering for a performance.

A strange nervousness besets him. He doesn't want to go in.

His son seems to sense it, places a reassuring hand on his father's shoulder.

"Pops, if you'd rather not?"

"Let us cross, Nolly."

The saleroom window has misted up. From the street, the room's contents are not properly discernible, seem like hulking wrapped objects in a nicotine fog. But the notice pasted inside the glass is clear.

EXECUTORS' PUBLIC AUCTION
OF THE LATE
SIR HENRY IRVING'S PERSONAL EFFECTS
APRIL 12th, 1912, 3 P.M. at these premises

Seven years having passed since the death of Sir Henry Irving, all matters of probate having now been resolved, the executors have felt it proper that some of his belongings may be disposed of to the public so that burdens on Lady Irving and his family might be relieved. Many curios, items of theatrical memorabilia, stage costumes by the house of Auguste et Cie, fancy objects, trinkets, sundries, a fob watch, reading spectacles, a good walnut desk, some of his clothing and boots, a fine billiard cue, an ivory paperweight of the Acropolis, a fine pair of fencing swords, good suitcases and monogrammed valise, daguerreotypes, sketches, mixed general lots (boxes of old newspapers, many back-numbers of Punch, Illustrated London News, Theatre Gazette), *phonographic cylinders, his Medal of Knighthood, & cetera. Advance bids accepted. Every lot must go. Cash or bank draft only. ALSO, the green beetle-wing gown of Miss Ellen Terry as worn by her in the role of Lady Macbeth, Royal Lyceum Theatre, 1888 ("The most marvellous and iridescent stage costume I have seen in my life," Mr. Mark Twain, American gentleman of letters), a memento gift from Miss Terry to the late Sir Henry. Also a collection of stage weapons, wigs,*

and other theatrical properties, all clean. Also, a very finely-cast
DEATH MASK.

Inside, the room is stuffy. The smell of mothballs and damp coats. Nearly every man here is smoking. Professional traders, they scurry about with notebooks and catalogues, their magnifying glasses and measuring tapes looped to their belts. There is an anxiousness, a fear of something about to be missed.

Long trestle tables have been set up and draped in black baize, the better lots laid out carefully and labelled. Autographed letters from Conan Doyle. A signed photograph of Queen Victoria. The scroll of honour on which his Freedom of Philadelphia is inscribed. Signet rings. Tiepins. A hall-marked silver comb. The pair of gloves given him by Lady Tennyson. A jewel-hilted dagger inscribed with his favourite quotation: *If you prick us, do we not bleed?*

A headless mannequin on a platform is wearing the beetle-wing gown, which has been lit by a circle of candles. Now and again, a white-gloved attendant picks up a candle and walks a slow, priestly circle around the pedestal, so that beams of emerald and cobalt and silver shimmer from the bodice and dance around the dirty, smoke-filled air like *eau de nil* turned to light. A woman is trying to photograph the effect, with a box-camera on a tripod. But no camera is able to capture magic.

He wheels himself further down the room to where a collection of bad sketches has been badly hung. He will not look at the death mask, which is in a glass case of its own. His son drifts away towards the gown.

A phonograph machine has been set up on a table and, through a sea of crackle and fuzz, begins playing what he realises after a moment is Irving's voice. So startling to hear it, after all this time. It's both like him and not, as though he's giving an impersonation of himself. *To tek. Up awms. Against a see. Of twubbles. And by oppeausing. End them.*

Such an old-fashioned style of delivery, plummy, over-declamatory, his speech impediment oddly more prominent than anyone who ever heard him speak would remember. The voice a bit in love with itself, not serving the text. That mode would be laughed at now.

Nearby, a trio of glass cases containing medals, picture frames, silver cigarette boxes, a presentation urn of Waterford crystal.

His clothes have been pinned to sheets of cork set leaning against the walls. Jackets, britches, waistcoats, even under-shirts. Two dozen pairs of empty, wrinkled shoes, in a line, like a detail from a nightmare set at a grand ball.

One dealer plucks a tricorn hat from a stack on a table, pops it onto his head, turns grinning to his chum, who warns him with his eyes that he'd better replace it or the attendants will ask them to leave. Remarkable, how much can be said with the eyes. But every actor knows that.

In a corner down at the back, near the exit to the lavatories, sits the junk no one but a scavenger or a rag-and-bone man will want, the stuff someone will have to be paid to cart away and dump. Bundles of mildewed theatre programmes, stained cravats, divorced slippers, envelopes of odd buttons, a bent sword. A notice has been pasted to the windowsill above the dismal huddle: ANY OFFER SECURES. BUYER MUST REMOVE IMMEDIATELY ON PURCHASE.

Beneath a length of old curtain, he finds a battered card-board box, MARKED ASSORTMENT OF SECONDHAND BOOKS. Many are missing their jackets, or silverfish have been at them. A *Complete Poe*, fallen to bits. A ninth edition of *Jane Eyre*. A pirated *Little Men* by Louisa May Alcott. Nothing anyone would want. Too damp even to use as kindling. The novels that never sold. The poems unread. The dead books where the publisher simply made a mistake, was in a falsely good mood the day he said yes, or wanted something from the author, or owed someone a favour. And now, in the bottom of the box, something he recognises, an old friend fallen low. Spineless, frayed, the first copy of *Dracula*. Chapter two has been torn out. Someone has scribbled what appears to be a grocery list on the yellowed, crinkled frontispiece. *Bread, wine, half pound of sausage, milk*. Below it, in his own hand, six faded words.

To Henry, from Bram. Eternal love.

As he looks away, through the blur, the scald of the weakening blush he doesn't want to have, an apparition arises near the steamed windows. There, across the room, by the luminescent dress, the ghost of her gentle young self. So fresh, full of the majesty and poise of youth, so possessed of the knowledge she could *not* have known at the time, that innocence is a kind of wisdom, more valuable than experience, that no moment will ever come again.

You wanted her desperately. You never made it clear. Because you knew what would happen if you did.

And if things had been different, things might have been different. But it is too late now. It was too late too long ago. The words go around in circles. Brittle little bits of acidy memory, tangy as lemon-ice, bitter as salt, overhung by the reek of rotting coffin. No wonder you were never able to make of it a novel, a poor tale it would have been, a bit of dressmaker's trash.

Perhaps to have known her was enough, to have been any part of her life. If her story were a book of poems, you would be no more than one line, but that is not nothing, not at all. To have her think of you as her ally, her confidant, her shadow. How many true friends can anyone have? For a woman, how few of those will be men?

Light in at the window, through the blears of dirty steam, the gaps in the auctioneer's shutters. He listens to the sound of the hail. He is picturing the Wicklow hills, the long beach at Killiney. Sea-foam flying over the Military Road. He knows it is sleeting there too.

Turning, she stares at the windows behind you, her violet eyes glittering in the sleet-whitened light. A ghost long-accustomed to being looked at.

Now she is approaching. Pushing deftly through the traders. Their hands are waving bids but she is not looking at the lots.

"Excuse me, sir?" she says. "You're not by any chance Mr. Stoker? You were a great friend of my mother. I am Edy."

THE LYCEUM PALACE OF WAXWORKS AND SPOOKS

3.32 P.M.

From a flower girl in Covent Garden she buys a single white lily, which she folds in a page torn from a cheap edition of *Hamlet*. The afternoon light is pale.

She collects the script of her lecture series from the typewriting service on Exeter Street but the Welsh girl she was vaguely hoping to see is not there, has left, is getting married. The old hatchet who runs the place is tight-lipped and falsely courteous, as though there is something in the story she disapproves of and doesn't want to reveal.

Along Exeter Street. Southampton Street. Nightingales chirruping in the plane trees. A notion looms up at her—so she tells herself now, but in truth it has been with her for days, even weeks, pushing against her will to push it away. Going up to town anyway, little errands to run. Visit the old place when you're up.

Today, on the far side of the city, they're selling off his belongings, auctioning his clothes, whoring out his ghost.

Poking grubby fingers into his buttonholes, his privacies. Unbearable the thought, how he'd hate the vulgarity of it all. Instead she will hold him by walking with his memory in the parterre. Sit a while in the foyer. Lay a flower on the stage. We have each our own kind of remembrance.

It's not the vulgarity I'd hate. I never minded a little vulgarity. Leave me be. Not yet.

She climbs the steps carefully, stick tapping on the stone, pushes gently on the door, which is new, one of those modern revolving affairs that slap you on the bottom if you don't hurry along. Honestly, what was wrong with ruddy doors the way they were for a thousand years? This modern mania for improvement. The lobby is empty, the Box Office closed. Dusty light streams in from the narrow cruciform windows. The walls have been papered a revolting mauve and green, the carpet is worn and reeks of stale tobacco. The dozen brass-railed marble steps up to the parterre are gone, in their place a scarlet-painted ramp too steep for anyone to climb. You can see the dark circle in the ceiling-rose where the Tiffany chandelier once hung. She remembers its breeze-made tinkle.

She had expected him to feel close here, to be part of the air, the dust. But he isn't. She can't hear him at all.

The old theatrical prints are gone, replaced with posters for variety acts and freaks. The Globe-Headed Lady. The Wild Man of Borneo. His Highness, King "Tattoos" Muldoon. On a table near the rusted drinking fountain, a jumble of roller skates and a thick book of yellow tear-out tickets.

Be gone, say the roller skates. *You do not want to know us. If we were you, we'd skate off while we could.*

That was the staircase where she was once photographed with poor Wilde, on a night when he wore his fame like an ermine stole. Shaking the hands of royalty, accepting kisses from dowagers. Signing autographs with quills dipped in vintage Château d'Yquem. Two years later, he'd be dead.

In that alcove, a peer of the realm sipped champagne from her slipper, whispered suggestions that would have made an iceberg blush, beseeched her to be what he called his para-mour. Men queuing at the Box Office would fall silent when she passed through the foyer to rehearsal, as though she were a fairy or a unicorn. Today, almost nobody has recognised her. They rarely do any more. Spectacles can be so disguising.

And through that doorway over there, which leads to the private boxes—no, too saucy to think about what happened. It was the First Night of *King Arthur*, he was the King, you Guinevere. The wildness, the wanting, Christ he was like a bull. Dear heavens, youth. The walls have eyes. She feels her-self scorch as they watch her.

Now an impossible apparition comes strolling from the auditorium. Clad in only a pair of bathing trunks which are leopard-skin patterned, he is himself tattooed from head to toe in leopard-skin pattern, so that he looks like a walking carpet.

"Afternoon, Treacle," he says, in a pleasant cockney bounce. He lopes into the Box Office, retrieves a packet of cig-arettes, strikes a match against the wall and lights up.

"Yes," she replies. "Indeed."

An afterthought takes him. "Smoke?"

"Thank you, no."

"If you're here to see Ern, he ain't in."

"Ah."

"Shall I tell him you've called?"

"No, I'll wait."

"You in the business yourself, Treacle?"

"A little. I used to be."

"Knew it, I knew it. Minute I've seen you, I've said, Frank, that's a lady was in the show game if ever I saw. Where'd you work then?"

"As a matter of fact, I often worked here at the Lyceum."

"Blow me down. With who?"

"Oh I worked with a very great artist at one time, the greatest of all, people said."

His eyes widen. "Not Billy the Bearded Baby?"

"Not quite as great as that, no."

"Want to take a little shufti about the old gaff, Treacle? Go in if you like? I'd escort you but I've thingummy to see to here. Before Ern gets back, you know what he's like. He'll have me hide in a bucket if I don't."

"Why, thank you. That is most kind."

He beams. "Anyfink for a fellow artiste."

What used to be the auditorium has been stripped of its seats. The floor and low walls of the roller-skate rink are painted silver—well, what might have been silver once but is now corpse-grey. The orchestra pit has been boarded over, and the opera boxes. A wooden safety-curtain plastered with advertisements for cocoa and dancing lessons is concealing the stage, which in a way is just as well, she wouldn't like to see that. She places her lily at the foot of the proscenium pillar, says a silent, aching prayer.

Thank you, my darling.

Never feel you are forgotten.

Around the perimeter of the skating rink where the stalls used to be, the waxworks have been placed, on badly painted pedestals. Were it not for their labels you wouldn't know who they are. "Henry VIII" might be any other fat man in doublet and hose, "Dr. Crippen, the Wife-Killer" a tailor's dummy in bowler hat. "The Virgin Queen" looks like Chancellor Bismarck forced into a bustle, "Robin Hood" like a municipal librarian dressing up. "Shakespeare" is missing his right hand. Did someone steal it as a souvenir? A buxom young woman in a ball gown is labelled "Ellen Terry." The hair colour, eye colour, height, complexion and figure are wrong. Otherwise it's a perfect likeness.

Remember poor Bram, the way he used to stand there on

First Nights like a sergeant major, snapping at the ushers to get into their places, mother-henning the ingénues, rushing about with his chalkboard. Everyone used to laugh at him, but fondly. Dear Bram. Wonder about him. Used to sometimes glimpse him in dreams. So long since we've met. Did someone say he'd returned to live in Ireland? Who was that?

Can't remember just at the moment what caused the loss of touch. Did we quarrel? Hardly. He'd have been too courteous or too afraid, was never much of a one for having things out, more for wanting them left in.

Perhaps it was just a drifting apart, one of those sunderings that happen unnoticed. The letters a bit less frequent, a birthday forgotten. One year a Christmas card not sent. Then the point at which it begins to seem that it's too late to catch up, too much time has elapsed; explaining away the silence would be embarrassing. If you don't see someone for years, there is always a reason, even if you don't know what it is or can't find its name. Wonder where he is at this moment.

Happy here, was dear Bram. Joy shining from his face, his pride like a Savile Row suit, quiet, tactful, but transmitting its signals all the same, aware of its place in the world. His childhood so full of illness. His parents abandoned him. Remarkable, in his books, the sheer number of orphans. No wonder he clung to the theatre.

Back in the chilly foyer, the tattooed man is nowhere to be seen. Nobody here. As though no one ever was. Only the revolving door turning slowly in the draught.

As she makes to leave, she has a sensation of being watched from the staircase. But sensation is not the word, this is knowledge, certainty. She knows who it is. So intense, she can see the eyes without having to look at them. They are too difficult to turn to, and in the end she doesn't.

Goodbye, Mina, she whispers. *God bless you, dear ghost. I shan't ever come here again.*

* * *

This is Noel, my son do you remember? And your mother is well? Dear crikey, little Edy, what a beautiful young woman you've grown to. Stand back and let me see you, my eyesight, you know. And I haven't my spectacles. Mislaid them. My eyes. Do you remember when we'd all play together, in the theatre sometimes? The truth is, I forget things since I had a little stroke. Oh, quite better, thank you. Hard to keep a bad thing down. And your brother is well I hope? Wasn't it Edward, his name? Oh yes Gordy, that's right. Works in theatre himself, do you tell me, isn't that a living marvel. Golly, this is a turn up, Edy, to see you again. Do tell Mummie I said hello. We'd better run along Nolly and I. We have an appointment, you see. Something pressing, I'm afraid. Do remember me to your mother. Such happy old days. There we are. Goodbye now. Goodbye, Edy. No, we must.

* * *

Covent Garden is busy. So much here has changed. Pretty shops, little pubs, municipal flowers. More tarts than there used to be, and younger, poor things, standing by the lamp posts asking passers-by for a light. What is there for the man who is reduced to paying? Or maybe that's what he likes—his abasement?

The image of the street-girl brings dark recollections. They never caught the Ripper. He could yet be in London, could be anyone. That leopard-skinned grinner. An old waiter at the Savoy. No Londoner will forget the dread, the filthy chill of those nights. Suspicion rolling in like a fog.

But onward, you must. Wouldn't do to give in. Will never back down before the cowards and bully-boys. Nicer things to think about. It's a duty.

For no reason, it comes back, that mortifying performance. To think of it still liquefies the heart. Him as Arthur, about to pull the sword from the stone at the end of Act One, solemn knights all about him, lady queen in attendance, but the stage-hands had misunderstood a cue and wheeled the wrong stone back on, so that no matter how wretchedly he tugged and sweated, Excalibur stayed where it was.

The audience cheering him on, thinking it an extraordinary performance, such commitment in an actor, you could see the veins bulging in his temples, the massive eyes popping like grapes. Presently he lost his temper, insulting and kicking the stone. "You granite little poncing bastard, come *out* I say." And then Merlin got involved, his long wizardy hat flapping. Bram glowering from the wings, more anxious. She'd had to run from the stage, gulping down the laughter, clutching at her stomach and trying to think of something sad. And Bram had laughed, too, afterwards in the Crush Bar, his stern face wilting, tears of gaiety streaming into his beard, while Guinevere downed her gin fizz. And after a while, in trudged Henry. Make-up stains on his dressing robe. Cigarette in mouth. Sword in hand. "Anyone got a rock I might stick this in?"

Poor Bram. Whatever happened? Where did it go? That mad, blazing time when we swirled the stars in the sky.

On a whim, she tries in Boots Book-Lovers' Library on Tottenham Court Road—she never leaves the house without her membership card—but no books from him are listed in their last four catalogues and they don't stock the literary newspapers. The librarian, a Scotsman, manages to get a lot of rrs into "literary." He is brusque in his manner, never heard of any "Stoker," no call for ghost stories anyhow, it's the 20th Century now, an age of science and discovery not bunkum and horsefeathers, and if anyone's asking his opinion (which nobody was) ghost stories should be banned from all librrar-ries.

Outside, she passes a pleasant few minutes in that most English of pastimes: composing a letter of complaint that is never going to be sent.

Try the bookseller's. You might find him there.

Dear god, let me alone.

Take me with you?

She dawdles a while at a dressmaker's window so as not to give him the pleasure of her obedience. What a ravishing gown. Pale organdie silk. When she believes he has returned to whatever silence he lives in, she finds herself crossing the street and entering Foyles.

The ting of the bell and the soothing balm of silence, the peacefulness of all places where old volumes are gathered.

Where to start is the question. Which shelf would be best? How gorgeous, the daylight through the dusty front window, like an illustration of God in a hymnal for children. The aroma of ancient leather and parchment.

An assistant approaches, a young man of remarkably kind eyes. As though afraid of awakening the books, he speaks quietly.

"Might I be of assistance, Madam? Or just browsing?"

"I was looking for anything new by an author called Stoker. I came in about three months ago when I was last up in town and left a note with some of his titles. He is a writer of fiction, mostly supernatural tales."

"The name does seem familiar, Madam, one's definitely heard it somewhere. If you wait a moment or two I can check in the lists. Please, do feel free to take a look about while I'm gone, won't you?"

She gazes out at the street, at the people drifting by. A young woman in black emerges from the piano store across the way, pauses, glances at the sky before hurrying on. Something Russian about her, a sable-wrapped mournfulness. Once seen, you wouldn't forget her.

"I believe I have found the person you're after, Madam. An Abraham Stoker?"

"That's him."

"Published *The Lady of the Shroud* a couple of years ago, and then *The Lair of the White Worm* last year. Nothing since. Rum titles, aren't they."

"Have you either of those in stock?"

"I'm afraid not, Madam. They have lapsed out of print, as have all his other books. You might try a Boots Library or one of the second-hand stalls on the riverbank."

"Do you know how I would write to him? The author. Is that possible?"

"Golly, I'm not certain how that would be done. Via his publishers, perhaps?"

"Well then, I shall try that. Good day. Thank you for your helpfulness."

"Good day, Madam," he says, reaching out to shake hands. "Won't you come and see us again. We are always here to assist." Odd, his sudden familiarity. How times are changing. But she accepts.

Now she realises that he is pressing a tightly folded envelope into her gloved hand.

"Thank you for calling," he says. "I wish you success with your search. Goodbye."

With his eyes, he asks her to leave. From behind the counter, he waves.

On Charing Cross Road, the pavement is crowded. People hurrying past barely notice an old lady in a bookseller's doorway, spectacles misting as she reads. The small shake of her shoulders. Her wrists brushing tears from her face.

Dear Madam. I go about with a person who works at Foyle's, the boy who has given you this note, a reply to yours of 9th January. Forgive the cloak and dagger if you will, skulduggery is not intended. My father sits on the Charitable Aid Committee of the Royal Society of Literature, and my brother and I sometimes assist him in small secretarial ways in that regard. The proceedings of this body are of course confidential and its decisions are effected with utmost discretion, as you will understand. I am honour-bound never to discuss publicly any workings of the committee. But I can tell you that, in various ways, it succours authors of a certain age who might benefit from tactful assistance. I happen to know that a certain old gentleman is one such case. A lot of our old gentlemen and ladies can be proud and not entirely forthcoming. But the fact is that the gentleman's employer died some years ago and the gentleman has found no position since. He has suffered a number of strokes, is in considerable want and has no friends of his old life. His wife is herself unwell and is staying with relatives in her home country. If you will write to the Society, I believe that more news may be ascertained. Your servant in confidence. A friend, Foyle's Books.

* * *

A TABLE AT CLARIDGE'S

4.43 P.M.

His eye picks her out immediately. Alone in the furthest corner of the café. Sipping tea, reading a slim volume of what must be poetry.

His impulse is to leave. Her solitude and stillness too beautiful to disturb. But her daughter touches his shoulder and eases forward his wheelchair. Through the rows of gorgeous tables, the lavish bouquets, the ice buckets.

"Mummie," she says.

"Edy."

"Look what I turned up at the auction."

Nothing is said for a thousand years.

"Oh, my dear friend," she says, rising slowly from the table. "Oh, my dearest, dearest heart. What joy."

He tries not to weep, will not be unmanned as he covers her outstretched hands with kisses.

"Sit a while with me, won't you, Bram? I say, waiter, another menu."

"I shan't eat, thank you, Ellen."

"You'll have something small."

"No thanks."

"You have ruined my eye-paint, darling. I shall stop in a moment."

After her daughter has left, they look at one another, saying nothing, hands clasped tightly on the stiff linen tablecloth. When talk commences, it is of old acquaintants; Harks emigrated to South Africa, she tells him, they keep in touch now and again, lives in Durban. Gordy is designing stage sets, frightfully successful, owns a motor car.

The waiter brings her meal, a plate of mixed grill, and places it silently before her, then fills her glass from the water jug.

"You'll let me buy you a bit of tea, Bram?" she says. "My treat?"

"I'm not hungry."

"Then you'll share this pile of stuff with me, it's far too much."

"I really—"

"Come now, you remember how infernally vain I am, you can't let me eat all this mountain of muck, I shall bloat." She turns with a brisk smile and beckons the waiter back, insists on a second plate being fetched, and a bottle of Mouton

Rothschild. The old-fashioned gaslights on the walls begin to dim.

"Your daughter is very beautiful," he says.

"Yes, she is."

"She would make a nice sweetheart for my Noel."

"That would be unlikely, old darling, dreamboat though he is."

"Why so?"

"Edy bats for the other eleven."

"Ah."

"Yes. Rum turn-up when one's only daughter turns out a tearing old lesbian. Often sorry I didn't give it a good go myself. Would have saved everyone a good deal of bother."

"Never too late?"

"What a thought."

"Your Edy knows how to spend your money at any rate. She bought up half the auction. Drat me if she wasn't actually boosting the prices on purpose."

"Yes, I sent her along, didn't want all the old bastard's clutter falling into the wrong clutches. You know what a frightful snob he was, the scamp. Couldn't go oneself, didn't care to be recognised. Also, wanted to find a way of getting a bit of decent money to his wife. Always felt for her, you know. Difficult woman, they say. Likes queening it up about the town in the role of Lady Irving relict, but Christ, imagine being *married* to the rascal, it would drive a bloody saint mad. No doubt a little guilt on my part too. But let us speak no more of such things."

"How wonderful to see you. Are you working much, darling?"

"A couple of jobs lined up in the provinces, where they don't mind an old carthorse clopping about the boards. I've Ophelia in Penge or some ghastly place like that, she'll be the cobwebbiest incarnation ever seen. Oh and I'm going to start appearing in these nonsensical moving pictures, such dreadful vulgarity but they fire pots of money at one. I don't give it a year, silly fad."

"Must admit I rather like the moving pictures. Guilty pleasure sort of thing."

"Oh everyone *likes* them, darling. That's why they are bad. Be honest, don't you ever dream some character you've written might appear in the moving pictures one day?"

"I should need to be insane to entertain any such notion."

"But enough about me, dearest Bram. How is your health?"

"Ruddy marvellous." He laughs quietly. "How does it look?"

"You must permit me to help you," she says. "Financially and in other ways. At least until you are back on your feet. I absolutely insist."

"I shall do no such thing, darling. Subject closed."

"You'll come stay with me a while at Smallhythe. I have oodles of room. Do say you will, what a hoot we should have together. Plain good food and God's fresh air and we could flirt and talk maliciously of old friends in the evenings."

"That does sound enticing but I'm not one for the countryside, I'm afraid."

"Oh you stubborn old owl. How you madden me."

"I'd rather forgotten how much fun maddening you can be. You look even more radiant when you're maddened."

"So you'll come?"

"No, I shan't come, darling. I'm set in my ways. Wander a mile from the Thames and I break out in pimples. I say, this lamb is good."

"Tell me, why did you go to the appalling old auction, darling? For auld lang syne?"

"No, I wanted to get a gift for my Florrie, a sketch of Noel as a little fellow. It's her birthday coming up soon. But it wasn't there."

"Shame."

"Odd, it was listed in the catalogue. 'Portrait of a Boy.' I suppose it was lost. Never mind."

"Wretched pity. Things are never what they seem, are they, *mon ange*?"

"Things not being what they seem is what things do best, don't you find? Like that time with the guns and the water."

"What time was that?"

"You know. In Norfolk. The day you held my hand."

"I don't recall?"

"But you must."

"I have never been to Norfolk, I don't think. Have I, Bram?"

"We'd gone there, the three of us and the children, to be away from London for a bit. Edy was there, and Gordy and Noel. Some kerfuffle or another was going on, problems at the bank, I think it was. The reporters had been snuffling about, sifting the trash outside his rooms, all of that. So off we toddled to Burnham for an August weekend."

"Did we? How lovely. Can you tell me the rest?"

"The children were visiting a farm for the day. We were out in a little rowboat, Henry, you, and I. Off Holkham beach. Near Wells-next-the-Sea. One of those golden autumn afternoons in England where the air smells like linen and white wine. We were singing, or trying to, you were teaching us a harmony. *Believe Me if All Those Endearing Young Charms*. And lazily trying to fish but catching nothing."

"Oh dear. What a shame."

"Henry started mucking about, saying he'd satanically summon them from the deep. He was merry after a good lunch. Making us chuckle. Oars into the oarlocks. Whips off his cap. Screwing up his eyes like a witch in the Grimms. And out with it, then, this great stream of cod Latin or some dashed thing, lots of 'orums' and forming the crucifix with his fingers."

"The crucifix."

"The crucifix, yes, with his fingers. And snarling."

"There weren't—*horses* by any chance?"

"Do you know, darling, there were."

"I seem to remember horses in the sea. Is that possible, Bram?"

"Darling, Burnham is where they send the cavalry horses from Buckingham Palace in the summer for a break. They're exercised on Holkham Beach, the soldiers ride them into the bay. You do remember."

"Good heavens. Great black stallions? I mean majestic sort of fellows? Irish Draft Cross thoroughbreds or some such beauties. Sixteen hands high if an inch."

"Black as the night. Splashing away up to their necks in the waves. One of the noblest sights I ever saw."

"What happened then?"

"We were laughing so hard at Henry, I almost fell out of the boat, you hauled me back in by the collar. But rot me if a minute or two later the fish don't start galloping up to the surface. Hundreds of the beggars. Thousands. Armfuls. We were scooping them out by the bucketful. Remember that part?"

"Crikey O'Reilly. No, I don't."

"What happened—we only discovered it later, back on the dock—we'd strayed near a section of the bay that the navy use for torpedo practice. They'd loosed off a ruddy torpedo a moment before Henry's incantation and up popped our finned friends in their multitudes."

"To pay homage to the commander of the deep."

"That exactly. He enjoyed it no end, the great fraud."

"I daresay, the vain devil. What a chump."

"Back ashore, we got him up the stairs and put him into his bed—he was still a bit sozzly—and then you and I walked the prom near the Strand for an hour. Arm in arm. Funny thing, we didn't speak. Not so much as a syllable. There was a carousel there and we watched it a while. The painted horses turning. A Wurlitzer waltz. The sun had burned me a little. We had to collect the younglings from the farm. And—just for a second or two—you held my hand. Then you kissed it. I kissed yours. And we walked back to the hotel."

"How strange, darling, not to remember something so delightful. I wish I did."

"Now you do."

"Weren't those horses magnificent?"

"Like creatures of myth, you said. You were right."

"I shouldn't have let your hand go, darling. I should have held it for ever."

"Of course you should."

"You know I was terribly in love with you I expect."

"Yes you were. For a week and a half."

She laughs.

"I see now that we were all of us a little in love with everyone," he says. "Which isn't the worst, when one's young."

"*Or* old."

"Or old. Yes indeed. Here's to folly."

* * *

OUTSIDE A NURSING HOME
ON BRICKFIELDS TERRACE

The church clock is striking eleven. It won't toll again before morning.

He asks the cabbie to leave him on the corner of Bishop's Bridge Road and assist with the wheelchair. A clear, cold night, the sky alive with turquoise stars. Past the closed Turkish Baths, the shuttered-up library. A lovely last cigarette before bedtime.

He had intended to smoke only four today, is into tomorrow's allowance. Oh well. Special occasion. Who'd have thought?

He pushes himself down the terrace, looks up at the ruined townhouse. Moonlight in the windows. Wild flowers sprouting from the walls.

The weekend will be pleasant. Good of her to invite him. Perhaps a day or two in the country, she has good fishing and shooting. Many years since he shot. Never truly liked it. But a little time together, to talk and to laugh. Perhaps go motoring down to Folkestone with her, would be lovely to see her drive. An image of him in his wheelchair beneath her pear trees arises, confetti of blossom, an old man in a blanket. Someone is playing Chopin.

The faintest prickle of electricity seems to sparkle through his cheekbones and the bones of his scalp. Now comes pain behind the eyes, shocking, snake-tooth-angry, hands of granite grip his throat but he is unable to cry out and the pain vanishes like the heat of a forge-reddened sword thrust into a quench of iced water.

Glancing up, he sees the piano teacher approaching through the smuts of ashy cold, hands outstretched towards him in sisterly gentleness. It is as though some layer that was previously around her has been scorched away by his pain; he sees her clearly, like a man coming out of a cave seeing light for the first time. Her smile is like music. He notices she is barefoot.

"*Bhfuil tú réidh?*" she asks. Are you ready?

Somehow he is able to answer, he doesn't understand how. He knows barely any Irish. But English is leaving him. It is as though they are conversing in starlight. There are things he will need for the journey, he tells her. Might we pop up to my room and fill a bag? She answers that there is no need, where they're going, everything is ready. He takes her hand and attempts to rise. It is easier than he thought.

The door of the ruined townhouse is opened by a bearded old mariner who might be a nightwatchman in a Rembrandt. Like the girl, he is barefoot. His eyes glitter like polished cents.

"Stoker," he exclaims. "My excellent fellow."

"Whitman, dear man. How was your crossing?"

"Come in from the cold, step right up, you fond rascal. Everyone's longing to see you. We're putting on a little play. I seem to be appearing as Homer."

Ice is forming on the steps. The piano teacher assists him. The hall is warm and dark; the doorways aglow. In the mirror he sees the face of a mild-eyed boy.

His sisters. His parents. A brother he never knew. Ophelia is here, with Desdemona and Juliet, conversing with Wilde about Paris. Prospero and Heathcliff and Catherine Earnshaw are chinking slim glasses of bubbles. Macbeth is showing Jane Eyre a portrait of Mary Shelley. In the firelight, the Little Match Girl plays marbles with Puck. Every room is full of friends, pushing forward to shake his hand, embrace him. Dead stagehands and steamfitters, lovers half-forgotten, lost sinners encountered in shadow now aglow in the limelight, a man he once saved from drowning, but new, seen as for the first time, as though with the names that belong to them, the long pseudonyms shed.

There is music in some strange scale he never knew existed, strong and yet fragile, impossibly beautiful. The windows are open to the night, the birds are speaking Greek.

"If you'll come upstairs with me now? Someone's waiting to see you."

"Let him wait," says Stoker. Turning towards the rooms. Drunk on the beauty of moonlight.

* * *

26 St. George's Square,
Pimlico,
London.
April 20th, 1912

Dear Miss Terry, dear Ellen, if I may,

You and I do not know one another well, having met so infrequently and hurriedly down the years at the odd First Night or gala, a matter of immense regret to me. But I thought you should want to know the sad news that, having suffered a stroke on Friday evening last, from which he never regained consciousness, early this morning my husband Bram died.

Noel and I are heartbroken. The only relief, for which I thank God, is that he was spared great pain at the end and that Noel and I were at his bedside, holding his hand and cradling him.

Bee and I were not entirely happy together, as you will have gathered; but we had what these days seems the rather unconventional arrangement that is a conventional marriage. Like the woman he married, Bee was by any measure not a saint. He could be sullen, for example, and overly private. And I was impatient, sometimes angry. But he was the only person I have known who did feel in every grain of his being that love is not love which alters when it alteration finds. He was utterly, patiently, endlessly loyal, incapable of purposely letting down a loved one or anyone to whom he had given his word. He was a funny, dependable, clever and gracious man, with a womanly heart full of mercy. What happy times we had were happy indeed. He was a person of fierce kindness, a loving, strong and besotted father. I am so blessed to have my son. He means that Bee will never truly go.

Bee spoke of you often, with great tenderness and love. When in recent times you and he did not see each other as often, as can happen between people what with the busyness and drift of life, he missed you. He took pride in all your artistic and professional success, and in the special and particular friendship you and he had once had. Proud, too, of his close and long loving friendship with H.I., as who would not be. I felt often that each of them was the healing to a wound the other had been hurt by. Or perhaps it was that they discovered, in their particular combination of solitudes, that not all wounds must be healed.

Bee would always have been brave. It was how his flames tempered him. But we women have so many kinds of bravery where those poor creatures, men, have only two. He could so easily and forgivably have become one of those narking old leather-skinned fellows who bore on about youngsters and take to poultices and Knowing Better and smashing the ice on Christmas morning so as to swim in the Thames in order to make everyone around them feel second-rate. But that was not my Bee. I am glad he escaped himself. To me, he will always be the intrepid and handsome boy running down towards the surf, whom I first saw when he and I were seventeen.

He wrote in his *Dracula*: "There is a reason that all things are as they are." I do not think so. But now he knows. What I can say is that the life he found at the theatre brought him great solace and purpose, as I hope you understand. He had a painful, lonely childhood and did not find the happy marriage that he perhaps was not made for, but was entirely devoid of self-pity or even self-consideration. It was his theatre-life that gave him the courage to face his many disappointments, which he bore, like his illness, with such stoicism and dignity. I am very thankful to you for all your close kindness and love for my Bee.

There are many kinds of love. I know that. He did, too.

Sincerely yours,

Mrs. Bram Stoker.

Florence

CAVEAT, BIBLIOGRAPHY, ACKNOWLEDGEMENTS

Shadowplay is based on real events but is a work of fiction. Many liberties have been taken with facts, characterisations, and chronologies, even with the publication dates of Stoker's lesser-known works. All sequences presenting themselves as authentic documents are fictitious. Readers in search of reliable material are directed to the following works and to the bibliographies they contain:

Edward Gordon Craig, *Ellen Terry and Her Secret Self*; Michael Holroyd, *A Strange Eventful History: the Dramatic Lives of Ellen Terry, Henry Irving, and their Remarkable Families*; Jay Melville, *Ellen Terry*; David J. Skal, *Something in the Blood: The Untold Story of Bram Stoker*, and Stoker's own *Personal Reminiscences of Henry Irving*.

The text of *Shadowplay* contains many references to Stoker's masterpiece, *Dracula*, as well as allusions to some of his other writings. The reference in the closing pages to the birds speaking Greek is borrowed from a letter written by Virginia Woolf.

In 1922, ten years after Stoker's death, a German company, Prana Film, produced *Nosferatu*, a pirated screen version of *Dracula*, which, like Stoker's other books, had been almost forgotten. Unfortunately for Prana, not by everyone. The redoubtable Florence Stoker sued and won, establishing her rights of ownership and important principles of copyright. All authors owe her a debt of gratitude.

Since then, *Dracula* has sold tens of millions of copies, been translated into more than a hundred languages, and been filmed 200 times. Bram Stoker would be astounded by the immortality of his character. The Count's afterlife is proving long and unique.

Sir Henry Irving's ashes are interred in Poets' Corner at Westminster Abbey, near the Shakespeare memorial. Forty thousand Londoners watched his funeral procession. In 1963, an admirer who for sixty years had placed roses on Irving's tombstone on the anniversary of his death made a gift to the Abbey: Irving's crucifix.

Ellen Terry's unparalleled career lasted seven decades. In 1911, she recorded five scenes from Shakespeare for the Victor Recording Company. She later appeared in a number of films. In 1922 she received an honorary doctorate from St. Andrew's University, and in 1925 she was made a Dame Grand Cross of the Order of the British Empire. Her grand-nephew, John Gielgud, performed *Hamlet* at the Lyceum in 1939. The surnames of Terry, Stoker, and Irving are engraved on the Burleigh Street exterior wall of the Lyceum, in commemoration of three remarkable artists.

I thank my editor, Geoff Mulligan, everyone at Secker and at Vintage, Isobel Dixon, Conrad Williams and the team at Blake Friedmann Literary, TV and Film Agency, Paul McGuigan of BBC Northern Ireland for suggesting the Henry–Bram relationship to me as a screenplay and Stephen Wright who directed my adaptation of that screenplay for BBC Radio 3. I thank my friends and University of Limerick colleagues, the fine writers Donal Ryan and Sarah Moore Fitzgerald, for enabling me to write this book, and I thank the University for granting me leave.

One of the reasons why I would like life after death to be

more than a story is that I would like to see the dedicatee of this novel again. Carole Blake was my friend and literary agent for twenty-five years. If the otherworld does exist, I know she will have found a very good restaurant there, with an excellent wine list, and, on a neighbouring cloud, a designer shoe shop. The medieval choral music she loved will be playing. And she will be arguing with a publisher on behalf of her latest client, God, who is not receiving sufficient royalties for the Bible.

As ever, my greatest debt is to Anne-Marie Casey and our sons, James and Marcus, for their love, kindness, and support.

JO'C, 2018